You May Kiss the Duke

By Charis Michaels

The Brides of Belgravia
Any Groom Will Do
All Dressed in White
You May Kiss the Duke

The Bachelor Lords of London
The Earl Next Door
The Virgin and the Viscount
One for the Rogue

You May Kiss the Duke

the Duke

A Brides of Belgravia Novel

Charis Michaels

AVONIMPULSE
An Imprint of HarperCollinsPublishers

YOU MAY KISS THE DUKE. Copyright © 2019 by Charis Michaels. All rights reserved. Printed in the United States of America. No part of this book may be used or reproduced in any manner whatsoever without written permission except in the case of brief quotations embodied in critical articles and reviews. For information, address HarperCollins Publishers, 195 Broadway, New York, NY 10007.

Digital Edition MAY 2019 ISBN: 978-0-06-268582-7
Print Edition ISBN: 978-0-06-268585-8

Cover design by Patricia Barrow
Cover illustration by Frederika Ribes
Cover photographs © Period Images (couple); © perlphoto/Shutterstock (background)

Avon Impulse and the Avon Impulse logo are registered trademarks of HarperCollins Publishers in the United States of America.

Avon and HarperCollins are registered trademarks of HarperCollins Publishers in the United States of America and other countries.

FIRST EDITION

19 20 21 22 23   HDC   10 9 8 7 6 5 4 3 2 1

For my sister-in-law Jennifer, because she gets it.

ACKNOWLEDGMENTS

A generous team of creative geniuses helped me with the medical technicalities of this book (which I distorted for my own devices) and the plotting and characterization of Stoker and Sabine (who I loved too much to wrestle into a viable story without outside intervention). Thank you, Barbara Taylor, MD, and JoLynn McEachern, RN; also critique partners Cheri Allan and Lenora Bell, as well as Wounded-Heroes Expert Sarah Goldstein.

As ever, thank you to my indulgent and loving family.

You May Kiss the Duke

October 1830
Pixham, Surrey

Before

Sabine Noble agreed to marry because of a cupboard.

It was a cedar cupboard, built into the wall of the green salon, formerly used to store table linens and silver. Now the linens were draped over furniture, and the silver had been long sold. The cupboard sat empty, a three-foot-by-three-foot space, secured from the outside with a wooden peg.

The cupboard represented a new level of humiliation for Sabine. She couldn't explain the cupboard away with a lie about a fall from her horse or an accident on the stairs; and dark, tight spaces elicited a particular sort of hysteria.

Perhaps it was understandable that Sabine was not herself when she was finally, unexpectedly, released from the cupboard after forty-five terrible minutes of dark, airless in-dignity. Perhaps the cupboard—or rather freedom from the cupboard—was the perfect storm of relief and opportunity and panicked going-along.

Perhaps she wouldn't have agreed to the marriage if her uncle hadn't locked her in the cupboard on the first day Jon Stoker came to call, but he did lock her in, and this is the story of what came after.

Jon Stoker agreed to marry because saving women had become a rather burdensome lifelong habit, and Sabine Noble was meant to be his last hurrah.

Stoker had turned up to Park Lodge that day, uninvited and unknown to Sabine or her uncle, due to an advertise-ment that Sabine and her friends had posted in London. The advert offered the girls' dowries in exchange for marriages of convenience. The girls hoped to gain access to London after speedy marriages to sailors who would be rarely, if ever, at home.

Stoker wanted no part of it, despite the unexplained en-thusiasm of his business partners. He'd called that day for no other reason than to tell her that he'd been volunteered out of turn; marriage was not in his future, thank you, but no.

He was met on the doorstep by an impervious old man who tried immediately to send him away. Stoker heard shouts of distress from inside, banging, muffled cries for help, and he forgot the advertisement and stepped around the sputter-ing old man to follow the sounds.

For ten minutes Stoker prowled the ground floor, his ear cocked to the cries, while the man threatened eviction and the sheriff. Stoker ignored him and located the source of the noise in a back parlor. A cupboard, its hinges rattling with blows from inside. He removed the lock and whipped the doors open and Sabine Noble tumbled out, gasping for air.

Jon Stoker's life was forever changed.

Sabine recovered with the speed of a woman prepared for the next terrible blow. She darted behind a chair, gasped for breath, and shook her hair from her eyes. When she looked up, she saw a stranger shoving her uncle into the very cupboard from which she had just been released.

"Duck," the stranger ordered Sir Dryden, his hand pressing the older man's head. "*Duck*," he said, louder. Sir Dryden ducked, the door was slammed shut, and the stranger turned calmly. Sabine gripped the back of the chair.

"I'm Jon Stoker," the stranger said.

Sabine nodded cautiously, too breathless and hoarse to speak. She touched a hand to her swollen eye. She tasted blood on her lip. He watched with solemn patience, no wincing, no reaching out, no bellowing for a maid. He waited.

"Mr. Stoker," she finally repeated, but she thought, *Who?*

When realization dawned, it was as swift and painful as Sir Dryden's backhand.

No, she thought, disbelieving. Her hands slid from the chair and she took two steps back.

No.

Not that *Jon Stoker. Not*—

Jon Stoker was the name of the man who had answered the advertisement posted by her friends. The advertisement *for a husband.*

Jon Stoker, her friend Willow had told her, had been the applicant most suited for Sabine.

Jon Stoker could only be here for one purpose—a proposal. To her. Today. On this of all days. As her face swelled and her lip bled. As her uncle began to slowly knock a bony knuckle against the inside of the cupboard door.

Surely not.

Sabine closed her eyes, willing herself to disappear. She willed Jon Stoker to disappear. She willed Sir Dryden to hell and beyond.

Stoker cleared his throat. "This man"—he pointed to the locked cupboard—"is a problem. Obviously."

This man—

Sabine did not answer, and she wouldn't answer. She wouldn't look at him, or make excuses, or thank him, despite the fact that he deserved her gratitude. And she certainly would not marry him. The advertisement had been her friends' mad scheme. Sabine had gone along because she'd never thought it would come to anything.

She turned and began to weave through the furniture to the parlor door.

"Is there somewhere we can go?" he called after her. "To speak?"

Sabine picked up speed. She darted through the door, bustling down the corridor.

Bustling? No, she was *fleeing*, and Sabine never fled. Her face burned with fresh shame. Was it not enough to suffer the humiliation of being beaten by a tyrant uncle and released from captivity in her own home? Must she also be chased?

"I'd like to speak with you," Jon Stoker called, striding behind her. "About the advert."

Sabine missed a step but kept moving.

The advert, the advert. Sabine swore in her head.

Her friend Willow had proposed the advertisement on a day like today, when Sabine harbored a broken rib and her future with Sir Dryden had seemed like certain death. Sabine had acquiesced, and now someone named Jon Stoker was here, witnessing one of the greatest humiliations of her life, and unbelievably, she did not hate him. Yet.

"I am interested in the advertised . . . arrangement?" Jon Stoker said from behind her. It came out like a question. "The offer is still on, I presume?"

Sabine stopped short and grabbed the wall to keep from pitching forward.

She glanced over her shoulder at the tall, dark man. She thought, *He must be as desperate as I am.*

Jon Stoker asked, "You are captive to this man? He is your father?"

If ever there was a statement to draw her out, it was this. "Absolutely not," she said. "Sir Dryden is my uncle."

"Where is your father?"

"Dead. Six months. Sir Dryden is his elder brother. His less accomplished, avaricious, cruel, and petty elder brother."

"Your father's will stipulated that control should go to this brother?"

"There was no proper will. My father died unexpectedly. His heart seized up, they say."

"I'm sorry."

"Yes. We are all very sorry."

"How many family members remain here?"

"My mother, myself, a handful of devoted servants who refuse to leave us. However, Sir Dryden's rages are reserved only for me."

"For how long?"

Now Sabine paused. She was not in the habit of answering personal questions from strange men. As a rule, she did not answer personal questions from anyone or speak to strange men at all. But Jon Stoker was so incredibly matter-of-fact, so level. She could not have tolerated hysteria or bluster. Sabine thrived on calm, and Jon Stoker appeared the very soul of calmness.

And, best of all, he didn't ask why.

Why did he lock you in the cupboard?

What did you do to invite a blackened eye or a bloody lip?

He did not ask.

The answer was, she'd refused to serve Dryden's cream tea. He'd proclaimed that a proper lady should serve the master of her house, and she'd said, *Pour your own bloody tea.* And off they went. To blows. To the cupboard.

"My father died in February," Sabine said. "Dryden installed himself after the funeral. He and I have been at odds since then."

"*At odds?*" Stoker choked.

Sabine touched her swelling eye. "We do not get on."

He allowed this incredible understatement to resound between them. Finally, he said, "Is this the worst of it?"

"There was a broken rib, I believe. Or two." Sabine hadn't realized the relief of actually *telling* someone. Especially someone she did not know and who would leave here in five minutes. She'd hid the worst of the abuse from her mother and her friends. She was so very ashamed—and what could they do? The helplessness was as terrible as the pain.

Yet, here she stood, telling this man.

"But his attacks," asked Stoker, "do not extend to—?" He stopped, ran a hand on his neck, and began again. "That is, he does not . . . ?" Another pause. His flat tone had taken on a stratum of something harder, something decidedly *less calm.*

She shook her head. *No. Thank God. Not that.*

Stoker nodded and looked away. He took a deep breath. "You cannot remain here," he said.

Sabine could not know it, but Jon Stoker had rescued hundreds of girls over the years—not because he'd married them, but because he'd beaten down doors or stabbed oppressive men or stolen them away under the cover of night.

Some said he'd been born a hero; others said he fought in memory of his desperate mother. Stoker said he was in the wrong place at the right time. All too often.

Regardless of the reason, regardless of their prisons, he

always said these same words. *You cannot remain here*. It was routine.

Sabine raised her chin. "I am in the process of cataloging my father's legacy. He was a cartographer of some merit, and he was scheduled to publish a collective of maps when he died. There are surveys and drawings and text—much of it out of order, all of it unfinished. There are apprentices living here at Park Lodge to curate the work, but I had taken the lead since his death. And my mother is not well. We are lucky to have a devoted caregiver, but her health is tenuous at best."

"And how effective are you at these endeavors when you are under the dominion of this man?" Stoker asked.

Sabine looked down at her hand. A bruise shined from her smallest finger, a remnant of the week prior, when Sir Dryden had come upon her at the drafting table and pressed a paperweight into her hand.

"The truth is," she said, "I cause my mother fresh grief the longer I remain. She cannot bear to see me hurt."

"This is why you advertised your dowry?"

Sabine looked at him. There were reasons, and then there were fantasies made up by well-meaning friends. The advert had been a fantastical, made-up thing.

"My friends engineered the advert," she said. "I have no wish to marry."

"*I* have no wish to marry," countered Stoker.

It was not what she expected him to say. He'd been asking for ten minutes if the advertised proposal was still on. He stood five feet away, feet planted. Leaving seemed the furthest thing from his mind. He studied her as if she knew the solution to a problem that could change both of their lives.

For the first time she allowed herself to look at this man, to *really* look at him. He was large, of course. Sir Dryden had not fought him because Jon Stoker was large and her uncle was a coward. Not simply tall, however. Stoker was broad-shouldered, with a substantial chest, flat middle, and long, thick legs. He had the physique of a farmer, someone who lifted heavy things, who plowed and chopped. His face was tan and weathered. He was older than she was but not so very old, ten years beyond her own twenty-three years, perhaps? He had black hair, rather like a pirate.

A farmer pirate?

Later Sabine would scold herself for standing before him, wounded and embarrassed, and inventing the label *farmer pirate*. *Vigilante stonemason* and *blacksmith warrior* also came to mind. Had she hit her head in the cupboard?

Stoker broke the silence. "What is your reason?"

"I beg your pardon?" Only a lunatic could follow this conversation.

"Your reason for not wanting to marry?"

"Oh. That. Well, I've realized in the past six months that I've no wish to live under the dominion of any man. Not ever. And I am very occupied with my father's legacy, as I've said. I haven't the time to tend to a husband. Or the desire."

He nodded, and she asked him the same question. "What is your reason?"

He paused, studying her, almost as if he weighed the benefits of answering.

Sabine crossed her arms over her chest. *Oh, you will answer. It's only fair.*

He cleared his throat. "Marriage involves another person, doesn't it? The combination of two lives? I'm certain that my life is not suitable for anyone but myself. I would not inflict it on an unsuspecting woman."

This made her laugh. "How dashingly cryptic, but hardly an answer. *Why not* inflict this life?"

Another long stare. "Very well," he said. "To begin, I was born in a brothel."

Now he crossed his arms over his chest. His expression said, *That should shut you up.*

"And I," countered Sabine, "just emerged from a locked cupboard. My father is dead. My mother is going blind. My uncle is a sadistic tyrant from whom I cannot seem to escape. This is not a conversation for the faint of heart."

He rolled his shoulders. "Right. Well, I was born a bastard, to a mother who could scarcely care for herself. I was brought up in the streets. I have seen more devastation than you can imagine. I have since acquired some means, and by some miracle I have been educated. I have an import business with two partners. I own a ship. I have sailed the world. But matrimony is not like money or knowledge or travel, is it? You don't simply *earn* marriage and use it to your advantage. Marriage will convene all of my terrible history on another person."

"And what if the other person does not wish to convene her life with yours? What if she wishes marriage in only a legal sense?"

He looked confused. "Every woman wants to convene."

"I don't."

He cocked his chin.

"Can you not see my face?" she went on. "Do you recall the locked box from where you, only moments ago, released me? I shall never, ever, put myself in a position of obligation or subjugation to a man again. Marriage is a union of trust, and trust, for me, is gone. But I would do it for the freedom of the thing—that is, I would *possibly* do it. As a way out. If the circumstances were correct."

If she was to pinpoint a moment in the conversation when she went from resisting this madcap scheme to actively campaigning for it, it was now.

The words *I have no wish to marry* had allowed her to reconsider.

Jon Stoker said, "But a traditional marriage to a kind man could deliver you from your situation."

"My uncle appeared kind before he backhanded me within days of my father's funeral. Would marriage to a loving girl vanquish all of your demons?"

"I don't have de—"

"I don't want to know, actually," she said, holding out her hand. "Forgive me, but I believe we might have reached some common ground. I want no part of a traditional union with any man. I could not be more serious about not wanting it. However, I would consider an alternative."

"And so the advert was meant to . . . ?"

"The advert was an aspirational daydream engineered by my friends. I never expected it to elicit someone like you." She looked him boldly up and down.

"And you know what I'm like, do you?"

"I know you released me from the cupboard without ceremony. I know you have been measured and steady in a very strange moment. I know you need my £15,000 dowry—you would not have answered the advert if you did not."

"These are but a fraction of the things to know about me."

She continued as if she hadn't heard. "And if *you* have no wish to marry, and *I* have no wish to marry, then we could, in theory, marry in name only and part ways. I will go to London with my friends and enjoy the freedom of a married woman. You may . . . go wherever you will go and do whatever you do. We shall live separate lives. Oh my God, this might actually work." Sabine felt a little breathless. The terror and humiliation of her uncle's dominion had been so oppressive, the possibility of some deliverance, any deliverance, felt like a gag had been removed from her mouth.

"You cannot remain here," he repeated.

It was not a refusal and Sabine forged ahead. "Swear to me now," she stipulated, "that you will never raise a hand in violence to me, not ever. That is, on the very rare occasion that we should see each other. And I do mean very rare. Once every five years."

"I do not strike women," he said.

"And swear to me that, if we marry, you will take my

dowry and go, leave me in peace. That we shall carry on separate existences in separate parts of the world. That we will have no sway on the life that the other builds."

Sabine's heart had begun to pound like she was running a race. This conversation felt very much like a race. They had begun to walk, and then he walked faster, and then *she* walked faster, and then he had begun to run, so *she* began to run, and now they were both sprinting side by side, trying to keep up.

"I swear," Jon Stoker said slowly, and Sabine thought, *My God, what if this actually works?*

It had been a true statement; Stoker did not strike women. Also true, she could not remain here. But he'd lost track of whether he was trying to convince her of something, or she was trying to convince him.

You will save her by marrying her, he thought.

She will die if you do not.

"This is madness," she said, letting out a little laugh, and she turned away. Stoker felt something like panic rise in his throat.

"I will take your dowry and go," he rushed to say. "You have my word."

She turned back. "You require the dowry money so badly?"

This, he elected not to answer.

She continued, "Or has your misspent life treated you

with such callousness, you have no aspirations to real happiness? You can simply marry anyone, no bearing on your future. It simply won't matter."

Stoker was not accustomed to women weighing his aspirations or his happiness. He also was not accustomed to lying. He was many regrettable things, but never dishonest. He opened his mouth to say, *I don't require the money, not in the way my partners do*, but the look on her face caused him to close it. He paused.

Stoker and his partners were embarking on an import voyage to bring guano fertilizer to the farms of England. It was new and untried and potentially a windfall beyond their wildest imaginings, but they could benefit from some financing to raise a crew and provision. They'd considered the girls' advertisement because their dowries would finance the first expedition and then some.

That is, his partners had considered the girls' advertisements. His partner Joseph had fallen into something like love-at-first-sight with his potential bride. And Cassin really did need the money.

Stoker was not in love nor destitute. But what if he married as a way to end the exhausting business of saving people?

No more Stoker as hero, Stoker as savior, Stoker as someone else's deliverance from . . . whatever.

The sacrifice of marrying Sabine Noble—of marrying anyone at all—would be so great, he could retire.

After her, he could walk away.

It was helpful that the marriage described by Sabine was

meant to be completely detached, with oceans between their lives, and wholesale unaccountability. It was really no marriage at all, except by name.

Stoker took a deep breath. He looked her over once again, and she raised up to her full height. She hiked her chin. He felt something twitch and sink inside his chest, like sand dropping into a hole on the beach.

This was a woman who had choices, he thought. She could have her pick of men. The dowry she advertised was significant and her beauty was dark and rare and, if he was being honest, took his breath away. Coal-black hair, long lashes that shielded emerald eyes, perfect nose, perfect mouth—perfect everywhere. Even beaten by her uncle, even desperate, he could not look away.

"Mr. Stoker?" Sabine prompted. "Why would you marry a stranger, if you've sworn never to marry?"

"For the dowry money," he heard himself say. He would blame it on the money but know it was one final act of altruism for a pretty girl in a bad situation.

"Right," she said, her voice tentative but also official. "You will do it for the money, and I will do it to leave Sir Dryden. I suppose it's all settled." She took two steps back.

"Do you have to gain your uncle's permission to leave home and marry? Does he control the dowry?"

She shook her head. "No. My father prepared the dowry years ago, thank God. Sir Dryden may remain locked in the cupboard until he rots, for all it would affect me."

"Are you safe from him tonight? Eventually, a servant will release him."

She shrugged. "I think we should do it as quickly as we can. I can go to my friend Willow's aunt's house in Belgravia. This has been Willow's plan. Let me speak to my mother. She has a devoted lady's maid who will see to her care when I go. She will miss me but be relieved that I am free of him."

"Right," Stoker said, working to keep his voice normal. "We shall do it as quickly as we can."

CHAPTER ONE

August 1834
London, England
Four years later

Some eight miles outside London, rising from the banks of the River Thames, **Greenwich** is a sprawling, leafy antidote to the crush of the city.

This former royal retreat is the first glimpse by which seaborne travelers view London, but landlocked visitors may explore it in person.

The royal palaces, now recommissioned for use by the Royal Navy, are open to the public and home to hundreds of maritime paintings. The so-called "Painted Hall" dazzles visitors with a floor-to-ceiling mural of ocean squalls, sea serpents, and nude sailors in repose.

Admission 1d. Royal Palaces closed Tuesdays and Sundays.

—from *A Noble Guide to London*
by Sabine Noble

Sabine Noble reread her last line and contemplated the prudence of "nude sailors in repose."

Too provocative?

Potentially, but she'd counted no fewer than thirty-five naked seamen in the overwrought mural, far too many not to mention. Sabine's travel guides had become best-sellers due in no small part to her plain speaking, not to mention her instinct for attractions that would stand out to rural visitors, in particular. Naked sailors fell well within this category.

Sabine left the phrase in and roughed out the sketch that would become the map that accompanied her description of Greenwich. The descriptions amused Sabine, but her true passion was the maps. Part illustration, part functional guide, Sabine filled each *Noble Guide to London* with eye-popping cartography. Not simply maps, but colorful works of art that told a story about each of London's many boroughs and neighborhoods.

"I think we have it, Bridget," Sabine said to the dog resting at her feet. "Measure twice, sketch until it leaps from the page."

The dog, a patchy, one-eared mongrel with a perpetually bared incisor, scrambled to her feet and stabbed her nose to the air, searching for threat. Few things triggered the dog's vigilance like the words *I think we have it*.

I think we have it meant the boring, civilized portion of their day was over, and the excitement would, at long last, commence. Little of interest happened while they surveyed serene parks and hushed museums, but what came after could be very exciting, indeed.

Packing away her drafting kit, Sabine turned her back on the stately order of Greenwich and squinted at the River Thames. Downstream, not a quarter mile away, bobbed the hulking, three-deck warship known as the *Dreadnought*. The boat had been decommissioned in 1831 and anchored in Greenwich to serve as England's floating maritime hospital. The ship took in gravely ill English seamen who had made their way to home to recover (or die) on its bed-lined decks.

Sabine had been mindful not to mention the *Dreadnought* in the *Noble Guide's* entry on Greenwich. Famous warship or not, a hospital was no draw for holiday seekers. Visitors to the *Dreadnought* came to call on the bedside of sick relations, not tour the sights.

Today, if she was lucky, Sabine and her dog would call on ten or eleven sick relations—or rather, she would *feign* some relationship to a dozen sick sailors on board.

"You must pretend to be very excited to see these men," Sabine told Bridget, striding down the riverbank to the looming, ark-like figure of the *Dreadnought*. "I've made an actual script today, loose though it may be. And you are the star."

Too much advanced planning, Sabine had learned, was a threat to flexibility, and flexibility was what allowed her to drift in and out of places that a lady would ordinarily never drift. She had become a rather accomplished snoop, which fit ever so nicely with her other identity as bestselling travel writer. She could pass a morning mapping a given area, making notes about statues and Norman churches, and then devote the afternoon to infiltrating a nearby dark alley or, in this case, a looming hospital ship. If she was detained or challenged, her alibi was the true story of her own life. She was the author of a popular travel guide, and she was in the area for research.

Sabine's father, the famous explorer Nevil Bertrand Noble, had enjoyed the dual role of adventurer *and* cartographer, so travel writer *and* snoop felt quite natural to Sabine, if considerably less esteemed. But Sabine couldn't care less about esteem. She wanted only two things: revenge against her uncle and to finally return home.

She'd arrived in London four years ago from her home in Surrey so very angry, reeling from what had become of her life. Her father had died and her uncle had moved into their family estate and turned on her. Touring the streets of the city had soothed her. She had walked and walked and walked, tears burning her eyes, thoughts racing, railing at the injustice of it all. But also making sketches, each one a little more detailed than the next, of the neighborhoods and boroughs she toured. Soon *A Noble Guide to London* was born.

Her father's map engraver agreed to publish the first installment, and they had invoked Nevil's reputation to promote the book. In no time at all, readers were clamoring for Sabine's clever writing and beautiful maps. By the second installment, bookshops were doing a booming business. By the third, the engraver was begging her to feature every borough and attraction of London in new installments of her *Noble Guide*.

Sabine had complied, choosing parts of town that would be of most interest to tourists. For weeks, she had prowled London's landmarks and hidden treasures, until one day, quite by chance, she crossed paths with one of her father's former apprentices. The young man had been a favorite of the family, and he and Sabine took tea in a café to commiserate about their lives since the great explorer's death.

Amid the pleasantries and remembrances, the young man bemoaned the fact that Sabine's uncle had cut ties with all of her father's students and turned them out of the student cottage at Park Lodge.

"But for what reason would Dryden dismiss you?" she had asked incredulously. "The engraver was paying your stipend, not Dryden. And when Papa's final maps are published, the estate will enjoy the profits. Your work would be a windfall for my cursed uncle."

The apprentice had shrugged. "Cannot say, madam, but he was quite emphatic about it. Between you and me, we students believe he has some alternate plan for the maps. He asked for every sketch, every note, every slip of parchment from our desks. He searched the cottage and our belongings, making sure we stole away with nothing. The same morning that servants carried every folio and map to your father's old library, new locks were installed. I was in the middle of a measurement when they swept through, and they wouldn't permit me to finish the line."

"But it makes no sense to stop work that would eventually bring more money," Sabine had said. "And Sir Dryden had no real interest in Papa's work."

The student had shrugged. "Before we left, I saw that Sir Dryden had guests to the library, a crowd of men in three carriages. He herded them inside and slammed the door."

"What manner of guests?" Sabine had asked.

Another shrug. "Older gentlemen. No one I'd seen before. No one from the world of cartography or engraving, I'll tell you that."

Sabine had left the encounter reeling. She'd raged at the sky and complained to her friends and walked the streets of London for half a day. Ultimately, she'd written to her lone, reliable source at Park Lodge, the longtime lady's maid of her mother, a woman called May. Sabine asked specifically about new guests to Park Lodge and the eviction of her father's students. May had dashed off a quick and detailed reply— names, dates, snatches of conversation overheard from the dining room—and Sabine's search for evidence against her uncle had begun.

Why were her father's students dismissed? What would become of their work? Who were these men, visiting Sir Dryden? How often did they turn up? What endeavor had Sir Dryden embarked upon using her father's unpublished maps?

Beginning with names provided by her mother's maid, Sabine began to nose around London for details. She hadn't known precisely how she would exact revenge against Sir Dryden, but a clearer picture fell into place, clue by clue, every day. One man worked in shipping. Another, munitions. A third man was a chemist. Sabine vowed not to rest until she could determine Dryden's business and return to Surrey to stop him.

Now she tossed a piece of bacon to Bridget and stared up at the *Dreadnought*. Somewhere inside were a dozen scurvy-ridden sailors who could fill in the gaps of her latest discovery. One of Dryden's known associates was, she had discovered, a London-based shipper. The man himself had proven impossible to interview and his sailors were, unfortunately, almost always at sea. But Sabine had learned that this particular crew had contracted scurvy and were, at the moment, laid up on the hospital ship. Pity about their health, Sabine had thought, but also perfectly situated to answer some pointed questions about their employer and his expeditions.

"We must be very charming and lovely, Bridget," Sabine reminded her dog, dropping another piece of bacon.

Bridget regarded every morsel of food as if it were her last, and she attacked the treat.

"You are not even trying, I see." She shaded her eyes, staring at the ship.

Sabine's capacity to beguile was nearly as limited as her dog's, but unlike Bridget, her face and body tended to take over where flirtation failed. Green eyes and sable hair had that effect on men, whether she wanted it or not.

But who would they beguile if no one was on deck? The *Dreadnought*, which she knew to be packed with ailing sailors, looked abandoned in the bright afternoon heat. Sabine's overt sweetness, already in short supply, was rapidly draining away. She ruffled her dog's ears and scanned the area again. In the distance she spied a lone uniformed crewman slouched against the trunk of a tree. His rank was undistinguishable, but he was young. He was savoring a smoke with an expression that Sabine would best describe as blankness. *Perfect.*

"Hello?" Sabine called, approaching the man with a shy wave.

He looked up, sliding his gaze from the top of her hat, down her face and body, and up again. "Hello yourself," he said hopefully.

Bridget growled deep in her throat. Sabine slapped a handful of skirt over the dog's snout.

"Are you," she asked, "a member of staff on the hospital ship?"

"Not for five minutes, I'm not," the man said. "Break."

"Oh, a break, of course. Good for you. But are you . . . a doctor?"

"Right, that's me. Doctor." He laughed. "Deck steward, more like. Who wants to know?"

"Steward? Oh, lovely, perhaps you can help me. Can you tell me how the patients are housed on the ship? That is, are they arranged by condition, or name, or perhaps the severity of their ailment?"

"Searching for a sweetheart, are you?"

Sabine shook her head vigorously. "Oh no, I'm a married woman." About this detail, Sabine never pretended.

Her wedding ring was concealed by her glove, but she raised her left hand by force of habit.

After the obvious escape from her uncle, the two most useful things about Sabine's hasty marriage to Jon Stoker were the wedding ring and the words *I'm a married woman.*

"My husband is a sea captain, in fact, but he is out of the country at the moment."

The third most useful thing about her hasty marriage to Jon Stoker was that he was always, *always*, out of the country. In fact, the last time she'd seen him had been more than a year ago, and even then, their exchange had been limited to a few pleasantries in the street. They did trade letters on occasion. Their correspondence had not been planned, but Stoker had business with an impoverished aristocrat trying to claim a familial relation. It was an old duke trying to finagle a piece of Stoker's growing fortune. At Stoker's request, Sabine sent clippings about the old man from London papers and had even done some snooping around town. She described what she learned in letters and posted them to whatever foreign port Stoker was due to drop anchor.

"Married?" the steward repeated resentfully.

"Quite, but I'm seeking several members of a ship's crew. They're meant to be patients on the *Dreadnought*. They . . . they'd all succumbed to scurvy when they were admitted, I believe."

"Which crew? You'll have a list of their names, I hope?"

Sabine was a miserable liar, but she could hardly reveal that she had no such list. She knew only the name of the last ship on which they sailed.

"Actually, the crew is attached to this dog . . ." she said gainfully, gesturing to Bridget. "She was their unofficial mascot on a particularly harrowing voyage. She has been left in my care while they recover. Scurvy, as I've said. It would bolster them to see her."

The steward squinted at the dog, who, with narrowed eyes and bared teeth, looked like no mascot. In truth, the dog looked a little scurvy-ridden herself.

"Mascot, you say?" he said.

"Indeed. Beloved and sorely missed, I should think."

"How did *you* come to mind her?"

"My brother was among the crew."

And now the lie grew. Sabine spoke more quickly, trying to prevent the story from taking a life of its own. "He died at sea, sadly. But the crew members who survived left the dog in my care. I promised to bring her to visit." She swallowed and added, "As my brother would have wanted."

Sabine snapped her fingers, and Bridget reluctantly lowered herself into a dejected squat, sitting in a crooked approximation of docility. Sabine smiled a sad, wistful smile and batted her eyelashes.

To further distract, she added, "But what is the nature of your work as steward? Do you care for all the patients?" She fidgeted with the button on her glove, flashing the pale skin of her wrist.

He nodded. "All. Except the dead ones, of course."

"The dead?" Sabine looked up.

To date, the investigation of her uncle had not brought her in the path of any dead bodies, and for that she was grateful. She'd been unsettled enough by the prospect of today's *sickly* sailors. Corpses would be quite out of the question.

The sailor looked philosophical. "Aye, dead bodies. Getting on a hospital ship is no guarantee that you'll get off a healthy man, is it? We stack the dead bodies in the ship's hold."

"How . . . efficient," murmured Sabine. This conversation had taken an unpleasant turn for the worse.

The man shrugged. "Can't rightly bury them at sea if the boat is docked. The River Thames is not the sea, is it?"

"No," Sabine managed. She had no interest in the topic of dead bodies or their disposal.

She redirected. "But might your expertise extend to helping me gain access to the ship? I should very much like to locate these men." She smiled her most beguiling smile. Bridget growled and she nudged the dog with her foot.

Ten minutes later Sabine and her dog were being admitted to the tidy, weatherworn gangplank of the hospital ship and directed to Deck Three.

Jon Stoker was in hell.

At long last.

His body . . . on fire. His skin . . . burned away, limb by limb. His throat stung. His very hair was in flames.

His eyes . . . seared. Wouldn't open. Couldn't see. Couldn't breathe.

Suffocation.

Needed to cough, needed to swallow.

Starving.

Thirsty.

Sick, so bloody sick.

Pain everywhere. Cold and hot all at once.

Call out? *No.*

Sit up? *No.*

Turn? *No.*

Draw breath? *No, no, no.*

Try.

Again.

Sleep.

Wake up. Still in hell.

Misery. Cold, burning, suffocating misery.

Now, a dog.

Barking. Barking so bloody loud. Hounds of hell?

And shouting. Deafening shouting. A woman, shouting in his burning ear. She took him by his burning arm. She pulled.

Pain. He was going to retch. So much pain.

Ceaseless barking. She would pull off his arm and feed it to the dogs.

"Stoker?! Jon Stoker! *Stoker!?!?*"

Profanity.

"Jon Stoker?!"

He was in hell, he thought, and the devil was a woman.

And she knew his bloody name.

Chapter Two

Londoners have crossed the River Thames by way of man-made bridge for nearly two thousand years.

History suggests that Romans built the first London Bridge in 55 AD, but a Scotsman called Rennie and his two sons designed and built the newest iteration, a stately, five-arched affair known as **"New London Bridge,"** in 1831.

Stretching from the City of London to Southwark, New London Bridge is a spare, clean overpass for wagons and pedestrians (some three hundred vehicles and five hundred people a day), devoid of the homes, shops, and public latrines that lined earlier bridges on the same site.

Open to the public day and night, densest crowds in early morning and late afternoon.

—from *A Noble Guide to London*
by Sabine Noble

Sabine covered her nose with a handkerchief, blotting out the stink of the River Thames. Today had been a day of terrible smells. The makeshift morgue on the *Dreadnought* exceeded expectations in terms of airlessness and rancidity, and now the crush of vehicles on London Bridge trapped their open wagon over the smoldering river, stewing in the afternoon sun.

Sabine shaded her eyes with her hand and looked down at the unconscious body in the bed of the wagon. Could a gravely ill man become sicker from a terrible odor alone?

She took up a broom from the bed of the wagon and nudged him with the handle. He groaned, and Sabine retracted the broom. She frowned down, her head spinning with questions.

Why, for example, had doctors heaped a not-dead man in a cold, airless room filled with dead corpses?

What condition had rendered the not-dead man so very nearly dead—unconscious, cold, with only the faintest of breath—but not fully deceased?

How had a capable sea captain, and one of the most successful men in England, wound up in a floating charity hospital, surrounded by impoverished sailors?

And finally, most important: Was the man really, actually, truly who he appeared to be: her estranged husband, Jon Stoker, a man she barely knew and had not seen in more than a year?

Well, to this, at least, she knew the answer. Of course the not-dead man was Jon Stoker. She would not have screamed when she'd seen him; she would not have run frantic through the ship for help—she would not have abandoned her own fact-finding mission, her first solid lead in weeks—if she hadn't been certain it was him.

Perhaps she did not know much about the man she married, but she knew he had a distinctive tattoo of a sea serpent on his right arm. She had recognized it immediately, the very thing that had caught her attention as she hurried through a narrow passage in the ship's hull. On closer inspection, she'd recognized his face. He was a pale, thin, sunken-cheeked version of himself, but it was Jon Stoker, there had been no doubt.

As for what she would do with him, the answer was unavoidable; she should maintain his not-dead condition (also known as his life) until she could hand him over to someone who could properly revive him, assuming, God willing, a revival was in his future.

"Can you not maneuver *around* the ox cart?" Sabine asked the driver. She'd hired a wagon to transport them from the *Dreadnought* to her cellar apartment in Belgravia. The crush of vehicles jamming London Bridge had slowed to a lurching crawl. A warm breeze mixed the rank smell of the Thames with the odor of standing livestock.

"And go where, missus?" asked the driver. "There's a carriage and a mail coach ahead of the cart."

Sabine frowned and looked again at Jon Stoker. Should she affect some manner of canopy to shield his face from the sun? It was a warm August day, no threat of rain, and she'd not brought a parasol. She looked around. She saw only her drafting kit, the fresh hay, and two barrels of an unnamed liquid that sloshed with each lurch of the wagon.

She sighed and pulled her dog into her lap. "He may have been better off in the morgue, Bridget."

Nursemaiding was an occupation about which Sabine knew virtually nothing—lack of skill combined with lack of interest with a dash of repulsion. *Not a natural caregiver*, her dear mother had always said, and this was a generous view.

Skill or no, it was common sense to protect one's face from the bright sun . . . unless sun was just what he needed after having been stashed in the dark, airless hull of a ship for God knew how long.

This same common sense had, for better or worse, caused Sabine to dismiss the doctors who hurried to the ship's morgue when she discovered his familiar tattoo and familiar face.

But we must examine him, the doctors had implored her. *He should not be moved. He could be contagious.*

This last exaltation had been the only remark to give her pause. She absolutely did not want to contract whatever condition rendered him so very nearly dead that he passed for a corpse.

But Sabine was proud to a fault, and she had already challenged their competency and humanity. She could hardly back down.

She'd arrived in Greenwich in a Hansom cab, but it wasn't feasible to depart in the same way, stuffing her husband's limp body beside her on the cramped seat. Luckily, the hospital provided wagon service for discharged patients who were too sick (or too dead) to ride or walk away. Sabine agreed to hire the wagon, and Jon Stoker's unconscious form had been loaded into the straw-lined bed of the vehicle by a shaken and repentant staff.

And now here she was, riding beside the very same unconscious form in the wagon, going to the only place she knew to take him, which was her own apartment in Belgravia, a suite of rooms she had taken with her two friends when she left her uncle and moved to London.

She had been a new bride then—a new bride who had spent all of one afternoon with her new husband.

By her request, Stoker had not even come inside the Belgravia house; how ironic that he would go there now.

God help me, she thought. *Please let him remain unconscious until his friends come for him.*

His friends. She was already building a plan for the next step in his care, which absolutely could not include convalescence in the care of Sabine herself. She'd meant what she said when she'd disavowed all men in her life, including men who were nearly dead. She'd been absolute—how could she not, after what her uncle had put her through—and the choice had served her well these past four years. Stoker's closest friends were his business partners, and they would simply have to come for him. One resided in Yorkshire and the other in County Durham. She would write to them at once. There was also a middle-aged London couple from his past, the closest thing he knew as "family." Sabine knew very little about Jon Stoker's personal affairs, but she had deduced over the years that he preferred not to saddle this charitable couple with fresh burdens.

She would write his partners first, she thought. One of them would retrieve him, seek out the care he required, learn how he'd ended up in such dire straits, and . . . set him back on the proper course. In the meantime, surely her spotty and reluctant care was better than slowly dying (the rest of the way) in the hull of a ship.

"*Water?*"

Sabine's head snapped up and the dog leapt from her lap, teeth bared. She leaned forward to examine the ashen face of the not-dead Jon Stoker, her breath held.

"Water?"

Sabine sat up. She had not misheard. Not only was he not dead, he was also *making requests.*

She narrowed her eyes, thinking of the doctors proclaiming that he might never reclaim consciousness or even survive the ride to her home. She would write a letter. No, she would write an editorial for the papers—

"Water?" Jon Stoker rasped again and then mumbled what sounded like French profanity.

Sabine glanced around the spare wagon. She looked to the vehicles to her left and right. She clasped both hands on the arms of the wagon seat, the posture of someone about to do something. *Water, water, how am I meant to produce water?*

"I beg your pardon," she called to the driver. "Do you happen to have a flask of water? Or perhaps these barrels of yours contain drinking water?"

The driver shook his head. "No water here, missus. Barrels have water, but I wouldn't drink it." He laughed, amused by how unfit the water must be.

Sabine nodded and looked again at Jon Stoker. His eyes were closed, dark lashes forming fringed half-moons against his stark cheekbones.

Was it strange that she'd known him from the moment she paused at the door of the *Dreadnought*'s morgue and cautiously peered inside?

She'd seen his tattoo first, winding its way up his biceps in the light of the steward's candle. She'd remembered it from their brief wedding. She'd not seen all of it, of course, but its terrible, sharp-toothed head could be just seen beneath the cuff of his sleeve. She'd asked him about it, one of myriad questions meant to discern his character as quickly and soundly as possible.

She had not thought of it again until the distinctive, fire-eyed sea serpent stopped her where she stood this very afternoon. She'd marched into the terribly dark, terribly fetid room, her vision tunneling to the ink on his wrist.

The steward she'd met outside—so far, a willing guide— had called her back in the high-pitched voice of disbelief. At her heels Bridget had barked and barked and barked, but Sabine had barely heard.

She'd crossed to a limp arm and extended hand, his palm open like a man waiting for a coin. The closer she had gotten, the more certain she had been. Her heart raced but she swam through fear and dread and stooped to see his face. She'd let out the breath she'd been holding and gulped in air; within moments the gulps had turned to sobs.

She had cried, she told herself, because that was what one did when one encountered death. She cried because the *Dreadnought* hospital ship was a terrible place, because he had been alone, because even his closest friends must not have known. She had cried because crying was easier than actually pausing to consider what it would mean if this person was dead. Or nearly dead, as it were.

And then, unbelievably, amid the shock and tears, the dead man whose face and serpent she had known, rolled onto his side and retched.

And swore.

And endeavored to sit up.

After a suspended moment of fraught silence, Sabine's sobs had turned to screams.

Even now, hours later, her voice was hoarse from the sobbing and screaming and rebuking of doctors.

Now she looked again at Stoker's face, wondering if she'd imagined that he'd called out at all.

"Water," he rasped again, causing her to jump. She cleared her throat and bent over him. Bridget growled, uncertain of the unconscious man, and Sabine wrapped her gloved hand around the dog's bony snout.

"Stoker?" she said lowly, with due practicality. "We haven't any water at the moment, but there will be refreshment when we've reached Belgravia."

She paused and added helpfully, "Which is where we are going."

After a moment she said, "Can you manage?"

Sabine did not expect him to respond—*please do not respond*, she prayed—but she waited, watching him for signs of consent. It seemed only polite.

To her alarm, he opened one brilliantly green eye, blinked it, and stared up at her. Sabine reared back and Bridget lunged with a yip.

"Bridget, please," Sabine warned softly, staying the dog with her hand.

"Wh—?" asked the not-dead Jon Stoker, one eye blinking in the bright sun.

Sabine puzzled over this. Did he mean . . . *What?* Or, *Where? Who? Why?*

It could be any of these. And she had so few answers. She elected to stick to what she knew.

"It's me, Sabine Noble. Er, Sabine Stoker. I've discovered you in a very bad way, I'm afraid. But not to worry. I'm taking you to my home and will soon hand you over to someone proficient in . . . in care."

Sabine winced at her own words. It sounded like the same treatment one might give a baby bird, fallen from its nest. She looked at him. He was nearly dead, but he was no baby bird.

With no warning, he moved. A protest? Agreement? Relief? It was impossible to say. He affected an agonized expression and seemed to coil his strength and heave upright. That is, he endeavored to heave. Instead, he shuddered, seized, and then collapsed, making a spine-clunking collision with the bottom of the wagon. He closed his eye again.

Sabine let out a breath and studied his large body carefully, from the toes of his giant feet, bare as they had been in the morgue; up his long legs, covered only by a loose white tunic; over his faintly rising chest, his broad shoulders, to his bearded face. He did not move again. Thank God.

Bridget barked and Sabine scratched the dog idly behind the ears. "Only because he's in such a very bad way, Bridge," she vowed.

She thought about this and added, "What harm could there be?"

Another pause. She said, "He cannot even lift his head."

She had not thought of his weakened condition as a fail-safe, not in as many words, but it was true. She would never have accepted a whole and animate male person into her life and into her home. She would not have accepted a male person who was *conscious*. Even her husband.

She leaned back and checked the traffic on the bridge for progress.

"Just for a day or two, until I can find someone else to take him," she promised the dog. "The partners in his business are very fond of him. It shouldn't take long."

CHAPTER THREE

Jonathon Gentry Stoker was not in hell; he was in a woman's bedroom.

I'm in a woman's bedroom, he thought, the sentence coming to him fully formed, no gaps or blackouts, no confusion, when he . . .

What had he done?

Come to?

Resurrected?

Resuscitated?

It was as if he had awakened, but he had no memory of going to sleep. His only memory, as disjointed and tortured as it was, had been of being dead. And in hell. Racked with chills and burning with fever and tortured. He remembered suffocation, muteness, and pain.

So much pain.

Stoker took a deep breath and focused his new lucidity

on his left side, which had been the distinct source of the most terrible of the pain. Carefully, he endeavored to prop himself up.

The jolt of pain was so immediate and intense, his vision swam and nausea pitched his gut. He collapsed against the pillow, sweat beading his brow.

For five minutes he forced himself to breathe slowly in and out, in and out, willing the revolt to subside.

When his vision cleared at last, when his heart slowed (he would table the notion of sitting up for the moment), Stoker looked around the room.

First, the door. *Am I captive or guest?*

The door to this room stood open. Limp cotton garments hung from a hook—not his clothes, but someone's.

He raised his right hand and examined the sleeve of what appeared to be a white nightshirt. He moved his right leg and felt bare skin against a crisp sheet.

He had the impulse to tear off the covers and examine everything about the alien clothes and his damaged body, but the memory of the pain was too great. He remained supine, sheet bracing him tightly around the chest like a bandage, and breathed in and out, in and out.

He turned his head and scanned the other side of the room. The walls were bright; the furniture was spare. A cluttered sort of casualness pervaded the space. Not unclean, simply . . . strewn. Bandages and paperwork were heaped in a scramble on a desk. Linens drooped in an uneven stack on a chair. A vase beside the bed held a profusion of flowers ranging from thriving to decomposed. Books were stacked in crooked towers across the floor. Morning sun poured through an open window, the breeze fluttering an apricot-colored curtain that sent a pile of newsprint skating across the floor.

Although his crew and his friends took him as careless and undomesticated, he would not, in his own room, allow newspapers to blow to and fro; he would not tolerate the scattered lack of order on the desk, or books on the floor, or the loosely folded wash. He would not, but someone, obviously, did.

He thought he should call for his host (captor?). Most people would do this; they would simply summon whomever was responsible for the soft bed and the sunny room. But Stoker was not most people. It was one thing to be bedridden but quite another to lie prone and cry out. God grant him death before he reached the point of bellowing from a sickbed.

Instead, he closed his eyes and forced himself to call up his last cogent memory, before the pain, and death, and descent into hell. Before this room. Before . . .

Had he been in Spain?

No—Portugal.

Yes. He'd sailed to Portugal to . . . to look in on a villa.

Cabo de San Vicente on the coast in Portugal, and then there had been—

Creeaakk.

His thoughts froze on the strained sound of hinges on

a door. Next, he heard a female voice, her words indistinguishable. He heard the *clunk-clunk* of possessions piling onto a wooden surface. He heard laughter and then . . . growling?

There were footsteps, a pause, and then the determined *click, click, click* of tiny paws on stone floor.

Moments later the ugliest mongrel Stoker had ever seen—part dog, part . . . weasel?—clicked into the room and continued to the bed as if they shared it. Stoker held his breath when he saw the dog's intention, bracing his damaged body for impact. The animal leapt and landed unevenly at Stoker's feet, scuttling up his legs and belly and stopping on his chest, sniffing along the way. The tiny tapping paws from the floor felt like talons against his skin. Only when the animal hovered over him, nearly nose to nose, did the dog pause and stare down into Stoker's face.

Stoker opened his mouth to say, *"Off,"* but the dog beat him to it, filling the quiet room with an explosive round of frantic barking.

Now Stoker did say, "Off!" but it was drowned out by the dog. The animal crouched in a defensive position on his chest, baring its teeth between barks. Four razor paws dug into the thin barrier of sheet and nightshirt.

"Bridget, down!" said a voice from the doorway, and Stoker craned his head, trying to see.

"Bridget," repeated a firm female voice, "I said, *down!"*

Footsteps—and then there she was, plucking the dog from his chest, its short, mangy legs windmilling in midair—a blur of yellow dress. Stoker lifted his head, trying to see around the dog to the woman. He saw yellow again, black hair, swift, efficient movements, and then—

He dropped his head back to the pillow.

Sabine Noble.

His wife.

Chapter Four

*The up-and-coming neighborhood of **Belgravia** sits atop colorful Mayfair like the stiff white hat. Uniform stucco crescents surround a verdant private garden. Shiny black ironwork cordons walkways and steps. The result is regal and important, not unlike the well-heeled Londoners and foreign dignitaries who have made Belgravia their home.*

But don't be fooled; these pristine terrace mansions only appear to be cut from ivory or marble; they're actually made of painted bricks fired from the mud that formerly moldered beneath the area's original landscape, which for centuries was Middlesex marshland and bog.

—from *A Noble Guide to London*
by Sabine Noble

Sabine deposited Bridget on the floor and rose, taking up a stack of clean towels from Stoker's bedside. She peered down at him, curious at what had set the dog off. After four days Bridget should be accustomed to a semiconscious man lying in their bedro—

Sabine let out a little yelp and dropped the towels.

"Good God!" she gasped, staring at the man in her bed. Bridget resumed barking, jumping, and spinning at her feet. "Bridget, quiet!"

The now-awake Jon Stoker stared straight up at the ceiling, ignoring her, ignoring the dog, and Sabine had the panicked thought that he had, at long last, died.

She took a tentative step closer, extending her neck for the best view from the greatest distance. He lay motionless, *eyes* unblinking.

He is dead, she thought, taking another step.

His eyes slid left, the alert gaze of a decidedly living man, and locked on her face. Sabine drew back. He looked back to the ceiling.

"Stoker?" she whispered.

Jon Stoker had opened his eyes several times in the four days, but his expression had been vague and cloudy. He looked but did not see; he'd been alert enough to take food and water, but he had not been sentient.

Today his gaze was sharp. His eyes stared at the ceiling with full consciousness. His body, previously limp beneath the sheet, was rigid; his jaw was clenched. Even his beard looked wilder.

Sabine hopped a step back. She'd taken to breezing in and out of this room at all hours; it was alarming, really, how comfortable she'd become with his inert form taking up silent space in her suite of rooms in the cellar of Arthur and Mary Boyd's Belgravia townhome. But of course he posed no risk if he was out of his head, too feeble to roll over. And if his friends turned up soon to reclaim him. If he simply remained mostly asleep.

But now . . .

Not taking her eyes from him, Sabine stooped and retrieved her dog, hugging Bridget to her chest.

"Stoker?" she asked again, more pointedly this time. Caution translated to timidity in her brain, and timidity felt like fear. When she left her uncle's purview, she vowed to never be afraid again. "*Stoker?*"

"Where am I?" he asked. His voice was raspy, hoarse—but his tone? Not vague, not even weak.

And not particularly friendly.

"It's me, Sabine," she said. "I've brought you home—er, to my home. This is the house where I reside in London. In Belgravia."

"Brought me *from where?*" He wouldn't look at her.

Had he gone blind? she wondered.

"From the morgue on the hospital ship *Dreadnought*. In Greenwich. You'd been left for dead, I'm afraid. You've a wound in your side—the doctors say you were likely stabbed. Infection has set in."

She saw him grimace and endeavored to shift beneath the covers. Bridget growled and Sabine fastened a hand around her snout.

"Careful," she said. "Perhaps it's best not to make unnecessary movements. I've hired a footman to care for your personal needs, and you suffer considerable pain when he, er, tends to you, I believe. From the sound of it, that is. I wait in the, er, corridor."

"I'm being *tended to*?" He gritted out the words.

Sabine frowned at this. "Well, you are hardly in the condition to tend to yourself. You were left for dead, as I've said. You are well enough to have this conversation, which is an improvement, but I'd wager that is the extent of what you can accomplish at the moment. You are rather sick, I'm afraid."

Stoker squeezed his eyes shut. "If I was left for dead," he ground out, "why did they summon you? What connection was made between a dead man and his estranged wife?"

"There was no connection," she said. "I came upon you quite by accident. I had other business on the *Dreadnought*. By sheer happenstance, a steward led me by the morgue and I noticed your—" She felt herself redden, thinking of the jolt she'd felt when she'd seen the serpent tattoo winding up his muscled forearm.

She began again. "That is, I noticed *you*. Upon closer inspection, I discovered that it was, indeed, *you* and you were not dead after all. The doctors wanted to move you to a proper bed and keep you on, but I could hardly abandon you there. Not when they had already failed to notice something as significant as your beating heart."

She made a face, remembering. "I cannot say I recommend the hospital ship *Dreadnought*, given the choice. Even the most fit patient was uncomfortable, to say the least. I could not, in good conscience, leave you there."

"You are under no obligation to me," he breathed, eyes still closed. He shifted again and winced.

Sabine squinted at him. "A simple 'thank you for saving my life' would be sufficient in this moment, Stoker." She forgot herself and stepped to the bedside, staring down at him. "I don't require gratitude, of course, or even expect it, but cordiality would be appreciated."

He didn't move; his eyes remained closed.

Sabine marveled over his detached rudeness. She'd hardly thought he would be cheerful when he came around, but she had gone to considerable trouble to affect what she thought of as his "rescue."

She reminded herself that she didn't know Jon Stoker, not really. Perhaps he was always like this. She'd spent all of two half days with him when they'd married; and they'd interacted only intermittently after that. Rarely did she see him in person.

She tried to remember her own demeanor when they'd first met, when she'd been the damaged one—eyes blackened, lip bloody. She'd been helpless and furious and embarrassed, and she'd tried not to look at him. But had she grunted out short sentences and failed to show gratitude?

No, she reasoned, *I did not.*

Sabine looked at him and said, "We are not well acquainted, you and I, and no one relishes infirmity, but I did snatch you from the jaws of death. Surely, you don't resent the effort."

Prudence demanded that she not lecture him, that she *not care* whether he was resentful or silent or wouldn't look beyond the end of his nose. Honestly, she'd hoped he would be gone or in the process of going when he came to. She'd sent word to his friends by private courier. Surely, they would arrive any day.

Now he turned his head and looked up at her. The brilliant green had returned to his eyes, the redness and cloudiness gone. She sucked in a little breath.

"Forgive me." His tone was not the least bit repentant. "I am not resentful, I am mortified. I am not accustomed to being *cared for*."

"Oh," she said, softening. "Well, I am not accustomed to providing care, so perhaps we are even. But never fear, I have written to your friends, and they will come for you soon, I am certain."

His head snapped back. "Which friends?"

"Your partners, Joseph Chance and the Earl of Cassin."

He considered this and then nodded. "I worried that you meant Bryson and Elisabeth Courtland. I would not want them to see me—" he looked down at his body "—in this condition."

Bryson and Elisabeth Courtland were the wealthy couple who sponsored Stoker when he'd been a street boy. They had provided his education and were the closest thing he had to a real family. The couple had endeavored to meet Sabine after she and Stoker married, but she had resisted. She was not really married to Jon Stoker, not in a traditional sense. When the time came to send for help, she had considered them, but ultimately she decided the explanations and assumptions would not be worth the bother.

"No, I did not contact the Courtlands," she said.

"Thank God," he said. "Elisabeth Courtland would make a fuss and be sick with worry. My debt to Bryson and Elisabeth extends two lifetimes already."

"Well, you have no debt to me," Sabine said briskly, "and you needn't be mortified where I'm concerned. My rooms are modest and there is almost no staff. You will find that I am a distracted and, dare I say, reluctant nurse. I never pounce. I will not wring hands or swab your brow or administer any treatment not explicitly directed by the doctor—and several of those I have omitted because they seem extraneous or I can't be bothered. As I mentioned, I have paid one of the Boyds' footmen—you'll remember the Boyds? I have paid one of their footmen to manage your, er, personal needs."

Now it was her turn to wince. She cleared her throat and released Bridget to the floor. The dog immediately leapt onto the bed, and Stoker grunted in pain.

"And I have a dog," she said. "She is terribly behaved and comes and goes from your sickbed as she pleases, which is frequent. Considering all this, you may yet have me send for the Courtlands after all."

Stoker eyed Bridget as she sniffed her way up his body, her short dog legs wobbling for balance on the uneven terrain of the bedcovers.

"I won't," he said, wincing. "But I will hire my own doctor and staff and relocate. I keep a suite of rooms in Regent Street when I am in London. There is no reason for me to intrude on you. Despite the fact that you discovered me on a charity ship, we are both aware that I can provide for myself."

This plan sent a jab of something sharp in the area of Sabine's chest. *Relief*, she guessed. *Or gladness?*

No . . . she was not glad or relieved. She was—

Well, to begin, the room felt suddenly chilled. She

frowned at the open window. Bright sunshine coursed in, mocking her. It was August, and there was no chill.

"Actually," she heard herself say, "the doctor has said you absolutely may not be moved while the stitching in your side heals—that is, if you expect your stab wound to effectively close and stave off further infection."

Bridget continued her scrambling progress up his body, stepping on his groin, his stomach, his chest—tiny paws painfully close to the wound in question. Stoker let out a ragged gasping sound.

"I will risk it," he said.

Without thinking, she said, "You're joking."

"No," he breathed, watching the dog root up his body. "I'm not."

"Are you mad?" she asked. She would not restrict his movements, of course, but she'd already invested four days in his care, and considering the rapidly approaching deadline on her next travel guide, not to mention the investigation of her uncle, it would be such a waste to have him leave and then do something as inconsiderate as *die*. Four days for nothing.

Now Bridget was on his chest, staring him in the face, her nose just inches from his.

"I am a grown man," he said to the dog. "I cannot tolerate being tended to by a hired footman or a wom—or *you*. I've a ship that is apparently missing and a crew with it. I must begin an inquiry that will locate them both. I've been attacked and left for dead, two circumstances for which there will be grave consequences. I need to discover who and why. None of this can be managed from your bed, regardless of how grateful I am for your care to this point. I don't know what day it is, I don't know what *month* it is, and I am ravenously hungry, but I refuse to lie prone in this bed and ask you, of all people, to hasten to the kitchen and feed me like an invalid."

She was just about to tell him that it was a Tuesday, in August, and that he *was* an invalid, but he pulled an arm from beneath the covers to push away the dog, and the combination of this exertion and his long proclamation of *I don'ts* and *I won'ts* overwhelmed him. His skin went ghostly white, his emerald-green eyes blinked and then rolled back in his head, and he collapsed against the pillow in a dead faint.

Even Bridget's fresh round of barking did not rouse him. Sabine scooped up the dog, sailed from the room, and went up the stairs to prepare his broth and cider. He'd said he was hungry—arguably the only sensible thing he'd said—and so he should eat. Although she did not have all day to wait around. Today she would return, finally, to the *Dreadnought*. Her plans to interview the scurvy sailors had been postponed while she settled Stoker into her house, but she'd always planned to go back.

She had time to feed Stoker and carry on—or argue with him and carry on—but she did not have time for both.

CHAPTER FIVE

Stoker was roused from a deep, dreamless slumber by the smell of food. Onion, cloves, poached chicken—*food*. His mouth began to water before he opened his eyes.

"Stoker, you must eat," said a voice—*her* voice—and realization struck him like a punch to the gut.

He squeezed his eyes more tightly shut, willing her away, willing himself dead rather than subjected to this helplessness. The hunger in his stomach and dull ache in his side receded. He knew only his pounding heart.

"Stoker," she repeated, more sharply this time.

"I'm leaving," he rasped. This had been his last thought before the pain and exertion had sucked him under.

He felt ridiculous speaking without opening his eyes, but he didn't want to look at her. Even more, he didn't want her to look at him, or touch him, or, God forbid, *feed him*. He wanted to be whole again. In absence of that, he wanted to be gone from this house. To be feeble and helpless and pathetic in the privacy of his own quarters. He wanted—

Clattery ministrations beside the bed distracted him from his long list. He blinked at the ceiling and then stole a glance from the corner of his eye.

He saw the yellow dress, a tendril of black hair bob against her cheek. A familiar yearning, faint but insistent, rose in the pit of his stomach; he felt it even over the pain, even over the mortification. She wasn't looking at him, thank God. She wouldn't see his regard in his face. He'd always been so careful not to reveal it in his face.

She dropped the salt cellar, swore, and then stooped to pick it up. Her hair was so black, it glinted bluish in the sunlight from the window. She'd twisted it on top of her head and secured it with a yellow ribbon. Never once had Stoker looked at her hair without the fantasy of seeing it long and loose down her back. For this reason, he so rarely gave himself the opportunity to look at her. Once or twice a year. Fleetingly. Ten minutes at a time. Long enough to notice her hair. And her skin, which was unblemished white, the color of fresh cream.

In their brief encounters, he always marveled at two things: her stunning beauty and that she'd married him. She could have had any man. Or, she could have had no man and been a gift to the world, simply by moving through it.

Now Stoker worked furiously not to stare. She didn't like it; and, despite his desire to study her, feature by feature, he had learned at an early age to keep a distance from things he would never have.

Now she was dragging a chair across the room, her movements more intent than careful. When she arrived at the bedside with the chair, she created a table by balancing five books on a footstool, topped by a wooden box, a sixth book, and now the tray of food teetering on top of it all. The makeshift tower listed slightly and she took up a napkin and spoon.

"I beg your pardon?" she said casually, indulgently.

Stoker snapped his head back to the ceiling. He hated being indulged.

"I said," he informed her, trying to sound sane, "that I will take my leave. Today—now." The pronouncement actually managed to sound more petulant the second time around.

"Oh yes," she said, "by all means, you should go. Heave yourself up and gather your things and walk right out the door."

"I will hire transportation," he said. He tried to shove up in the bed, but the jolt of fresh pain made him breathless and he collapsed against the pillows.

"Yes, I know you can hire a great many things," she said, "but that does not mean these are wise or healthy things. It doesn't mean it would be the rational behavior of a man of sound mind." He heard the clink of her spoon against china and the thud of something being lifted and replaced to the floor. Liquid sloshing into a goblet. His throat burned. He was so bloody thirsty.

"Will you take some broth and water?" she asked.

"My mind is sound," he informed her, even while he wanted to say, *Yes.*

"Brilliant. If your mind is intact, then we've made real progress. The doctor said your wits should eventually return, but there was never a guarantee."

Stoker groaned at the thought of Sabine spoon-feeding him under the assumption that he might never regain his wits.

"Look," she went on, "it's obvious you are displeased with the arrangement, but I'll not be responsible for the setback that would surely result from a . . . a *hired transport*. The doctor means for you to stay, and I am inclined to follow his orders. His directives have been very effective so far. And this includes the order that you should eat and drink as much as possible. So, while you glower and tell me how you will soon take your leave, can you also open your mouth and eat this soup? I've quite a full day, actually. You were much easier to feed when you were barely conscious."

Stoker considered refusing the sustenance; turning away was quite literally the only stand he could take at the moment. But then his stomach growled audibly, the rumble filling the room, and it felt more ridiculous to pretend.

"There's a good man," said Sabine briskly, moving in with the spoon.

"Oh God," mumbled Stoker, wincing at her encouragement, and Sabine said, "What?"

"No platitudes," he said. "I will eat, but do not praise me like a child."

"Oh right," said Sabine, but then she drew back, dropping the spoon into the bowl. "This position flat on your back will never work. Can you—?" She stood up. She opened her hands over him, and then stopped. She snatched her hands back. "Harley the footman usually hoists you up to sitting before I feed you," she said.

"I can sit," he said. He had no idea if he could sit.

"Can you?" Her tone said that he could *not*. She crossed her arms over her chest.

Stoker ignored this and concentrated on animating his arms and planting his palms on the bed. His heart pounded; the sheets weighed at least a stone. Pain dragged along every limb like a match. He bit his lip and pushed on.

"Harley has midday duties," Sabine mused, watching with a worried look, "but I could ask him to come down for five minutes."

"I can sit." Sweat poured down Stoker's neck and he gasped, unable to contain the agony of shoving up. It took three tries, but he would not *not* sit.

Sabine did not reach out to help him, nor did she look away. She observed his gaspy, red-faced struggle as if she was watching a stuck wagon slowly roll from the mud. Stoker closed his eyes.

"I would congratulate you," she sighed, reclaiming her seat, "but you've said no platitudes. Can you still take the broth?"

"I can feed myself," he rasped. This was likely untrue.

"Of course you can," she mocked. He heard chair legs slide closer to the bed, the clink of the spoon. "Open."

Stoker forced one eye open and looked at her.

"Your mouth, not your eye."

"I will not be spoon-fed like an invalid," he said.

"You are not *like* an invalid, you *are* an invalid, and spoon-feeding is the only way to get this delicious soup down your gullet. Open."

He blinked at her, wondering how long he could resist. His stomach growled again.

"Did I mention," she sighed, "that I have a very busy day?"

"When did you write to Cassin and Joseph?" If he must consent to her ministrations, he would know for *how long*.

"Four days ago," she said, bringing the spoon to his mouth.

He could not look at her and accept food from her hand, so he closed his eyes again. The warm, salty broth pooled on his tongue, the most delicious food he had ever tasted, and he gulped it down. She spooned another dose into his mouth, and another, and another. His pride melted away, and he forgot about closing his eyes. He was ravenous for the next bite.

"Good, isn't it?" she said. "I've been rather spoiled here with the Boyds. Their staff is impeccably trained and the cook in particular is a great talent."

"No word at all from Joseph or Cassin?" Stoker asked.

"Oh yes, they've sent concerned letters, two and three a day, but I have hidden them from you, so that I may relish your convalescence as long as I can." She offered a goblet of water and he drank greedily.

"Never you fear," she sighed. "I will relinquish you to them as soon as either of them makes an appearance. In the meantime, you are stuck with me."

"I am not ungrateful," he said, gasping between gulps.

"You are wholly ungrateful," she said, refilling the goblet, "but my dog likes you, and I can look after you around my other work, so it could be worse, I suppose."

"The travel guides?" He was so weary of talking about himself.

"There is that," she said vaguely. She took up a baguette and flapped it back and forth over his face like a fan. "Would you try some bread?"

"I can manage," he gritted out. He forced his right arm to rise, and he snatched the bread, a small triumph. He raised his left hand and tried to rip the baguette in two, but his strength failed him. He blinked and looked at the ceiling, raging.

Sabine snatched the bread as if she hadn't seen and tore off a hunk. She tucked a chunk into his hand. "I'm actually balancing the work of the travel guides with another project," she told him importantly.

Whether she meant to distract from his weakness or actually wanted to share her work, he could not say. She stared thoughtfully into the distance. Stoker raised the bread to his mouth with a shaking hand and took a pathetic bite.

She glanced at him, waiting for some encouragement, and he felt compelled to go along. "What other project?"

"Piecing together criminal evidence. Against Dryden."

Stoker opened his mouth to take more bread, but he snapped it shut. He looked at Sabine. "What sort of criminal evidence?"

"Well, I've always thought *criminal* was an apt *general* description of my uncle, but—clever me—I believe I've stumbled upon actual proof. Legal proof of crimes punishable by law."

"What crimes?" Stoker forgot the bread. Sir Dryden

Noble was a tyrant and a sadist, and he'd thought he'd delivered her from ever tangling with him again.

"Crime enough to oust him from Park Lodge and allow me to return home," she said. She began to collect the bread and spoon and tidy the tray. "The Boyds' home is comfortable and London has been diverting, but I cannot remain here forever. My real home is Park Lodge, and I always meant to go back. My mother's health grows worse every year. But I can't return if I do not remove my uncle. How much more effective to have the authorities do it for me?"

Sabine reached to press a napkin to his lips, and he turned his face away. He summoned all his strength to wipe his own mouth with his sleeve. He said, "Sabine, *what crimes?*"

Sabine looked right and left as if they might be overheard. "I learned in the spring that he's dismissed all my father's students and put a stop to their work on his last folio of maps. He's using the maps for some other purpose—that's what I believe."

"What purpose? What illegal thing could be done with *maps?*"

"Well, the maps chart the landscape of the barrier islands that cluster around the shores of Great Britain. This had been my father's last project. And . . ." now she lowered her voice ". . . I believe that Sir Dryden has taken some role in illegal *smuggling*, using these barrier islands to bring contraband goods into England."

"Smuggling?" Stoker choked. His mind leapt to every blackguard smuggler, every rotting boat, every danger he'd ever witnessed in his ten years as a sea captain.

"Yes, smuggling," Sabine went on. She sounded triumphant. "There are more than a hundred barrier islands around Britain, and none of them had ever been properly mapped until my father's last expedition. Intimate knowledge of these islands is a smuggler's dream. Contraband can be unloaded, hidden among the rocks and caves, and rowed to shore in small lots. The islands have been used for this purpose for centuries, but I believe Sir Dryden is organizing a *fleet* of smugglers to navigate the barrier islands on a grand scale."

Stoker blinked at her; the words *fleet of smugglers* and *grand scale* spun in his head. He said, "Sabine, who is helping you?"

She stopped in the process of hoisting the tray. "Helping me? Why would I need help?"

Because smugglers are deadly serious about their work, and you have no idea what you're doing, he thought. But he said, "Because collaborations can be . . . useful."

She shrugged and continued with the tray. "My mother's nursemaid, May, writes me with any gossip she overhears from Dryden's many meetings and dinner guests. Her letters to me could be considered a collaboration, I suppose."

Stoker opened his mouth to contradict but Sabine had warmed to the topic. "According to May, one man returns repeatedly to Park Lodge. Mr. Walker Leaver. We know his name, but it's been nearly impossible to learn his occupation. We have ferreted out the workplaces of every other Park Lodge guest, but I've found so few details on Mr. Leaver. Only a vague connection to shipping. Finally, at the end of last month, I overheard a conversation in Blackwall."

"Blackwall?" Stoker repeated in a strangled voice.

Sabine nodded with enthusiasm. "The two men talking suggested that the illustrious Mr. Leaver is not so much a *shipper* as a *smuggler*. And that's when I knew I had him. Dryden is consorting with known smugglers, and I need only learn how and why. When I discovered that sailors under the employ of Mr. Leaver could be found recuperating on the *Dreadnought*, I knew my next step. And *that* is why I was on the hospital ship—well, that, and to discover your lifeless form, of course. Assuming one believes in fate. But now I shall return to the hospital ship to speak to the sailors about the nature of their work for Mr. Leaver." She rattled it off like plans for the market. She was halfway to the door.

"Sabine," Stoker called, trying to keep his voice level, "the men who work as smugglers would not think twice about taking a life to protect their profits."

She did not miss a step. "Perhaps, but I am very careful. And I have the travel writing to disguise my investigation. No one knows I am snooping around, piecing together my uncle's business." She smiled and sailed from the room, her dog trotting after her.

For the first time since he'd awakened, Stoker forgot about the pain, the helplessness, or the mortification of being an invalid. He thought only of Sabine in her pretty dress and yellow ribbon moving through the underground network of pirates and smugglers on London's docks. His mouth went dry. "Sabine?" he rasped.

There was a pause and she stuck her head back into the room. "Yes?"

"Do you mean to return to the *Dreadnought*—now?"

"Of course." She looked at him like true madness had finally set in. "Don't worry. I won't acquire any additional corpses. I went there to interview sailors who are still very much alive. Or at least they were four days ago," she said, smiling vaguely and ducking away.

Stoker was left to stare at the empty doorway and realize a new level of helplessness. The *Dreadnought* was likely the safest of the places Sabine would venture. Clearly, she'd been to Blackwall, and more than once. She was hounding the steps of a possible smuggler. God only knew the business of these other men or how it all tied together. Stoker allowed himself to think, perhaps for the first time, of all the places his wife had snooped before he'd washed up on England's shores. He knew her well enough to acknowledge that she would not stop with scurvy sailors on the *Dreadnought*.

No, he thought, helplessness was not being spoon-fed by his wife; helplessness was being too bloody infirm to protect her.

Chapter Six

Five hours later, as the setting sun cast long shadows on Belgrave Square, Sabine hurried home from interviewing the scurvy-ridden sailors in Greenwich. Her boots struck a confident *clip, clip, clip* on the walkway, and Bridget scuttled to keep up. She'd made such progress in one afternoon. Names, dates, the port from which they sailed, the barrier islands they'd dropped anchor—the details crowded her brain like unmarked roads on a map.

Her instinct had been correct; Sir Dryden was furnishing her father's channel-island maps to seasoned smugglers. Together they were sneaking illegal goods into England, and on a grand scale. The sailors could not have been more clear. She now knew Dryden's particular interest was to a barrier island off the Dorset coast called the Isle of Portland. It was only a matter of time before she learned what they smuggled and how the newly mapped Isle of Portland came into play. Then she would have solid, actionable proof of illegal smuggling, including names and dates. His certain imprisonment would be her freedom. And her revenge.

When Sabine reached home, she clipped down the cellar steps, bypassing the Boyds' front door. She typically spent a few minutes chatting with the older couple when she returned for the day, but not tonight. Tonight she had pages of notes to transcribe and consider. She'd jotted down a few things while she was interviewing the sailors, but not every word. She'd visited them under the guise of charitable caller, visiting the sick, so most of the visit had been spent tsking and fawning and allowing them to play with the dog. But they spoke so very easily about their role in the last smuggling run, the conversation had been a veritable goldmine of evidence. She wanted to get down every detail while it was still fresh in her mind.

Sabine unlocked her door with haste and flung her satchel and scarf in the direction of the bench. Bridget was hungry, yipping at her feet, but she ignored her, tugging off her gloves as she made her way down the corridor to her study.

When she passed the bedroom containing the inert Jon Stoker, she shot him a quick glance, certain he would be asleep, and hurried on to the—

Sabine stopped so quickly, she nearly stepped on the dog.

Jon Stoker was not sleeping or inert. He was gone.

The bed containing Jon Stoker contained no one at all. Jon Stoker appeared to be gone.

Sabine blinked twice, pivoted, and stared into the room. The empty bed was lit by the last orangey ray of sunset. The crisp sheets were folded back like a carefully opened envelope.

She let out a little gasp and scanned the room. The chair by the bed was vacant. The desk unoccupied, the window unobstructed, the bookshelf clear. She looked back to the front door. The entryway was empty and the small parlor adjacent to the bedroom was—she spun around—empty.

"Stoker?" Sabine called, her voice hollow. She felt an unexpected surge of something like panic. *But could he have actually gone?*

The words *Not yet* formed, unbidden in her brain. He was still so ill, his friends would surely be rushing to his bedside at any hour. And she was going to tell him about the sailo—

But no, she thought.

He couldn't have managed to drag himself away. He couldn't even hold a spoon. He—

"I'm here," said a gravelly male voice from the study.

Sabine's head shot up. She was flooded with a strange rush of emotion.

Relief? He had not gone.

No, not relief. Anger.

How in God's name had he managed to leave the bed?

She looked at the door to the room down the corridor. *Her* room. No, so much more than a room, her *sanctuary*. Sabine had taken over the room as her study when Tessa and the baby had gone. She slept in the bedroom, she took meals with the Boyds, but her life and future were carefully drawn in her study. She'd moved in a proper desk and leather chair, castoffs from the Boyds. She'd assembled shelves and bought a used drafting table.

She used the study for her cartography and writing and,

most recently, her growing evidence against Sir Dryden. She didn't want anything disturbed, she wanted to come and go at all hours, and she did not want anyone looking at her evidence. Even the maid was not allowed inside.

It had been one thing to install Stoker in her bedroom, but it was quite another to discover him inhabiting this, of all spaces.

"Stoker?" she called. "Are you there?" She strode down the corridor, swiping a glowing lamp from the sideboard. The dog darted ahead.

"Stoker?" she repeated, her voice all business. "I am not—"

She paused at the threshold. There was an open-flame candle on the desk, illuminating the study with an eerie yellow glow. In her desk chair sat Stoker, freshly shaved, hair trimmed, wearing a dressing gown and breeches she'd never seen before. Even in the shadowy candlelight, she could see his face was as white as cold ash. He appeared to be five seconds from rolling to the floor.

Sabine held up her lamp. "You've left your bed. You're dressed. How, in God's name?"

He turned his head slowly, an old man in pain, and studied her. With the beard gone, she could see the gauntness of his face. His lips were thin. His shoulders were hunched.

"Your footman, Harley," he said simply.

"You've paid Harley to serve as valet?"

Stoker shifted in the chair and winced. "I made it worth his while to run errands to my rooms in Regent Street and do something about my madman's hair and beard."

"And to install you in my private study?"

He made a scoffing noise and winced again. "*Install* is a very apt description of how I arrived here—but yes, he was good enough to help me. I've rather urgent letters I need to get out—the small matter of my missing brig and crew, the fact that I was left for dead, et cetera. And the desk in the bedroom had no ink."

His words were matter-of-fact, but she could hear the underlying struggle. He was winded and hoarse.

Even so, she felt compelled to repeat: "This is my private study."

"I was endeavoring to make today's post."

"Four days ago you were as good as dead, and today you are endeavoring to make the post?"

"Yes, in fact. Making the post is one of many steps I intend to reclaim my life. I will also do things such as venture beyond my sickroom and wear breeches if I can help it."

"Are you suggesting that you've been restricted under my care?"

"*No*," he said with forced patience, "I've been undyingly grateful for your care. But now that I'm up—or at least now that I'm not quite so low down—I am running mad with all the things that I would have done."

Sabine understood his madness, truly she did, but her own anxiety overshadowed it. She was unnerved by the sight of the large form in her chair. Her desk was hardly tidy, but she could see he'd moved books, flipped pages on her calendar. Heaps of fresh parchment were scattered about in the room in wads. But how long had he been here?

"I understand your urgency," said Sabine, taking a step inside, "but I really must impose a restriction on roaming the apartments when I'm not at home. I can provide writing materials for the bedroom desk. I can provide whatever you require. You need only have the patience to wait for my return and to ask." She stooped to pick up a wad of parchment.

"I am not a patient man."

"And I am not the proprietress of a coaching inn." She took another step. "These rooms are not yours to inhabit as you wish."

"In the very near future, I hope to be removed from these rooms entirely."

And now she was angry. Not only was he intrusive, he was also so very *ungrateful*. She picked up another wad of paper. "*At present*, I would prefer that you removed yourself from *this* room. I'm not accustomed to sharing my private office, and I've work to do." She set down the lantern with a clunk and tossed the parchment into the bin.

Stoker opened his mouth to say something and then closed it. He looked away.

"Stoker?" she prompted sharply.

"I'll go," he said simply, but he didn't move.

She narrowed her eyes. *Yes*, she thought, *you bloody will.* She said, "You may take the ink. Take any writing materials you require. Whatever else you need, I can—"

She reached for the ink pot on the desk in the same moment Stoker made a grunting noise and shoved from the chair. The motion caught Sabine off guard and she skittered back.

"Damn, damn, *damn*," he said lowly, falling back into the chair with an *oof*.

Sabine frowned down at him. "Stoker?" she asked cautiously.

He shook his head. He sat stiffly in her chair with his eyes squeezed shut. His entire face was squeezed, every feature creased, the expression of extreme pain.

"Are you—?" she ventured.

He made a little growling noise and shoved again, this time while sucking in breath. She held out a hand, but he ignored it. When he was up, he paused, one arm out as if balance eluded him. After listing there for a long moment, he took one cautious step.

"You're in pain," she realized. "*You cannot move* for the pain."

"I can move," he gritted out. He took two shaky steps, staggered, tipped, and began to crumble.

Sabine shrieked and lunged, ducking beneath his arm just in time to catch him. She looped his arm around her neck and shouldered his weight.

"*No*," he said, but his body came down on hers, heavy and burning hot. Sabine widened her stance and braced, struggling to hold them up.

"Are you fainting?" she gasped.

He shook his head.

"Are you . . ." she began but stopped because she was losing her grip. She cast around for his hand on her shoulder and grabbed it for leverage. She searched his face, his legs, the spot on his side where the stab wound—

Sabine let out a little shriek. "*Stoker*, you're bleeding! Your stitches—have you ripped them? Why didn't you mention this?"

There was so much blood. His left hand covered his bandaged ribs, and blood had soaked through his dressing gown between his fingers.

Stoker said nothing and clung to her, his eyes shut tight, his body a strange combination of tautness and dead weight. He shook his head once, a sharp jerk to the left.

"*Stop*," she demanded. "Open your eyes. Martyrdom will get you as far in this house as trespassing. Can you walk?"

He nodded and made the smallest possible step; one foot dragged in front of the other. "You haven't the strength to hold me up," he said.

"There's only one person here lacking in strength," she said, "and it's not me. Can you take another step?"

"I'm hurting you," he ground out, his words barely audible. "Too heavy."

He was exceedingly heavy, and the giant mass of him hung unevenly on her right side. One of his hands clenched his wound and the other held hers in a vise grip. Each step was a slow, careful slide.

Sabine felt around beneath his arm, searching for a handhold that would not further damage his wound. She widened her stance, stooped to readjust the arm on her shoulders, and then pushed up, evening out the weight.

Bridget had begun a low growl, circling them in nervous rings. Sabine jerked her head, dismissing the dog, but she would not leave them.

"Stoker, *what* happened?" Sabine asked. They continued to the door in small, sidewinding steps.

"I've been stabbed," he growled, "or so you've told me."

"Hilarious. Did the footman know you were in such pitiful shape?"

"Must we . . . use the . . . word . . . *pitiful?*" he breathed.

They passed the drafting table and he reached out, trying to brace himself. The table tipped under his weight, and Sabine gasped, staggering to correct them. He reached out again, finding the correct balance, and leaned over the table.

"Harley was ultimately called away by Mrs. Boyd," Stoker panted. "He was meant to come back. He said he would come back."

Sabine shook her head. "His first duty is to his actual employer. I've only borrowed him for small tasks when he was on break." She took three deep breaths. She disentangled her free hand from his fingers and wiped her brow. "I hope Mary hasn't missed him today. How many errands did he run on your behalf?"

"A handful. I will wait for him. Leave me here, and I will wait."

"Wait on my drafting table? No."

"I am not helpless," he said.

"You are entirely helpless," she countered. "The longer you remain upright with the wound unchecked, the more blood you will lose. The doctor was very explicit about your remaining in a constant *prone position*. You must return to the bed immediately."

"No." He shook his head.

"*Yes*," she countered. "Is your vanity so inflated that you cannot allow an irritated woman, and that defines my mood very mildly, to drag you to a more comfortable position?"

"It's not vanity."

"Whatever it is, I haven't the patience, Stoker, honestly. Take a deep breath, and let's carry on."

"You are the devil," he gritted out, but she felt him coil his strength, and he shoved up.

"That remains to be seen," she breathed, "but I am also all you've got."

Chapter Seven

Oh my God, the pain, Stoker raged in his head, limping like a ninety-year-old man, using every fiber of strength to hold his considerable weight off his staggering wife.

He drew in a long, slow breath, trying to balance the gnawing pain in his side with their peg-leg wobble down the corridor.

Sabine kept on a steady stream of encouragements and scolds, and Stoker left off trying to contradict her. She was correct to scold him. His protestations were ridiculous, bordering on belligerent.

They wobbled around a particularly harrowing corner, Sabine murmuring, "Nicely done," and, "There you are," and Stoker heard himself actually growl in frustration. He paused, stricken by the thought that she'd felt threatened, and he blurted out, "I nearly died when I was a boy."

"Oh," she said, pausing to wipe her brow with the back of her sleeve.

He glanced at her, grateful she had taken this admission in stride. He continued, "It's no excuse for my . . . lack of graciousness, but you might as well know."

"Is graciousness what this situation lacks?" she teased. And then, "What was your boyhood brush with death?"

"Typhus," he said. "I was living on the streets at the time. The winter I was eleven or twelve. A miserly woman saw me through. She was truly terrible. She actually mocked my recovery, but I was too ill to refuse her. The experience left me with a lifelong aversion to relying on other people. I . . . I vowed never to be helpless again. I am not trying to be difficult."

"Rarely does anyone *try* to be difficult," she said. "God knows I do not."

For this Stoker had no answer. He'd never thought her difficult, merely—strong willed. Her strength was thrilling to him. It meant, he hoped, she would not shatter from his coarseness.

"I'm sorry to learn you didn't have proper care when you were so ill," she continued. "My friend Willow nearly died from an infection when she was a girl. Of course, she had every advantage and comfort. I cannot imagine enduring a childhood illness alone, at the mercy of the world."

Nor should you, he thought. It was one of the reasons he'd kept mostly away these four years. He drifted through life on a raft of terrible memories that tended to surface and haunt him at the worst possible times. She'd had a proper childhood with loving parents, a grand house, fine manners, safety, and security. Until her uncle's season of abuse, she'd not known a moment's ugliness. He would no sooner expose her to his wretched past than haul her to Covent Garden and expose her to the bawdy disarray inside a brothel.

She lived on, unsullied and undisturbed by the darkness inside him, while he surreptitiously borrowed the lightness of their rare visits to distract from the dark memories when they came. From the afternoon of their first meeting, Stoker found himself basking in his memories of her, taking comfort, distracting himself. No other woman had ever captivated him in this way. Even with a bloody lip and a swollen eye, she had been pure and perfect but also strong and defiant.

After they married he was afforded a handful of fresh memories of her, but the occasional letter, and eventually her travel guides. He pieced these together like a sort of refuge in his mind, a safe place he could go if the phantasm of the past howled too loudly. If this imaginary refuge alarmed him, if he was obsessive or strung along with schoolboy devotion, he told himself it was his own secret. A way to enjoy her in his life with no burden to her.

In person the effect would not be the same, he knew. Her memories distracted him, but her living, breathing person would drive him mad with want. Stoker already wrestled with the lifelong curse of a lustful nature, a shameful mix of what he'd seen as a child and what he desired as a man. He only needed her lush beauty and high spirit to push him over the edge into lunacy.

On the rare occasions when they met face-to-face, he

allowed himself to endeavor nothing more than a glance, a stolen look. One moment to memorize her. He liked to look at her because she looked like a survivor, and Stoker prized survivors above all others. But he also liked to look at her because it was the next best thing to touching her, and he longed to touch her like a drowning man longed for one more breath. He alternated between lust, which spun her face and body into every torrid fantasy his depraved brain could concoct, and iron-willed control. The control was preferred, obviously. He placed her securely on an untouchable pedestal, a protected saint, chaste and revered.

Now they were near the end of the corridor, and his eye was on the bedroom door. Before he could reach out, Sabine's dog, previously trailing behind or marching ahead, began to leap and bark, jumping onto their legs.

"What's wrong with it?" Stoker groaned. Pain shot through his side with every impossibly high collision of paws on his hip.

"Bridget is a girl," Sabine reminded him over the barking.

"She's a petulance," Stoker said.

"She thinks we might go out. She loves a ramble above all else."

"Can you call her off? Her bark is deafening and if she knocks you over, we both go down."

The barking increased, and Sabine said, "Now you've done it. You've said her favorite word."

"Deafening?"

Sabine laughed. "No, it's *go*."

Stoker exhaled painfully and ground out, "Make. The vermin. Stop."

Sabine laughed again, a happy musical sound, a sound Stoker would remember and call up in his brain for years to come.

"Bridget, stop," Sabine commanded through her laughter, and miraculously the dog dropped to her four paws and fell silent. She told Stoker, "It's not her fault you're out of bed. My dog is not the problem, as you well know."

"Your dog *exacerbates* the problem."

"Poor Bridget," cooed Sabine, "maligned by her new best friend."

He chuckled and she said, "No laughing." Stoker bit his lip and carried on, sparing a glance at her face. Her expression was determined as if she saw a finish line at the end of the corridor. She held herself slightly away, despite the burden of his weight. She looked like a woman caring cautiously for a wounded animal. It unnerved her to be so very close to him—he knew this. At the altar when they'd married, she'd stood three feet away. She never accepted his help on or off a horse. There were no handshakes or, God forbid, a proffered hand when they said hello. They had been friendly enough these past four years, but her evasiveness was ever present, an unseen sentry that stood between them. He did not question it. He had, in fact, encouraged it. Evading him was one of her best instincts.

But she could not evade him now. Now she bloody carried him.

"Have you heard lately from the duke?" she asked lightly.

"You are trying to distract me," he grunted.

"Perhaps, but I also would not mind knowing. I got rather caught up in researching the illustrious Duke of Wrest, I must say. It prepared me to investigate Sir Dryden. How proficient I've become at watching old men stagger from their clubs or rendezvous with their mistresses. Trailing His Grace was good fun while it lasted, but then your letters stopped."

Stoker missed a step and groaned. It allowed him to postpone his reply, and he took a deep, pained breath.

The letters.

She was referring to their one sustained exchange over these past four years. He'd sent her a series of letters asking if she might undertake an errand now and again to check up on an aging aristocrat—the impoverished Duke of Wrest—who, through a solicitor, had mounted a campaign to claim Stoker as his long-lost son.

This old man, of whom Stoker had previously never known, insisted he had been one of his mother's customers long ago. Not merely a customer, a great favorite who had actually *sired* Stoker some thirty-six years ago. Certainly, Stoker's mother, Marie, had entertained many men, but Stoker was quite certain that none among them was a duke. Now the old man apparently lived in a crumbling mansionette in Chelsea, just blocks from Belgravia.

Stoker, away from England for months at the time, imposed on his estranged wife's proximity and cleverness to play the role of spy. It was the only time he allowed the never-ending scandal of his childhood to brush up against the bright tidiness of Sabine's own life.

The man didn't really know Stoker, and certainly they were not related. The grasping nobleman had read about Stoker's success in the papers, and when he'd learned a few basic facts, he'd embarked on a scheme to cousin up. Research into Stoker's humble beginnings had been the only backstory he'd required to cast himself as long-lost papa.

When Stoker wrote to Sabine and asked if she, living so very close to the duke's home, might quietly discover anything about the old man, her response had been immediate: *It would be my pleasure to snoop on an opportunistic old duke.*

And so began their chain of spirited correspondence. That is, her letters were spirited, clever, and wry. Stoker's replies were cynical and to the point. It was the one and only time in his life when he awaited the post with bated anticipation.

But then Wrest's overtures to Stoker turned from imploring and sentimental to demanding and downright threatening, and Stoker felt that Sabine's involvement, even her confidential involvement, put her at risk. He would not have her harassed or menaced by a desperate old man who, by all accounts, was out of money and saw opportunity in an invented bastard son (who was also a newly minted millionaire). Despite the pleasure of corresponding with Sabine, Stoker put her investigation to an end.

"I did not like the tone of the letters I was receiving from the duke's solicitor," he said now. "It's one thing to pretend to be my long-lost papa, and quite another to suggest that he is owed some recompense from me. He was a curiosity for a time, and then he was a nuisance. He is not worth the bother."

"It was no bother to me," she said. "I rather liked spying on the man."

For this, Stoker had no answer. He'd stopped her snooping because it seemed unsafe. She'd promptly embarked upon the investigation of her uncle, putting herself in the path of a far more dangerous set.

"You're a natural sleuth, it would seem," he said.

She shot him a look but shouldered on.

They'd staggered onward, walking nearly cheek to cheek. He could smell her—wind and grass and just the faintest whiff of . . . butterscotch. He tried to turn his face away, but it took all his strength just to make his way forward without crushing her. He breathed her in, filing away the memory. He felt her skirts, heavy against his legs; her thin shoulders, strong and upright. Her hand was small but tight in his own. *Remember,* he thought through the pain. He would fall asleep to these details for a year.

Sabine was tall compared to many women, with deep curves and legs that ate up the ground with long, purposeful strides. She did everything, including carry his damaged form, as if it was the most important task of the day. When Sabine applied herself to something, everything else fell away. Distraction was never a threat. Time and again since his arrival, he'd found himself caught up in the simple pleasure of watching her. He was thoroughly entertained by the sight of her diligently rolling a bandage or tossing a ball to the dog.

Now that he actually touched her, he thanked God for

his wound. It was the double-edged sword that allowed him to hold her without disgracing her, or himself.

"How did you manage to get so very far from the bed?" she asked now, glancing up to catch his stare.

Stoker jerked his gaze to the floor. "The stitches tore when Harley helped me into your chair. I was quite mobile before that, actually."

"Congratulations," she said, "for reversing days of progress in the length of one afternoon. *To write correspondence*."

He grimaced, allowing the excuse of extreme pain to preclude any answer. What could he say? She was exactly bloody right.

Jon Stoker was a lot heavier than he appeared, and that was saying a lot. He appeared very heavy indeed. He was a foot taller than Sabine and twice as broad. He could scoop up Bridget with one giant hand. His sleeping body made Sabine's comfortable bed look like a cot.

With drunken progress, they skidded along one wall, then the other. It was strenuous, sweaty work, with copious *oofs* and profanity and a litany of excuses and denials from a gasping Stoker.

Sabine was surprised by none of this—of course he was large and heavy, and of course it was a trial for him to be dragged, especially by her. What surprised her was how little it bothered her to be so very close to him.

Sabine had avoided men, all men, even those who appeared too old or too drunk or too stupid to be a threat to her. Sir Dryden had spoiled men for her in that way, and she had no real hope of recovery, even after all this time. Today, on the *Dreadnought*, a sailor grateful for her visit had opened his arms for a brotherly embrace and she had recoiled.

She'd never been overtly open to uninvited closeness, even before Sir Dryden, but after she escaped his particularly sadistic reign of terror, she found herself entirely unable to indulge anything more than the quickest of handshakes with a male. The notion of being handed down from the saddle, sitting crushed together in a crowded carriage—or, God forbid, dancing—was entirely out of the question. The very thought lodged a sharp knot of dread in her throat.

All things being equal, she had not missed it—not like she missed her mother or her bedroom at Park Lodge or working on her father's papers. She employed a ready selection of dismissive looks and curt withdrawals that kept most reasonable men at bay, and all things being equal, they hadn't really been that difficult to avoid.

Until a staggering, swearing man, only half in control of his motions, draped himself across her and forced her to drag him twenty yards. She should have been terrified, sick with anxiety. She was not.

Once she got over the initial touch—hot male body through cotton and silk; straining muscle; heavy breath; raspy, stubbled cheek—she found she was not so much afraid of touching him as she was afraid of dropping him.

They broached the bedroom door after ten minutes of effort, and his weight seemed to increase; his footfalls dragged longer. His strength was waning.

Oh no, you do not, she thought, and she said, "You mustn't stop now, Stoker. We've nearly made it." She stooped to get a better grip. It was impossible not to feel the muscles of his body constrict and stretch with every movement. He had been laid low by the knife wound, but he'd not succumb, even to the infection. This, she felt sure, was due entirely to his preexisting fitness. "You can make it three yards."

"I'm too heavy, and I'm less able to walk than when we began."

"You are not so heavy," she countered, but she thought, *You are so incredibly heavy.*

"I've damaged you."

"Stop," Sabine breathed. "I am not a piece of china in a shop, and I know my own endurance, thank you very much. Keep walking."

"Leave and allow me the dignity to crawl to the bed on my own."

"You and I will make it to the bed together if I have to drag you by your hair. Go, Stoker. *Walk on.*" Biting her lip, Sabine squeezed him tightly and they staggered to the bed.

"Let me go," he rasped when they were in reach.

"You will fall on your wound. We must pivot."

"Let me go."

"I will lower you down," she insisted.

"You'll be crushed."

"I've already been crushed a half dozen times. At least now I will be pinned against the mattress rather than plaster wall."

Before he could broach another argument, Sabine took

a deep breath, bent at the knees, and pivoted, pitching both of them in the direction of the bed. She felt her feet leave the floor, felt the mattress take her hip, and—*flop*, she found herself pressed beneath him in the center of the bed. His weight was like a dead horse. She could hear his sawing breath and feel his chest heaving up and down.

Sabine remembered to draw her own breath and she wiggled her fingers and toes. She waited for some distress or alarm, but she felt only weariness—and gratefulness. They'd made it. She'd said they would, and they had. She turned her head and breathed in, willing her heart to slow, giving him time. Bridget stood beside the bed and looked up at her. Sabine smiled down, and the dog sat attentively and studied her mistress squashed beneath their new houseguest. She cocked her head, opening one bug-wing ear to a potential command.

After a long moment Sabine said softly, "Stoker, you're alright."

Her face was flush with his neck. She could see a faint pulse throbbing above his collar. She had the strange, unfamiliar urge to press her lips to it. Just a swipe. The work of a moment. To test the temperature of his skin and feel the texture against her lips. To breath him in.

She ignored the impulse and looked again at the dog. "You're alright," she repeated.

"Can you move?" he asked.

"I'm not the one clinging to life. Of course I can move."

Then why haven't I? Sabine wondered. The soft mattress was, indeed, a great relief. The sheets were clean and cool.

The living, breathing weight of Jon Stoker felt . . . not anything like she had expected.

"Are you crushed?"

She shook her head, and her lips grazed the skin of his neck. Stoker stopped breathing for half a beat and she sucked in a little breath.

"I told you we would manage," she said, trying to sound matter-of-fact. She looked again at the dog. "Is this not preferable to the study?"

"Preferable?" he said shakily.

She chuckled and she heard him wince. It could not be useful for him to drape across the curved landscape of her body. She began the slow, strange process of disentangling their arms and legs. By inches, she slid from beneath him. There was no graceful or impersonal way to do it. She touched every plane of him, every crook, every hollow and swell. When, at last, her arms and legs were free, she rolled right and tumbled onto the floor. Bridget barked and he let out a moan.

"I am fine," Sabine announced.

"This was not worth the letters I posted," Stoker said to the ceiling.

"Obviously," she said, "and we haven't even gotten to the truly terrible part."

"No."

"No—what?" She sighed, brushed back her hair, now loose and wild.

"No to whatever you believe to be worse than what we've just done."

"I must look in on your stitches," she said. "If you've torn them, I will have to send for Dr. Cornwell."

"For God's sake, Sabine," he breathed, "send for the bloody doctor. Please." He sought out her face with red, weary eyes. His skin looked grey beneath his tan, and his hair was wet with sweat. "I will pay for the man to call every ten minutes if that is what I require. Spare yourself bloody stitches, if nothing else."

"Fine," she said, and she realized she was relieved. He had won this point. Dragging him through the apartments was one thing; torn stitches were quite another.

She brushed her hands briskly over her dress, avoiding his gaze. "I'll just dash off a summons. Don't move," she said, and he actually barked a faint laugh.

Five minutes later she'd written to Dr. Cornwell and sent the note to Harley Street with a groom.

"I suggested it was urgent," she said, returning to the doorway. "He won't be long." She paused, watching him. He hadn't moved from the spot where they had flung themselves. His gasping breaths had subsided, and she wondered if he'd fallen asleep.

"Stoker?" She took a step into the room.

"I'm here," he said, staring at the ceiling.

"Are you . . . comfortable?" It seemed like the correct thing to ask.

"No," he said.

"Should I—"

"No," he said.

"You would be an easier patient if you were more demanding," she said.

"You say that, but it is not really true."

"I feel rather helpless, now that you're awake. If I'm being honest."

He chuckled and then winced. "May you never know real helplessness."

"Oh, but you forget. I already have."

He raised his head. "Yes, I suppose you have."

A flash of recognition passed between them. She looked into his eyes and they saw the same memory. She could not think of the next thing to say. She took another step into the room.

Stoker said, "Will you tell me what you discovered when you were out today? With the sailors?"

"You're joking," she said, a test. She wanted to tell him.

"Not a joke," he said. "Why would you say that?"

"Because you're half-dead."

"Possibly. But if that is true, I am also half-alive. You may be shocked to learn that the living part of me knows quite a lot about smugglers."

She shook her head because she did not have the conviction to say no. She must refuse him, mustn't she? They were not collaborators. They were not even friends.

"You do not trust me," Stoker guessed.

"I do not know you," she said, the truth.

"You knew me enough to marry me."

"I would have married anyone."

"I don't believe that."

You shouldn't believe it, she thought. *I would not have married anyone.*

He asked again. "Tell me only what you've learned today."

She hesitated.

"It will become clearer in your mind to relate it," he said. "Only until the doctor arrives, perhaps? To take my mind off the pain."

"The pain is your just reward for today's recklessness," she said, sighing, but she drifted closer.

He waited. After a moment she said, "I have an idea. I'll tell you about the sailors if you tell me what's happened with the Duke of Wrest."

Stoker made a sound of regret.

"What?" she asked. "It's only fair. My investigation in exchange for yours. You cannot include me in the early days and then filch on the ending."

"There is no ending," he sighed.

"There is more than has been revealed to me.

"Tell me about the smuggling."

"Tell me about the duke."

"Ladies first."

"Why?" She laughed.

"I am half-dead."

Another laugh, but she drifted to the bed and settled on the corner of the mattress. Bridget leapt into her lap and Stoker winced.

"Today," she began carefully, "I met twelve sailors who claimed to have served as crew on a small brig owned by my uncle's associate—this man, Mr. Leaver. The boat sailed from Portsmouth across the channel to France, making delivery of one hundred bails of wool. When they returned from France, however, they sailed with fifty barrels filled with some unknown . . . something. The sailors were not told." She paused for effect, relishing his attention. "They did not return to their home port of Portsmouth with the unidentified barrels," she said. "They sailed west instead, just off the coast of Dorset, to a tiny barrier island called the Isle of Portland . . ."

CHAPTER EIGHT

Stoker found the doctor to be a competent man, practical and reasonable and in no way alarmed that a beautiful woman was tending to a half-dead man who she discovered in a morgue. Dr. Cornwell was more concerned with what he referred to as Stoker's "escapades" of the day—possibly the first time the act of getting out of bed had been considered an escapade—but the older man did not scold or coddle. He unpacked his satchel and set to work, pulling away Stoker's blood-soaked dressing gown and sending Sabine for whiskey and a piece of wood on which to bite. He did not say the words, but his message was clear: This would hurt.

Sabine returned quickly with the wood and whiskey, but Stoker wanted only the liquor. He took a long drink from the bottle, relishing the fire in his throat.

"Will you leave us?" he rasped, looking at Sabine.

She glanced at the doctor and back to the bed, and then nodded. It was clear that she had no wish to bear witness to whatever the doctor would inflict. In this, they were agreed. But still, she lingered. Stoker grimaced and turned his face away. His pride was at the breaking point.

He took another drink, purposefully ignoring her, *willing her* to go. Finally, thankfully, she stooped to pick up her dog and stepped from the room, closing the door behind her. Stoker let out an uneven breath.

"Am I meant to survive this?" Stoker asked the doctor when she was gone.

"You'll survive," said the doctor, rummaging through his tools with a foreboding clink and rattle.

"Can you make out what happened? And how long ago?" Stoker asked. The fire in Stoker's side raged hotter, and he took another drink. He closed his eyes and concentrated on breathing in and out.

"Stab wound," said the doctor. "I'd say about two weeks ago. Infection has set in. It was very bad indeed when your wife rescued you from the so-called hospital ship, but you've made great progress since then. Until today, of course." Dr. Cornwell prodded gently at Stoker's side with a metal tool and he let out a howl of pain. The doctor *tsked* and replaced the tool with shears.

"Can I be safely moved from Mrs. Stoker's bedroom?" Stoker grunted, speaking around the pain. "Assuming you can repair the damage of today." He paused, hissing out a breath. "I have a suite of rooms in Regent Street and can raise a full staff. I'll be very cautious, and the most attentive servants can be hired to manage the move."

Cornwell jabbed and tugged at his wound but gave no

immediate answer. Stoker grimaced, bracing against the anticipation as much as the pain. It was madness, of course, to remain here. Sabine was unsettled and inconvenienced. He was in considerable pain, obviously, but her constant presence was an even greater challenge. He endured a terrible mix of desire and helplessness.

Say no, he thought, in spite of it all. *Say I must remain.*

"I wouldn't," Dr. Cornwell finally said, carefully snipping at his burning side. "Your body is fighting for life, Mr. Stoker. My advice would be to work in accord with the fight and not against it. Stillness, rest, nourishment, a clean room, and an attendant with a vested interest in your improvement. Staff is very handy except that they frequently couldn't care less if you live or die. Nothing like the motivation of a loving wife. Unless you mean to move her to Regent Street too. Even so—why risk the health of this wound? Why inconvenience yourself when you already battle an infection? Stay put, that's what I say."

Stoker let out a breath and nodded. It was irrelevant to point out that Sabine was not a loving wife but a charitable acquaintance. It was unbelievable to say that his time here would be devoted to tracking her movements among London's maritime criminal element, not to battling infection, although theoretically he could do both at the same time. Regardless, he'd been given permission to stay, at least a little while, and he would seize it.

"Ah, bloody hell, man, what have you done?" said the doctor, poking and prodding with what felt like searing blades.

"What indeed?" Stoker breathed, taking another swig of whiskey. The doctor reached for a swath of fabric, dipped it in boiling water, and applied it to the raw, damaged flesh of Stoker's side. The new pain was immediate, overwhelming, cold and hot at the same time, high and low, deep and shallow. Consciousness flitted, spun, and finally, thankfully, dissolved to pink then red and then blessedly black.

Chapter Nine

The northwest London borough of **Marylebone** is renowned for an Anglican church of the same name and an eighteenth-century pleasure garden. The church has been rebuilt three times since 1200 AD, but the pleasure garden, including its once remarkable shell grotto, now languishes in ruin.

The only remaining feature is the garden's musical venue, The Rose of Burgundy tavern, which has remained in business for two centuries and stages concerts daily. Likewise, the church, as ever, carries on.

See bills outside tavern for showtimes and ticket prices. Libations and lite fare available for purchase.

Church tours twice daily, weekly services Sundays 11:00 o'clock.

—from *A Noble Guide to London*
by Sabine Noble

A week later Sabine stood in the shadow of the grotto ruins in Marylebone High Street and transcribed the not-so-discreet conversation being volleyed some five feet away.

One Thomas T. Toose of T. T. Toose Wagons and Carts was giving orders to a foreman regarding an undertaking to which he referred as "Orion's Light." Fortuitously, Sabine had learned that "Orion's Light" just happened to be the code name for the smuggling operation commanded by her uncle. (Thank you, scurvy-ridden sailors from the *Dreadnought*.) After five days of lurking around Marylebone, she had finally stumbled upon a conversation with value.

The illustrious wagon master, Mr. Toose, had been named again and again in the letters from her mother's maid. Sabine had since discovered that he was a purveyor of wagons, but that was all she knew. Wagon-letting was a legitimate profession, of course, but he would not have been such a frequent guest to Park Lodge without a more nefarious purpose.

Under the guise of research for a Marylebone installment for her travel guides, Sabine had been up and down the high street, just waiting for him to say or do something useful to her investigation.

But now he had invoked the code words, "Orion's Light," and she knew she had finally lit on a conversation worth overhearing. Standing beside the wagon house, her drafting kit open and a half-finished map of Marylebone in plain view, Sabine listened carefully and took down every word.

"The barrels leave for the Isle of Portland at the end of the month," Mr. Toose told the underling. "A quarter of them will have nothing in them, so get your hands on something to fill them with. We'll sell whatever it is in Dorset. I mean to make money coming and going. You think Dryden and the others aren't lining their own pockets every chance they get?"

"Get my hands on something . . . like what?" asked the younger man.

"Don't care," said Toose. "If it fits in a barrel and will travel easily, it'll do."

"How much are you willing to pay to for this *something?*"

"As little as possible. And then we charge double when we sell it to the good people of Dorset."

Sabine scribbled madly. When they changed course and began discussing calendar days, she gave Bridget a friendly kick, sending the dog darting between them. The men cursed and leapt back—a disruption that allowed Sabine to catch up.

Five minutes later the men had gone their separate ways and Sabine tucked away her notebook and drafting kit and walked to Oxford Street for a hansom cab. If Stoker was awake when she returned, she could go over every word while it was still fresh in her mind. In Sabine's estimation, Mr. Toose supplied a fleet of wagons to distribute . . . whatever it was Sir Dryden smuggled into the country. Also the barrels to transport it, apparently. Sabine couldn't care less about middlemen like Mr. Toose, but she must follow every lead until she knew exactly Dryden's game. What was inside the barrels that were not empty? What would go inside the empty ones? These were the persistent questions that kept Sabine and Stoker up nights. She'd paced Stoker's bedroom for the past week, explaining to him what she'd discovered, showing off her map of London with pins that marked each cog in Dryden's wheel of smugglers. She recounted notes she'd made, newspaper clippings she'd saved, and every letter received from May, her mother's nursemaid, which detailed who Sir Dryden entertained at Park Lodge.

Sharing her evidence with Stoker, a man who knew the business of importation and who had a sense of England's strategically situated barrier islands, was gratifying to Sabine in a way she could not have imagined.

Ultimately, he said very little, but he listened so very well, as if Sabine was explaining the most troubling problem in the world. And when he did ask questions, they made the whole conversation feel like . . . like a collaboration.

How long had it been since she she'd known the thrill of working on something with someone of like mind and abilities? Her friends had embraced their marriages and moved away. Her father had been dead for five years. Perhaps Stoker only humored her, too ill to do anything else but listen; perhaps he did it to distract from her questions about the Duke of Wrest. Either way, he clearly understood her ultimate goal. And he endorsed it—or if he did not endorse it, he did not discourage it.

And all the while, he struggled with very significant problems of his own, the greatest of which was his painful recovery. There was also the mystery of his missing boat and absent crew and the fact that he'd been left for dead. Yet, he was wholly attentive and engaged whenever she drifted into his sick room with a question or new evidence, and he tolerated mealtimes dominated with talk of her investigation.

Of course, what choice did he have at mealtimes or any time? She fed him, or rather she helped him eat; his strength returned with greater force every day. Talking came naturally to her, and he was not prone to chatter. It was a little bit like having her own useful captive, she thought, a capable man who did not intrude or countermand or do much more than entertain her chosen topic of conversation.

But of course he was not a captive, nor did she wish for him to be. He was a virile man in the prime of his life, suffering from a momentary setback. When he was well, he would leave her and her investigation and go on his way and she would not hear from him again for months.

As well it should be.

As she preferred it.

A quarter hour later, Sabine and Bridget reached Belgravia to see Dr. Cornwell's carriage parked outside the Boyds' townhome. Sabine checked her timepiece, cursing her tardiness. She'd known the doctor would call this afternoon, but she'd been disinclined to leave Marylebone without listening to everything Mr. Toose might have to say.

"At least we've caught him before he's left," she told Bridget, clipping down the cellar steps.

"Ah, Mrs. Stoker, there you are," said Dr. Cornwell, pushing through the door.

"Oh yes, hello, Doctor. I'm so very sorry to be late. I was detained in Marylebone. How is he today?"

"Doing much better, in fact," said the doctor. "Now that he's finally consented to actual bed rest, the true healing has begun. Of course, the sustenance and mental stimulation has also been a boon. He is a strong man and you are a devoted nurse, luckily. He's just told me you'd gone out to fetch fresh herbs to make a healing tea."

"Oh yes, a healing tea," Sabine repeated, biting her bottom lip. Original. She went on, "It's imperative to keep him drinking and eating, and I've had no end of luck with this particular . . . er, tea."

"Carry on, then," said the doctor, putting on his hat. "Just take care you don't poison him. I find one cannot go wrong with chamomile or jasmine."

"Of course," Sabine said, patting her drafting kit.

The doctor went on, "I've cleaned and redressed the wound. Always a painful process, but the bandages are fresh now and he is resting. Mind you, I've left him without a shirt, and I should like him to stay that way. The wound should air out during the mild part of the day. Assuming the sunshine remains, keep him uncovered while daylight remains, keep the windows open, and let mind and body breathe."

"Mind and body," repeated Sabine vaguely, "right."

Dr. Cornwell clipped up the steps. "I'll be back tomorrow, Mrs. Stoker."

Sabine bid him farewell and pushed her way into the apartments, pulling off her gloves. She dropped her satchel and coat on the bench and paused, staring at the open door to her bedroom.

Shirtless. Stoker. Just inside the room. Right. Not a problem.

Sabine had never felt shy about hosting Stoker; she'd strode in and out of his room, lecturing him, inquiring about evidence, retrieving her dog without a second thought. All the while, he'd lain there in his shirtsleeves, the sheet pulled tightly, and been wholly . . . well, inert. Even when she dragged him down the hall, she had not been shy or nervous.

So the doctor said he would be shirtless—so what? She may have not seen a shirtless man before, but surely such a paltry thing as the lack of a shirt would not change the fact that he was a very sick man, completely harmless, and really more of a resource now than whatever he was—

Sabine forced herself around the corner and froze in the doorway.

Jon Stoker without a shirt changed everything.

She pushed out a breath. The room shrank to the expanse of tan skin above the white of the sheet. He appeared to have doubled in size. All at once, she saw shoulders and biceps and a tapered waist. She saw ribs and hair and broad, bare chest. She saw old scars and fresh bandage and the aggressive serpent tattoo weaving up his right arm and coiling around his chest.

He was sitting up against the pillows, reading a broad-sheet newspaper folded into a rectangle. In no way did he appear infirm or harmless, except for the bandage. Sabine was struck by the dual impulses to duck back into the hall-way but also to stand and stare.

Stoker looked up from his paper. "I'm sorry," he said, narrowing his eyes. His expression was sincerity and chagrin with a touch of bashfulness. He spoke as if he'd promised something and failed.

"Don't be silly," she said, but the words came out with too much force. She cleared her throat. Bridget was not fazed and progressed to the bed with her usual sense of entitlement.

"Bridget, no," Sabine said weakly, watching the dog leap.

"Oh, now you call off the hound," he said.

"I have very little control over my dog."

"You have keen control over your dog. I've never seen anything like it."

I've never seen anything like you, Sabine thought.

She wondered how he could be both so very ill and also so imposing. Had he expanded in height and breadth when his shirt was removed? Was his tan darker? And that tattoo up his arm and across his chest? She'd not known the extent of it.

She blinked up at the ceiling, uncertain of where to look. It was missish and awkward to stare at the floor or out the window, but staring at his chest was hardly appropriate. She settled on his face. He watched her in silence.

"You are enjoying this," she said.

"I do not enjoy making you uncomfortable. I would tell you to go, but I would like to know what happened in Marylebone. You were gone for an age."

She gave a little laugh. "Nothing happened." She retreated to the bench to retrieve her notes. "Why should something happen?"

"You were eavesdropping on suspected criminals, Sabine. Any number of things could have happened." There was a bite in his voice she'd not heard before.

"Are you . . . worried about me?" The prospect of Stoker taking stock in potential danger had not occurred to her. It had been so long since anyone regarded Sabine's safety but Sabine herself.

He shook his head. "I never worried about my own well-being before I was nearly stabbed to death, and look at me now." He gestured to his wound, and Sabine's eyes migrated to his expansive chest and thick, muscled arms. "Caution is not a weakness. It is self-preservation. I know you've been independent for many years, but I—" He stopped and began again, "I am so incredibly useless here in this bed."

Sabine thought of Stoker out of the bed, accompanying her to Marylebone or wherever else the investigation might take her. She had not considered the possibility of this. Surely, when he healed, he would not devote time or energy to her. That had never been the nature of their relationship. He was here now, because he was convalescing. She tolerated this, she told herself, because he was hobbled and dozing.

He went on, "Today I cannot even wear a shirt."

Sabine looked at his chest again. He was not dozing. In no way did he appear to be dozing.

He finished, "I am of little help to you. But I am still curious."

"Nothing happened," she repeated, "but I did overhear a very pointed conversation from the suspected associate, our Mr. Toose, and he used Dryden's name in particular."

Sabine began to read off the transcribed conversation, drifting closer. When she reached the mattress, she sat at the foot of the bed near Bridget and began to stroke the dog.

"What do you make of it?" she asked, looking up. "Clearly, Toose's wagons are used to transport the smuggled goods from the Isle of Portland and the coast of Dorset to . . . whomever buys them. But why send some of the barrels with goods to sell in Dorset—making them effectively empty after they arrive—and some filled? Filled with what? So many barrels. Will the smuggled goods not arrive in their own barrels?"

"It's true," he mused. "Most goods, whether they come illegally or through proper channels, arrive in barrels or sacks or crates or trunks. We sailed with the guano in barrels. It's odd that Dryden is dealing in something that requires a fresh barrel when he makes landfall . . ."

Sabine nodded and flipped through her notes for their growing list of possible smuggled items. "Clearly, he does not require *clean* barrels if his man is going to fill some of them with something else before they are met with the smuggled cargo. You don't suppose they intend to wash them between usages, do you?"

Stoker chuckled. "Smugglers are not overly concerned with how pure or clean or unblemished their cargo may be. They work quickly, under the cover of darkness, with anonymity and stealth."

Sabine made a note and looked up in time to see Stoker raise his right hand to scratch the back of his head. His chest broadened and the muscled knot of his biceps bulged, expanding a link of his serpent tattoo. Sabine stared, openly marveling at the beauty of his body. She wondered if all naked male bodies were this fascinating. Was it the bareness or . . . was it him? She thought of the scrawny footman Harley or middle-aged Arthur Boyd without a shirt and tried immediately to erase the image from her brain. She peeked at him again and he caught her gaze.

"Sorry," he said quietly, lowering his arm. "I know the tattoo is . . . alarming."

"I quite like the tattoo," Sabine heard herself say. Her voice was too loud and she cleared her throat. She tried again, "I am fond of serpents from an artistic standpoint. They can be frequently found on maps. I've never seen a nautical map without one, in fact."

He narrowed his eyes and considered her, almost as if she had offended him and he dreaded the next thing she might say.

"That is," she went on, "I was able to make the snap decision to marry you because of the tattoo." *Did I just say that?* she wondered idly, looking again at the ink on his arm.

"Because of the tattoo?" he repeated. "The tattoo is designed to traumatize respectable women."

"That's not what you told me on the day we met. When I asked about it."

"One thing that was very clear to me the day we met was that you were not easily traumatized."

"Perhaps I was simply not respectable."

"No," he said softly. "My respect for you was—*is*—very great."

Sabine felt her eyes go big, much larger than when she looked at his chest or his arms or his tattoo. She glanced down at her notes again and saw nothing. "Well," she said softly, "you alone would feel that way, especially considering the condition in which you found me." She thought back to her blackened eye and bloody lip. Her hair loose down her back, her dress a sweaty tangle.

He said, "Why did the tattoo influence you?" His voice was low.

Sabine's mind raced for some joke, some way to change the topic, but his face was so very serious. She glanced at the serpent on his arm again. Bridget lay nearby and she snatched her up, holding the dog close.

She shrugged. "It was in the chapel, before the ceremony. My commitment to our snap decision was wavering. I noticed the serpentine head poking out of the sleeve of your jacket, and I asked you about it. Do you remember?"

He nodded slowly.

"Well," she said, "you answered honestly, didn't you? And you were so matter-of-fact. You did not try to deny it or explain it away. You did not try to shield me from it. *That* appealed to me. And you had just the slightest touch of . . . chagrin? Almost as if you'd outgrown your choice."

She glanced at him. He was still staring. Had the room grown overwarm?

Stoker waited, and Sabine heard herself continue. "You said that after your first windfall as a shipping captain, you'd wanted to squander a large purse of money on something foolhardy—something that took the shine off any unwanted respectability that might come with success."

His expression softened just a little. "Surely not."

She chuckled. "That's what you said."

"I cannot imagine saying something so milquetoast or devoid of manly swagger."

You embody manly swagger, she thought. It surprised her, because she was not in the business of considering manliness or swagger, except perhaps to avoid it—but it was true. Jon Stoker exuded a sort of quiet, watchful stoicism; a fierceness; a hard edge that was pure male. He'd been every inch a man, even when she dragged him, half-dead, to this bed.

Now he seemed entirely alive.

"Why did *you* agree to marry *me*?" Sabine asked. They'd spoken at length in the days since he'd come, but not about personal matters, not really. Sabine was hardly an idle gossip, but she could venture from the topic of wagons and barrels and smugglers, just this once. The question of why he'd married her had crossed her mind a thousand times in the past four years. She'd wondered about it after their brief encounters and after she'd read his letters. Sometimes simply as she lay in bed at night, dreaming of where in the wide world he might be at that moment and if he ever thought of her.

He was here now, and they'd finally stumbled into an intimate conversation. She repeated the question. "Why did you agree to marry me?"

"Because of your brazen tattoo," he said.

She laughed. "Valiant effort."

"Because of the dowry money."

"We both know this is a lie. Tessa and Willow have told me that you were the richest man in the partnership at the time of our marriage."

"Just to be clear," he said, "I'm still the richest."

"High time for another tattoo." She smiled. "Take the shine off that respectability."

"I will never be respectable."

She laughed with incredulity. "Why not? Joseph Chance is a former serving boy who is running for Parliament. He's every inch the respected statesman."

"Joseph was not—" Stoker stopped and looked down at the newspaper on his lap.

"Oh yes," Sabine said sarcastically, "your terrible past. Your courtesan mother and the brothel and your life on the streets."

Stoker looked up and crossed his arms over his chest. Sabine blinked at the new shape and breadth of his muscled arms. He said, "Never let it be said that Sabine Noble is overly sympathetic."

"My name is Sabine Stoker, actually. And I should like to know why you did it. Come on, then, it's only fair. I told you why I agreed to marry."

"Ah, you told me some part of why. I know the tattoo wasn't your only reason."

"Oh, and now you would have me say more? Fine. I agreed to marry you because you seemed to pass no judgment on my miserable situation—you didn't even appear shocked. You took remarkably creative initiative when you stuffed Sir Dryden into the cupboard. And you were available."

"Available?"

"Right time, right place. So fortuitous."

"I am the fortunate one," he said quietly, "marrying you."

"Stop," she said, but she felt a flutter of warmth shimmer in her belly. "You don't even know me. We never see each other—" He opened his mouth to interrupt but she spoke over him.

"I'm not complaining," she said, "God knows I would not complain. This was our agreement. But you are present now, and we are having this conversation, and I've shared my part—twice, in fact—and now it's only fair that you share yours." She leaned across the bed, a bridge over his legs, propping herself on her hand.

Stoker breathed in, either to brace himself or make some pronouncement, she couldn't say. He rubbed his jaw and the back of his neck. He shook his head slightly.

A proper woman, Sabine thought, her heartbeat suddenly very loud in her ears, *would drop the matter. A proper woman would have shied away after his first evasion. A proper woman would not be inching closer to his half-naked body, forcing him to reveal bold truths.*

Perhaps I am not a—

Well, I'm not so much improper as tenacious.

"I'm tired," he tried.

"You don't look tired to me."

"At any moment I will drop into a deep sleep."

"It's far too bright in this room for sleeping."

"You're holding me captive in this bright room to interrogate me, and I feel threatened."

"You know no threat, from me or anyone else," she said. "You are impervious to threat. But I am beginning to believe you had no wish to marry me at all, you saw no benefit, and you did it only out of pity."

"It wasn't that."

"Then why?"

"You want me to tell you?"

She cocked her head in frustration and stifled the urge to demand, *Say it.*

"Fine," he said. "I did it because I had grown weary of saving women."

"What?" Sabine sat up.

"And children," he added. "And every other victimized soul I stumbled upon. Or who stumbled upon me. *You* were my swan song, so to speak."

It was not what she expected to hear. And not simply because it made no sense. His answer had absolutely nothing to do with her.

"Explain," she said, scooting closer to him on the bed.

He let out a heavy sigh. "You know Bryson and Elisabeth Courtland?"

She nodded.

"I met this couple—well, I met Elisabeth—because she was actually an old friend of my mother's."

"Your mother the prostitute?"

"My mother the prostitute, yes. Never let it be said that you mince words, Sabine."

"Well, perhaps she was, but I'm certain there was more to her than her profession."

Stoker looked at her carefully. It was as if no one had ever suggested this notion to him. Sabine shrugged. "I am more than a travel-guide writer. I am more than an amateur smuggler hunter. I am also a compassionate nursemaid, for example."

Stoker barked out a laugh but continued, watching her closely. "Yes, well, Elisabeth Courtland was kidnapped as a girl and my mother helped her escape a dreadful situation. They became . . . friends. My mother's *only* reasonable friend. And when I was ten or eleven and took to the streets because I could no longer tolerate life inside the brothel, my mother sent me to call on Elisabeth, who was a charity crusader and niece to an esteemed countess in Mayfair. It was the one piece of useful advice my mother, God rest her, ever gave me. For weeks I followed Elisabeth. I was bored and curious and a little dazzled. I eventually approached her. A collaboration ensued."

Sabine wrinkled her brow. "A street boy and a wealthy Mayfair maiden. What a collaboration."

"She was a friend at first."

"A very unlikely friend," said Sabine.

"Elisabeth is very unlikely."

Sabine nodded and looked at her lap. She'd seen Elisabeth Courtland on two occasions, both happenstance encounters around London, but they had never spoken. She was older than Stoker, although only by ten years or so, and she was still very beautiful, despite being a married matron with three children. She obviously regarded Stoker as a member of family. Still, Sabine felt a twinge of something unsettling. Stoker always spoke of her with such clear fondness, almost reverence.

Sabine nodded. "Go on."

"Elisabeth's life's work is saving young girls from prostitution. Her charity aims to stem the tide of helpless, unwitting girls from being scooped up into this life. But her organization has always operated the way all charities do—through proper channels. She works with the church and the government. Because of the limits of traditional charities, she always felt her work was incomplete. She was powerless to actually physically extract entrenched girls from this life. And that is where I came in. I was from the streets, I knew every street and dark alley, I knew the dens of iniquity, and the lavish courtesan townhomes. The lawless underworld had been my home for as long as I could remember. I was also fifteen and seized by a restless energy that was well suited to knocking down doors, spiriting away girls into the night, fighting, conning, setting things ablaze—whatever it took. And so, working together with Elisabeth, I began to raid brothels on behalf of her charity."

"And by *raid*," asked Sabine, "you do not mean you approached these establishments formally and led the girls away? You did not negotiate with whomever was in charge? You literally stole them?"

He nodded. "We stole them. I organized a band of street boys and we began sneaking into brothels, rescuing these girls, and delivering them to Elisabeth's care."

"Did she pay you for this work?"

"No." He looked a little offended. "We survived on righteous fervor and the sheer thrill of it. I raided ten, twenty, fifty brothels in those early years, removing hundreds of girls. Young girls, old girls, grateful girls, girls who were belligerent and who I had to toss over my shoulder and haul away screaming. I rescued small boys and old men and dogs and—it simply became a habit, really. Once you begin seeking out injustice to liberate, you find that injustice seems to flourish everywhere you look. There was always someone else to rescue."

"But you were educated, Stoker. You went to university. I know you did not raid brothels and rescue these girls forever."

"Well, I stopped with you, didn't I?" he said, raising an eyebrow.

Sabine considered this. Should she somehow be offended that he placed her rescue on the same level as that of prostitutes?

No, she decided, she was not offended. She had been just as desperate as anyone else, trapped with an oppressor and unable to find her way free.

He went on, "Elisabeth saw potential in me beyond muscle and cunning, and forced me to sit for tutors. When I excelled at lessons—I was pathetically desperate to please her—she discovered a university that would take an unrefined but promising blighter like me." He exhaled loudly. "And she forced me to go. So you asked if she paid me to rescue the girls. Not in money. Only in opportunity."

"Surely, you are grateful."

"Surely," he said.

"But that was years ago," she prompted.

"Yes, that was years ago. But since I met her, I had never stopped stumbling across people who required my help in some way. Girls in subjugation. Widows beholden to cruel landlords. Children in workhouses with unthinkable conditions. Slaves in every port in the world. Entrapment. Blackmail. Terrorizing. Advantage taken at the cost of another. The strong dominating the weak." He sighed as if it pained him to tell the story. "Joseph says I have a 'heroism affliction.' God knows it's not that. The things I have seen and done?" He made a noise of misery. "I'm no hero—I'm . . . I'm trying to save a mother who had no wish to be saved, trying to change a boyhood that has already come and gone." He made a bitter laugh. "I've never said that out loud. I'm not sure I've ever thought it."

"Are you saying you did not do it for the girls, but for yourself?" Sabine asked. She'd never been more rapt. She scooted closer.

"God knows why I did it," he said. "All I know is, when you begin busting through walls and knocking heads as a very young man, it's difficult to simply stop. I have the strength, I have the skill, I've seen virtually every evil known to man—seen the very depraved source of it and seen desperate people do desperate things to survive. Most important, I've come to know that putting a stop to most evil is simply a matter of strength and confidence. The larger dog compels the weaker to piss off. I am good in a fight. Why shouldn't I deliver helplessness when I see it?"

"But you haven't . . . enjoyed it?" said Sabine. "Not once? Have you not known some sense of righteousness or satisfaction from standing up on behalf of these people?"

He let out a deep breath and lay back on the pillow. "I'm tired, Sabine." He rolled his head to the side and looked at her with half-lidded eyes. "So bloody exhausted. Just because I know how to vanquish petty evil does not mean

I have the energy to do it forever. As I've said, it changes nothing, for me."

"And so why not simply . . . stop? God knows you've done enough. You've done more than most people do in ten lifetimes."

"I did stop. I stopped with you."

She laughed at the simplicity of his answer. "Why did *my* predicament qualify as permission for you to cease being . . . being a hero?"

"Because the thing required to save you was such a very great departure for me. It felt like . . . enough."

"Freeing me from a cupboard and locking my uncle inside was *enough?*" she asked.

"*Marrying you* felt like enough."

"Ah," she said. "Because I am so terrible?"

It felt a little wrong to say this, considering Sabine knew she was not terrible at all. She'd not given much thought to suitors or marriage before her father died, but she knew that when the time came, she would be reasonably easy to marry off. She was pretty enough, if you liked strident, bold, wildish girls; she was well-dowried enough, and she was clever. She was not, perhaps, biddable and pliant, but she could offer intelligence and self-reliance in exchange.

Stoker didn't answer, and she tried again, "Marrying me felt like enough because you said you would never marry?"

"Yes," he said, sounding a little cornered. "I felt like I could give myself permission to stop being a . . . oh—is *vigilante* the wrong word?"

"You seem far too rich to be a vigilante," she said.

"Whatever I was, I felt like I could stop, because I was doing this thing I'd sworn never to do. Marry."

"But you did anyway."

"Yes, but only in a manner. As you well know. Our 'arrangement.'"

"And was it enough? This convenient marriage we have? Have you spent the past five years feeling absolved from saving anyone, ever again?"

He did not reply but looked away. After a moment he gave one quick nod.

Now Sabine felt indignant. She felt childish and maligned and . . . indignant. She was not someone's penance. She was not a healing broth that one ate despite how terrible it tasted.

She asked, "So you've simply stopped? You've seen the guano venture through to the end and . . . done whatever else it is you do when you sail around the world, and you've ceased rescuing people?"

"I have," he said simply.

Sabine thought about this. She considered his demeanor each time they met for their rare, brief encounters. Had he seemed fulfilled and carefree? Had he seemed happy?

No, he had not. He seemed as glowery and brooding as ever.

She narrowed her eyes and asked, "And has your retirement been the liberating, revitalizing thing that you hoped it would be?"

He opened his mouth and then closed it. He shifted his

position in the bed. Finally, he said, "I have been very busy. When Cassin and Joseph left the partnership, someone had to do the work of two absent men."

"But the guano is depleted. You've sold it all. You've made enough money for ten men. That was a year ago, wasn't it? Since then have you been so fulfilled?"

She saw him swallow hard. "I've been looking for some property in which to invest. To put down roots. I want to build a house. I . . . I believe I will feel more settled when I have a proper home. I've not had one, not really. It's why I was in Portugal when I was attacked. There is an eighteenth-century villa for sale in Cabo de San Vicente."

She stared at him. Slowly, she began to shake her head.

He offered, "You've said you seek the same thing. For a home. To return to Park Lodge."

Park Lodge could not be further from her mind. Even the investigation and the smugglers and seeing her uncle imprisoned felt like an afterthought.

Sabine took a deep breath and looked away from his face. She stared down at the crisp sheets of the bed, over to the dog, out the open window. She could think of fifty questions to ask him, but perhaps he'd said enough. He'd never been so vocal, not remotely, in their four-year association. Her mind spun with all he'd shared. Had she expected him to say, *I married you because I fancied you?* No. She didn't suppose she had expected that. She'd asked the question with no expectations so that she would not be disappointed.

She looked back. He watched her with curious reservation. His expression suggested he wanted some response, but he was afraid of what she might say. Stoker afraid of her? If so, she understood the sentiment.

She was suddenly desperate to change the subject. She looked again at his tattoo and asked, "Did it hurt terribly? When you got it?"

Stoker's eyes narrowed and he hesitated.

She raised an eyebrow.

Slowly, he said, "It was not the most comfortable undertaking. I don't really remember. I was not entirely sober at the time."

"Do they use a . . . knife?"

"Needles," he said. "Hundreds of needle pricks that push dye beneath the skin."

Sabine scrunched up her face. "Needles . . ."

The thing she said next could be blamed on impulsiveness or impetuousness or pique or any number of unaccountable reasons, but the truth was, she said it because she wanted to. It had suddenly become *all* she wanted. Even their incredibly personal conversation, as fascinating as it had been, fell away to make room for this.

"May I touch it?" she asked. She released the dog to the floor.

Across the bed, Stoker went very still. His half-lidded eyes opened wide.

Sabine raised her chin. The instinct to flinch or flee the room did not even enter her mind.

Stoker said nothing but extended his hand to her with careful slowness. She watched him reach out, realizing suddenly that she had touched him, really touched him, so few times. When they'd married, they'd barely shaken hands. When she'd discovered him on the *Dreadnought*, staffers had conveyed him to the wagon; when she'd gotten him home, footmen had put him in the bed and Harley had tended to him. There was the incident in her study, but that had felt less like touching and more like *transporting*. She'd fed him for a week, but they had been separated by the length of a spoon.

What she asked now was touching for the sake of touching. Whether it was years of latent curiosity, or his openness when they spoke, or simply his bare arms and chest spread before her—she did not know and did not care. She wanted her brain to shut down for five minutes and simply . . .

She ran four fingertips along the surface of his forearm, the motion of smoothing down an imaginary sleeve. His skin was warm, and she felt tendons and muscles twitch beneath her touch. The dark pattern of the tattoo was risen ever so slightly, barely discernable through the dusting of hair on his arm.

"Was it painful for days?" she asked softly.

His voice was a rasp. "I don't remember."

She glanced at him. His eyes had not moved from her face. She looked back to his arm. When her fingertips reached the large bone of his wrist, she slid her hand back up. At the pit of his elbow, she extended her index finger and traced the coiling serpent around his biceps, under, over the top again, under again. The buckles of muscle in his arm felt like knots of thick rope. When her finger reached the widest point of his biceps, she stretched out her hand. Her hand spanned less than half of his arm.

"Dr. Cornwell was correct," she whispered. "You are improved today."

The truth was, he seemed hardly sick at all. The bandage around his torso had been wrapped fewer times, and the dressing on his wound was considerably smaller. He was warm and muscle-hard and tightly coiled. He seemed like an animal that had been sleeping but was now very much awake. She gave his biceps a small squeeze, testing the hardness. The latent strength mesmerized her. She was intrigued by the hair on his forearm, the smooth skin of his upper arm, the rock of his shoulder.

"Sabine," he said.

She looked up.

Ever so slightly, he shook his head.

"What?" she said lightly. His denial could mean a hundred things, all of them applicable to this moment, but Sabine hated being told no.

"You don't want this," he said.

"Don't want what?" She could not put specific words to what she might want, but she knew she did not want to stop. Curiosity and something akin to . . . well, it felt like a new stretch of terrain into which she wanted to properly venture, to make note of the landmarks and unique features, to measure and admire and map. He was *unexplored*.

She slid the cuff of her fingers down his arm, jostled them around his wrist, and grazed them back up again, marveling at the sinewy landscape of his muscles.

"Stop," he said, his voice agonized.

Sabine narrowed her eyes. She felt her familiar stubbornness rise like a blush. "Am I hurting you?" Her voice was matter-of-fact. In no way was she hurting him.

"Yes," he said, but he sounded breathless, and not the kind of breathless that came from pain. She glanced at his face.

No, not pain.

Dubiousness had left his expression. Now she saw shock. Bright, excited shock. She sucked in a small breath and smoothed her hand up his biceps and over the hard rock of his shoulder.

Chapter Ten

Jon Stoker prided himself on never being caught off guard.

He anticipated crises and planned for disaster. Every morning he assumed that the world would fall apart.

It made him a proficient captain and an even better rescuer of women and children and dogs and every other wretched soul he'd somehow admitted to—

Stoker drew a ragged breath. One minute they'd been talking about barrels and the next he was prattling on about being an—Oh God, had he really used the term *vigilante*? What in the bloody hell had he been thinking?

He hadn't thought; he'd only felt. He'd been swept up in Sabine's closeness and attention; wanting, just once, to feel clean and pure in living flesh rather than in his mind.

She hadn't needed to know. Her life could go on forever without the lurid truth of where he'd been or what he'd seen or how he'd survived. The less they knew about each other's lives, the less complicated their relationship would be.

Not to mention, Stoker's priority at the moment was locating his bloody brig. He needed mobility, to provision and sail from London as soon as possible; he needed to return to Portugal. If he could also keep tabs on Sabine's personal vendetta against her uncle, all the better.

There was no time to be caught off guard by her request to touch his bloody tattoo.

The irony was that women had been asking to touch his tattoo for as long as he could remember. It elicited a thrilled sort of reverence from a wide range of women—everyone from rescued prostitutes to old grandmothers and little girls. He'd gotten the damn thing because being mistaken for a gentleman scared the hell out of him. He'd had no idea at the time how many females were invigorated by the notion of . . . of—whatever a gentleman was not. He'd never understand why the tattoo intrigued so many women, but *Sabine?*

Sabine asking to touch it, her eyes filled with wonder, her cheeks flushed, the notebook containing her precious investigation bouncing to the floor?

He'd been given no choice but to offer his arm. He'd watched her reach out, watched her trace first one finger, then five fingers, down his forearm. When she'd slid her hand around his biceps, he'd stopped watching and closed his eyes. For the first time since he'd regained consciousness, the burning pain in his side left him. The earth shrank to her cool caress.

This is not sexual, he recited in his head.

This is not attraction; this is not even affection.

This is curiosity.

She is curious, and I will go out of my bloody mind.

"Am I hurting you?" she asked softly, breathlessly.

No, he thought, but he said, "Yes."

"How?" she demanded, her voice still soft, but a demand, just the same. "How is this hurting you?"

By killing me, by teasing me, by offering me something that will not happen.

He said, "This cannot happen."

"What cannot happen?" she asked. Her hand was gentle on his biceps. Slowly, she began to fan her fingers out, a featherlight touch of unfolding sensation.

Stoker cleared his throat. "You were curious about the tattoo, and now you've seen it."

She looked up, trying to read his eyes. He leveled her with what he hoped was a most intimidating scowl.

She laughed—*laughed.* "Are you glaring at me?" She did not release him.

"Sabine," he warned, "you're too close."

"I know," she said softly, the laughter dying away. "I am too close and you are too . . . unclothed."

She chuckled again, a short burst of disbelieving laughter. "I'm not sure why I haven't fled the room, except that I hate being told I cannot do something for no reason. And I never flee. This is why Sir Dryden and I didn't get on."

Stoker's eyes flew to her face. "You said Dryden never touched you."

"Well, he never touched me like I am touching you, but he—"

Suddenly, she snatched her hand away and stood. She gaped at him. "But is this how I've made you feel? Do you feel like I'm taking advantage by touching your arm when you've asked me not to?"

And for the third time that day, Stoker was caught entirely off guard. He blinked, he opened his mouth, he closed it. "Ah—no," he said.

The skin on his arm sang where she'd touched him. He lowered it, pressing his palm into the mattress until his wound stung. He wanted to snatch her hand back; he wanted to tug her back to her spot beside him on the bed. He made a strangled noise and closed his eyes, willing his self-control to catch up, to catch on, to *resist*.

"Oh," Sabine said, and she returned to her spot beside his hip. He opened his eyes. No amount of self-control could prevent him from seeing her sit beside him.

She said, "I should never want to take advantage."

"Sabine . . ." he began, struggling to find the correct words. "You cannot take advantage, because the benefit of you touching my tattoo or my arm or any part of me would be *entirely mine*. So you needn't worry about taking anything from me or a misbegotten balance."

"Really?" She looked confused. "The only gain? Because I quite liked it, too. You are very strong, but you are also very controlled. It's intriguing. I cannot say why I want to touch you, but I do."

And then to his mounting disbelief, she lifted her right hand and reached halfway to his arm. A question. She raised her eyebrows.

Stoker's body surged in response, even while he thought *no, no, no, no.*

This was a woman who refused to convene with him for more than five minutes twice a year to exchange mail. This was a woman who had struggled to drag his bleeding body down the hall because of her great distrust of all men.

"Sabine," he rasped, "what are you doing?"

"I don't know," she said honestly, extending her hand farther. Her fingertips were nearly to him. His skin sizzled with anticipation, the muscle twitching. His body had begun to betray him, part by part. He was weak and voracious at the same time. Failing and surging. Shrinking back and grasping.

"May I speak frankly?" he asked. It was a reasonable question that came out in broken, cracked tones. He cleared his throat.

"Can you?" she challenged.

He narrowed his eyes. And now she would be coy? Without thinking, he reached up and snatched her hand, entwining his fingers. She sucked in a breath and endeavored to pull free, but he held her firm. This was allowed, he thought. This, too, was not sexual. This was a taste of his strength and speed, but it revealed none of his roiling desire.

"Sabine." He spoke quickly, lowly, a confession. "Forgive me if I make assumptions or misread your intent, but the touch of your hand and the look on your face do not feel curious or clinical or even friendly. Do you know how it feels?"

Her beautiful green eyes had gone wide. "Let go of my hand," she said, and immediately, he released her.

"Forgive me," he said, feeling panic soak him like a driving rain. *That did it. I've frightened her, damn it all to hell. I've overstepped. I've—*

"How does it feel?" she asked.

"I beg your pardon?"

"You *asked me* if I know how it feels. I don't know—so tell me."

"It feels sexual," he answered immediately. He meant to shock her with bold, coarse talk. It was also the truth. He meant to tell her the truth. "It feels sexual. In nature. Do you know what that means?"

The cream of her skin turned pink and her beautiful lips opened to a pouty O. Slowly, she shook her head. It was one of the most sensual gestures he'd ever seen. His brain leapt, missed, leapt again, trying to catch hold of something he could add to this already brazen statement. Would she make him say it? Would she—

"What?" she demanded, and then boldly, confidently, she wrapped her hand around his forearm.

Stoker's vision shrank to her fingers. Sensation frothed beneath the skin. His arm buzzed and tingled and radiated warmth.

Of course she would make him bloody say it.

"Are you a virgin, Sabine?" he heard himself ask. It didn't matter; it *wouldn't* matter, but it would inform what he would say next. His mouth went dry. He wondered if he would manage to hear her answer over the pounding of his heart.

"Of course," she said.

Stoker was pulled under with an undeserved and unaccountable wave of relief. He struggled to catch his breath.

"Of course," he managed to repeat. He paused, picking around the chaos in his brain for words that might safely end the journey on which they'd somehow found themselves.

"At the risk of explaining something that you already know," he began, "sex, when you have it, is . . . is like a transaction." He felt his face go red, but he did not look away.

"A transaction?" She repeated this as if he'd said, "Sex is like a garden rake." Or ". . . a baby giraffe." Or, ". . . a bad clam."

"Yes," he said. "Sex is something to which women consent in exchange for something they require—such as money or protection or a name or even a child."

Sabine scrunched up her face in distaste. "Is that what you believe?"

"Sabine," he sighed, "I, perhaps more than any man alive, have seen the beginning, middle, and end of every part of human desire. It is not my opinion. It is what I have known since I could hear my mother 'at work' across the room while I was meant to be asleep on the floor. Sex was a *transaction* into which she entered, again and again, until it killed her. I have rescued countless girls from a similar fate. I have seen it dressed up in luxury, and diversion, and flower-trimmed romantic trappings. I have also seen it reduced to minutes—

nay, seconds—against alley walls. But every time, I have seen the same basic trade—a man's pleasure for some payment to the woman. It troubles me to assume so much and offend you with my bluntness, but it cannot go unsaid. I hold you in too high esteem to enter into any such transaction with you."

He'd looked away, unable to hold her gaze. It was too much to hope that she would flee from the room. It was too much to hope that she would slap him. Was it too much to hope that she would say, "Very well, I am grateful to finally know the truth of it"?

He glanced back to her.

Yes, it was too much.

She was staring at him as if he'd just explained that Sunday would not follow Saturday.

"But are you certain that *everyone* views . . . relations in this manner?" she asked. "That is, not suggesting that I wanted to, er, 'transact' with you in this moment, but since you have brought it up."

He ran a hand through his hair and scratched the back of his neck. And now she would force him to elaborate. And now he must *debate* the topic.

"Sex," he lectured patiently, "is viewed in every possible light, I'm sure, but few people have seen what I have seen. As much as I am loath to admit it, I really am somewhat of an expert."

"An expert on sex?"

"An expert on the motivations and ramifications of sex."

She nodded and looked at the ceiling, thinking this over.

Stoker tried to watch her, but her pensive expression, so stark in profile, was too beautiful, and he looked away.

After a moment she said, "And what of your business partners? Cassin and Joseph Chance?"

"I beg your pardon?" His voice broke.

"One cannot help but wonder about the Earl of Cassin and his countess, my friend Willow? Or, what of Joseph and my friend Tessa? Willow and Tessa have been quite open with me, and they reported nothing transactional about sex with their husbands."

Stoker sighed. "I have not discussed it with Cassin or Joseph, but I have no doubt they have managed it with decorum and respect and made the effort very worth it for their wives."

Now her expression was even more confused. "This is nothing like they reported it to me."

"I . . . don't like to speculate on the relations of others," he said.

She stared at him. He could see wheels of thought turning in her head, but she did not seem embarrassed; she did not seem chastened or threatened. *That's all that matters*, he thought. *Protect her*. The least he could do in return for her care and the stolen thrill of her attention was to protect her.

Now she said, "And so *you* never . . . engage in the, er, transaction of sex? I mean, your own self?"

And now I will die, he thought. "Sabine . . ." he pleaded.

"What? Surely you cannot mean to demand that I reveal *my* virginal state but refuse to discuss your own."

"I am not a virgin," he said quickly, praying this was enough.

"And you are racked with guilt because of the advantage you've taken of the women in your past? Is that it? It all began so innocently—she wished to touch your tattoo—and then it spiraled into fantastical sex, for you, not for her, because she only wanted to touch your tattoo and then earn some reward?"

"Sabine," he groaned. He wondered how many times he could skate by on simply saying her name.

"I want to know," she insisted. "You have been so gracious to educate me, and now I am captivated and want to hear all of it."

"Sex with me never begins innocently," he said. He couldn't look at her; he stared at the paper in his lap. From the corner of his eye he saw her agitated posture perk up. Her full attention. Of course.

He wondered why his wound couldn't begin to hemorrhage? Why couldn't the doctor return to tell him he had ten minutes left to live?

"So you *pay* for this non-innocent sex?" she theorized.

"No, never, not in as many words. If you must know—"

"Oh, I must know."

Stoker squinted at her, working to string together words that would . . . end this. In truth, his assignations with women had been limited strictly to middle-of-the-night encounters with partners both sexually aggressive and financially independent. These were wealthy widows, businesswomen of a certain age, the odd bored monarch. He'd never, not even once, entertained young women with aspirations to marriage or a conventional life. He'd never paid for sex, but he was generous with gifts or some security concern he might manage on their behalf. He was racked with guilt after every encounter, but he was a man, just like any other man, and his desire for sex did battle with his self-control. A gnawing hunger that was never fully sated. An emptiness that ashamed him as much as it drove him.

"Stoker?" she prompted.

He sighed. "The women I've taken to bed have all been carefully selected to require nothing, expect nothing, and want no part of me after I've gone," he said. "They are generally older or widowed or both. They are independent beyond traditional standards for most women, so privileged in rank or social standing that they do as they please."

"And so the transaction is . . . ?"

"I cannot say exactly. It has never been an ideal arrangement. These interludes haunt me, actually, and the reason for this entire excruciating conversation is to avoid anything of the sort for you. You will not be haunted, and I will not have the sin of defiling you on my conscience. We made this deal from the beginning." He glared at her.

She looked back with a pensive expression. "You find this conversation excruciating, don't you?"

"Yes."

"I quite like it. Although, one thing is unclear. How does my touching your arm have anything to do with sex?" She accompanied this question with a flutter of her cool fingers on his arm.

Stoker's body surged in response and he made a pained growling noise. "This is what I said from the first, Sabine. You cannot run your hands up and down my arm. You cannot caress and lean in and . . . look at me with wide-eyed . . . bloody . . . wonder. You are too innocent to know it, and I cannot fathom what has come over you, but this is how sex begins. No man could withstand it, least of all me. I'm sorry."

Sabine crinkled up her nose and fluttered her fingertips again. "And what if I wish to *challenge* your theory that sex is always a . . . a transaction or an exchange? What if I'm to say this is not what I've been told, not at all."

"Then I would be forced to say that you know virtually nothing about it and I know quite a lot. Again, I'm sorry."

Sabine sucked in a breath, a flash of anger deepening her features. "I *detest* being told that I 'don't *know* something.' Even if I don't."

"Well, you don't, and it's a gift. Be glad you don't know."

She was shaking her head. "Tell me I have something to learn, tell me I'm wrong, but please never say that I 'don't know anything about it.' It's infuriating. It goads me on, actually." Her fingers closed around his arm and Stoker ground his teeth.

"Do you know what infuriates me?" he gritted out. "Being bloody taken by surprise. Being unprepared. Casting around for a solution to a problem that I could not have anticipated. And your sudden interest in my bloody tattoo, and your hands on my skin, and asking provocative questions about sex has taken me wholly off guard. So forgive me if I have not been gracious or articulate or clear. You've consistently claimed to want no part of any man, myself in particular, and yet your hands have been everywhere."

"Come now," she said. "Everywhere?"

Was she teasing him? Could she not see how he struggled to remain calm and reasonable and in control?

"Look," she said, "I'm sorry if you are surprised, but perhaps I am as surprised as you are. I've not given your tattoo a second thought until now. I've never thought of touching you, and certainly I had no intention of discussing sex. *You* were the one who . . . who . . ." Her voice had risen; she was sucking in air to speak, but now she stopped. She blinked. She let out a deep breath and leaned in.

"What if," she said lowly, but with a hard edge, "I concede that that last bit was a lie?"

Concede? A lie? This sounded like a trap.

Or a dare.

"What if," she went on, "I tell you I *am* interested in touching your arm, *and* your shoulder, *and* leaning in, and giving you . . ." Here she paused, and Stoker's heart stopped. "A kiss? What if I tell you that?"

Stoker's brain went completely blank. He saw only white. His last useful thought was of whipping off the covers and staggering from the room, down the hall, and into the street.

"Sabine—no," he managed.

"I hate being told no," she said defiantly. She leaned closer. Oh God, he was inundated with the scent of her—sunshine and butterscotch. Loose tendrils of her hair dropped against his arm.

He grabbed a fistful of sheet on either side of his body. "No." He shook his head.

"If kissing is a part of sex—which I can concede, yes, it is—then let us invoke this transaction of yours. What would you like me to give you so that we might share a kiss? Just a small kiss. Just so that I may see what it is like."

"Oh God." He made a strangled noise. His heart was drumming in his chest.

"You aren't attracted to me?" she guessed. "You find me difficult and domineering. My hair is too black. My eyes are too green."

He heard the ocean in his ears, like listening to a shell.

She went on, more guesses. "There is no token or favor on offer that is worth kissing me."

"That is not the way the transaction works," he managed, sucking in the smell of her skin. "I would give *you* the token or favor in exchange for *you* allowing *me* to kiss you."

"But what if I want the kiss outright? What if, irrationally, unexpectedly, the kiss is suddenly the only thing I want?" She leaned closer and whispered, "What if only a show of great disgust would dissuade me? Do I disgust you, Stoker?"

Stoker swallowed hard and locked eyes on her mouth. She swiped her pink tongue across her top lip, and his mouth watered.

She sat up suddenly and he almost gasped out loud. It felt like she ripped out his heart.

"Unless," she said sharply, "you have a mistress."

"No," he breathed.

"One of those old, rich women for whom you dole out favors?" she theorized.

"There is no one since I married you. But Sabine, you will regret this," he whispered.

She cocked an eyebrow and leaned down again. "Why do I feel like I will regret it if I do not?"

"I've no idea," he breathed, and just like that, his power of speech dropped off. He searched the beauty of her face, just as magnificent at close range. His gaze settled on her lips. His hand moved without his permission to grasp her waist. She sucked in a small breath. He thought, *Thank God, I've finally alarmed her*, although he would howl if she pulled away.

She did not pull away, or slap him, or exhibit even a tremor of traumatized behavior.

Instead, she fell against him.

Stoker made a noise of defeat, capitulation and desire combined, and she scrambled up. "Oh, I'm so sorry! Your wound!"

His hand reached of its own accord and took her up by the wrist, pulling her back. "I feel no pain," he rasped. In his head the words *Do not, do not, do not, do not* spiraled in time to his pounding heart.

"Oh," she said. She turned her head and said, "Bridget, *out*." The dog leapt, stretched, yawned, and tapped from the room. Just like that, she allowed herself to be pulled back to his chest.

Stoker felt everything. The small ruffle trim furling along

the seams of her dress. The lush landscape of her body—flat stomach giving way to ripe breasts, round hips. Her hands scrambling for a hold on his bare shoulders. She'd landed nearly nose to nose and was too close for him to see more than creamy skin, red lips, and black eyelashes.

"I've no idea how to go about this," she whispered.

Stoker closed his eyes. Her innocence should not matter, but every reference was a double edge of possession and desire.

"Oh," she said, clearly still watching him. "Eyes closed. Right."

Before he could look again, he felt her breath on his cheek and the tickle of her hair on his ear—and then he was swimming in the fresh butterscotch smell of her.

He tightened his grip on her waist, his most base instinct ordering him to never, ever let her go. With his other hand, he cupped her face.

Gently guide her away, said some hateful, cruel part of his brain, but it was already too late. He felt the light, cool cushion of her lips. He felt her nose nuzzling his. Her hands left his shoulders and slid around his neck.

I'm dying, he thought, a phrase never more accurate in his life.

Ever so slightly, Sabine began to move her lips.

Stoker tried, weakly, the weakest bloody effort, to turn his head away. *She has no idea; she is better than this; she is better than you; she does not exist in your world; she is—*

Sabine let out a noise of frustration. The smallest, sweetest sound, and something in Stoker snapped. His hand clenched at her waist; he dug his fingers into her hair; he pressed her face fully against his. He moved his mouth the fraction of an inch that precisely aligned their lips, and he kissed her. One small, delicate nibble. And then another, and another.

He heard her small exhale of breath, felt her hands flex against his neck. Her eyelashes brushed his cheek and he opened his eyes to find her staring at him. She pulled back far enough to see him, really see him, and Stoker opened his eyes wide, his heart cracking open. He braced himself to witness shock-alarm-tears-trauma-whatever, but she stared only at his mouth, studying it with an analytical, determined look.

Before he could react, she descended again, her hands cinching around his neck, her nose against his, her lips fitted more perfectly against his.

She mimicked the movement of his own mouth, searching for the correct rhythm. Stoker kissed her back, trying to contain the torrent of desire evoked by the erotic combination of her eagerness and innocence.

Without thinking, he sank his fingers into her hair, relishing the silkiness as it slipped from its pins and fell down his arm. Sabine copied the movement, sliding up her own hand.

He heard her breathing, heard himself panting; he invoked colossal effort to try to slow down; he ordered himself not to gobble her up. And yet, the hand on her waist slid upward, glossing over her ribs, feeling the side of her breast.

My God, her breasts. He had survived entire voyages

on mere speculation about the feel of Sabine's breasts. She sucked in another breath and his hand slid away, back to her waist, and then lower, to the lush roundness of her hip.

Meanwhile, she kissed on and on and on. It was a labyrinth of kisses, and he was so lost, so immediately lost. Witless. He was teaching her even as he lost his mind. She kissed the corner of his mouth, his bottom lip, his upper lip, and then full on the mouth again. When she came up for air—*no*—he pressed his palm flat against her hip and cupped her head, unwilling for it to end. But then she lowered her head, kissing him again, more deeply, more thoroughly.

Without thinking, Stoker swiped his tongue against her bottom lip. It was in and out of his mouth before he'd realized he'd done it. She made a little jump, sending pulses of pleasure at every point of contact from hip to shoulder, and made a noise of alarm.

Stoker panicked—*it's finished, she's afraid, you've*—but then she met his tongue with her own, a tentative swipe and then another, and then another, and Stoker groaned and slipped his tongue deeper, and she said, "Oh!" with a delightful lilt that he would hear in his head every night until he died.

Stoker was lost. He'd known all along it would come to this. His body took over; his mouth and his hands and his rock-hard manhood, pressing insistently against her hip, and all control, all regard for her chastity and honor, would be gone.

If his brain could function, he would have questioned her enthusiasm, questioned her ardor, questioned her motivations and intent and why she would lower herself—to him, of all people—with his dark past and his warnings about sex and his haunted regard for every pleasurable touch. But his brain could *not* function; his body moved on instinct. She was a melody and he was silence. She was an unlocked door and he was a thief.

When she turned her head to the side to breathe, he kissed her ear. When the weight of her body finally, unbelievably, pained his wound, he shifted with a grunt and she drew her knees onto the mattress, kneeling beside him, taking the pressure off. He looped his free hand around her bottom, holding her against him.

He was just about to move to the side, to guide her long legs down beside him on the bed, when a loud, insistent knock sounded from the door.

From the next room, the dog began to bark wildly.

Stoker froze, even while Sabine continued to kiss and kiss and—

Knock-knock-knock-knock-knock-knock. It sounded like an insistent bird with a very blunt beak. The dog could be heard running circles by the door, barking to raise the dead.

Sabine lifted her head and brushed her hair from her eyes. It was impossible to control their breathing, and she made no effort. She sat up and endeavored to gather up the cascade of ebony hair that now rained down her back and shoulders in loose curls. She glanced at him and then away.

"I'm sorry," he said. There was nothing else.

"Stop," she said.

"What?" He didn't understand.

"We'll discuss this later," she said. "How do I look?" She hopped from the bed, bouncing on one foot to find her balance. "Bridget! Quiet!" she called.

You've never looked more beautiful. "Who could be at the door?" he asked.

"I've no idea. No one bothers me here. It's one of my favorite things about the apartments. Visitors usually call first to the Boyds' front door."

"Are you . . . hurt?" he asked.

"Hurt?" She frowned at him.

"I'm sorry, I . . . lost control."

She glared again. "Are you?"

"Am I sorry?" He didn't understand.

"Stop saying that. Are you *hurt*?"

He shook his head, still trying to catch up.

"You are mad," she said.

"I'm not mad," he said, but the dog's barking and the insistent knocking drowned out the words.

She took up her skirts and gave them a shake. She wiped the back of her hand across her swollen lips and spun away, shouting for the dog. When she glanced back, he opened his mouth to apologize again, but she shook her head—*Do not.*

He blinked and said nothing, and she swept from the room.

"Coming!" she sang, meeting the dog in the doorway and scooping her up. "Who is it?" he heard her ask through the door.

Stoker heard a mumbled, high-pitched reply and then Sabine could be heard to say, "*Ooooooh.*"

He heard the locks snap open, door hinges, bustling, footsteps, possessions hitting the floor in a clatter.

"Miss Sabine!" said an excited female voice that precisely matched the enthusiasm of the knocks.

The dog barked once, and the new voice and Sabine shouted in unison, "Bridget, stop!"

"Perry?" exclaimed Sabine. "What on earth are you doing in London?"

If Stoker remembered correctly, Miss Pippa Perry was the lady's maid who had originally accompanied the three brides from Surrey to London, and who was currently in the employ of Willow Caulder, the Countess of Cassin.

"I've traveled all the way from Yorkshire to you, miss," said Perry.

"Yes, I see that, Perry," said Sabine, "but why have you come? Is Willow unwell?"

"Oh no, Miss Sabine, the countess is quite well. But when she received your letter about Mr. Stoker being half-dead, she was in such a state. The earl is in Italy at the moment, acquiring new treasures for the castle . . ."

This she said as if Cassin were in heaven buying golden harps. Stoker rolled his eyes. Cassin and his new countess had saved his Yorkshire castle by transforming it into a luxury hotel with healing-water baths. It was a raging success, clearly a point of pride for the maid, but Stoker liked to tease Cassin about being the only earl in England who also worked as an innkeep.

The maid continued, "And his lordship isn't due to return for a month. Lady Willow could not come because—well, she doesn't even really know Mr. Stoker, does she? And also, who will manage the castle if both the earl and countess are away?"

"Who indeed?" Stoker heard Sabine say.

"But never fear," boasted the maid, "Lady Willow asked me if I would come instead, and here I am. I shall look after Mr. Stoker, and without complaint, mind you, despite how disagreeable I find London *or* how swollen or putrid or bilious he may be. This is the promise I have made." Her voice had taken on the tenor of a vow.

"How fortunate we are," said Sabine, clearing her throat. Stoker thought, *Thank God. Save her from me, save her, save her . . .*

"Now," said the maid, "where shall I begin? Does Mr. Stoker require—"

"*So* fortunate," Sabine repeated, cutting her off. "I will write Willow straightaway and thank her for sparing you. Your ample talents will be put to good use, never fear. But Perry, you will be assisting *me*, not Mr. Stoker. His care is managed by me alone, I'm afraid."

"Mr. Stoker's care?" Perry confirmed.

"That's right. I hope you don't feel as if you've come all this way for nothing."

Stoker took up the newspaper, now mangled against the sheet, and laid it over his face.

He heard the maid let out a sigh. "Oh no, I prefer it, honestly. Lady Willow said you would be overwhelmed, having to look after Mr. Stoker all by yourself, but I said I never knew Miss Sabine to be overwhelmed, not once."

"Your faith in me is gratifying, truly," he heard Sabine say. Next he heard footsteps, and Stoker swiped the paper away and stared at the door. Sabine closed it in one quick swing. The last thing he heard before it slammed was Perry exclaiming, "Well, if nothing else, I'm glad to have come because something really must be done about your hair—"

Click.

Stoker was locked in his room, restricted to this bed, and prisoner to his riotous body, a stew of lust and fear and regret.

CHAPTER ELEVEN

Within an hour of Perry's arrival, Sabine had dispatched the maid to the servants' quarters and holed herself up in her study for what she considered to be the "foreseeable future." Perhaps she would never leave. Perhaps she would grow old in the study, eating food brought in and out by servants, growing pale and wizened like a crone. Sir Dryden would carry on, unchecked, with his smuggling, and country tourists would wander the streets of London with no guide. Her dog would go blind for never seeing the light of day.

All of this, she thought, would be better than reckoning what had just transpired with Jon Stoker. *With her husband*, she reminded herself. Well, her *convenient* husband. The phrase had suddenly taken on new meaning. Not convenient to marry, but conveniently located in her bedroom to kiss whenever she willed it. Clearly, she willed it very much.

Was it wrong that some part of her wanted to return to his room and carry on kissing him again? Was it wrong that she wasn't scandalized or ashamed by the kiss but really rather invigorated? Was it wrong that her lifelong vow to live independently and solitarily suddenly seemed very short-sighted?

Oh God, the kiss. While her friend Tessa had spent far too much time fantasizing about kisses, and her other friend Willow had devoted an entire childhood to vowing she would never do it, Sabine had not really thought of it one way or the other. She'd not had a featherheaded, beau-chasing youth. She'd been so taken by her father's cartography, so interested in travel and sketching and maps, there hadn't been time to fantasize about kissing. And then Sir Dryden had put her off men in general.

Now she wondered if she'd ever think of anything else. No, that wasn't true; there was plenty to think of—smuggling, Stoker's health, getting back to Park Lodge—but the thought of intimacy with Jon Stoker had elbowed in with significant prominence among her other interests and pursuits.

Perry came and went with a supper tray, and Sabine sat down with a stack of clean parchment to compose a letter to Willow. She must make some show of gratitude for sending Perry. And she must apprise Willow and Cassin of Stoker's progress. And she might also . . .

Well, obviously, she had only just kissed Stoker, so it was too soon to draw conclusions or even put too fine a point on what had just happened. But would a few carefully worded questions allow her to cast around for some generalized answers about . . . well, about intimacy among husbands and wives? Hiding in her study felt safe and prudent at the moment, but she would run mad if she did not communicate with someone.

Dear Willow,

How to begin this letter?

There is the obvious: Perry has been a godsend, thank you.

But also, perhaps more accurately: Perry? Willow, how could you?

(I hope you'll consider this in the good humor in which it is intended.)

Of course, Perry is a godsend. There has been more of every kind of household chore since Stoker came to Belgrave Square, and I haven't had the time or energy to train someone new. My travel guides and my investigation would have fallen so far behind if Perry had not arrived. Her constant chatter and general enthusiasm will be a boundless reminder that patience is a virtue. Would that we all were as guileless as Perry.

But of course you knew that, which is why she's come. Thank you. Truly.

Perry has mentioned your regret that Cassin himself was not able to race to London to look in on Stoker. Please put this concern out of your mind. Stoker is comfortable and recovering nicely. Surprisingly, it has been far easier than expected for me to accommodate his care.

If anything, I wish for your presence—this is not a cry for help, merely wishful thinking—as I find Stoker's time here to be marked with . . . oh, how can I say this?

I find Stoker's time here to be marked with . . .
philosophical questions and behavioral challenges I could
not have anticipated.

(And now that I have your full attention.)

I run the risk of misleading you or misrepresenting the
situation when I allude to this, but before you galloped away
to fall in love with your husband and his castle, you and I
did speak freely about such things.

"What things?" (I can hear you speaking to this letter.)

Indeed. Plainly put, I have one or two questions about
marriage and, in particular, so-called "marital relations."
Ahem. I dare not commit these to paper in specific terms
but in general, (and here is the real point of this letter, I
suppose):

Would you say, as a happy wife, that relations with
your husband feel like a . . . sort of . . . trade-off for "things"?
And by "things," I suppose I mean tangible gifts or for
preferential allowances that you would like? That is, is . . .
congress among the two of you always a matter of his bed
in exchange for . . . oh, let's say, a new piece of art or having
your way in some conflict?

Or, in contrast, would you say marital relations are
more of a joint effort that ushers in, well, joint contentment,
with no sought-after prize for your participation?

It is my great hope that you can consider this question
without jumping to conclusions. Stoker is very ill and
determined to recover both his health and his brig with
no distractions, marital or otherwise. I am committed to
unmasking my uncle's smuggling plot, whatever it is, and

to my travel guides. Our "arrangement," which is the only
one of the "Brides of Belgravia" unions to align with your
original vision, is unchanged.

This is an idle question that has simply come up, and
Stoker feels one way, and I know very little on the topic, but
had always been led to believe the other. Let's call it a debate
that I am bullishly motivated to win. (You know me.)

Please do not share this with Tessa as she will never
believe my question to be theoretical, and I cannot tolerate
her gushing and romanticizing. As I've mentioned, Stoker is
a very sick man, and I . . .

Here Sabine paused, raising her pen. She looked over her
shoulder at the open door to her study, auditioning denials
in her head.

Stoker is a very sick man . . . and I hardly know him.

Stoker is a very sick man . . . and I remain averse to all men
in the wake of Sir Dryden's abuse.

Stoker is a very sick man . . . and I believe him to be planning
his immediate departure upon recovery.

Finally, she settled on:

Stoker is a very sick man . . . and I am very busy.
    Fondly,
    Sabine

Before she could change her mind, she sealed the letter
with wax and sent it upstairs to be posted.

Returning to her desk, she tried to focus on pinning

notes to the wall mural she'd drawn to display all the evidence amassed on Sir Dryden. Every few minutes she would pause to listen for Harley. She'd summoned the footman to sit with Stoker as he took his supper, cowardly, no doubt. Perry had offered, but Sabine had meant what she said. She would manage his care. Although simply not . . . today. And perhaps not tomorrow.

Sabine was not ashamed or abashed about the kiss so much as . . . uncertain about how to proceed. And nervous, perhaps? Just a touch. She felt a little like she'd drawn a beautiful map to a magical location, and now it was in the hands of a traveler. She could, theoretically, ask this traveler how he enjoyed the map, but she was afraid. What if it had not been useful? What if there were wrong turns? What if he had been confused by the route? Worst of all, did he make the journey but hate the destination? Did he wish he'd never left home?

Sabine was also terrified that she'd somehow injured Stoker during their passionate . . . passionate—whatever it was. Passionate *moment*. Passionate *interlude*. It had been so much more than a kiss.

Her skin tingled at the memory of his hands in her hair and down her back and up the snug side of her bodice. Her stomach flipped when she thought of the noises he made, desire and satisfaction at once, exactly as she felt. And his chest. Bare and muscled and furred with hair, exposed to her searching hands. The tattoo had only been the beginning.

The memories mingled with her nerves and she kept away.

Surely, he would call for her if she'd harmed him. He would tell Harley. He would send word that he needed the doctor.

Sabine shook her head, trying to return her focus to the evidence mural, when Perry bustled into the room with a tea tray, Bridget trailing behind her.

"Oh, Perry, you needn't bring refreshment this time of night," Sabine said. "I know you're exhausted after your journey. Let us both stop for today and go to bed. Did you find your old room in the servants' hall?"

"Oh yes, miss, just like I left it. But where do you sleep? Now that Mr. Stoker is—" and now she lowered her voice to a whisper "—*in your bed?*" Her face suggested an ogre in their midst.

"Oh, I've taken a guest room on the second floor. The Boyds have been so generous about Stoker's convalescence. And he's not so very bad. His condition is not contagious."

"Well," said Perry, pouring the tea, "he's not contagious in any way that we know about."

Sabine hid a smile. "Perry?"

"Yes, miss?" Perry shooed the dog off a chair and pushed it toward the tea service.

"Back in Yorkshire, at the castle . . ."

"We prefer to call it by its proper name," corrected Perry, "which is Caldera. And there are certainly no dogs inside the castle."

"Oh yes, I remember this from my visit," said Sabine with a smirk, feeding Bridget a biscuit from the tray. She started again, "At *Caldera*, does your work as Lady Willow's personal maid require you to maintain a separate bedroom for Lady Willow? Or do the earl and countess share one bedroom?"

"Oh, they share the most beautifully appointed master suite you've ever seen," reported Perry reverently. "With a stained-glass window and chandelier and a canopied bed the size of a barge."

"Right," said Sabine. "And Lady Willow sleeps in this room . . . every night?"

"Oh yes, every night," assured Perry. "And myself and lordship's valet? We are only permitted to enter when they ring for us or when they are out. They make their own fire and dress for bed themselves. They are very private and it is part of my job to protect their privacy from the upstairs maids and footmen. Well, mine and Marcus's. That's his lordship's valet." Perry rolled her eyes and repeated her colleague's name with a haughty affection. "Marcus."

"Oh yes, of course," mused Sabine. "It sounds . . . exclusive."

"Well," sniffed Perry, making her way to the door, "they are an earl and countess, aren't they?"

"Indeed they are, but Perry?" called Sabine, and the maid turned back. "Thank you. For coming all this way. I know life in the city is not your preference, and your work for Lady Willow at Caldera has great value. I'm grateful that you've consented to lend your time and talents back at Belgrave Square."

The maid beamed. "You're quite welcome, Miss Sabine. How could I not come, when Lady Willow explained how gravely ill Mr. Stoker was, and you here all alone, not able to abide his company."

"Yes," said Sabine, clearing her throat. "As I've said, he's not so terrible."

The maid paused. "Not so terribly sick or not so *terrible?*" She scrunched her face into an angry scowl and raised her hands like claws.

Sabine bit her lip and then said, "Neither."

The maid went away, looking unconvinced, and Sabine slipped upstairs to her own bed an hour later.

Despite Stoker's distinction of "non-terrible," Sabine managed to avoid his presence for the next four days. Perry's household contributions allowed more freedom to Harley, and he managed the meals that she had formerly overseen.

It felt cowardly to stay away, not to mention duplicitous—she veritably sprinted past his half-open bedroom door when she came and went—and for all practical purposes her dog was lost to her. Bridget had taken up full-time residence in Stoker's bed, and Sabine dare not retrieve her. But she was not yet ready to face him.

On the second day after the kiss, they received a letter, at long last, from Joseph Chance, Stoker's second partner in business. In short, the letter apologized profusely but claimed Joseph could not possibly travel to London due to the impending birth of his and Tessa's third child.

Sabine added the letter—which had been addressed to them both—to the other mail on Stoker's meal tray and allowed Harley to deliver it with his supper.

On the fourth day Sabine lit on an intriguing lead in the investigation of Sir Dryden, and she was out of the house, first to snoop around the laboratories of the new Royal

Polytechnic Institution in Regent Street, then to observe a charcoal kiln in Hampstead.

If Sabine missed sharing meals with Stoker, checking on his condition, and discussing her investigation, especially these two new leads, she did not miss it so much that she was prepared to actually face him. She simply wasn't yet ready. She continued to mull over every ramification and possibility in her mind. And she still blushed at the memory of what they'd done. She would take it up with him personally very soon. Not yet, but soon.

On the fifth day after the kiss, the day she vowed she would, absolutely, without a doubt, return to Stoker's room, Mary Boyd sent a note asking Sabine to make time for tea in her attic workshop.

The note surprised and worried Sabine, because a formal invitation from the Boyds was very rare. Sabine came and went from the Boyds' house as she pleased, and the middle-aged couple—both of them busy artisans in their own right—did the same. They shared an evening meal four or five nights a week, but with no expectations, and Sabine could never remember making time in the middle of the day for tea, certainly not since Tessa and Willow had moved away.

Sabine allowed Perry to dress her carefully. She'd grown perhaps too familiar and casual around the Boyds. It showed lack of respect and ingratitude, especially in a home as stylish and well-appointed as Belgrave Square. Sabine rehearsed excuses or alternatives she might offer if, for some reason, Mary announced that she and Arthur had grown weary of housing a half-dead sea captain in their cellar apartment or (her greater fear) that they could no longer spare Harley the footman to assist in his care.

The date of Stoker's arrival—some three weeks ago— weighed heavy on her mind. Was this reasonable? How long could a recuperating husband lodge in the borrowed cellar bedroom of his estranged wife? The circumstances were simply so odd. No hosts could be more generous than the Boyds, and Sabine did not wish to take advantage.

Not yet, Sabine thought, watching in the mirror as Perry piled her hair ever higher on top of her head. *Not yet, not yet, not yet.* The words spun in the back of her mind.

Despite Sabine's avoidance, despite the imposition he might pose to an already generous family, she could not stop thinking it.

Not yet.

He's not well enough. I've not finished collaborating with him yet. I need more time. I need—

Not. Yet.

"Thank you so much, my dear, for coming," called Mary as Sabine climbed the winding stairwell to the attic studio.

"I don't know why we don't do this more often," said Sabine, looking around the cluttered workshop of furniture, mirrors, and art. She went on, "I so rarely make time for a proper afternoon tea these days. What a treat to indulge."

"Well, I'm not sure it's proper, not in the clutter of the attic," said Mary, stepping back to squint at the curved leg of an upturned chair. "But the topic at hand warrants informality. The parlor would never do. Too stuffy."

Sabine stopped ambling, unprepared for the woman's bluntness. "Oh dear," she said, recovering, "that bad, is it?"

"Oh no, 'tis not bad at all," cooed Mary, returning to the chair leg and massaging it with a cloth. "Forgive me if I'm distracted. I can't seem to get this stain exactly right."

"It's beautiful."

"It's too red."

The woman wet the cloth with fresh stain from an open pot and applied it to the shiny wood, rubbing firm, circular strokes. Sabine fixed what she hoped was a pleasant smile on her face and watched in miserable, impatient silence.

After what felt like an eternity, Mary Boyd said, "I've a letter here from Willow." She nodded to an open envelope on the workbench behind her.

"Willow?" repeated Sabine. She stared at the letter, immediately recognizing the regal stationery of her friend's Yorkshire castle. "Is she . . . well?"

"Oh yes, quite well, but she's very worried, I'm afraid—about you. Will you sit?" Mary gestured to a sofa and Sabine wound her way through stacks of furniture and lowered herself into the seat.

"Worried about me?" There was a tea trolley beside the sofa, and Sabine began to pour. "She's sent Perry to look after me."

"Yes," said Mary, "Perry. How lucky for us all." She looked up from the chair to wink at Sabine.

Sabine made a sheepish face and extended a cup of tea to the older woman.

"Lovely, I'd nearly forgotten about the tea. Thank you."

She took a sip. "Tell me, Sabine, how is Mr. Stoker getting on? Harley has assured us he will not die in our cellar, thank God. But that is all we know." She settled the cup and saucer on her knee.

"He is doing quite well, thank you. My own work has kept me busy these past few days, but when last I spoke to the doctor, he gave a very encouraging report. I . . . I cannot tell you how grateful I am for Harley's assistance. And that you've allowed us to make over my bedroom as his sick ward."

"He is your husband, Sabine, and Arthur and I said when we invited you girls here that this would be your home just as it is ours. That makes it his home, as well."

Sabine looked into her teacup, overwhelmed by the four years of boundless generosity from the Boyds. "Thank you, Mary. You and Arthur are the very souls of kindness."

"You girls are like the daughters I never had—which brings me to the reason I have called you here." Mary wiped her hands and set aside her cloth, taking up Willow's open letter. She narrowed her eyes at Sabine.

Sabine's heart had begun to pound.

Mary gazed down at the letter. "Willow is very worried about you, which, in turn, makes me worry. Do we need to be worried, dear?"

"Worried about . . . ?"

"Right," said Mary, taking up her tea. "Do you mind if I speak frankly, dear?"

"I prefer it," said Sabine.

"Willow says here that there is some . . . *confusion* among you and Mr. Stoker about . . . the marriage bed."

"Oh God," said Sabine, dropping her teacup on the saucer with a clatter.

"Indeed," said Mary, not looking away. "I would not normally insert myself into a quandary like this—these matters do tend to work themselves out—but Willow could not be here and she believes you have no one else to talk to."

Sabine considered taking up the open pot of furniture stain and drinking it.

"The confusion is . . . not all that troubling," Sabine said, unable to look up. She stared into her lap, seeing nothing, feeling nothing but a full-body blush, inside and out. Even her hair, she was certain, had turned pink.

"Can you tell me if Mr. Stoker is well enough to . . . engage with you in some manner, Sabine? Obviously, this is something I cannot ask Harley."

"*Oh God*," breathed Sabine. "Please do not ask Harley."

"Of course not. I am asking you, and honestly, I'm surprised by your shyness. You were always the boldest of the three brides, weren't you?"

"I know I'm being . . . silly. Forgive me. I've—that is, when I took him in, I never expected to enjoy his company quite so much. And after that, I never expected to . . . to—"

She looked up and shook her head. She wasn't sure how to say the rest.

Mary Boyd reached again for her tea. "Ah, so the answer is yes. He *is* well enough in some way. Lovely." She took a sip and glanced again at the letter.

"I've no wish to interrogate you or embarrass you, Sabine," Mary went on, "but I share Willow's concern for your—oh, let's continue on with the notion of *confusion*. This is yet another area of life kept shrouded in mystery and shame for females, isn't it? It's not as if you can locate a book on the topic and research the answers, can you? You must rely on other women to speak plain truth. In the absence of Willow or Tessa or your own mother—here I am. I am an old woman, but I have been married for many happy years, and I try very hard to speak plain truth whenever I can."

Sabine nodded. "Thank you."

"Now, lucky for us," said Mary, waving Willow's letter, "there doesn't seem to be a mechanical question per se—although I can happily answer those, too, should the need arise." She glanced at Sabine.

Sabine, finally recovering some of her signature cheek, raised one eyebrow.

Mary laughed. "Right. Very good. But Willow is concerned that Stoker has suggested to you that marital relations between husband and wife involves some sort of . . . barter? Is that correct? Does he want something from you, Sabine? Surely not?"

Sabine shook her head wildly. "No, no, it's the other way around. And please understand. We've only shared so much as a, er, kiss—thus far. I mean, at all. He is still recovering—and when he is healed, I believe he will sail from London, just as before. There is no guarantee that 'marital relations' are in our future. But he made such a big fuss about the kiss, it raised the question. And *that* is why I wrote to Willow. Although I see now I should have simply come to you." Sabine slumped on the sofa. "How has her reply reached you so quickly?"

"Private courier," said Mary, waving the envelope. "Willow felt this conversation was very urgent, indeed."

Sabine shook her head and choked out a laugh. But then she thought of Stoker, whom she hadn't seen in five days despite her mounting desire to see him. Perhaps it was rather urgent. Perhaps she had been avoiding him because she needed some ruling on this issue.

"But what do you mean," asked Mary, "*it's the other way around?*"

Sabine nodded. "As part of this new . . . er, closeness between Stoker and myself, we have shared a kiss. Or two." She took a deep breath. "I believe we both felt the kiss was rather . . . er, lovely, but he resisted the kiss at first. He was strangely resistant to embarking on anything remotely like, well, like physical affection—despite his obvious, at least to me, desire. Er, desire for it. He seems to believe—he seems to *stridently* believe—that all affection leads to sex, and that all sex takes advantage of the female in a way. As a result she must be compensated with a gift or protection or some favor. He *further* believes that this transaction, this *trade*, even in a loving marriage, is always damaging to the woman. Or something." Sabine looked at Mary Boyd and shrugged.

"*Really?*" marveled Mary. She tapped her index finger to her chin.

Sabine told Mary some of Stoker's terrible childhood and his years of crashing in and out of brothels. "He uses these experiences as his proof," she said. "He has seen the worst of humanity, I'm afraid.

"And so my question was," Sabine finished, "could his

view possibly be accurate? For all couples? Every time? Is there never mutual pleasure for pleasure's sake?"

"Absolutely," enthused Mary lightly, taking up her polishing rag again. "You are right, and he is wrong, God save him. I can assure you, as a married woman of some thirty years, *and* as a woman who left a respected family to marry a carpenter who could offer me nothing but pleasure for pleasure's sake, these sorts of relations happen all the time. Every night and day."

"I knew it," said Sabine, a little breathless. She stared out the window at the treetops of Belgrave Square. "I knew Willow did not feel that Cassin takes advantage of her. Tessa, of course, was sorely abused—but not by Joseph. Joseph treats her like a queen. But I never got the sense that he did it to repay her for . . . for . . ."

"There is no payment for sex in a happy marriage," stated Mary, dipping her cloth in sticky mahogany stain.

"But what about in a *convenient* marriage?" asked Sabine, the words out before she'd realized.

"That is more difficult for me to define," chuckled Mary. "My marriage was entirely inconvenient. My family disowned me, as you know. But perhaps this question is less urgent. And I can think of two women very dear to you who might expound on this at length by letter." She winked and nodded to Willow's envelope. "In the meantime, I believe you will be surprised how quickly you discover the answer for yourself. Assuming you can challenge Mr. Stoker's notions about this bartering nonsense, whatever it is." She applied the wet cloth to the chair and began to rub.

Sabine watched her work for a moment, sipping her tea. "To him, it's not nonsense. That is my fear."

"Yes, but you are hardly nonsensical, my girl. You are confident and proud and clever and your opinion will matter to him. If he truly wants you, it will matter."

"Oh, he doesn't—"

Mary cut her off with a tsking sound. "I've only met Mr. Stoker on two occasions, but I saw the way he watches you in both instances. Trust me when I say that he very much wants you. The real question may be, do you want him?"

The real question.

Indeed.

Do you want him?

"Well," Sabine began slowly, "it has been far more pleasant having him here than I expected. He is very useful to the research I am doing on my uncle. He is not oppressive or demanding. I enjoy spending time with him—that is, near him."

She laughed. "I want to be in his room all the time." She looked up. "I can't believe I've just said that."

"Is it true?" Mary asked.

Sabine considered this, trying to find truth in her jumble of feelings and fears and desires.

"It is not untrue," Sabine began. "And when I am in his room, and we are talking or he is taking his meal, I . . . I want to touch him. I've never been so overwhelmed with the desire to put my hands on another person." Sabine stood up. "Does this sound mad?"

"Not at all. It sounds very natural, in fact. There is a name for what you are describing, but I dare not say it. Not yet."

Sabine barely heard Mary as she began to pace. "But he will not stay in London. When he recovers, he'll show his gratitude in some detached, informal way, and sail away. That was our agreement, and he speaks daily about recovering his ship and his crew. When he leaves, it won't matter what I want. He only married me because I swore we would always live apart. He . . . he's told me he is in the market for a piece of property to call home—his first ever home. He is hoping to settle down and find some peace after a lifetime of restlessness. It won't be in London. It won't be in England at all."

"Oh, lovely," said Mary brightly. "Please remind him that I should be happy to design the interiors when he settles on a place. We've clients around the world. I'm so very good at helping wealthy men spend their money on peaceful first homes. He's said to be one of the richest men in England, isn't he?"

"That is what is said," said Sabine.

"*Imagine*, one of the richest men in the country, convalescing in my cellar." Mary glanced at Sabine. "Of all the places for him to recover. I wonder why a man such as this might linger . . . here . . . with us? When he could be anywhere?"

"Oh, he is very ill," Sabine assured her. "Far too ill to relocate."

Mary gestured to the letter again. "Forgive me if I don't think he sounds quite as ill as one might be led to believe." She gave another wink.

Sabine considered this, drifting among the stacks of half-completed furniture.

Mary called, "Will we see you tonight at dinner, dear?"

"Perhaps not tonight, thank you," said Sabine. "I . . . I will send Perry for a tray."

"Very well. Carry on. Lovely chat." Mary Boyd smiled, took hold of the chair, and flipped it. "I'm always here when you have need of me. Do not forget."

"Thank you," Sabine mumbled, drifting out the door. *Thank you, thank you, thank you.*

Chapter Twelve

"Perry?"

Stoker heard the rapid scuttle of footsteps that he knew belonged to the harried maid. It pained him to shout through the apartments, but he knew of no other way get the girl's attention. "Perry?" he called again, swearing in his head.

The girl had taken very seriously the edict that Sabine and Harley alone would manage his care. He'd yet to see more than the blur of her uniform zip by outside his open doorway, although a blur was more than he could say for how much he'd seen of Sabine.

Sabine.

He'd not seen her since The Lapse, as he had come to think of the afternoon of their kiss. Five days ago. She'd sent notes, apologies, forwarded letters from friends through Harley and even Dr. Cornwell, but he had not seen her.

It was exactly as he had expected. Actually, he'd expected immediate eviction, but perhaps she clung to some guilty notion of Christian charity. He was, as she said repeatedly, nearly dead.

But how near dead could he have been to erupt into a torrent of desire so stunningly aggressive, she'd kept away for five days? Stoker had devoted the solitary time to ruminating in utter misery, trying to second-guess how overwhelmed and . . . plundered she must feel. It was no wonder she'd not shown her face—despite her pride and her resilience. There was a possibility he would never see her again in this life.

No, stop. He reminded himself not to become operatic. Sabine was not a coward, nor was she missish. No doubt she'd tolerated the ministrations, but it would take more to compel her to actually flee from him. Instead, she had abandoned their easy regard. They would return to the thrice-per-decade in-person meetings, and she would be civil if not warm. Warmth, in particular, would be out of the question because she would not wish to encourage him. Little did she know (and thank God) how very little encouragement he required. Even now, even racked with guilt and anxiety, he wanted her still.

He detested himself for his own weakness and the ever-present strumming lust. What before had been an underlying throb had been elevated by her presence to the thunder of a thousand horses. His blood ran hot, his body was hard, and his mind drifted to private, unspoken things. Even before, when he was burning with fever and light-headed with lack of blood, he'd watched her in the most elemental way. His skin had buzzed beneath her most innocuous touch. How could he be expected to resist when she moved so very close, when she reached for his arm, when she bade him explain such base, torrid things?

When she'd passed along the letter from Joseph, and Stoker had realized he had no friend who could be bothered to leave his happy life to assist him when he was nearly bloody dead (he would address this with Joseph and Cassin at a later date), he'd vowed, then and there, to hire his own team of caregivers to move him to his own suite of rooms in Regent Street. But then Harley had mentioned Sabine's plans for the week—stalking a chemist in Regent Street one day, followed by (Stoker's throat still closed at the thought) poking around a bloody charcoal kiln in Hampstead the next—and he realized there was no way he could go. She put herself in too much danger.

Oh, the irony. She was in danger here, from him and his lust, just the same as she was in danger when she tailed suspected criminals around London. A fair comparison? Possibly, also possibly an overstatement. There was always the chance the chemist and kiln master were harmless.

I can resist, he told himself. *I'll not meet her half-dressed again. She won't lean in, or rub my arm. I won't give explanations for explicit things that invoke coarse words and vivid images.*

She'd already kept away for five days, which proved his point. Her regret would be safeguard enough.

As to the London smugglers and her investigation, he could offer no effective security, invalid that he was, but at least he could track when she left, where she was going, and when she returned. And perhaps, by some miracle, she might have some question or theory urgent enough to supersede the damage caused by The Lapse. If she needed him, he would not be in Regent Street; if she needed him, he would be here.

Except not this afternoon, he thought, swinging his legs over the side of the bed. *This afternoon I will walk around the bloody block if it kills me.*

Stoker listened for the maid's footsteps outside the door and called out again. "Perry?"

He heard a small intake of breath and faint throat-clearing.

"Perry, if that's you," he went on, "might I beg a favor?"

Silence.

Stoker squinted at the doorway. "Perry?"

Ever so softly, he heard four hesitant footsteps. He stifled the urge to shout, waiting instead. Eventually, after what seemed like five minutes, the slight, head-bowed profile of the young maid appeared in the open space of the door. She did not look up.

"Perry. Good. There you are. Ah, do you remember me?" he asked gently.

The girl nodded.

"Right. Harley tells me that you've come to London to assist Sabine. I'm grateful to you. I've arranged for a substantial bonus to appear in your wages for the month."

"Oh, his Lordship the Earl of Cassin pays my wages, sir," reported Perry, shaking her head at the floor, "and quite generously, I might add. A pension too."

Stoker exhaled, thinking of his formerly impoverished friend Cassin, before the guano fortune rolled in. "Of course," he said. "I presume too much. You honor the earl with your service, and you honor Sabine by coming all this way. If you've no use for an increase to your salary, I wonder if I might beg a favor outright?"

"A favor?" Perry said to the floor. Her voice was deeply suspicious.

"I'm suffocating in this bedroom and I should like to step outside, walk around the block or into the gardens of Belgrave Square. Harley has helped me dress, but I wonder if you might lend a hand to locate my cane. I'll need a hat, if possible. You get the idea."

"Oh no," scolded Perry, shaking her head, "Miss Sabine has given strict orders that no one should look after you but herself or Mr. Harley. I couldn't possibly—"

"Yes, but Miss Sabine is not here, is she?" Stoker said. "And Harley has been called upstairs. I can see sunshine from the window but there's no guarantee it will remain. I should like to take some air while I can."

"But sir?" challenged Perry, "what would the doctor say about—"

"Perry? Look up, if you please. Look at me. I'm fully clothed. I am unarmed. I am merely asking for a favor."

The maid lifted her head but kept her eyes squeezed tightly shut.

Stoker sighed. "You've suggested that you're immune to monetary incentive, but I've got a ten-pound note for you if you'll simply spare five minutes to help me out the bloody door."

Perry gasped at his language, but she also opened her

eyes. Stoker had managed to heave himself to standing and now hovered beside the bed. He raised his hands, palms up. *There, you see?*

Perry gasped again. "But you're not half-dead!" the maid exclaimed.

"'That remains to be seen," he chuckled, taking a careful step. "Can you find where they've hidden my hat and a cane?"

"But you look just the same as before, Mr. Stoker!" the maid praised, gawking from the doorway.

"Is that a compliment or an insult? Where is my hat?"

"They told me you were burning with fever, starved down, thin as a blade. They said you were swollen with infection."

"Thin as a blade *and* swollen with infection," Stoker mumbled. "Well, I don't do anything half measure. Do you see a cane in the corridor? I could find my own hat, if I only had the cane."

"But what will Miss Sabine say when she comes home to discover you've gone out?"

"Likely she will be relieved. How warm is it? I despise London weather. I became a sailor to escape this frigid island."

The maid had finally moved from her spot and dashed about, producing items Stoker might find useful for a walk. She piled her arms with an umbrella, a week-old broadsheet, two shillings from her own pocket, a stack of biscuits from a discarded tea tray, a lady's fan, *his hat*—praise God—and two editions of Sabine's *Noble Guide to London*.

"Would you like to take a chair into the gardens, sir?" she asked.

"Just the cane, Perry, if it can be found."

"Oh right." She piled her armful of provisions on the bench and produced the cane from behind the door.

"*Thank you,*" he said. Slowly, taking care to protect the pulling stitches and soreness in his side, Stoker walked through the door and out into the September sunshine.

"**S**toker?" Sabine called, stomping through the overgrown path that led deep into the gated garden of Belgrave Square. The builders of Belgravia had made great strides, constructing an exclusive neighborhood out of former marshland in only five years' time, but garden pathways had been an afterthought, clearly. "Stoker?" she called again.

She held her breath and listened, expecting to find him collapsed on the ground. She rounded a large birch tree, its trunk crowded with overgrown rhododendrons, and stumbled into a sunny clearing with a stone bench and birdbath. Thick foliage, lush from September rains and just beginning to turn red and gold, hung over the bench, filtering sunlight like stained glass. Swirling leaves fell intermittently, floating on the surface of the birdbath and dotting the soft green grass. Jon Stoker, dressed in trousers and shirtsleeves, stood at the outer edge, where sod met hedge.

Sabine came up short when she saw him. He was dressed in day clothes, his head was bare, but a hat rested on the bench. He was steady and tall on uneven sod and his broad shoulders pulled against the white linen of his shirt. He was . . . whole.

"Stoker?" she said again, more softly.

He turned, cringing a little, putting a hand to his wound. When he saw it was her, he said, "Sabine." A statement, not an invitation.

"You're here," she said, the first appropriate thing that popped into her mind.

You're well; you're dressed; you're beautiful—it was all wrong.

"I could not lie inside another hour," he said. "I'm reading correspondence by the light of the sun instead of your smoky lanterns."

"You must be recovered," she said, surprised by his progress in just five days. *Now he will leave,* she thought. She felt her chest deflate.

"Not recovered so much as . . . improved," he said.

"I'm glad," she told him, even while *Now he will leave* circled round and round inside her head.

"What are you reading?" she asked.

He looked at the paper in his hand. "I've hired an investigator in Portugal, and he finally has something to report. My ship has been found. One by one, members of my crew are sending word from ports around Spain and the North of Africa."

Now he will go, she thought again. Before she could stop herself, the words were out of her mouth. "Now you will go."

"Go . . . ?" He looked confused.

Her heart was pounding. She hadn't seen him for five days, and now he would go. "You will leave Belgravia."

"That depends," he said.

"On Dr. Cornwell's assessment?"

"On whether *you*," he said, walking to the stone bench, "can be compelled to curtail your dangerous sojourns around town, trailing after criminals." His tone did not accuse so much as complain. He sounded weary and worried and impatient. He tossed his papers next to the hat.

"My what?" she asked.

"Where were you today?" And now he did accuse.

"Today? I went to Hampstead. To a charcoal kiln."

"*A kiln?*" he said with emphasis, crossing his arms over his chest. "A kiln in Hampstead?"

"Yes, that's right." She took a step toward him. "You wouldn't believe what I've discov—"

He cut her off. "Hampstead Heath is miles from the city, Sabine. A kiln is an ancient furnace, hot enough to—"

"I am well aware of the nature of a kiln."

"I suppose you also know they are operated by rougher men than you'd find in a workhouse or the docks, and yet you went there alone?"

"I had Bridget—"

"Stop." He glared at her.

"Forgive me if I'm surprised that my whereabouts are of any concern to—"

"Do you know why I haven't gone?" he asked.

"To Hampstead?" She was lost.

"To my boat and my crew and the suite of rooms I keep

across London?" he gritted out. "Why I impose on your home, and your time, and the Boyds' staff?"

Sabine thought of Mary's suggestion that he remained to be nearer to her, but he did not sound interested in nearness. He sounded frustrated and temperamental.

She ventured, "Because your health is still very much at risk?"

"Because," he gritted out, "it scares the bloody hell out of me that you come and go to places like a *charcoal kiln in Hampstead* and no one is the wiser."

"Perry knew my plans for the day," she countered. "I may have even mentioned it to the Boyds. I am not accustomed to reporting my location to—"

"I know you relish your freedom, and I understand why. But it's one thing to visit tourist sites in London and sketch maps—"

"I give equal time to the investigation *and* the guidebook maps, so please don't deceive yourself that I've been plotting walks through Hyde Park until now. I was gathering clues in every corner of London well before I stumbled upon your weakened form. I might remind you that I *found you* because of the investigation. Next came Marylebone—"

"Forgive me for worrying when I learn that you are lurking around a *charcoal kiln in Hampstead*!"

She stared at him, trying to decide if his anger was rooted in concern or control. She said, "If you care where I've been these past few days, why didn't you call for me?"

The bluster drained from his face, and he looked away.

"This is my fault, I am well aware," he said lowly. "I . . . I dishonored you and . . . and struggled to know the best way to proceed. I apologize." Color rose to his cheeks, and Sabine realized he was *blushing*.

"Oh yes, well," she rushed to say, "perhaps it's not entirely your fault. I am also to blame. I myself stayed away because the . . . er, encounter between us was new and untried and a bit overwhelming—although not in a terrible way. Certainly, I don't feel *dishonored*, as you say. I have been trying to understand how I felt about it. The silence was rude, I'll admit, but I required some solitude. I should have made some sign of wellness, but I—" She stopped and took a deep breath. "This is new to me. As I've said."

"*This?*" he said, spinning to her. "There is no *this*. What happened between us was a one-time lapse in my self-control, and it won't happen again. You owe me no excuse for your distance. I . . . I am surprised to see you, even today."

Sabine blinked up at him, trying to keep track of all the *won'ts* and *one-times* and *distances*. "You do not control our experience, Jon," she said, invoking his given name for the first time. His eyes went wide and she felt a burst of gratification. *Yes, I will call you Jon.*

She continued, "You cannot dictate how I will remember it or how I will respond to what happened."

"You are in control," Stoker vowed stoically, raising his hands in surrender. "That is what I said."

"No," she said patiently. He'd missed her point entirely. "*You said* that you lost yourself, and you said you won't do it again. You've suggested that I should stay away if I know what is good for me. Do you deny it?"

Stoker opened his mouth but then shut it.

"Well, please be aware," she said, stepping closer, "that is not how I see it, and I don't appreciate having you characterize what happened on my behalf. I would never assume how you felt about it."

Did you like it? she wanted to ask. *Would you do it again?*

He let out a harsh bark of laughter. "I think it was obvious how I felt about it."

"Actually, it's not. You are cryptic by nature and this is no different. I won't guess at your feelings, but I also won't make you say them. In return, you will not tell me how *I* feel."

Tell me your feelings, she willed in her head.

"You want to discuss what happened? In detail?" he asked lowly, turning a little white. "After avoiding me for a week?"

She plucked a leafy frond from a hydrangea bush and spun it in her fingers. "I do, in fact," she breathed. "But perhaps not . . . right this second. You've blustered at me about my investigation without even saying hello. You've had some breakthrough of your own of which I know nothing. We've not spoken in days. This conversation has become too adversarial, too quickly."

She took a deep breath and tucked the leaf in her hair. "May I first ask simply how your wound is faring? Are you comfortable out of the house? Perry told me she helped you out. According to her, you are entirely recovered and I'm holding an able-bodied man captive in my bedroom."

He huffed, but his posture relaxed. He ran a hand through his hair. "Do not blame Perry. She feared she was betraying you, as you alone are meant to care for me."

"As any self-respecting captor would insist."

He nodded, staring down at her. She felt him look at her, really look at her, not in guilt or worry, but to simply see her face. She smiled up at him. He held her gaze, his green eyes appreciative and hungry.

"I am much improved, thank you," he said, looking away. "The wound is closing. The infection is entirely gone."

"So, you *are* ready to move on from my—From us?" She looked at the ground.

"Are you ready to cease this trailing around London after known criminals?"

Her head snapped up. "*No.*"

"Would you tolerate a security detail to accompany you?"

"Absolutely not. They would bring attention to my otherwise stealthy investigation."

"Will you allow me to call in a runner from Bow Street or the police?"

"And have them bungle the investigation or scare Dryden into hiding? Not until I have enough solid evidence to put him away."

"Then no," he said. "I'm not ready to move on."

Sabine turned her face away to hide the relief. He wouldn't go. But it was not because he wanted to be near her.

"I'm not trying to evict you. I hope you are aware," she said. "I was always prepared for you to stay until you are fully healed. But I would be mortified if you remained merely to check up on me." This was true. She felt a little mortified already.

"I'm not checking up, Sabine, I'm . . . I'm—"

"Shall I tell you what I've discovered, and you can see for yourself that there is no threat?"

"The world is a threat, Sabine, when you are a beautiful woman prowling the streets alone."

"The only real threat I've known in my twenty-seven years is Sir Dryden, and *he* is the reason I investigate the smuggling."

"Fine. Tell me of these past few days, when a kiln in Hampstead was so very safe and justified."

"Actually, I began in Regent Street," she said, excited to finally tell him, "looking in on a chemist."

"Oh yes. The chemist."

"Another frequent guest to my uncle's meetings at Park Lodge. The reports sent by my mother's maid mention him repeatedly. He's a young professor at the London Polytechnic Institute."

Stoker limped across the clearing to the hedge. "Go on."

"I observed the professor lecturing to students, doing some desk work in an office, puttering around a laboratory."

"How long did you follow him?"

"A full day. I also made detailed notes on Regent Street and roughed out a preliminary map. I am always doing two things at once."

"And what of the chemist?"

She shook her head. "I couldn't make sense of it. Through

the window, I saw him weighing something on a scale and making notes. God only knows what he was doing. But earlier in the day, he gave a lecture to students on combustible substances."

"What?" Stoker had been pacing, exercising his legs, but now he stopped short. His alarm was so very satisfying.

"Explosives," she confirmed proudly. "Compounds that blow up mines or cause cannons to—"

"I'm aware of the function of explosives. *This* is the man who frequently calls on your uncle?"

Sabine nodded. "The very same. And at teatime, this man left the institute and made his way to a public house in Piccadilly, and Bridget and I followed from a safe distance."

"You followed him into a pub?"

"I am a married woman," she reminded, dropping onto the bench, "and I can patronize a pub if I choose. I took a table adjacent to his, and within ten minutes another man arrived, and they began a conversation about charcoal."

"Charcoal?"

"Yes. It took me some time to determine what, exactly, they were discussing, but then the new man said something like, 'We'll have to burn the kiln for a fortnight, working 'round the clock, to turn out that much charcoal, but it can be done.'"

"Charcoal is a major component of most explosives," Stoker said. "But a chemist whose research deals with explosives could require charcoal for any number of things that have nothing to do with smuggling or your uncle."

"Except that the next thing the professor said was, 'It must be absolutely dry when it reaches Dorset. We take a great risk, acquiring the charcoal in London . . . putting it in barrels and on wagons.' And then the other man said, 'Yes, but not every furnace master is willing to take the risk, is he? There are ways to keep it dry.' And then the professor said . . .'"

Now Sabine was overcome with enthusiasm, and she strode to Stoker and smiled up into his face. "And then he actually said, 'Dryden Noble chose me for a reason.'"

She beamed, and then forgetting herself, she reached out and grabbed him by the arms. Stoker frowned into her smiling face but she pressed on, squeezing his biceps and giving him a shake. "He actually said Dryden's name. They are all working together. The chemist and the charcoal kiln master and the man with the barrels. It's a coordinated effort to do . . . something off the coast of Dorset."

Stoker dropped his gaze from her face to her hands. Sabine rolled her eyes—he was so touchy—and stepped away.

"So of course," she said, "I was given no choice but to seek out this kiln in Hampstead." She stalked back to the bench. "The professor eventually left the pub and I followed him the rest of the day. If I returned again so soon, I would risk suspicion. There was no choice except to go to Hampstead and poke around."

"Sabine," Stoker said, lowering himself onto the bench, "do you never feel unsafe, poking around pubs and furnaces?"

"No," she said simply. The bench was small and he was sitting very close. Her arm tingled where their sleeves brushed.

"Do you feel unsafe with me?" he asked.

"No." This was the truth.

"When we met, you told me that you would never allow any man close to you. You told me you'd never put yourself in a position of danger from any man."

"What I told you was, I would never *adhere* to a man. I would never be bound to the dominion of a man. These men I investigate have no hold over me. They barely notice me. And you? You've never tried to dominate me. You don't force me to adhere to you."

"I dominated you when we kissed."

She laughed. "No, you didn't. You just . . . lay there."

Stoker ran a hand through his hair and squinted into the distance. "This just keeps getting worse and worse."

"Stop," she said. "There is nothing *worse* about this conversation. It's a good conversation. I'm rather enjoying it. I can't believe I've kept away for five days."

"You kept away because I embarrassed you."

"I insist that you stop telling me how I feel. Honestly. I was never embarrassed."

"You were ashamed."

"No."

"You were confused."

"Possibly. But not because of anything you'd done. Stoker, you do not intimidate or subjugate me. If anything, *I* took advantage of a sick man. But will you *always* be so very sick and so very stranded here? Will you always *just lie there* in my bed? No, you will not." She paused, gathering her nerve. "Would you like to know what I've been considering these past five days? I've been asking myself if it feels prudent to explore a physical relationship with you when I know you will eventually sail away and leave me."

"Sabine, we will not have a physical relationship."

She looked up at him. "Truly? You've decided this? After what we . . . shared? Simply to—leave it?"

"God save us from *what I want*, Sabine, we're dealing in—"

"Because I'm not so sure we should leave it. *And*," she said, "I believe we should decide together."

"You don't know what you ask," he rasped.

"I know you must stop trying to protect me," she cut in. "You sought to protect me from the Duke of Wrest, just when that got interesting. You seek to protect me from the smugglers. And now it feels as if you endeavor to protect me from . . . yourself? Have I got that right?"

He stared at her, not answering.

She went on, "You said you gave up rescuing women when you married me. *Stop*, Stoker. I don't need rescuing. I'm not a victim."

"You are not a victim *yet*," he said, speaking to the ground. "But only because these smugglers, or saboteurs, or whoever the hell they may be have not caught on that they're being followed by a woman bent on their demise." He looked up, leveling her with his intense green glare. "And *only* because I've not unleashed the . . . the . . . maelstrom of my desire for you and ravished you, mind and body."

Sabine sucked in a little breath. His words felt like a lightning strike to the newly awakened part of her, so attuned in his presence. After a moment she said, "I'm sorry to tell you this, Jon, because you don't seem to like it, but I find statements like that very exciting. And they only make me want it more."

He blinked. "Make you want the smuggl—"

"Make me want *you*," she corrected, cutting him off. The bashfulness and indecision of the previous week were suddenly nowhere to be found, gone from her head and her heart. Even his confining protectiveness was forgotten. She glanced at his mouth. The words *unleash* and *maelstrom* and *desire* heating her skin and places deep inside her.

"*Sabine*," he warned lowly, fixing his own gaze on her mouth.

"*Yes?*" she whispered. Her breathing hitched and accelerated. Their gazes locked; the air was charged between them. Sabine felt something monumental was about to snap or implode or burst into flames. She bit down on her bottom lip.

"Do not," he said, not looking away from her mouth.

She laughed, a mix of nerves and excitement. There was no help for it. His resistance in this moment felt comical. "It can't be helped," she said, laughing again. "I quite like the idea of being ravished, mind and body." She crossed her arms over her chest. She scooted closer to him. He flinched, toppling his hat and his cane to the ground.

He swore and swung his gaze back, looking at her the way a Spanish bull stares at a matador's flag. He shook his head. Once, twice. He swore in a language she did not know. She raised her face, tipping up her mouth, leaning in.

He swore again and descended on her mouth. Sabine

stopped breathing, joy exploding in her chest. He was so close now, finally, after five days. She swam in the musty, soapy, male smell of him.

He'd taught her how to kiss in his bedroom, and five days had not dulled the lesson. She would never forget how to kiss him. She tasted, and sucked, and sought his tongue with her own.

He did not reach out. He didn't touch her at all. He claimed only her mouth, feasting, breathing hard, kissing her as if his life depended on it. Sabine lost her balance— she lost rational thought—and fell a little against him, clasping his shoulders to stay upright. The bench spun, the garden spun, the world spun, but they were perfectly still, the only spot in the world that mattered, doing the thing that Sabine had wanted to do since she came upon him in the clearing.

He wants this, she thought, consuming his need. *He wants me.* His desire could not have been clearer. He would easily kiss her off the edge of the bench and onto the grass if she had not pressed back, insistent with her own return kisses. She could barely breathe. It was thrilling and wonderful and not enough, all at the same time.

She was just about to wrap her arms around his neck, crawl up his body and into his lap (his wound be damned) when the wind picked up; a sharp, cooling gust. It lifted the escaped tendrils of her hair and also the letters on the bench, strewing them across the clearing.

He made a noise of frustration and kissed her harder, ignoring the wind and the mess and everything but her lips, but Sabine opened her eyes, catching a glimpse of flying parchment.

"Stoker, your letters," she said, pulling away.

He followed her with his mouth. She kissed him once more, a firm smack, and then pressed him upright. "Look, your papers. Are they not important?"

He looked at her through half-lidded eyes, blinking as if he'd been slapped. She pointed to the dervish of papers flying from the bench.

While he blinked himself back to consciousness, Sabine leapt from the bench and began to pick up the dancing paper. Her fingers trembled and her insides were molten, throbbing need. She swore quietly, trying to pounce on one letter after the other.

Behind her, Stoker mumbled something bitter and tried to push up. "Ow!" he groaned, grabbing his wound.

"You've overdone it," Sabine scolded, darting after flying paper.

He made a grunting noise and dropped back on the bench.

"I hope you can make sense of these," she said, looking down. "They've been completely scrambled, but I think I have them al—"

She stopped mid-sentence and squinted at the paper in her hand. Her eyes flew over the words and froze on one sentence. Her rib cage grew tight. She drew the paper closer to her face to read it again.

She looked at Stoker.

"This letter mentions the Duke of Wrest," she said.

"Yes, right here. 'His Grace Saul Newington, The Duke of Wrest.'"

She turned back to him. "Has the duke begun to plague you again about your paternity? Why didn't you tell me? Are you looking again into his claim?"

"No. I'm not."

"Then what of this letter?" She tried and failed to scan the illegible scrawl on the wrinkled sheet of parchment.

"That letter is from my investigator," Stoker said, trying again to stand. He winced in pain but pushed on.

"Oh yes," Sabine said faintly. "You've investigations unfurling at every turn. Forgive me, I forget there is the certain matter of your missing ship and the attack. I am—" She stopped and began again. "I am accustomed to only considering myself."

"I like that you look after yourself, Sabine. Despite my worry. You should consider yourself above all."

Sabine would file that away to consider later. Now she shook her head and waved the papers at him. "But why would your investigator mention the old duke?"

"Because," Stoker said, "my man uncovered more than the brig and crew in Portugal. He believes he's found my attacker. A paid mercenary."

"You mean someone hired another man to kill you?"

"Well, someone hired another man to *try* to kill me."

"Oh yes, I keep forgetting how invincible you are," she mumbled. She was rereading the letter. "But why haven't you told me of this?"

"Sabine, I haven't seen you."

"For this, you should have summoned me to you," she insisted, but in her head, she thought, *I should have gone to him. I should have gone to him days ago.*

Stoker was quiet for a moment, watching her. "Apparently, the would-be assassin has been found, and after a rather costly negotiation, the hired man revealed who wanted me dead. Would you believe it was the old duke?"

"*No,*" Sabine marveled. She dropped her hands, pressing the letters into her skirts. "The Duke of Wrest tried to have you killed?"

Stoker shrugged. "I was as shocked as you. The duke was named by the assassin out of thin air. I'd never mentioned Wrest's previous contact with me to the investigator, and the mercenary is an Italian, someone who's been following me for months."

"But why would he try to have you killed?" Sabine asked, scooping up his hat and cane and thrusting them at him.

"Another attempt to get a piece of my fortune, I assume. The duke's overtures to me had become very petulant and demanding. I had finally stopped taking delivery of them. At the time I thought him half-mad and entirely pathetic, but I never dreamed he would have a thirst for blood. My God, when I think of the danger I put you in when I asked you to look in on him." His expression twisted into a scowl.

"But what of the danger you're in now?" she asked, waving the letter.

He shrugged. "I believe my invincibility has already been referenced."

"Do not joke!" she said.

"I'm not worried about it, Sabine," he sighed. "When I think back to the afternoon I was attacked—and my memories are blurred—the man lured away my crew, occupying them elsewhere. He paid a sham estate agent to lead me down an isolating road. I thought I was being shown a private estate for sale. Instead, I was ambushed. It was an amateur mistake for me to be so taken in, but Portuguese is not my strongest language and I was caught up in the idea that my future happiness rested in this coastal mansion—whatever it was. Buying a big house on a high cliff was perhaps the most civilized undertaking on which I'd ever embarked. I'd let down my guard because that is presumably what civilized people do. I nearly died for my error, but it won't happen again. I am now . . . aware. Hilltop mansion or no. I'm not worried, and you needn't worry, either."

Sabine thought about this, thought about this civilized house he meant to buy in another country. There was so much yet to discuss. But he was limping toward the path. She looked down at the letters in her hand.

"If there is no worry," she said, "then we must seek out the old duke immediately."

"No, *we* must not," he said levelly.

"Not to accuse him, of course—not yet, at any rate—but to discern how guilty he may . . . look? How desperate or calculating. I wonder if he knows you survived?"

"My investigator and I are doubtful he knows I washed up in England."

"But what is your plan?" asked Sabine, following him down the garden path. "A man who hires an assassin is as guilty as the murderer himself. The duke should be prosecuted."

"My plan is to sail my investigator home on my recovered brig. When he's in London, we'll take the matter to the police."

"So casual," she said softly, "about an attempt on your life."

He shrugged. "I still draw breath, and the Duke of Wrest is not my first enemy, Sabine. Perhaps my convalescence altered my perspective, but I'm not set on vigilante justice like you are. My years of score settling are over. If the statements and evidence found by the investigator hold true, the case will be easy enough for the authorities to manage. He's a pathetic old man."

"He is truly doddering and his station is quite humble," she said, falling in step beside him. "I am shocked he had the wherewithal to hire a mercenary, to be honest."

"I have seen desperate old men do terrible things in service to their vices all over the world," he said. "I've no doubt."

They walked in silence for a moment, and then she said, "I'm not set on vigilante justice, by the way. I simply cannot risk accusing Dryden and then having the charge dismissed or shoved to the side. I'm a woman, don't forget, and Sir Dryden has cultivated his respectability and aplomb for years. He will challenge any charge brought by the police. He will play Lord of the Manor. The more obviously, *plainly* guilty he appears, the better chance I have. That's my entire goal. To be taken seriously, and for Dryden to be obviously, plainly guilty."

They walked on a moment, the leafy path giving way to the green grass and the road ahead.

After a moment she asked, "What is your goal, Stoker?"

He did not answer until they'd reached the edge of the park. Finally, he said, "I'll not achieve any goal until I've healed, will I?" He winced a little.

That's no answer, she thought, but she'd pressed him enough. She simply said, "No. I suppose you will not." She laced her shoulders beneath his arm because—well, why shouldn't they walk home arm in arm? She found she could not *not* touch him.

He stiffened briefly and missed a step.

"Stop," she said. "Seriously, Stoker, you must stop."

Chapter Thirteen

The problem, Stoker thought, with touching Sabine, was that once he touched her, he did not want to let her go. Ever. Not to walk home (or in his case, *limp* home) from Belgrave Square; not to instruct servants to carry a summons to the doctor, which she had insisted on; not even to eat bloody supper, an endeavor he'd waited five long days to experience in her company rather than across the tray from Harley.

Now that she was finally back, elaborating on her findings at Hampstead kiln, all Stoker wanted to do was upend his tray and reach for her.

Instead, he stared at his food. He answered her questions about explosives and charcoal and how she might discover what they, along with barrels and wagons and the Isle of Portland, had to do with her uncle's illegal smuggling business. Her dog, blessedly absent from the gardens, now sat beside his bed and begged for scraps from his plate.

Thankfully, Sabine seemed to have set aside the topic of

the Duke of Wrest, although he was not so naive as to believe she'd forgotten it. It had never been his intent to conceal from Sabine what the investigator had learned. When he'd said the conversation had "gotten away from him," it had not been a lie. The list of things he'd *not intended* in the garden were legion. He'd not intended to scold her about her ramblings in Hampstead. He'd not intended to translate her own feelings into his terms. And then of course, there was the thing he intended least of all.

He'd kissed her. Again. After he'd spent five days vowing to get a handle on his control. No matter how she provoked him. No matter how his desire for her raged. Because kisses, as he knew, led to other things, all-consuming, violating things, and he would never, ever violate Sabine. He would not be a source of distress or shame or pain in her life; and his ferocious lust would not be the end to the brief meetings they had always enjoyed or the simple knowledge that she existed somewhere in England, not hating him.

If these stopped, if she shut him out, he would embrace the demons of his terrible boyhood and wild youth and stop making any effort to be a gentleman. He would simply allow the memories and fears to consume him.

And no one wants that, he thought cynically, acknowledging his penchant for melodrama. Perhaps there would be no consumption, but there would be wretchedness, nightmares, and hopelessness. For the time being, she kept it all at bay.

Stoker passed another haunch of chicken to the dog and tried to keep up with the conversation. Sabine had set aside her own tray and now tacked pieces of parchment to his bedroom wall, explaining that she'd prepared the parchment as an evidence mural. Now securely hung on the bedroom wall, they could digest the evidence together. He admired her organization and artistry but also felt a heavy weight roll from his chest. She was back, back in his room and back in his life. For now, at least. If he could manage not to scare her away again.

She'd headlined the mural, "Known Facts Regarding Dryden, Smuggling, and Barrier Island Maps," and used sketches and notes to form a representative path of what she'd discovered so far, with dates, places, names, and suppositions. There were arrows and question marks, newspaper clippings darkened with underlined text.

Her devotion to this research astounded him; hours and days and her considerable talents all brought to bear. When she'd mentioned her challenges as a young woman bringing accusations against an older relation, he'd wanted to remind her that she was married to a wealthy man who would happily call down the undivided attention of law enforcement, or he could put another investigator on the case. He could also simply travel himself to Surrey and pound on Sir Dryden's door and demand to know what the hell he was doing. But he dared not interfere with her work or usurp the satisfaction it gave her. No one would be more thorough or effective than she.

"The key missing piece is this Phineas Legg of Portsmouth," she said now. "He owns a small fleet of ships. According to the sailors on the *Dreadnought*, it was on one of this man's vessels that they sailed."

Stoker nodded and tried not to stare at her mouth. Was it redder since their kiss? Had his whiskers abraded her cheek? Had he marked her? His mouth watered, remembering the kiss. She seemed to have some misguided curiosity about it. Thank God she was too innocent to know where kissing led.

He'd succumbed today because—he succumbed today because he'd wanted it so bloody much. He'd wanted it since she'd left his bed five days prior. He had become a vessel of desire for her, and when she had, remarkably, unbelievably, seemed to want the same thing? He gave in. Restraint was an afterthought; no, restraint was forgotten, and he took and took and took.

For perhaps the first time in his life, he wanted and seized in the same glorious moment.

It was a kiss. Well, it was several kisses. He told himself that, of all the dark, dangerous paths to sex, kissing (for kissing's sake) wreaked the least amount of havoc.

She was curious, he thought. Most young women came of age fantasizing about a kiss. Why she would transfer this fantasy on to him, an enigmatic man twice her size, damaged, churning with lust, he could not fathom. But the only thing that exceeded Stoker's desire for Sabine was his possessiveness of her. And the thought of any other man putting his mouth on her made him consent to the kiss. Just once more. Lest she endeavor kissing with any other man.

If nothing else, he had taken fastidious care to keep his hands at his sides. The assault was to her mouth alone, a brief taste of what she believed she wanted.

Meanwhile, he gripped the bench with enough force to crack the stone, and rational thought had dissolved. He floated in the taste and smell of her.

Was it any wonder they'd gotten nowhere in their discussion of the smuggling or even how long he would remain in Belgravia?

No, he thought wearily, setting his tray aside, *it was no wonder.* The dog leapt to the bed and availed herself of the uneaten chicken.

"Stoker?" Sabine called from across the room. "Did you hear what I said? You're certain you can recall no knowledge about this man? Phineas Legg in Portsmouth?"

"No, nothing," Stoker said, forcing himself to keep up. "His fleet must be very small, indeed, because I know of most shippers in London and the ports along the South Sea."

Sabine crossed out a note on her mural. "I've not had the time to travel to Portsmouth to look in on him. He was meant to be my last stop before venturing to the Isle of Portland itself."

Stoker thought of Sabine traveling to the Dorset coast to look in on a nest of smugglers, and his stomach turned. Naturally, she would not limit her investigation to London. He cast around, trying to think of a strategy that would keep her safe until he was well enough to travel with her. He thought of the maritime vendors and sailors he knew from Portsmouth . . . the dock masters . . . and—

"Bryson Courtland," he said, sitting up in bed.

"What?" She turned from the mural.

"I'm just thinking that we might apply to Bryson about this shipping man in Portsmouth. Bryson is one of the most respected shipbuilders in England."

"I thought you didn't want to bring injuries to the attention of Bryson?" Sabine said, glancing at him. "Or that is, you mentioned protecting his wife, Elisabeth Courtland? We cannot approach him without alerting her, I'm certain. And the Courtlands do not even know me. What time or interest would they have for my revenge plot against a cruel uncle?" She turned back to the mural.

Stoker frowned, confused by her resistance. After a moment he said, "I wished to conceal my injuries from them when I was on death's door, but now that I am—" he paused, looking for the correct word "—going to survive, it's rude of me to not send some word. Elisabeth's feelings are wounded when I am in London and I don't call."

"Oh yes," murmured Sabine to her mural, *"Elisabeth."*

"How would you feel," he went on cautiously, "if I send them a note and explain my recovery here in London? I could ask if we might interview Bryson on a confidential topic related to shipping? I can vow for their complete and total discretion. And his support in whatever we may need."

"I don't need support," she said, still facing the wall. "This investigation is my own. Mine."

He opened his mouth to tell her she would require considerable support when her investigation moved from observation to action, but her tone gave him pause.

He tried again. "You've used my support, or at least my knowledge, and see what we've managed to deduce?

But look at me, Sabine. I'm back in bed. Today has proved that I'm unable to even walk to the garden without paying the price." He shifted in bed and winced. "I'm a very weak lieutenant, indeed, and I detest myself for it. Can you . . ." He paused, almost losing nerve. This was too important to bungle. Bryson could help with information, but the Courtlands could also help protect Sabine. He couldn't believe he'd not thought of it sooner.

He started again. "I would consider it a personal favor if you would allow us to include them in your investigation." He watched her shoulders tighten as she scribbled notes on her mural. "It kills two birds with one stone. I cannot, in good conscience, remain in London much longer without sending some word. Elisabeth would never forgive me."

Sabine said, "I doubt that."

"Sabine, what is it?" he asked. "I—your hesitation is beyond my ability to interpret." He waited, but she did not turn.

He pressed on. "You will like them, I promise. They have asked to meet you for these past four years. They have begged for an introduction. The reality of my marriage to a woman they do not know has been a . . . sore spot. The tension was avoidable when you and I lived separate sort of lives. But now that we are friends . . ."

And now he did lose heart. Sabine had stopped writing, stopped breathing. Slowly, she turned.

"Is that what we are?" she asked. "Friends?" She leaned against the mural.

He swore in his head. "I don't know."

"Because if we call on the Courtlands, they will wish to know. It will be their first question."

"I have conditioned the Courtlands not to pry," he said. "They will accept us. Whatever our relationship."

Sabine nodded and looked out the window. He'd said the wrong thing, that much was clear. Possibly everything he'd said had been wrong. This was one of the many reasons he preferred to say so very little at all.

After a moment Sabine looked back. "They will wish to move you," she informed him. "Their home is one of the grandest in London. You would have every luxury there. Elisabeth will want to care for you. They are your family, you've said it yourself. And I am merely your . . . *friend*." She looked at the floor.

Stoker stared at the top of her head. He had no working memory of Sabine ever betraying a moment's insecurity. Not when he'd rescued her from the locked cupboard, or when she'd trailed around the Duke of Wrest. But this . . . ? It sounded like she was afraid to lose him.

It sounded as if she *wanted* him.

For the second time that day Stoker tried to engage his brain, to think and reason, but he heard only the sound of the ocean. He blinked, trying to stay ahead of his shock and . . . and . . . something else he could not name, something he'd never allowed himself to identify.

Carefully, slowly, he ventured, "I am comfortable here."

"In my cellar apartment?" she asked sarcastically, casting him a wry glance.

"Yes."

"With my dog?"

He looked at the vermin dog, licking the last vestiges of chicken and potatoes from his plate. "Yes," he lied.

"And Perry, and being looked after by a footman who is unavailable most of each day?"

"I am comfortable here," he repeated, the only phrase that seemed to have been right.

Sabine pushed off the wall. "With me kissing you when clearly you hate it."

"I don't hate kissing you, Sabine. I hate what comes next."

"Avoiding me?"

"Look," he shot back, "I am immovable in a sick bed. *You* avoided me. That's not what I mean."

She laughed at this. "You are the strongest, heartiest man I've ever known to claim a sick bed."

"Thank you, I think, but that's beside the point. I want to be clear—" He stopped and took a deep breath. "Please be aware: I will never pursue you after we . . . after the—"

"Because you dislike it," she guessed.

"Because I want it too much, Sabine," he breathed. "I want it with a ferocity that you cannot fathom. May you never fathom how much I want you. Yes—I am a strong man. Yes, I am determined to resist you. But please be aware, when it comes to how much I relish the look of you, to *the years* I have fantasized about touching you and how much I want to take you to bed, I don't believe that I have the strength to resist you forever.

"So," he continued, his voice rising, "if you continue to test your curiosity on me, when I am in this bed and cannot escape you, I would ask you to *rethink* the way you view our marriage, because it will rapidly cease being 'convenient' or 'detached.' We will also cease thinking of each other as *friends*. It will become a marriage in every sense."

Sabine stood very still for a moment; her expression was thoughtful, almost placid. A tantalizing pink color rose on her cheeks. After a moment she asked, "A marriage like Willow and Cassin or Tessa and Joseph?"

"No," he said. "*Not* like our friends'." He slid his legs off the bed and shoved up, biting back a growl of pain. "Cassin is a gentleman and Joseph is almost a member of bloody Parliament. I am no gentleman or politician, Sabine. I'm from the streets, with no notion of manners or refinement or gentility. My needs are raw, my desires are wholly untamed, and I have discovered during my time here that I have only the loosest hold on my self-control."

He expected her to back away, to collide with the wall and slide toward the door. Instead, she took a step toward him. He continued, "Do you remember what I said about a transaction, Sabine? About sex being a man's pleasure in exchange for some item or aid a woman requires?"

"Of course."

"Because if you continue on, if you instigate these provoking conversations and encourage the kisses and the proximity, I will, eventually, crumble. Your innocent curiosity will spark, catch fire, and flame into something not innocent at all."

Sabine's eyes grew huge and she put a hand to her throat.

Stoker hated speaking so coarsely; he hated threatening her, but this could not go unsaid.

"It turns my stomach to say this to you, of all people, but if you continue to press me, Sabine, then select your bauble or your property or whatever your heart desires, because I *will* owe you. When it's finished. I will take you, and I will not be able to hold back, and I will be in your debt."

He was sweating now, unsteady on his feet. He flung his arm out to take hold of the headboard and Sabine jumped. Stoker swore and closed his eyes, hating to unsettle her.

Better with words than with deeds, he thought.

Now she understands.

Now she will leave me in peace.

The room fell silent; his breathing was the only sound. Even the dog had gone still on the bed, staring back and forth between them.

After a long moment Sabine said, "Alright. Let us call on the Courtlands. Will you write to them? How correct you are. It has been shortsighted of me not to invoke more help."

Stoker dropped back onto the bed. "That's it? You've decided?"

"Let us just say that I'm . . . *satisfied* with your answer."

What answer? Stoker remembered only growling and threatening and flailing?

"About wanting to remain here, with me," Sabine said. "*Satisfied,*" she repeated, "puts it very mildly, I'd say." She turned back to her mural. "We are on the same road, if not at the same place at the moment. Luckily, I am a cartographer of some merit, and I know how distance can be drawn to scale."

He shook his head, looking at her through narrowed eyes. "I was serious, Sabine, about . . . about the potential of our intimacy."

"I believe you are very serious. I shall be very serious too. We shall both be so very serious. In fact, I've already begun to think about the thing."

"*What. Thing?*"

"The thing that I want. In exchange for the moment you stop."

"Stop what?"

"For the moment you stop holding back."

CHAPTER FOURTEEN

October 24, 1834
Belgrave Square, London

Dear Cassin,

I am writing to inform you never to call, or write, or bloody cross to my side of the bloody road to say bollocks, you worthless rotter of a former friend. Thank you for absolutely nothing. This letter has been dispatched in duplicate to Joseph.

I understand that Sabine has sent word that an attempt was taken on my life and my subsequent abandonment in a morgue. I have rallied, no thanks to you, and I urge you to reverse any plans to call on me in London. I would rather return to the morgue than receive such a disloyal friend.

Your indifference will live with me forever, you selfish whoreson. I cannot believe you left my moldering form,

half-dead, as a burden to my wife. Your true mettle has been
revealed. Go to bloody hell.

    Sincerely,

    Jon G. Stoker

Brent Caulder, the Earl of Cassin, tossed the letter aside
and steepled his fingers beneath his chin. He looked at his
friend Joseph Chance across the desk. "That's putting it
lightly."

"He's livid," said Joseph. "I can't say that I've ever heard
him write so much in one letter."

"It's partly in jest," said Cassin. "Surely. He's angry but
it's hardly his style to harangue us for being *rude*. What he's
really trying to say is this: *Don't come.*"

"Yes, buried neatly beneath profanity and accusation,"
said Joseph.

"I'm relieved, at least, that he's out of danger. If he can
write this letter, he's clearly recovered. He's tougher than all
of us put together. I never doubted it."

"Who would have guessed. A knife fight to bring them
together. Cupid's arrow can take many forms, I suppose,"
said Joseph. "Naturally, Stoker, of all people, would require a
blade to the spleen to be brought 'round. He always was the
dashing one."

"One thing's clear. We were correct to keep away. Despite this obvious temper-fit letter. If we'd rushed to his aid,
Sabine would have never considered him."

"She might send him away yet."

"If Sabine's letters to Tessa can be believed, there is quite a bit more happening in Belgravia beyond bandage-changing and soup-eating."

"Whatever it takes," chuckled Cassin, leaning back. "I should have stabbed him myself, years ago."

"Well, you might say we've stabbed him in the back by not coming. That's what he believes. *Abandoned*."

"Well, abandoned for his own good," Cassin sighed. "He will thank us in the end."

Chapter Fifteen

Grosvenor Square, Mayfair's lauded neighborhood of noble families and respectable wealth, was developed on swampland beginning in 1724. Although planners originally considered constructing a uniform block, a more heterogeneous design prevailed, and nearly every townhome boasts a different facade and color.

The great irony of the square may be that its center garden is actually an oval. The park is gated, but the privacy of the gardens is often breached. As early as 1727, vandals dismembered the mounted statue of King George in stately Roman martial dress.

Grosvenor Square, Grosvenor Street, Brook Street, and Park Street all public thoroughfares; Park Square open to residents only, although the still-vacant King George pedestal is visible from the street.

—From *A Noble Guide to London*
by Sabine Noble

They waited a week and a half to call on Bryson and Elisabeth Courtland. Sabine claimed she was under deadline for her next installment of travel guides (not entirely untrue), and Stoker abided. His manner since their heated discussion after the garden was careful and . . . if not abiding, then a little stunted. He did not challenge her when she ordered him to eat; he did not strain his stitches; he rested and slept. He did not make good on his threat to ravish her. He was, at long last, a compliant patient.

It made her even more resolved that they should put off the call to Bryson and Elisabeth Courtland until he was almost fully healed. It was ridiculous, perhaps. Stoker was not her personal invalid to keep locked away from his friends. If he was still sick, would they not take him from her? *Yes*, she thought, *they would*. And she was not prepared to let him go.

And so they passed twelve more healing days in Belgravia, and now they were due at the Courtlands' for tea by four o'clock. Stoker had sent for a fresh set of clothes and had Harley dress him in waistcoat, cravat, and jacket. The finished ensemble belied no trace of infirmity; he was a handsome gentleman on morning calls. Even the tattoo was hidden.

Sabine, for her part, endeavored to match his aplomb. Perry prepared her orchid-colored day dress and hat, and dressed her hair with loose curls piled beneath the brim. It was silly, but she wanted to look worthy of Stoker when they met this couple. Sabine was a gentleman's daughter, after all, despite the fact that she worked as a travel writer and lived alone in a cellar in Belgravia. Would it matter that she entered into a convenient marriage with a stranger and now kept him restricted to her bed? Possibly. It never hurt to look one's best.

It was unlike her to be nervous about a simple afternoon tea with new acquaintances, but she found herself slamming down combs and stomped into stockings, her behavior to Perry nothing short of petulant. She had dreaded the meeting for days, but then she had swept down the stairs and the look on Stoker's face when he saw her—a whipsaw double take, a sweep of his eyes, obvious desire—made calmness settle in. It shouldn't matter, but his obvious appreciation was worth more than any approval she might receive from the Courtlands.

And then they were off, lurching through midday traffic to reach Grosvenor Square. Despite the fact that they spent their evenings together and most days just a corridor apart, something about the close confines of the carriage felt new and uncertain. Sabine found herself commenting on the autumn weather (although she loathed idle chatter) while Stoker retreated into his most stoic, silent scowl. Their short journey was so forced and awkward, she had half a mind to call off the visit and send him on alone.

But then again, she wasn't a coward; she wasn't afraid of his sulky moods and she did not want to go home. If she went home now, he would not be there and she was not prepared for an empty apartment. Not yet.

And how full the days had been since their time in the garden park. If Stoker had become an easy patient, she had also become a more cooperative host. She did not purposefully invite undue risks with the Dryden investigation just to worry him; and she did not start again with her surveillance of the Duke of Wrest, despite the fact that he was now the suspect in Stoker's attack. She had plenty to do, keeping a safe but observant eye on the wagon master, the chemist in Regent Street, and the charcoal kiln master in Hampstead. She also had her very real deadlines to make, and she looked after Stoker's rest and nourishment and . . . and . . .

Well, Sabine wasn't certain what, exactly, to call the third (although no less pressing) component of Stoker's care. As a sea captain, world traveler, businessman, and general outdoorsman, he was not accustomed to bed rest or even prolonged captivity inside of doors. It fell to her to . . . if not *entertain* him, then certainly to distract him. The doctor had begun to wean him from the sleep-inducing pain medicine, and a restless, glowery demandingness settled into his copious waking hours. He wrote countless letters and devoured every available newspaper (and thereby used up all but forty-five minutes of his morning). After that he summoned a steady stream of hired men to his bedside. Her cellar apartments became a spinning top of sailors, shipbuilders, runners, property managers, clerks, and secretaries. The ruckus was almost enough to wish Elisabeth Courtland would step in and take him off her hands.

Almost.

"Would you allow me to take in Mr. Stoker's supper?"

Perry had asked one night as Sabine carried down trays of cod and turnips at nine o'clock. "You must be exhausted, after being out of the house all morning and locked in your study all afternoon."

"I am perfectly up to the task," Sabine had called with a smile.

"What a good wife you are, Miss Sabine," Perry had praised.

Sabine had had no reply for that. Was this what a good wife did? Busied herself with her own pursuits all day and then brought supper so late, most reasonable people were already abed?

She had never guessed that marriage might allow her to occupy herself all day with her own work while her husband occupied himself with his separate undertakings, only to convene together in the evening to leisurely discuss the events of the day. The model of her own parents' marriage involved the exalted hero-worship of her father, with all meals and the daily routine in service to the rhythms of his work or the provisions for and countdowns to his journeys. So complete was her mother's devotion to her father that her own tenuous health had taken a terrible turn when he died. It was as if a part of her mother's very purpose for living had perished with Nevil Noble.

In contrast, Sabine availed herself of all of Stoker's business; they talked for hours about it every night. With everything she heard, she challenged or intruded, praised or rebuked. He told her of every person he assigned and hired and dispatched throughout the day, the letters he wrote, the things he bought and sold. He talked about his investigator's impending arrival from Portugal and his work with the man to build a case against the Duke of Wrest.

Stoker, in turn, listened to her new conclusions and discoveries about the case against Dryden, weighing in on what he thought and what he did not believe.

These were lively discussions that stretched late into the night. They also spoke of books and music, his travels, and her guides and maps. Sabine could not remember ever looking more forward to time spent with another person. She worked very hard all day, and happily so, but she *lived* for the evening meal with Stoker.

Only two topics seemed glossed over or omitted. The first was his most immediate personal plans for the future—his next voyage or his vague references to buying an estate somewhere and setting up "a real home."

The second was any reference to some intimate, physical . . . "something" that would take their relationship from fulfilling and captivating to intimate. To touch or, God forbid, to kiss. But nothing was said and nothing was done. Her desire to reach for him was so very great, but also so very uncertain. It was like looking out at distant mountains but having no map to show the way to reach them.

There had always seemed like too much to say, he was too prone, she too upright, there was crockery in the way, the dog was barking, Perry or Harley were in the room, on and on it went.

The truth was, Sabine was too inexperienced as a seductress to know how to parlay dinner conversation, no matter how scintillating, into, well—her touch. What was more, she didn't want to seduce him; she simply wanted to touch him and to kiss him, and for him to do those things in return. She'd spent considerable time and energy weighing the consequences to her heart if and when they did touch and kiss again. By all accounts, he would leave her when he was whole and able. She'd finally decided the thrill was worth the risk. But now he would not even meet her halfway.

In theory, the carriage ride with the vehicle's velvet seats and close confines offered a more ideal environment to finally, at long last, lean against one another (at the very least). But they were in the carriage for some purpose, and social calls introduced the complication of tight wool clothing, stunting leather gloves, and hats that would collide if ever they ventured too close. Not to mention, they rode in a sort of uneasy silence rather than the familiar banter of her bedroom.

Sabine could, she knew, simply put it to him plainly—she was not shy—but she also had her pride, and if he denied a bald statement such as, "I believe we should have another kiss," any such future requests would be even more fraught and difficult. She did not want to make things worse.

And, she thought, he probably would deny her. She knew this deep down, no matter how hotly he watched her or how suggestively she teased him. He'd made it very clear that denying himself (as he put it) was, in his mind, the same as protecting her. It was an obstacle she had no idea how to get around. Was the guise of "protecting her" simply a gentle way to say he did not fancy her? She did not think so, but this assumption did nothing to make his detachment go away.

Meanwhile, she herself had grown fixated on the *reason* he believed she required protecting. She'd not been able to get the threat of his . . . feral, rough, and raw desire from her mind. Night after night she sat opposite his bed and listened to stories of his adventures around the world, of fights with pirates, survivals in the face of ocean squalls, and near misses with sharp, rocky coasts. It was impossible not to be stirred by such stories, and even more stirring was the prospect of being held by a man with the courage and skill to fight and sail and *survive* as Stoker had.

My needs are raw, my desires are wholly untamed, he had told her, *and I have discovered during my time here that I have only the loosest hold on my self-control.*

Sabine examined this threat on a nightly basis. She thought about it while he perused one of her maps, or slipped food to her dog, or relayed some daring rescue from his past. All the while, she thought, *Yes. Yes, I should like to experience all of that.*

And yet, the notion of how to manage it escaped her. She'd grown so frustrated one evening, she had burst in on Mary Boyd in her workshop.

"Is it possible," she had asked, "that some women enjoy . . . wild, untamed relations with their husbands—and the pace and, er, ferocity of that kind of exchange is appropriate? That is to say, decent?"

If Stoker would not subject Sabine to such passion, at least she would learn if anyone else ever did. Or would. Or had.

"Well, it's clear why you've been taking your dinner in your rooms with Mr. Stoker this past week," Mary had chuckled, arranging swaths of fabric across a sofa.

"Oh no, nothing has happened. I was just wondering. In general."

"In general?" asked Mary.

"In theory. Because, when I was younger, if ever I gave any thought to the type of husband I might one day have—a very rare thought, I assure you—I suppose I had the rather vague notion of someone quiet and bookish. Accommodating and helpful. Someone who would never contradict me or endeavor to inflict anything upon me or restrict me."

"Quite so," clucked Mary. "The girlhood Sabine wished for a sort of *eunuch steward* as her husband, and how useful he would be. I dare say most women have thought the same one time or another. But now?"

Sabine had shrugged. "And now all I can think about is Stoker, and how he might, er, inflict or restrict me. I mean, in a manner." She'd blushed to the tips of her ears and turned to go. "I can't believe I've come to you with this. I'm sorry."

"Pray don't succumb to bashfulness now, Sabine," Mary had called. "Our days with you are diminishing rapidly, I fear. I'll not waste a single opportunity to relish your thoughtful questions before you fly away."

Sabine had stopped and looked back over her shoulder. "Oh no, Mary, you mistake me. This is only supposition. I've no plans to go away, none at—"

"Deny it all you like, but I have a sense about these things. I made the same predictions with the other girls, and how right I was."

Sabine had slowly turned back. "Perhaps, but Willow and Tessa never regarded their arrangements as true marriages of convenience. They were always going to fall in love."

"And what were you always going to do?"

Sabine had shrugged. "Remove my uncle from Park Lodge. Go home. Look after my mother. Curate my father's work."

"Well, there is nothing that says that you cannot do all of those things *and* fall in love."

I'm already in love, Sabine thought, shocking herself.

She spun around.

"Are you quite alright, dear?" asked Mary.

Sabine blinked at her. "I . . . I believe I may already be in love with him." Her voice was a rasp. The tower of teetering footstools beside her could have crashed down on top of her and she would not have been more stunned at this revelation.

Sabine asked, "Is this possible?"

Mary chuckled. "But of course it is possible. I find it highly unlikely that you would harbor a sick man in the cellar if you had not fallen in love with him. You are a generous girl, I'm sure, but you are not *that* generous."

Sabine laughed, but she wasn't really listening. She thought back over the weeks since Stoker had come. Was it possible that she did not host Stoker in her bedroom so he could heal, or so he could advise her about smuggling, or even because she enjoyed his company? Certainly, all of those things were true; but was it also true that she kept him in her bedroom because she could not bear to let him go? It is why she waited twelve days to share him, even for an afternoon, with the Courtlands. She awakened each morning, thinking about him, and she tossed and turned in her bed at night, fantasizing about him.

"I think I do," she whispered, more to herself than Mary. She lowered herself into the chair.

Mary went cheerfully on, "Of course you do, dear. And you may rest assured that there is no impropriety in loving your husband with a bit of wildness thrown in. Likely you were attracted to some ferocity in him all along. His passion will answer that need inside you. The reason I could foretell of eventual love matches for all of you brides is because otherwise sensible young women do not consent to marry disagreeable strangers, no matter how dire their situations. All three of you agreed to marry, however suddenly and anonymously, because of some spark of promise each of you saw in these men. It was a great stroke of luck and more than a little bit of providence. And now you will have to see it through to the end, won't you? Passionate lovemaking and all."

"I had not thought that far along," Sabine had admitted. She had barely allowed herself to consider kissing Stoker—in fact, she was quite preoccupied with it—and had not looked beyond. But the moment Mary had said the words, a vague, distant tableau began to flicker in the back of her mind, like a disjointed reflection on the surface of a pond. It was hazy and unclear, with blank gaps representing missing details that were not yet formed, but she saw herself and Stoker—

Well, she could not say where they were and what they were doing, but she realized that the image of them sharing a life together had been hovering there for quite some time— and whatever it was, she wanted it, very badly.

Suddenly, she'd leapt up. "Thank you, Mary!" she had called and darted from the workshop. Her question about wild lovemaking had not necessarily been answered, but an entirely new question had taken shape. What did it mean to love Jon Stoker and what of their futures together after he had his own life back?

The next day, as they had planned, Stoker sent a note to Bryson and Elisabeth Courtland, which prompted an immediate reply by the same messenger: *Please come to us straightaway. We have been desperate to see you. This afternoon would not be too soon.*

And now here they were, that very afternoon, trundling up to Denby House in Grosvenor Square. Stoker flashed Sabine a rare smile, young and carefree, one she could not remember seeing. Something about the newness and the eagerness of it unsettled her, and she found herself grinding her teeth as he handed her down from the carriage.

Stop being ridiculous, she scolded herself. Of course he hadn't smiled youthful, carefree smiles in Belgrave Square. He'd been fighting for his life, not to mention frequently at odds with her about smugglers and assassins and Bridget, who left a thicket of fur on his bed and hounded him for table scraps. It was shocking, actually, that he had remained in Belgrave Square, subjecting himself to her headstrong ways, when he could have been recovering here, in the relative splendor of a townhome mansion in the company of a woman who made him *smile*.

To his credit, he did not bound up the steps and abandon her on the sidewalk. He waited patiently for her to frown up at the towering facade of the Georgian townhome and stomp resolutely up to the great steps together.

"How is your wound?" she asked. Every day he leaned on her less and less. His strength was returning.

"I could do without these stiff layers of clothing cinching the scar," he said. "But I could hardly languish about in pajamas forever, could I?"

"And here I thought you'd dressed to impress the Courtlands," she said.

"I've dressed to suggest how very fit I am. Only you know the staggering invalid beneath."

Sabine felt a rush of strange pride that she, alone, had discovered him, and nursed him (however distractedly) back to health.

Get hold of yourself, she ordered just as the door swung open, revealing a beaming Elisabeth Courtland.

"It's them!" Mrs. Courtland called over her shoulder, shouting back into the house. "Come quickly, Bryson, it's them!"

Elisabeth Courtland, beautiful but understated in a simple blue dress, swept the door open and ushered them inside, shooing away a confused butler.

"Oh, but what a welcomed sight. Just look at you," Mrs.

Courtland exclaimed. "But I thought you said you'd been hurt? I can't remember ever having seen you so tucked and polished and upright. Are you certain you were stabbed? Come let me get a hold of you."

"Careful," Stoker mumbled before Elisabeth Courtland pulled his cheek to hers and clasped his hands. "I could collapse at any moment."

Elisabeth drew back, alarmed. "You could?"

"No," he clipped dryly. "I've quite surpassed collapsing, haven't I?" He shot Sabine a conspiratorial look.

Sabine affected a small, uneasy smile, standing awkwardly at the edge of their affectionate greeting. Mrs. Courtland followed his gaze and then pivoted, smiling at Sabine.

"Please forgive me," Mrs. Courtland said, reaching for her with two hands. "At last, Sabine. What a pleasure it is to meet you. Welcome. You must meet my husband, Bryson." There were footsteps and she motioned an unseen person to her side.

"How do you do?" Sabine murmured, putting on her most genteel and pleasant face. Mrs. Courtland didn't answer as she clung to Sabine's hands, squeezing and shaking, staring into her face with a hopeful smile, searching for . . . for . . .

Sabine could not exactly say what she wished to find, but some instinct told her that it was not necessarily gentility or pleasantness. Mrs. Courtland's expression was open and honest and hopeful, with no trace of the expected judgment or superiority. She looked as if she expected very little of Sabine, except for perhaps to know her. Her expression seemed to simply say, *Please.*

Sabine exhaled, letting go of a long, fraught breath. She felt her own expression relax into something more natural, something that answered the entreaty in Mrs. Courtland's face. Sabine ducked her head, looking at the plush rug between their joined hands, and when she looked up again, she smiled a real smile. Happy and curious and a little bit afraid.

"Thank you for inviting us," Sabine said. "That is— inviting Stoker. This is his first foray out, and I cannot think of any errand that would motivate him more. He was so eager to see you."

"Well, there is a first time for everything," said Mrs. Courtland, squeezing her hands. "We have learned through the years to take what we can get when it comes to Jon Stoker." She continued to stare into Sabine's eyes, her expression almost . . . grateful. It was nothing like Sabine had expected.

Behind them, a middle-aged gentleman emerged from down the great hall, both arms extended in welcome. He winked at his wife and descended on Stoker to vigorously shake his hand and slap him on the back.

"*Oof,*" Stoker said, cringing at the force of the slap.

"Oh sorry, man," Bryson Courtland said. He looked uncertainly at the women.

Stoker closed his eyes, pain tightening his face, and Sabine stepped up to take his hand. "Not to worry," she said lightly. "He's alright. The stitches have not completely fused, and he makes an effort to brace for sudden movements if he can help it. You simply caught him off guard. He has also been known to whinge to great effect, haven't you, Stoker?"

She eyed him carefully, hoping he wasn't really harmed. He looked down at her with narrowed eyes.

What? she tried to silently ask. *Put your friends at ease. It's the English thing to do.*

"Yes," he rasped, "whinging is now second nature."

Sabine laughed and turned back to their hosts. The Courtlands smiled uncertainly, clearly as unsettled as Sabine and Stoker.

"May I introduce myself," Sabine asked Mr. Courtland, trying to move the moment along, "Sabine Stoker. It's a pleasure to meet you."

Her introduction interrupted the odd moment and propelled the couple into apologies and handshakes and sentiments of general delight. They ushered them into an adjacent parlor and sent a servant for tea.

"How beautiful your home is, Mrs. Courtland," Sabine remarked, taking in the soaring ceilings and lavishly furnished rooms. Bright fires warmed the large parlor.

"I insist you call me Elisabeth," she said. "And thank you. Denby House belonged to my aunt. I came to live here as a young woman, after my parents died. Bryson and I were in a lovely home in Moxon Street when the children were born, but then Denby House went up for sale a second time—my aunt and her husband live in the Caribbean now—and Bryson bought it as a surprise. It's useful as the children grow and so much better suited to entertaining. Throwing parties is a necessary evil for charity work, I'm afraid, but Bryson relishes these events. We've a ball next week, in fact, don't we?" She looked at her husband with a scrunched nose.

"The twenty-five-year anniversary of my shipyard," Mr. Courtland replied. "A cause for celebration, if ever I've heard one."

"And you hear many," Mrs. Courtland replied. She went on, "But this is the house where Stoker first came to me and we began our infamous association as brothel raider and—" she laughed at Stoker "—and whatever role I played. *Charity Administrator*, I suppose."

"You are the one who changes lives," Stoker said. "I merely knocked heads and ran in the streets after dark."

Mrs. Courtland winked. "Do not listen to him. Stoker cut a far more dashing swath through London because he *is* more dashing—in every way. Even our first meeting. He climbed up the rose trellis outside my room and tapped on the window. The first of hundreds of times. I daresay you've never entered this house through the front door before today, have you, Stoke?"

Stoker gestured to a sofa, settling Sabine and then eased himself uncomfortably beside her. "Who can say?" he said.

If Sabine expected him to slide into a reverie of remembering days gone by, she was mistaken. He seemed far brusquer and less willing to elaborate than usual, which was saying a lot.

"But you must tell us the nature of this injury of yours?" Mrs. Courtland asked. "What happened? Where were you? My God, I was beside myself when I read your note."

Stoker apologized for the alarm and gave a brief description of the wound and ensuing infection. He and Sabine had not discussed what he would say, and she was surprised to hear him leave out key details. He said nothing of his suspicions about the Duke of Wrest and, more affectingly, he did not relate Sabine's role in discovering him. Instead of the great coincidence of the morgue and the *Dreadnought*, Stoker simply suggested that he "went home to Sabine" in Belgravia to recover.

Sabine listened quietly and said nothing, turning to smile at the Courtlands as they clucked and sighed, clearly horrified by the unbelievable story. Stoker dismissed their obvious concern, insisting he was nearly fully recovered. Sabine, too, listened quietly, contributing little to nothing. She simply sat beside him and, in some small way, cherished the knowledge that the two of them had their own secret version of the story.

She wanted, suddenly, to settle her hand on his leg, to scoot closer to him on the sofa. Quite out of nowhere, she felt bold enough to make the small physical overtures that had escaped her for the past week and a half. She refrained, of course, but she did relax. She sat back and relished the hot tea in its beautiful, delicate cup. His friends were lovely, just as he'd promised. He was not their son or their brother or their nephew—he was simply Stoker, and he did not belong to them any more than he belonged to her. And yet, there was something that he and Sabine shared . . . some undefined, unspoken bond that tied them to each other and their shared history as they sat across the tea service from his friends. They did not touch, they did not explain, but they were . . . united. At least for now.

Sabine glanced at Mrs. Courtland and saw her watching them over the rim of her teacup. Sabine smiled and blushed a little. She was suddenly very glad she'd not given in to her impulse to touch him.

"Sabine?" Elisabeth said. "Would you like me to show you some of the work that I do?"

"Oh," said Sabine, nearly dropping her teacup, "that would be lovely. Thank you, Mrs. Courtland." She'd prepared herself for Elisabeth Courtland to steal away with Stoker, but she had not expected the older woman to require time alone with her.

"Elisabeth—*please*," the older woman corrected, kissing her husband on the cheek. "Just a short little turn about the house," she said with vague promise, leading the way to the door.

CHAPTER SIXTEEN

Sabine followed Elisabeth Courtland down the great hall, chatting about her travel guides. She had clearly read all of Sabine's books. It had been rude, Sabine now thought, not to make Elisabeth's acquaintance before. Even if she and Stoker were estranged, Sabine might have just said hello. The woman wanted, clearly, to know her.

Sabine vowed to do better, no matter what happened. If the Courtlands would see her, she would make a point to be friendly after Stoker had gone.

"Here we are," said Elisabeth, gesturing to an out-of-the-way door that led to a cramped stairwell. The sound of voices, clanging, wood chair legs on a stone floor rose from below.

"I assume Stoker has told you about my foundation?" Elisabeth asked, preceding her down the stairs.

Sabine nodded. "He said that you seek to rescue prostitutes and then retrain them for honest work?"

"Oh, very good, so you do know. And look at you, able to say the words without blushing. Stoker has done his duty by me. I never know if he spares us a thought when he is away."

"Stoker regards you so very highly and he admires your work. You were one of the first people he mentioned when I—That is, when he regained consciousness."

"He begged you not to bring him here, didn't he?"

"Er . . ." Sabine missed a step. "I believe he did not wish for you to worry."

"I worry anyway," she said on a sigh.

They reached the bottom step and turned a corner into a bustling kitchen and scullery. Elisabeth led her to an unoccupied spot in a corner and began to point out servants diligently at work on tasks around the room, stirring pots, scrubbing dishes, kneading dough, carrying baskets heaped with vegetables. The fragrant smell of baking bread filled the room, and the idle chatter of the women rose and fell amid chopping knives and clanging copper pots.

"You put the rescued girls to work as your servants?" Sabine asked, trying not to sound a little alarmed.

Elisabeth laughed. "Ah, no. Not exactly. The brothel raids are not a means to staff my own kitchen, but wouldn't that be handy? My foundation offices are across town, and it includes a boardinghouse where the girls live. They rest, receive medical care, and slowly, when they are ready, learn some trade. Some do become maids of kitchen staff—although rarely for me. Others become typists or store clerks. We do not encourage factory work, but sometimes the girls don't feel suited for working in service. The foundation is staffed with caring older women who hold no contempt or judgment over the girls, but want only to help them discover some different life. I am there most days. It is a very demanding enterprise, but it gives my life meaning—that is, along with my family, of course."

"Of course," Sabine said. If Elisabeth Courtland meant to impress her, she had.

"The reason I am able to bring such direct help to so many girls," Elisabeth went on, "is because Stoker came to me all those years ago and volunteered to begin physically rescuing young prostitutes from their situations. Without him, I would have been just another fund-raiser, raising money so that some man at a church or in government could decide how to spend it. He was . . . he was the perfect combination of daring, and capable, and willing to help. He was only a boy, but certainly no adult man would have consented to do it. And a boy of less courage or cunning would never have succeeded." She sighed and shook her head. "I'll never forget the first girls he brought to me. He and I had only discussed *in theory* what might be achieved by raiding a brothel. And then suddenly here he was, standing outside the kitchen door"—she pointed to the door across the room—"with three bedraggled women and a little girl." She shook her head, remembering.

"I believe it is a cause about which he feels very strongly," Sabine said, watching her face.

"Do you think so?" Elisabeth asked quietly. "Because I can never be certain. That is, I know he despises prostitution and I know he believes I've worked hard to improve many lives, but I never knew for certain whether he was fighting against prostitution or simply . . . fighting. Do you understand?"

Sabine smiled weakly and said nothing. She had no idea why Stoker fought. A man had tried to kill him a month ago, and he did not even seem particularly motivated to find him or seek vengeance.

Elisabeth said, "I worry that, at some point, a young man like Stoker might reach his capacity for witnessing so many horrible things. When he's seen too much, he might simply stop believing that things can be made better. This has been my worry for Stoker, a loss of hope."

Sabine spoke without thinking. "He has spoken to me about the horrible things he has known."

"Has he? But does he seem to know the good he's done? The lives he's saved? I forced him to move on eventually. I made certain he obtained an education. He had honorable friends with ambition. Now I have teams of men who go into brothels on behalf of my foundation, but they follow his same basic methods. His legacy. Does he know this?"

"I—" Sabine began and then paused. She glanced at Elisabeth. "He is rather haunted, I believe, by his boyhood in general. I can say that you are the one bright spot in that part of his life. In every part."

"You mean he struggles to . . . to—To do what? Sleep? Carry on? Find joy in the simple pleasures of life?"

"No—That is, I cannot say. Forgive me for speaking out of turn. He—"

"But it affects your marriage?" Elisabeth assumed. "I know the circumstances surrounding your wedding were . . .

practical rather than romantic, but we were so encouraged by Joseph and Tessa's relationship, and Cassin and Willow's. And then to learn he's been staying in your home for nearly a month? I was elated. I didn't even care about his stab wound, as heartless as that sounds. I was so very grateful that he went to *you* to heal."

"Yes, well, he came to me for convenience's sake in the beginning, I'm afraid," said Sabine. "And then he was too very ill to move. And now? Now we have settled into something like a congenial sort of . . . accord."

This was a lie, she thought. *He remains so I will not prowl the countryside, hunting smugglers.*

"But your feelings are . . . warm, I hope?" asked Elisabeth. "I have lain awake at night for years, hoping for a girl who could make him feel warm."

"Oh, I'm certain there are plenty of girls with warm feelings for Jon Stoker."

Elisabeth laughed. "No, I mean true feelings. An authentic caring that embraces all of him, even the haunted parts, especially the haunted parts. A girl who sees beyond the dashing outer shell."

"I am finding it difficult to broach the haunted parts," Sabine said, looking away.

"Oh, but you mustn't give up," said Elisabeth breathlessly. "Please, Sabine, I've only just met you, but the moment I saw you standing by his side in the entryway—proud and confident but also . . . cautious—I knew you were a young woman who was up to the challenge of loving him. And then to see him follow you with his eyes, to hear him use discretion when he speaks of details that might bring you unease? His fondness is obvious. The only thing that matters to me is that Stoker finds someone to love him as he should be loved, and that he may love her back.

"Forgive me if I assume too much," she went on. "I promise that I did not lure you to the scullery to . . . set upon you with my hopes for your marriage. It is not like me to prattle on," she said, swiping a tear away. "No brother could be dearer to me than Stoker. And when I hear that he is haunted, I can but assume the worst and blame myself. In this, I am quite at your mercy. Please, Sabine, I implore you, stay the course if you can bear it. He has so much love to give."

Sabine blinked at Elisabeth, entirely at a loss. "I do not intend to abandon him," she heard herself say. "And I do not intend to be abandoned myself."

Elisabeth laughed a tearful laugh. "Oh, I could not have put it better." She reached out and squeezed Sabine's hand. "But let me introduce you to someone. *She* is the reason I have dragged you to the scullery. Let me see, where is she? Ah, there she is."

Elisabeth whispered to a passing hall boy who went to the giant worktable in the center of the kitchens and tapped on the shoulder of a tall woman. The boy jabbed a thumb in their direction, and the woman craned to see. She nodded and put aside her bowl, crossing to their corner as she wiped her hands on her apron.

"Hello, ma'am," the woman called to Elisabeth, smiling as she emerged from the bustle of the kitchens. The closer she got, the more clearly her face could be seen through the smoke and flour. At first glance, Sabine thought the woman had a large smear of batter or perhaps ash across one side of her face, but as she neared, Sabine could see that she had been, in fact, scarred, most likely by a terrible burn, from scalp to neck. Scar tissue pulled damaged skin tightly across her eye and cheek, and her mouth and ear had puckered into a disfigured sort of droop. Part of her hair had been burned away.

"Hello, Constance," sang Elisabeth, smiling. "Sorry to disturb you, but I've someone I'd like you to meet. What are you making?"

"Tarts, ma'am," said Constance, smiling her crooked smile. "Using the last of the raspberries."

"Oh, the children will be thrilled, and I shall have dessert for breakfast for a week." Elisabeth turned to Sabine. "Constance is responsible for all the pastries and pudding in our house, and how fortunate we are to have her. I've had foreign dignitaries, duchesses, members of court endeavor to hire her away. But I could never part with her, and she is loyal enough to remain in my meager kitchen."

"Oh, you do go on, ma'am!" enthused Constance. "Weren't nothing but a bit of sugar and flour."

"*And* she's as tight as a drum when it comes to her recipes, as you can see. I cannot complain. I quite like having the finest pudding in London." Elisabeth turned back to the cook. "Constance, I thought you might like to meet our guest. She has been enjoying your currant buns with our tea, so your reputation precedes you. May I present the wife of Jon Stoker—" she held out an open palm "—Mrs. Sabine

Stoker. He's brought her home to meet us. At last." Elisabeth beamed back and forth between the two women.

Constance made a sharp intake of breath and clapped her hands over her mouth, sending a puff of flour into the air. Her eyes filled with tears.

"How do you do?" said Sabine uncertainly.

The woman dropped her hands from her face and took up Sabine's right hand, shaking it vigorously in both of her own. "I'm so thrilled to know you, ma'am, so very thrilled. Stoker . . . Stoker. . . ." She broke off, tears spilling down her damaged cheeks. She looked at Elisabeth miserably.

Elisabeth gave Constance a half hug. "Remember when I said that I don't hire girls from my foundation in my own household? Well, that is not entirely true. Sometimes, on occasion, in special circumstances, someone from the charity *does* make her way into our lives here at Denby House. And Constance is an example of that—much to our delight, as I've said. She has been with us since just after Bryson and I married. Constance was rescued from a terrible situation in Cripplegate, and it was Stoker, then only fifteen or sixteen, who rescued her. Along with several others."

Constance nodded tearfully along, looking between Elisabeth and Sabine. She sniffed loudly and wiped her nose. "I would have died if he'd not crashed in on the house where I was being held—and I tell you, I would have welcomed death. He wasn't even a grown man. He came in through the window with two other boys. He worked quick like, locking doors and gathering us up. He took us out the window, the same way he'd come. We told him that he'd gotten us all, but when we were in the street, he went back and crawled in and out of every room. And did you know he came out with another girl? I'd been there nigh on two years, and I didn't even know the whoreson who held us had someone else locked up. That girl didn't make it, God love her, but she didn't die in that hellhole, and that is a small blessing." She shook her head as if to clear away painful memories, and smiled at Sabine again. "I've so much to be thankful for because of Stoker. And now he's taken a wife!" She looked at Sabine up and down. "But how beautiful and proper. He always deserved the most beautiful and proper wife, didn't he, ma'am?"

Sabine cut in, "I'm not sure about how proper I am. I can be demanding and stubborn, I'm afraid."

"Oh, Stoker won't mind that. It's the shrinking violet what would bore him to tears."

"Well, I'm certainly not that," Sabine joked. If Stoker knew she was in the basement claiming to be his actual, loving wife, God only knew how he would respond.

"But can you cook?" asked Constance, gesturing to the kitchen.

Sabine cringed. "I'm afraid not. I'm a cartographer by trade, actually. I make maps."

"Has a trade, does she?" marveled Constance. "Stoker was right to wait for the correct girl, ma'am."

"I couldn't agree more," said Elisabeth, beaming at Sabine.

They chatted a moment more before Constance excused herself to return to her dough. Elisabeth gave Sabine a grateful look and then led the way back to the parlor.

"I hope you didn't expect us to discuss weather on this little tour," she said, climbing the dim stairwell.

"I did not know what to expect, honestly," said Sabine.

"Bryson will say that it was wrong of me to inundate you with this history, but I am not prudent in that way. When you witness matters of life and death on a daily basis, you lose patience with idle chatter."

"Was the woman Constance injured . . . in the kitchens?" Sabine asked.

Elisabeth shook her head. "The man who held her captive in his brothel pressed a burning torch to her face each time she refused to accommodate customers. A terrible story. One of many, unfortunately. But she has done so well since. She has so much talent to give and she enjoys her work. I wasn't exaggerating about her exploits in the kitchen. We are lucky to have her." She climbed a few more steps. "We are lucky to have every girl. Some might consider the cost of helping them to be very high. Bryson takes my work in stride and loves me for my conviction, but it was never the life he envisioned. My children have always had to share me with my commitments to the foundation. And Stoker—Stoker has witnessed the worst of humanity firsthand. I see degradation and despair when the girls are delivered to me, but it is nothing compared to what Stoker had encountered when he entered these establishments to extract the girls. It could not but take its toll, especially on the way he views men and women and sex. He has so much love to give, of this I am certain, but there may be some . . . some memories to overcome." She turned to Sabine and gave an apologetic smile. "Not to impose undue pressure."

Sabine laughed. She felt more resolved to help Jon Stoker find love with every breath.

Elisabeth laughed, a clear, musical sound. They spilled from the stairwell into the great hall, wiping their eyes and fanning for fresh air.

The men were still in the parlor, their voices louder and more relaxed than the stiff, formal conversation of before. Elisabeth rushed in.

"Stoker, I must congratulate you on your wife," she said, sitting on the arm of her husband's chair. The men scrambled to stand. "Sabine has my wholehearted approval. I adore her."

"This comes as no surprise," Stoker said simply. Sabine drifted to his side. She wanted desperately to take his arm, to throw her arms around him, but she hovered instead.

Mr. Courtland said to Sabine, "Stoker tells me you wish to look in on the Portsmouth ship owner, Phineas Legg?" He retook his seat.

"Oh yes. Stoker said he might be of your acquaintance."

"Well, I know *of* his family. The ships from my shipyard are beyond their means, I'm afraid, but he has inquired after retired equipment and even out-of-service boats that we sell at a reduced price."

"When Stoker is well enough," Sabine said, "I intend to travel to Portsmouth to look in on him. I'm not sure what Stoker has said, but I believe him to be working with my uncle at something not entirely legal. I am determined to have them reported."

"Yes, Stoker has told me," said Mr. Courtland. "But rather than travel to Portsmouth, why not bring Legg to London? As I mentioned, Elisabeth and I are hosting a ball next week. Most of maritime London will be invited, as well as mariners from other port cities. I had not included Legg on the guest list, but he would be an easy addition. The crowd will represent a step up from Legg's usual acquaintances, if I had to guess. I cannot imagine he would turn the invitation down, even at last minute. It would allow you to get a look at him here in London before taking yourself off to Portsmouth. Would this be useful?"

Sabine was nodding before he finished. "Oh, but that would be a huge convenience and great benefit to us—er, to me. Thank you so much. Are you certain you don't mind?"

Mr. Courtland looked at his wife. Elisabeth made a dismissive wave of her hand. "What's another wealthy sailor staggering around the ballroom? You know I have no opinion about the ball, except to complain about having to attend it."

Mr. Courtland turned back. "It's all settled. I will invite Mr. Legg this afternoon."

"Thank you," breathed Sabine again, and now she did reach out to wrap her arm around Stoker's biceps, clinging tightly. His muscle tensed under her hand, but she did not let go. She glanced at him. Stoker and Bryson were sharing a look. Sabine realized that perhaps the invitation to Mr. Legg had already been decided. The men had solved the problem of Portsmouth and dear Mr. Legg while she'd been in the cellar with Elisabeth. How clever they must feel, but two could play this game.

Sabine cleared her throat. "But Mr. Courtland?"

"*Bryson*, please," the older man corrected.

"Bryson," she continued. "Would it trouble you terribly to add just one more unexpected guest to the party? That is, if it really is a large affair and hangers-on won't be noticed?"

"Not at all. How could we be of service?"

"Our research has also brushed up against an old aristocrat living in Chelsea—the Duke of Wrest? Do you know him?"

Sabine could feel Stoker tense beneath her arm.

"Wrest . . ." mused Mr. Courtland. "I cannot say that I do."

"He's rather old and not out of society," said Sabine. She hurried to finish, "Even so, would you consider including him, as well?"

"Consider it done," said Bryson, and Sabine let out a satisfied breath. She released her grip on Stoker's arm. Smiling, she reached for a second cup of tea.

Chapter Seventeen

Stoker had done many things in service to Elisabeth Court-land's sponsorship through the years. He sweltered in waist-coats and strangled in neck cloths; he passed mind-numbing twenty-course meals among stupefying lesser royalty; he learned French. But one thing he had never done—one thing that never occurred to him to do—was attend a ball. As a guest. Who . . . reveled.

Oh, he had lurked around Courtland events, but he'd never loaded his plate from the heaping buffet like a starv-ing man or gambled irresponsible sums in the smoky card rooms. Certainly, he had never danced.

And yet now here he was, descending the steps to the Courtlands' glowing ballroom with *his wife* on his arm.

"Are you in pain?" Sabine asked, glancing at him.

"No," he said. "That is, not because of my wound." Actu-ally, his wound was more like a scab now, and the only residual pain was from the broken ribs. He was fit enough to be at a ball or anywhere else for that matter—except that he resented trussed-up society functions. He had nothing to contribute to female gossip or male boasting. He was bored almost immediately and appalled by the dancing (how did full-grown men keep a straight face as they hopped in a line?).

"Can you untwist your face, perhaps?" Sabine whispered. "You look as if I'm leading you to a funeral pyre."

"Would that you were," he sighed. "I haven't the slightest idea what we're to do now that we've come. Is it typical to feel oddly conspicuous and gratingly idle? Like we're wasting time and showing off all at once?"

"If we are conspicuous, then we're on task. Everyone hopes to be noticed at a ball."

Stoker thought Sabine would be impossible not to notice in her elegant, cherry-red silk gown and golden gloves. He'd seen a dozen men turn to follow her with their eyes, jackals watching unassuming prey, and he'd felt a pang of possessiveness so acute, he'd almost slid his arm around her waist and hauled her against him. But good sense prevailed, and he scowled at the room in general and the men in particular. Sabine carried on not knowing or not caring, wholly focused on identifying her suspected ship owner, Phineas Legg.

"How will we identify your illustrious Mr. Legg if we don't ask?" Stoker said.

"Pray do not forget that Legg isn't the only reason we've come. The Duke of Wrest accepted Bryson's invitation, so we shall get a look at him too."

"We're not approaching the Duke of Wrest," he told her.

"*If* we approach either of them," she went on, "we must

blend in with the other guests. Never fear. I shall navigate for us. You may rely on me."

He glanced at her, wondering if she realized how completely he had allowed himself to *rely on her* in these past five weeks, more than he'd ever relied on anyone in his life, even his business partners. Not for clinical care: she was an average nurse at best, despite having saved his life. But he had grown to rely on her presence, her nearness, her attention. He'd discovered delicious insights into her personality to which he'd not been privy. He knew now that she was reliably diligent, up early each morning; amusingly disordered, with strewn paperwork amid drafting tools and half-eaten apples; she was fiercely loyal to her dog; she was clever—so very clever—and bossy. He awakened each morning, straining to hear the sound of her footsteps on the stairs or whipping open the door. He fell asleep after hours of conversation and long, silent stretches, where they stared into the fire.

He'd stored away every memory, every nuance, for *after*, when he was fully recovered, and this business with the smuggling was settled, and she was restored to Park Lodge in Surrey and he was . . . and he was . . . on to whatever his next act would be.

A more prudent man might have tried to curtail the slavish sort of attachment he'd allowed himself to develop for her—to *rely on her*—but honestly, he didn't care. So what if he admired her? So what if he thought of her to the exclusion of anything else? His proximity to her was worth any prideful restraint. Worse, his proximity to her was fleeting. He would not remain in her bedroom forever. He was in love with her. This truth had hit him like a boulder to the chest late one evening after she'd gathered up her notes and the supper tray and bustled from the room. *Come back*, he wanted to call after her. *Not yet. I'm dying, even as you heal me day by day.*

I love every moment that we are together.

I love . . . I love . . .

I love you.

His love had become such a fundamental truth, the admission didn't even alarm him. It felt, in fact, more settling to simply acknowledge it.

He loved her, but he was not stupid with love. He knew they would part ways. Another settling acknowledgment: He should savor her while he could.

Savor her at an arm's length, of course. Always and above everything else—perhaps his greatest achievement. By some great miracle, he was *not* guilty of taking her virtue or pawing her body. His desire for her, which seemed to intertwine itself with his love for her, confused and unnerved and worried him. He worked, daily, to tap down his persistent, driving need to touch her.

He laughed now, thinking he'd been tempted by the impersonal annual exchanges of previous years. These were nothing compared to spending hours every night talking, listening to her laugh, watching her face as he told her stories of his life at sea.

The days of merely savoring the *idea* of Sabine Noble were an afterthought; now he bloody *knew* her. He knew her wit and her artistry. He knew what she found ridiculous and what pricked her fierce sympathy. And he knew how she looked at the end of a long day, when she had burrowed herself into the chair beside his bed, long legs doubled up beneath her skirt, stockinged feet poking out, chin resting on her knees. And her hair—God, her hair—falling down from whatever hasty twist or braid that had survived the day but finally slipped free.

"Look, there are the Courtlands," Sabine exclaimed now, nodding to a bunting-draped alcove, thick with potted palms. "Let us say hello and thank them. And then we will eat something. We'll get a broad view of who is here and also save you from dancing."

"I will not dance," he vowed, not for the first time. She'd tucked her gloved hand so tightly around his biceps, he could feel the shape of her fingers. The lushness of her body pressed against his; her skirts lapped at his leg as they walked.

He glanced at her, hoping that she hadn't noticed he was overwhelmingly aware of every bat of her eye, every swipe of her hand. Other men, he knew, did not nearly incinerate at any idle touch from their wives. He would die if she knew he went nearly out of his mind when she touched his arm. She smiled up at him and Stoker jerked his head away. She was easily the most beautiful woman in this ballroom, likely the most beautiful woman in London, and it almost hurt him to look at her.

But it hurt worse not to touch her. To *really* touch her. To this end, a bloody ball was actually quite useful. Three hundred revelers closed in on all sides. Candles shone, food and drink kept them occupied. Beyond her escort on his arm, it would be impossible to touch her. The cellar bedroom had been a different story, and he'd fought a daily battle with his mounting—nay, avalanching—physical attraction to her. So deep was his desire for her, he could feel the sharp points of it sinking into his very bones, the heavy pressure of it expanding inside him. He would die for wanting her, he thought.

And so he had frightened her instead. The words had come out before he'd known it, but they had worked. The most reliable safeguard against his desire that he knew: threatening her with the truth. He'd used language coarse enough to offend a veteran sailor and swore to her what would happen if she continued to press. It was a sharp nail in the door to her curiosity, and it hit his mark. She'd not asked again. He'd been shocked that she'd not disappeared for another week, but she'd carried on sharing dinners, asking him about her investigation, and allowing him to fall deeper in love. His baseness and his darkness and his raw, pounding need were his own cross to bear.

"Stoker," Sabine called, trying to keep up, "we cannot simply walk to the front of the receiving line." He pulled her along the perimeter of the dance floor, skirting a throng of guests queuing to shake hands with the Courtlands.

"Oh, let us simply try," muttered Stoker, stepping up to Bryson and whispering in his ear. Bryson glanced at him, said farewell to the gentleman shaking his hand, and then reared back to pull them in beside Elisabeth beneath the festooned trellis.

"Look who's turned up," Bryson whispered, catching Elisabeth before she drew in the next guest.

Elisabeth turned. "Oh, thank God you've come," she breathed. "I'm saved."

"Not quite yet, darling," Bryson said with a smirk. The queue was rapidly growing.

"Oh right," she said, sagging a little, pulling a defeated face. But then she rallied, winking at them. "Shouldering on," she said brightly. "You look radiant, both of you."

"Have you eaten?" Bryson asked. "I can have drinks brought 'round, or a footman fetch plates from the buffet. Your Mr. Legg can be found very near the drinks table, I believe. Although I recommend you fortify yourselves."

"He's here?" asked Sabine breathlessly, craning to see.

"He was among the very first guests to arrive," imparted Bryson.

"He turned up at four o'clock in the afternoon," said Elisabeth conspiratorially. "I've never done this before, but I turned him away until a more appropriate hour. The staff was absolutely not ready. None of us were. His first London ball, I daresay."

"He's entirely ridiculous, isn't he? I'm so sorry. I hope he does not spoil your beautiful affair. I never meant—" She looked pleadingly at Stoker.

"I assume this means he'll be easy to spot," Stoker said, unmoved.

"*Do not* give him a moment's worry," assured Elisabeth. "We are glad to help, and there is always a contingent of boorish guests at these affairs. They provide valuable gossip, and no self-respecting ball would occur in this town with-out some number of early arrivals or tardy hangers-on. Oh, and the other honored guest—who was it?" She looked at Bryson.

"The Duke of Wrest."

"That's right, the old duke. He also sent his thanks and should be here somewhere . . ." She squinted across the ball-room. "But why did you say you're looking for him—?"

"Just another suspect," cut in Sabine vaguely, taking Stoker's arm. "But we are keeping you from your guests. Please carry on. We're not so single-minded that we cannot enjoy a lovely night out for the sake of diversion."

She laughed a little and beamed up at Stoker, and his throat went tight. He couldn't breathe when she turned her smile on him alone.

Enjoy a lovely night out for the sake of diversion.

And here he'd been congratulating himself for not pouncing on her. He was a bore and a social cripple and he had no idea how to relate to her as a woman and certainly not as a wife. She'd spent nearly six weeks beside his bloody *sickbed*, for God's sake. Of course she wished for diversion. Instead, he'd brought her to a ball to hover about a sus-pected smuggler and a suspected *murderer*.

Had he ever failed more spectacularly in his life? This was why he'd stayed away for four years. He would never be re-motely enough for Sabine Noble.

You don't need to be enough, he reminded himself. *You only need to protect her and leave her in peace.*

On his arm, Sabine was thanking the Courtlands again.

"We will seek you out when you're not so inundated with guests," she called, tugging him away.

"When we find Mr. Legg," she informed Stoker, diving immediately into her investigation, "one of us will prove better suited to coax information out of him than the other, but it's impossible to guess who. He may dismiss women on sight and have nothing to say to me. Or he may know who you are, considering the success of the guano venture."

As always, Stoker experienced an unjustified rush of gratification when Sabine mentioned the guano venture. He and his partners had been the first importers to bring nitrogen-rich guano fertilizer to the British Isles, revolutionizing agriculture in the country and making them three of the richest men in England. Stoker had given Sabine her due profits—hers was one of three dowries that financed the first expedition—but they'd never discussed the great windfall in detail. The fortune bored him, honestly, and she didn't seem to care. But she knew. Each time she mentioned it, the money was a little less boring and a little more worth the months he'd spent chipping bird shite off an island in the baking Barbadoes heat.

"I am your apprentice in this investigation," Stoker said, scoping out the long buffet table, heavy laden with colorful food and gleaming china and silver.

"Good God," Sabine whispered, gaping through a dispersing crowd of young ladies to a high table crowded with bottles of liquor and tiers of empty crystal. Beside the table, standing exactly in the path of busy footmen conveying trays of drink, leaned an over-pomaded, snugly trousered young man—twenty-two if he was a day—strangled by a cravat so voluminous, it looked like a lion's mane. He wore tall boots polished to a blinding gleam, a puce waistcoat, and a moss-green jacket so festooned with quivering gold buttons, he resembled an apothecary cabinet with fifty drawers and copper pulls.

Two older women waited before the table while a footman ladled punch into crystal goblets, and the young man lunged forward to intercede. The women chuckled at his overblown gallantry, thanking him as he dispersed the goblets with a bow and a wink.

"Surely not," said Sabine, her face scrunched.

"Shall I have a go or will you?" sighed Stoker.

"Let me begin," said Sabine, squaring her shoulders, "and if he cannot be taken in, you may take over."

CHAPTER EIGHTEEN

Stoker swore inwardly, and then reminded himself that of course Sabine would approach Phineas Legg. Stoker had an instinct for detecting maliciousness and threat, and Phineas Legg gave no suggestion of either, thank God.

No risk, Stoker said in his head, ambling behind Sabine. He promised himself he would not strike this person unless absolutely necessary. He would not cause a scene; he would not disrupt Sabine's work; he would not be a raging jealous lunatic unless rage or lunacy were required as last resorts.

". . . but have we been introduced?" Sabine was already trilling to the man at the drinks table. He cast an appreciative look up and down Sabine's body and appeared overjoyed by her suggestion.

No risk, Stoker chanted in his head.

"Mr. Phineas Legg, at your service, miss," the man was saying. He affected a sweeping bow over her hand.

"Oh, Mr. Legg, of course," said Sabine, "of Southampton." She made no effort to correct his "miss" to "madam."

Mr. Legg chuckled, "Of *Portsmouth*."

"Oh indeed? Portsmouth. But then perhaps we are not acquainted. I don't believe I know anyone at all from Portsmouth. I am a resident of London these past five years. What luck for you to attend all the way from Hampshire." She shot a glance over her shoulder at Stoker, her eyes bright with excitement. Legg looked up, noticing Stoker for the first time, and frowned.

"Yes," Legg said haltingly. "And who do I have the honor of meeting?" His eyes darted back and forth between Sabine and Stoker.

Sabine fretted over her rudeness. "Oh, but do forgive me. I am Elaine Toble." She extended her hand again. Legg smiled and descended slowly over her knuckles, casting another frown at Stoker.

Sabine quickly added, "And this is the man employed by my late husband to guard my welfare . . . when I am out of the house."

"To guard you?"

"We own several businesses that claim some . . . notoriety," she said simply, waving the notion away.

Stoker took a small step closer. Low risk or not, he did not relish being waved away, even as part of a ruse.

But now Legg was clarifying, "Your *late* husband?"

"May God rest him," said Sabine. The words were enthusiastic and dismissive at the same time.

Phineas Legg raised his eyebrows, a suggestive, knowing look. Sabine raised one of her own perfectly arched brows as they shared the look. Stoker bit back a growl.

"I assume your work is in *shipping*, Mr. Legg, like the other gentlemen here?" Sabine asked.

"It is indeed, madam," Legg said, pleased by her assumption. He motioned to the punch bowl and procured two glasses, handing her one. "I run a fleet of ships from Portsmouth Point. Across the channel to France and back mostly."

"A *fleet*," marveled Sabine admiringly. She nodded to a nearby column, just steps away from the bar, and began to drift. Legg did not hesitate to sweep his hand beneath her elbow to guide her along. Long, pale fingers brushed the skin just above her glove, and Stoker's heart lodged in his throat. Every muscle in his body went rigid. Even as they reached the column, Legg did not let her go. Sabine said something, but Stoker couldn't hear; his ears had disengaged. Possessiveness was a roar in his head.

You knew all along she would invent some identity, he told himself. Over meals in her bedroom, she'd explained the roles she played to elicit information. She did not aspire to widowhood; she was not an accomplished flirt. She was not affected by this man's hands on her.

Sabine tossed a glance in his direction, a casual tilt of her head, but the look on her face was very clear. *Do not.*

Stoker stared back, not blinking, not breathing, his gaze homing in on the place the young man held her arm. He stepped silently behind her.

"Your man is attentive," commented Legg, narrowing his eyes on Stoker.

"He is very good at his job, I assure you," Sabine said. "But tell me, what do you transport on these ships of yours . . . ?"

She engaged him for a time, exclaiming over his answers like they were the most fascinating truths of human history. Legg gave teasing, one-word answers at first, clearly expecting female shallowness, but she skillfully led him down a path of specific detail and self-important boasts. Within ten minutes he'd rattled off the boring history of his five meager boats, his itinerate crews, and his end-of-quay dock, all of which he inherited from a cruel mother.

"The reason for my questions," Sabine was now saying, "is that one of my late husband's businesses is a staffing office that places seasoned sailors with boat captains. I am endeavoring to maintain the business, and we are in constant search for owners or captains who might benefit from our men. I can only guess that your location in Portsmouth means you compete with the Royal Navy for crew?"

"You are a . . . businesswoman?" Legg asked carefully.

Sabine shrugged. "I have many occupations."

Legg considered this. Finally, he said, "I may have some need for crewmen."

"One of the useful things about my sailors," Sabine continued, lowering her voice, "is that they have very short memories." She looked at him through lowered lashes.

"I beg your pardon?" asked Legg. He'd scarcely taken his eyes from her face, but his expression tightened now from appreciative to something harder. Stoker stepped closer still.

Sabine exhaled prettily and looked right and left. "May I speak freely, Mr. Legg?"

"Please," he invited. Everything about him was a randy invitation.

"I . . . I'm afraid I have not been perfectly honest with you." Sabine raised a gloved hand and pressed her fingers against his arm, drawing him in.

Sabine went on, "Perhaps I *have* heard of you, Mr. Legg. Perhaps there has been gossip here and there about certain voyages of certain ships registered under your name that have returned to port with a hull as empty as—" she held out her punch goblet "—this cup. Yet, with a crew that has clearly been worked to the bone as well as handsomely paid. Does any of this sound familiar to you, Mr. Legg?"

"Some sailings deliver goods to France but return to Portsmouth without taking on new cargo."

"Come now. What shipper leaves a foreign port with nothing to sell in England? Not one as successful as you, I'm sure." The words were accusing but her inflection was playful. Clearly, Legg was intrigued by the combination, and he relaxed. He traced a line from her finger to her wrist with the back of his hand. Stoker felt his stomach pitch.

Legg said, "What precisely are you saying, Mrs. Toble?"

"I'm saying that if you require sailors to staff a forthcoming voyage, especially something with a very high potential to make us all rich, I should like the opportunity to throw in my lot. The sailors that I can provide are not faint of heart, nor are they particularly watchful, or as I said, known for their long memories."

She allowed this to sink in and then gave a little gasp, jerking her hand away. "Just to be clear, *I* should like to know. There are certain enterprises in which I don't care to dabble. The nasty business of slavery, for example. But beyond that—?" She let the sentence trail off. "Does this sound like something that might interest you, Mr. Legg?"

Stoker listened to her wind him up, oozing conspiracy and a promising sort of vague illicit behavior that could mean anything. It was very effective, he had to acknowledge. A strange skill, unexpected; but his own twitchy jealousy aside, Stoker felt a new pride in how smoothly she had dazzled and duped Phineas Legg.

In the next ten minutes Legg revealed to her that he devoted two of his mother's five ships to smuggling. He confirmed that the reason these ships returned empty was because their cargo was unloaded on the Isle of Portland, in Dorset—just as she had suspected. Finally, after they'd enjoyed another cup of punch and she allowed him to touch her arm a dozen unnecessary times, he finally revealed what he transported: two of the minerals in powder form, sulphur and saltpeter. They were purchased from mines in Italy and India respectively and smuggled through France.

Sabine listened carefully and then screwed up her face into a confused pout. Stoker could anticipate the next question— *But why sulphur and saltpeter?*—and he finally, after what felt like an eternity of restraint, stepped forward, and cut in.

"Beggin' your pardon, *madam*," Stoker said, "but you said to tell you when a certain lady was leaving the party?"

The intrusion was not welcome. Sabine and Phineas Legg

looked up from their bent-headed conversation as if they were in the midst of solving all the problems of the world. Legg glared. Sabine feigned irritation, but Stoker knew well what she looked like when she was truly angry, and it was not this. She scolded him, which he ignored (he was not the actor she was), and put a possessive hand on the small of her back. Legg puffed himself up to his full height, sucking in a breath to protest, but Sabine went smoothly along.

"Forgive me, Mr. Legg," she said briskly, "but my guard only follows expressed instructions from me. There is a certain woman that I must speak to on another matter. I came tonight for the purpose of catching her unawares. I'm afraid that I cannot afford to allow her to leave. But I am urgently interested in this business we might do together. May I seek you out later in the evening? Perhaps on the terrace, where we can be more private?"

Stoker slid his hand from her back to her waist, scooping her along.

Mr. Legg agreed reluctantly, and Stoker hustled Sabine into the crowded party, plunging them through dancers who swallowed them up in whirling silk and ostrich feathers.

"*What?*" asked Sabine breathlessly. "What's happened? I almost had it. He was just about to tell me the great mystery of what the smugglers are doing!"

Stoker kept walking, shouldering around old women with two heaping plates of food and three debutantes comparing their fans. "He doesn't need to tell you the bloody mystery. I already know."

"You do?" She took two steps to his one, scrambling to

keep up. Her face was flushed with excited exertion. It was her authentic face, the face that he thought of as only for him. She laughed anxiously. "What is it?"

"They're making their own gunpowder, Sabine," he said lowly, dragging her through a line of dancers. "Sulphur and saltpeter, when mixed with charcoal from your kiln in Hampstead, create the type of gunpowder that ignites hunks of rocks and the sides of mountains. It blasts open mining shafts. They're not smuggling in any one thing, they are buying minerals and mixing them with elements they procure here in England."

"On the Isle of Portland?" she surmised.

"Why not?"

"They're mixing it themselves on this uninhabited island," Sabine deduced, "then loading it on wagons in Dorset." She looked at Stoker. "Is gunpowder mixed?"

Stoker nodded. "That's the most rudimentary way to do it. Liquid can also be added to the mix and a little brick can be formed and dried. They call it a mill cake."

"Could this process happen on a deserted island, perhaps inside a cave? The Isle of Portland is riddled with caves."

"Absolutely," Stoker said.

Sabine thought about this. "But gunpowder wasn't on the list of things smuggled into this country," she said. "I'm not aware of any tax on gunpowder at all." She tried to stop walking, but he ushered her along.

She went on, "Where's the great profit in that?"

"There is *no profit* in importing gunpowder, because it's against the law to bring it into the country. The government stiffly regulates the gunpowder trade. There is an abundance of it in Britain, but the crown controls who makes it, how much, and who may buy it. It's nearly impossible to procure it if you are not a trained expert, cleared to work in mining, in the army—or . . ."

And now she did stop walking. They were at the edge of the ballroom, near double doors that led to the family rooms of the Courtlands' house. Sabine strode out of the way of lingering couples to a dark spot behind a large potted fern. She waved him over.

"Or . . ." she said, almost giddy, "unless a high price is paid to smugglers?"

He stepped up to her, shoving a palm frond out of his face. He was breathing hard after winding their way across the ballroom. "It's more than smuggling, Sabine, it's *treason*. Concocting illegal gunpowder and distributing it outside the bounds of crown regulation is considered treason in England. You have them."

Her expression opened up, happiness and relief and justification shining in her eyes. She raised both hands and squeezed, like she wrung victory from the air. "*Treason*," she marveled. "Of course. I never dreamed of a result so damning. My uncle . . . my uncle might be hanged. But to prove it and turn them in might save lives."

"Undoubtedly it will do," Stoker said. His hands slid to her waist and he fought the urge to pull her to him. He wanted to peel off her gloves and fling them away; he wanted to touch her everywhere that Legg had touched, imprinting her with his own hands.

She looked up, happiness and satisfaction and something like expectation in her eyes. She seemed to be holding her breath. She let her hands fall and moved backward deeper into the small forest of ferns. He could either follow or leave her to her personal triumph. He followed.

He was just about to let himself let go of everything but her. She was so very happy and he'd played some small role in that. The moment felt pure and almost sacred. He could kiss her to celebrate. He would not let it get out of hand—

"Johnny?"

Stoker froze at the sound of the name he had not heard in more than thirty years. Sabine jumped.

"Johnny Stoker? Marie's boy?"

It was a male voice. Close. Too close. Sabine scuttled up beside him.

"Are you the son of Marie Stoker?"

The familiar intonation of his mother's name filled him with a hurt and a longing he'd worked a lifetime to block out. He squeezed Sabine against him.

No, he thought. *Not here, not now.*

He shut his eyes.

"Johnny Stoker?"

Of course he could not have a single moment of sweetness with Sabine without some intrusion. It had been far too much to ask, just one kiss.

"The note from Bryson Courtland said he'd invited me on your behalf, so I know it's you," the voice said again. "Come on, give us a look. Don't try to hide it."

Stoker was a coward not to step into the light, but he

found himself unable to move. He was a boy again; he was Johnny. The street-hardened toughness of Stoker had not yet locked around his body or his heart.

A very old man with white hair and pale green eyes stepped heavily toward them, squinting into the ferns. Sabine sucked in a little breath. The sound broke Stoker's reverie and he slid his hands from her and stepped away. He was not a boy, he *was* battle-hardened, and the only man who scared him was himself.

Stoker considered the man. He'd known, of course, who he was. The voice was unmistakable. The childhood name he invoked. This was Sauly New, one of his mother's old customers. What he was doing here, at a society ball, Stoker could not guess. Stoker had seen him often enough as a boy, although he looked so very old now. He'd dressed finely once upon a time, but now his suit was faded and tight.

Stoker told him, "I have no business with you, sir."

Sabine stepped to his side. "Stoker?" she whispered.

Stoker made a low wave, trying to push her back.

"*Stoker?*" she persisted, her voice still low. "Do you know who this is?"

"Yes," he sighed.

"You *know* him?" Sabine tried to confirm.

Sauly New swayed crookedly, old or drunk or blind in the dim light. He huffed out sawing breaths like a man who'd climbed a thousand steps.

"This is a ghost from my other life," Stoker said. "It's nothing to do with you."

"*Right*," said Sabine, drawing out the word. She grabbed his hand and began to tug his head down, to whisper in his ear.

The man slurred. "I thought I saw you dart through the dancers. I . . . I would know you anywhere. You always were running." He coughed violently, his lungs drowning in fluid. "I'm too old and sick, damn you."

"Sabine?" Stoker said calmly. "Will you go to Bryson and Elisabeth? Just for ten minutes? Do not leave their side, do not speak to Leg—"

Sabine cut him off with a noise of frustration and yanked on his arm hard.

"That," she whispered harshly, "is the Duke of Wrest."

Stoker shook his head, barely hearing. "No, he is a man from my boyhood. I'm afraid that my old life has the uncanny tendency to crash in on my new. Generally, it happens when I am the least able to manage it. It was always meant to be far removed from you. I never wanted it to touch you."

"Stoker, you're not listening," Sabine said, all but climbing up his arm. "I mailed you a description of the Duke of Wrest when you had me follow him around. Did you not read it? I even made a sketch. *This* is the man."

Stoker simply stared. Sabine made a noise that was half shout, half scoff and clapped both hands on either side of Stoker's face, turning his eyes to stare into hers. "*That man*," she whispered, "is the man"—and now she barely mouthed the words—"you had me follow. His name is Lord Saul Newington, the Duke of Wrest."

Stoker staggered back, jerking his face from her hands. "*Him?*" he rasped.

But this man had been no *duke*, Stoker thought. He'd referred to Stoker as Johnny and given him sweets and broke his mother's heart again and again for years.

This man, who (it was no use in denying it) looked like a very old, very swollen, very stooped version of himself, had not been the man in Sabine's beautiful sketch.

This man was the bloody Duke of Wrest?

"No," Stoker gritted out, shaking his head, his mind racing with memories and misunderstanding and lies, lies, lies, so many lies.

This meant the same man who'd sent an assassin to *kill* him was standing here in a bloody ballroom, saying . . . saying. . . .

But what was he saying?

"How are you enjoying your evening, Your Grace?" Sabine asked flatly, taking hold of Stoker's arm.

"I've had better nights, to be honest," he said. "But you must be my son's doxie?"

My son?

Stoker saw red. He lunged but Sabine squeezed his arm with all her strength, tethering herself to him. "Let us be thoughtful about this," she said calmly. Her voice was a cool splash of water in the inferno of his anger, but he ignored her. He tried to shake her off.

"Stoker," she said again, louder this time, "wait." She would not let go.

"There's nothing to think, this is a lie," Stoker ground out, trying again to pull free.

"Your Grace?" she called to the teetering old man. "May I call you, Your Grace?"

"Of course. And what shall I call you? You're a pretty little thing."

"You will not speak to her!" Stoker growled, his voice breaking.

This was not the way the night was meant to go. Stoker had not spent his life running, and rescuing, and sailing the bloody backside of the world to stand in a ballroom, facing down a man who used to tie his mother's heart in knots. His beautiful Sabine was not *conversing* with a belligerent, inebriated, caustic shadow from his past—the same man who put a price on his head.

For the first time in his life, Stoker felt like he might actually howl—scream like a madman, shout down the walls because of the bloody, futile defeat of it all. He'd worked too hard and made too many correct choices for his life to circle back to *this*. While Sabine witnessed it all.

"Tell him," Sabine snapped to the old man. "Tell him that you are the Duke of Wrest. Let us begin there. So that we are all perfectly clear."

"Oh yes," sloshed the old man. "I am he."

"And you are claiming to be Jon Stoker's father?"

"Well, I supplied the living-giving essence that got his mother breeding. There was no union, save a mutual affinity for—"

"You blackguard!" Stoker raged and lunged.

CHAPTER NINETEEN

Sabine let out a cry and scrambled after Stoker, catching him around the waist and pushing him like a large piece of furniture, through the ballroom door.

"Leave it," she ordered, her voice ringing with authority. "Leave it for now. Let us be the reasonable ones."

Behind them, the duke warbled, "I must speak to my son . . ."

Stoker made a growling sound and Sabine tugged him toward the rear of the house. They walked a few steps before Stoker pulled free and reversed back into the ballroom. Sabine shouted again and scrambled after him, catching him by the arm and pivoting, spinning them back into the hall.

"And you said you didn't want to dance," she said, straining with effort.

"Let me go."

"I will not. Walk. Where does this corridor lead?"

"I don't remember," he said, but he began to walk.

"We will discover it, then."

He seemed to have abandoned the idea of returning to the ballroom, striding away at a fast clip. She hustled to keep pace with him.

"Slowly, Stoker," she said, "your wound, your ribs."

"I feel no pain," he said.

"We are not being pursued. We need not sprint. I merely wanted to prevent a scene."

"Then why ask Bryson to invite him?"

"I can see now," she confessed, "that this was a terrible mistake. But please remember, I did not know you actually knew this person. How could we know his claims of paternity were . . . were—true? Or, how could I know, Stoker? Is it possible that he actually sired you—"

"*That* is the man . . . ?" Stoker demanded, ignoring her question. "That is the man I asked you to follow around London for a month last year?" He glanced at her.

"I've said yes—the Duke of Wrest. He was not difficult to discover. He is not out in society but he is hardly a recluse."

They reached glass doors that appeared to open into a garden, and Stoker turned right, stalking down a second long corridor.

"I knew him," Stoker said. He sounded like he spoke to himself. Or the furniture. The paintings on the wall. "But I had no idea he was a bloody duke. And I had absolutely no notion that he was my—That he'd known my mother before—" He couldn't finish.

They strode in silence for twenty yards, and then he said, "She must have known. My mother. She knew all along that he was my father, and the two of them never said a bloody word."

"Would it have mattered?" Sabine wondered. "Considering he . . . he never meant to claim you, and he is obviously a man of diminished character."

Stoker stopped suddenly and rounded on her. "I want you to know that I would never, ever have charged you with trailing around a man who was my actual illegitimate father, let alone someone who would later try to have me killed. Please believe me."

"I believe you," she said, panting to catch her breath.

"I thought the paternity claim had come from an anonymous nobleman who'd read about me in the papers and was casting around for an easy source of money. I thought it was a hoax."

"I believe it is something like a hoax. He is no *real* father to you, obviously. Was he . . . cruel to you as a boy? When you knew him?"

Stoker thought for a moment and then turned on his heel. Sabine swore and hustled to keep up. "Stoker?" she called. "You obviously know him."

Stoker made a noise of disgust.

"Will you slow down?" she demanded. "Please. I cannot keep up."

"His name when I knew him was Sauly New," Stoker said, not looking at her.

"Sauly New," Sabine repeated. He was known in London as Saul Newington, the Duke of Wrest. "That's original."

"This from *Elaine Toble*," Stoker scoffed.

"I am not a duke, impersonating . . . whomever Wrest was pretending to be," Sabine retorted.

She knew he'd been displeased with the role she'd affected to dupe Phineas Legg. She hated to play the flirt, but it had been the fastest and most effective way to extract the information she wanted.

She tried again. "Who was Wrest pretending to be when he was Sauly New?"

"It doesn't matter."

"I think it matters a great deal."

"It should not matter to you."

"I alone decide what matters to me. We've discussed this."

"*Sabine*," he warned.

"Say it, Stoker," she sighed, taking two steps to his one. "Tell me!"

They came to another dead end, but a third corridor turned to the right, and he made the corner.

"I don't want to bring my terrible memories down on your head. These are things you should not have to know." He sounded angry, desperate; he was begging her without saying the word *please*.

Sabine was not too proud to beg. "Please tell me." She stopped walking. "Please."

He made an agonized sound of frustration and spun back. "You ask too much."

"I've only begun to ask, Stoker," she sighed, "and I am agonizingly persistent."

He swore and pivoted and walked five paces. "Fine," he said, not looking at her. "You wish to know?"

"I wish to know," she said softly. The outer wall of the corridor was lined with windows that overlooked a dark garden. Cushioned benches were positioned at intervals against the glass. Sabine trudged to a bench. "Will you sit?" she asked.

He shook his head. He began to pace back and forth, a jerky, angry march.

"My mother's life was not what I would call pleasant," he began. He stared at the floor. "Neither of our lives were *pleasant*." He stopped walking and looked at her. "I cannot do this."

"You will do this," she said.

He glared at her then resumed his pacing. "*In our unpleasant lives*," he said, "she traded hunger and cold for her service to men. An unending line of terrible men. Sometimes there was considerable money, but in exchange, my mother suffered black eyes and broken bones. Sometimes there was money but also the constant, lurking presence of some man and his friends, lumbering through her rooms at every hour. Sometimes we had money but my mother was sick from the very nature of her work."

Sabine blinked slowly once, twice. *Oh, my poor Stoker,* she thought.

"Always, always she was unhappy. Bitter, cynical, maudlin—a woman who knew her life had been spent in service to hateful men."

"But she had you," Sabine said softly.

He shook his head. "My presence was not a reason to live. I was a burden."

Sabine scoffed. "You cannot mean—"

"Sabine," he said sharply, stopping again. "I've told you that I have no wish to bring down my terrible past on another person, least of all you, and that is the honest truth. If I *must say it*, there is no benefit to pretending it was different. Please. I exaggerate nothing, I misrepresent nothing. I was there, and I have no confusion about what our lives were like and no reason to overblow it. It was wretched, but it was not her fault. She did the best she could."

"I'm sorry," she said quickly. "It is your story." She wanted to leave the bench and hold on to him. She wanted him to drop onto the bench beside her and lay his head in her lap. She wanted—

"But sometimes," he went on, "maybe once or twice a year, a different sort of man would turn up." He gestured behind him. "Sauly New was, I suppose you could say, such a man. He was not a drunk and he was not cruel. He dressed in finer clothes than ever I had seen. My mother actually appeared . . . well, lighthearted when he came around."

He paused and ran his fingers through his hair and squeezed his eyes shut. "Forgive me, the possibility that this man is actually *my father* is still taking shape in my brain. I cannot quite accept it, and yet—" He let the sentence trail off.

"Now that I've seen you side by side," Sabine ventured, "I must say that you do look rather alike. That is, he looks like you if you were aged forty years, sedentary, gluttonous, tangling with gout, and you rarely saw the sun."

Stoker opened his eyes. "Yes, I can see how the resemblance shines through."

Sabine gave a sad smile. After a moment she asked, "Did he—?"

"He paid me very little mind," said Stoker. "Which was my strong preference. Sometimes he gave me a peppermint. Or a toy musket. Once he brought me a pair of boots." He stopped pacing. "I was suspicious of the gifts—uncertain of what my mother would be required to do to earn them—but I was so bloody desperate for any attention and any . . . frivolity, that I took them anyway. I liked him. He was . . . happy. He made my mother happy."

Now he resumed pacing. "Until he made her unhappy, which was generally in three or four weeks' time—a month at most."

"He turned cruel?" Sabine guessed.

Stoker threw up his hands. "He simply got bored, or they quarreled, or he went home to a wife or off with another whore—I was not privy to why he left. I only knew the ceaseless crying. My mother would sob for a week, and we'd have no money for food. I would suffer this strange stew of anger and guilt. I was angry at her for doing whatever she'd done to make him go and guilty for wanting to subject her to him again."

"Oh, Stoker. How old were you?"

He stopped walking again. "Seven? Eight? Considerably younger than I am now, although still tortured by it, as you have the very great misfortune of witnessing."

"The last time you saw him was—?"

Stoker took a deep breath. "When I was about nine years old, he turned up to announce that he was moving us out of the brothel and into a proper flat in Blackhall. It wasn't lavish, but it was our own place, with a lock on the door and shelves for our possessions and curtains on the windows. He came and went at odd times, but he visited regularly, three or four times every week. When he was home, he ate a proper supper with us. He retired to my mother's bedroom only after I'd gone to bed. There was plenty of money, so my mother could go to the market and bake fresh bread and buy a winter coat. She awakened in the morning instead of the middle of the afternoon. She sang idle songs while she cleaned and mended. She seemed . . . truly *happy* for the first I could ever remember.

"I had always been a quiet, stealthy, distrusting boy, always on my guard—I'd had to be. I could disappear in plain sight, meld into the shadows. I could escape any room out of a window. But after a month or two in Sauly's flat, I had begun to relax. I spoke at mealtimes. Sauly offered to teach me to read and I accepted. He brought me books, maps, even parchment and pens.

"After another month I began to believe my mother and Sauly had fallen in real love—whatever notion of love I had at the time. I allowed myself to hope we'd begin to live a proper life, that this flat would be a proper home. I believed my mother had finally done it. She'd escaped the constant struggle to survive and the wretchedness of her work. I lay in bed at night and hoped our lives had changed for the better."

"Oh God," Sabine said softly, "I'm afraid to hear the rest."

"I can stop," he said, looking over his shoulder. "I would relish permission to stop this story."

She shook her head. She reached out a hand to him. "Will you sit?"

"Please don't pity me. I could not bear it."

"It's not pity, Stoker," she said, peeling off her gloves. "My heart is breaking for you. This is a wretched story, your boyhood was truly horrible, and my heart breaks for all of it. I'm sorry if that distresses you, but pride should not apply to your horrible history, the circumstances over which you had no control. You were a victim. You are still a victim of this story, it's plainly clear, and now I am too."

"Not you." He stared at her. "You may listen, but it will have no bearing on you."

"If it affects the way you relate to me," she told him, dropping her gloves on the bench, "if it has some bearing on whether we—"

"You will not be tarnished by this story," he vowed.

"Fine," she sighed. "I'm not tarnished. Finish."

He stared at her.

"Please," she said.

Something about the pitch of her voice, or the softness of her expression, or the bloody tilt of her head must have finally been correct, because he trudged to the bench and sat heavily beside her. He took a deep breath.

"The truth is," he sighed, "there are worse stories with worse endings." Now he laughed. "You would not believe the children I've seen and the fathers they have endured. *Sauly New* is inconsequential compared to some fathers." He dropped his head in his hands and stared at the floor.

"Yes, but we are not discussing other children at the

moment. We are discussing you and your boyhood and your father."

Stoker said nothing. She stared at the broad expanse of his back and weighed the risk of touching him.

Sabine waited a beat and then said, "Does it help to remember that you are no longer a child? You are a very rich man and a courageous one. This person cannot hurt you now."

Stoker looked up. "Can he not?" he whispered.

She could not promise this; the man had already sent an assassin to kill him. Stoker was incredibly hard to kill, which had been an oversight on the part of the Duke of Wrest. But the harm he could do him was emotional, and it could be very great, indeed. Sabine vowed in that moment to do everything in her power to shield him. She wanted Stoker to know wholeness and hope and happiness more than she wanted anything else she could think of. More than her uncle's arrest, more even than Stoker's love, and that was something she wanted very badly indeed.

"Tell me the rest," she said.

Stoker stared across the corridor at the portrait of someone's fat ancestor. "I have to tell of our life further back," he said, taking a deep breath. "Before we moved into the flat, we lived inside a brothel, one of several. In this . . . establishment, it was not uncommon for me to be awakened from a dead sleep to fight grown men out of my bedroll. I fought men for the stash of money I kept beneath the floorboard. I fought men for my mother's safety. Once I used a brick to break off a door handle to reach her, because I heard cries of distress from her room. When I finally pried the door open, the man in her bed backhanded me, and she ordered me to get out and close the door."

Sabine made a miserable sound of sympathy, and Stoker closed his eyes. "If something happened to Sauly's sponsorship, it would be this to which we returned. My fear of this was constant." He glanced at her. "Perhaps you can guess the rest.

"One day," he went on, "I returned to the flat to discover that my mother had packed up our meager belongings, and she announced that we were moving home.

"I said, 'Home? Which home? We live here.' She shook her head and named the last brothel.

"I shouted the word 'No!' so loudly, the walls shook. I trembled with anger and fear and the sense of unfairness that only a child can feel. I'd had one taste of comfort and I was outraged at the suggestion that someone might yank it away.

"I assumed immediately that Sauly had turned my mother out. I demanded to know what he'd done. When she said nothing, nothing at all, I confronted her with a ferocity born of sheer desperation.

"I said, 'Does he hit you, does he steal from you, is he depraved in a way that you think I can't understand? What is it? Has he betrayed you?' And she said he'd done none of those things. She said that it was simply time to move on.

"And I'll never forget, I fought her, actually tussled with her over the bags. I was shouting, 'But why? Why must we go? If he is not a cruel man and you are happy?'

"And she said to me, 'Happy? You think I am happy?'"

Stoker shoved off the bench and turned his back to her.

"I'll never forget the piercing bitterness of her words. I dropped the bags and stumbled back. I shouted at her, 'But we are warm and dry here in this place! We have proper meals! He is not mean or jealous or demanding. He's taught me to read! He's . . . he's not bad.'"

Stoker turned around. "And she got the saddest look on her face, and she said tiredly, 'Well, you don't have to sleep with him, do you?'

"I was old enough to comprehend her meaning. The burden of her 'work' was a constant refrain, and I can never remember *not* feeling guilty for the manner in which she provided for us. It's why I left for the streets at the earliest possible age. Just after this, in fact."

He shook his head. "But I fought her on this. Just once. I didn't care. The security had been too glorious. I shouted at her, 'But you like him, I can tell you like him. He is good to you. What we have here is a good thing.'

"And I'll never forget what she said. 'What we have here is an *even trade*. I give him my attention, and we get this flat and all the comforts you love so much. *Yes*, I like him, and I like this flat, and I like all the rest of it. There is a lot here for us to grow accustomed to, isn't there? Meanwhile, there is only *one thing* he likes, and we both know that *that kind of like* never lasts forever, does it?'

"I . . . I didn't understand," Stoker said. "I screamed at her that I didn't understand, and she said, '*He's bored*, Johnny. He's bored, and he'll move on to the next girl. No one knows the signs better than me. And we'll do better to leave now, before he boots us out. It hurts less,' she said, 'if we leave now.'

"And then she was crying too. I didn't understand at the time, but later, as I watched her grow old and sick, pining for this man—" Stoker pointed behind him "—for *that man*, I realized that she wasn't leaving him because she did not fancy him. She left because she fancied him too much. When her work became her own passion, she thought that she had nothing to contribute. She loved him, but she could not afford to love anyone. Not and survive."

"But had he really evicted the two of you?" Sabine asked, rising up. "Had he truly grown bored?"

Stoker waved the question away. "I've no idea. She dragged me away and I never saw him again until tonight." He raised his hands, running them through his hair, and then strode off down the hall.

Sabine swore and pushed off the bench, hurrying to catch up. "You said he was in and out of your life—but was this always? Did your mother seem to know him from before your . . . life?"

"Yes," he said. "She always knew him. Why didn't I see the signs that he might be my father?"

"Well, if they never told you . . ."

"How could any man see his son and the mother of his child exist in such squalor and depravity *for years*? If he could not keep my mother as his lover, why not install us in a bloody cottage in the countryside and provide for us? Any meager offering would have been better than what we endured. Why neglect us for years? How could he put her through the emotional strain of repeated, unrequited affairs? How?"

"He is not a decent man, Stoker," Sabine said.

"I nearly died of typhus the next year, after he'd gone. I slept in a shed to keep out of the snow because the madam in my mother's brothel did not want the disease spread to her girls."

The corridor ended at a vestibule that connected back to the great hall. Around the corner the ball rollicked and spun. Stoker paused, staring in the direction of the sound, and Sabine had the panicked thought that he would return to call out the old duke.

She was just about to pull him back in the direction that they had come, when a woman's laughter pealed from the ballroom doors. Sabine looked up and saw Phineas Legg staggering out, arm in arm with a laughing woman in a daringly cut purple gown.

"Oh God, it's Legg and a paramour," Sabine gasped, pulling Stoker behind a ceramic vase on a thick pedestal.

"Where?"

"Leaving the ballroom."

They watched in alarm as the couple danced in a fumbling sort of embrace, kissing hungrily. When they reached the curled staircase bannister, they fell against it and plunged into another kiss.

"He seems to have made the acquaintance of another . . . friend," Sabine said.

"He is insatiable," said Stoker.

Behind them the ballroom music crescendoed to a rallying final note and then fell silent. The new quiet was followed by a spike in voices, and Mr. Legg scowled in the direction of the ballroom. The woman reared up, yanking on her bodice.

They whispered for a moment and then Legg kissed her again, dragged her to him, and they embarked up the stairs at a fast clip.

"They would not," said Stoker, pushing off the wall.

"I believe they would," said Sabine. "But let us—"

He started toward the stairs. "This is Bryson and Elisabeth's home," he said. "They have children here—"

"I thought their boys were in school."

"This is not a winter-solstice bacchanal in bloody Portsmouth," Stoker ground out, ignoring her, walking on. "This is a family home, one of the finest in London."

Sabine darted after him. By the time he reached the bottom of the stairs, Legg and his friend had disappeared into the shadows of the landing.

"*Stoker,*" she warned. "This is not wise."

"I'll tell you what's not wise." He began stomping up the stairs.

"It's not prudent for the two of us to roust them. You are meant to be my bodyguard, remember?"

"Crass, ungrateful, salacious . . ." He was halfway up.

"Let us summon a footman," she said, two steps behind. "Or alert Bryson if you are so bothered. I don't think—"

"Which way?" He reached the top step and looked right and left. Dim, doorway-lined corridors stretched on either side. The couple seemed to have vanished into the shadows. Stoker chose left and stalked down the landing. "They are trespassing," he said. "What if every guest stole away to bedrooms when the bloody orchestra takes a break?"

Sabine called to him again, whispering now, but he didn't

hear. His tirade continued, all hope of coherency lost. He was angry and hurt and likely in pain, and he'd not liked Phineas Legg on sight.

Sabine hurried after him, still hoping to drag him away before Phineas saw, but he came to a door standing halfway ajar and shoved it open.

Sabine closed her eyes.

"*Empty,*" she heard him scoff from inside. She said a silent prayer and hurried after him.

"Stoker," she said, imbuing her voice with authority. "You must stop. You're behaving like a man possessed. We've had quite a shock, you especially, and there is much to consider. You are tired, I am tired, but listen to me. We cannot challenge Legg in a bedroom of Denby House like a . . . like a rogue chaperone. He mustn't see me again—this was your own proclamation. I must turn in my uncle and his lot anonymously in case something goes wrong. None of them must ever know I was behind the investigation. *For my own safety.* I cannot have Phineas Legg learn another thing about me or who I really am. Be reasonable, please."

Stoker had come to stop by a giant bed. He closed his eyes and breathed in and out.

She went to him. "Remember how you chased me away from Mr. Legg after we'd learned of the gunpowder? We are finished with him."

He made a growling noise and walked in a circle.

"We're going home," she said.

"Yes. You're right. I've lost my mind." He looked at her guiltily. "Forgive me. I'm—This house is—My friends."

"Legg is ridiculous and I owe Bryson and Elisabeth a very great apology, especially now that he is roaming freely with his . . . er, new friend. But we cannot risk—"

She was cut off by a familiar gurgle of laughter.

Legg. Footsteps. Rustling outside the door. Sabine froze.

Stoker swore and stepped in front of her, tucking her behind him. They were blocked from retreat by the large bed in the center of the room.

"No, not that way," she whispered, "they cannot see your face!"

She spun him in the same moment the amorous couple crashed against the door, laughing and grappling for handfuls of fabric.

Sabine squeezed her eyes shut. Stoker widened his stance and broadened his shoulders, expanding to shield her. She tried to more thoroughly disappear behind him. She gathered up her distinctive red skirts, but the silk would not cooperate; every handful seemed to produce another flouncy swath. And the effort made too much noise. She began to silently panic.

In the doorway the laughter continued; they heard the rattle of an entwined couple rolling this way and that against the open door; fabric ripped, and there were smacking kisses and low moans.

Stoker swore softly, and Sabine glared at him. *Quiet*, she warned with one firm shake of her head.

"Oh, Phineas," cooed the woman in the doorway, and Sabine squeezed her eyes shut again.

Sabine was just about to bury her face against Stoker's

chest when she felt him fasten his hand around her waist, lift her, and drop her on the big bed behind her. She hit the satin of the coverlet with a soft *puff*, her head bobbed on the pillow, and her skirts sprawled out like a fan. Her eyes flew open in time to see Stoker's giant body, following her down.

Sabine made a small sound of surprise, and Stoker cleared his throat, covering the sound. They'd landed in a stack in the center on the bed, Stoker's considerable weight pressing her into the mattress, his cheek against her cheek, his face against her neck.

"What's that?" demanded Legg's voice from the doorway. "Who's there?"

They heard giggling, and the woman said, "There's already someone in this room, Phin!"

Phineas Legg could be heard swearing; the woman laughed again. There was a small grunt, footsteps, and the loud slam of the door.

Silence prevailed. Stillness. A low fire jumped in the grate.

Stoker lay prone atop her; she felt his weight and heat everywhere. Their combined shallow breaths sawed in and out. Neither of them moved as they clung together in the dark.

CHAPTER TWENTY

Sabine waited two beats, every function of her body held motionless by shock.

She did not blink, she did not swallow, she did not feel a single thud of her heart. She knew she breathed because she could hear the sound, but she'd forgotten how or why.

Above her Stoker felt as taut and tense as the string of a bow. She did a quick mental check of her own well-being. Was she hurt? No. Could she breathe? Apparently. Was he hurting her or frightening her or trapping her? No, no, no.

It occurred to her that she had been in this position before. They had collapsed on the bed when she'd moved him from her study, the first week of his convalescence. But that had been an exhausted, sprawling, stranger-in-my-bed sort of fall. Now Stoker's body felt healthy and tight and not the least bit tired. Or sick. Or unknown to her.

He smelled like shaving soap and potted palm and *himself*. His cheek was rough with whiskers; his nose bussed her neck. His shallow breathing had given way to deeper, faster breaths.

She had been waiting weeks for this.

Almost, she called his name. Almost. She was *this* close. Instead, she sucked in a slow, even breath, turning her head so that the sound was so very close to his ear. If possible, Stoker's taut body went even tauter.

Next, she pulled her right hand from between them and sank her fingers slowly, lightly, into his hair. When her fingertips touched his scalp, she slid her nails along the crown of his head, one long, satisfying scratch.

She waited, her heart beating in her ears.

He didn't move. He didn't speak. His breathing grew harsher against her neck. Every exhale sent goose bumps along her arms.

Sabine had the sense that her next move would decide their future. He was waiting for some trigger, some invitation he could not resist. Mentally, she cataloged her body. One hand cradled his head and the other was pinned between them. Her head was turned and she breathed into his ear. Her left leg was tangled in her skirts, but her right leg was free. She made a command decision. Slowly, idly, she raised her right knee, canting her body ever so slightly and hemming him in.

His response was immediate. He let out a harsh breath, pressing his face firmly against her neck. "Sabine," he growled.

"I want this," she said, trying to be very specific.

He repeated her name, moving his lips against the skin of her neck. She squeezed a handful of his hair, pressing his head to her. "I want it," she said.

"I . . . I—" He lifted his head and looked down into her eyes, his face a beautiful twist of desire and emotion.

"Do it," she whispered. "Enough. Do it."

He made a feral noise . . . the sound of letting go . . . and pounced on her mouth.

What came next was a frenzy of lips and tongue and teeth and his lips pressed roughly against every part of her face. He kissed her eyes and hairline and nose and cheeks and her mouth again and again, a torrent of kisses. He kissed her like a feasting animal after a long, cold winter.

Sabine closed her eyes, thrilling to the ferocity and the sensation, breathing when she could, kissing his mouth when it was there, arching her neck and offering herself when he kissed some other spot.

He lurched up to his knees and elbows, yanking her squarely beneath him, his strength and demonstrative command of her body taking her breath away. He gathered her up, scooping his hand beneath her shoulders and balancing her head between his thumbs so he could guide her face to exactly where he wanted her to be. He tipped her back to scrape his beard across her neck and eased it forward when he was ready for her mouth.

Sabine allowed it all. She was a rag doll, relinquishing herself to everything he would do to her.

Yes, she thought, wrapping her arms around his neck. *Take me. Use me up. Love me.* She wanted what he wanted.

"*Sabine,*" he rasped, again and again, saying her name like there was no other word in all of language. She answered with sighs and moans and rolling sounds of pleasure that she'd never before heard but that sounded exactly, precisely, the way she felt.

"This dress," he said, moving lower, kissing her chest above the bodice of her gown. "No man in the ballroom could look away from this dress but you are mine. *Mine.* I wanted to scream it. I wanted to throw you over my shoulder and haul you back to the carriage."

This image made her laugh. It thrilled her and she wanted to ask him why he didn't avail himself of her when they were alone in the carriage but words failed her, and she could only giggle and cradle his head against her. She pressed his head lower, lower, lower, to the lace edge of her neckline, tight against her corset, and to her breasts, heavy and straining upward beneath.

He growled when she laughed, which only made her laugh harder, and he pounced on her mouth again, swallowing her giggles, kissing her until the laughter died away.

When she was panting for breath, he rose up on his knees and stared down at the straining bodice. His green eyes were hot, molten emerald and his beautiful mouth was turned up in half a smile, half a smirk. Not taking his eyes from her, he ripped off his coat and hurled it to the floor.

"Do it," she said, panting.

He shook his head but did not meet her eyes. He stared at the tops of her breasts, rising and falling beneath the tight neckline of her gown. On some instinct Sabine arched her back and bowed up from the shoulders, offering herself to him.

"Please," she breathed, arching higher, and something

like a growl tore from deep in his chest. He took up the front of her gown and ripped. The straining fabric resisted but was no match for his strength. The silk rent with a clean tearing sound, and Sabine laughed again. The moment was too exciting, too theatrical, too final.

Stoker ignored her, his eyes feasting on the sight of her full breasts bulging at the top of her corset. She arched again, and she felt her breasts rise, her nipples barely contained. Stoker reached out with both hands and claimed each breast, sliding a finger beneath the stiff satin to scoop. Sensation coursed through Sabine; she cried out, and arched again.

Stoker slid his fingers beneath a second time, and then he cried out and grabbed the top of the corset, pulling it down. Her breasts bounced free and he gazed down at her body like a man who had just been privy to the most spectacular view the world had ever known.

The cool air of the room hit Sabine's nakedness, a contrast to the heat of his gaze. She drew a breath and arched again, offering her body to him. He descended, his mouth everywhere at once—breast, nipple, neck, clavicle, and breasts again. Where his lips were not, his hands roamed, pressing firmly, exploring, teasing—*claiming*.

Inside her, Sabine felt a low pressure flicker, pulse, and then begin to burn, rising like the simmer of water in a pot. She arched her body again, lifting from her hips this time. Her body surged up of its own accord, seeking the hardness she'd felt when they lay still.

He called her name again and she ignored him. A second

call, and she whimpered, irritated that he would try to engage her in conversation now. She hated the gap between their bodies. He was on his knees, leaning over her, and she wanted all of him, now, answering her rising need.

"Down," she cried breathlessly. Her hands left his shoulders and fell to his hips, fumbling ineffectually at the waistband of his trousers. "Come down."

"It's enough," he panted.

"It's not enough," she replied.

She peeled his waistcoat upward, away from the waist of his trousers, and dug her fingers between the dark wool and the cotton of his shirt, seeking some leverage. When she found her grip, she pulled with all of her might, forcing his knees down the bed and the hard weight of his body to settle on top of her.

He came down with an *oof*, holding perfectly still for a charged moment and then grinding into her, setting off a cascade of sensation that shimmered from her belly to the tips of her fingers and toes. She answered back by surging up again, seeking the sensation through layers of silk skirts, seeking to satisfy the burn. He pressed down, and she was rewarded with another cascade. She gasped and tried it again. They found a rhythm that felt familiar but also wondrously new.

Meanwhile, the pressure continued to build, threatening to boil over, but there was more; her body told her there was more, and she wanted it all.

It occurred to her that they were fully clothed. She was wearing her shoes, for God's sake. Her skirts were a constricting tangle around her legs.

"More," she mumbled against his mouth, the only word she could manage.

He growled and scooped her up, gathering her beneath him. He rocked once to the left and rolled, transferring himself beneath with her on top, balancing astride him.

Sabine blinked and raised up on her hands, shaking the tangle of her falling coiffeur away from her face. She stared down at him and frowned.

No, she thought.

She used the position to yank her skirts free from her legs, hiking them up around her hips.

She shook her head, *No*, and slid back to the mattress, landing beside him on her back.

He snapped his head to the side, frowning into her face, and she frowned back. She reached over and grabbed a handful of his shirt. Heaving, she hauled him back on top of her. Stoker resisted for half a second and then rolled with a groan, mounting her in one swift movement. Sabine sighed in relief.

"*Please*," she breathed, pressing her hips up. She raised a leg against his hip, and his hand locked down on her stockinged knee, pressing it up. That felt exactly right. It canted her center more firmly against his hardness. She raised the other knee.

"Sabine, have some mercy," he ground out. "I'm warning you."

"I'm warning you," she said between kisses.

He kissed her hard, like he was trying to put the words back in her mouth. When she turned her head to breathe, he followed her, dropping his head on the pillow beside her face. She kissed the whirl of his ear, his earlobe, the place where his neck met his hair. Meanwhile, their lower bodies rocked together, building toward something, something. Sabine marveled that it was not impeded when she hitched up her skirts. How much better, she wondered, with their clothing removed? He'd ripped her dress to expose her breasts, but would he dare push her skirts entirely up? And what of his trousers? She moaned in frustration, wanting to feel him and love him and receive him and not work out the logistics of how to undress.

She opened her eyes, blinking in the dimness. His face was inches from hers, his eyes squeezed shut, his expression one of restraint and also pleasure. She loved the sight of his face in every mood. She'd watched him sleep, she'd watched him speak, she'd watched him glower. Tonight she'd watched him lose his mind, just a little. There was no expression that she didn't adore—even this one, even holding back what they both wanted, what frightened him as much as it thrilled him. But Sabine was not frightened. Sabine was impatient.

She tipped her face down, hovering her lips directly over his ear. "Stoker," she whispered softly. "Stoker, I love you. Stoker, I—"

In a flash Stoker's body went tense and still, the words sinking in. With stiff, jerky movements, he shifted up from the pillow, hovering over her.

"Oh," she said, thrilled by how forcefully he squared himself over her. She smiled up at him, squeezing his hips with her knees, pulling her legs closer to her chest. Every wiggle brought his body more intimately pressed against hers. She felt heat and sweetness and solidness all at once.

Stoker let out a moan, kissed her hard once more, and then reared back, pulling the buttons free on his trousers. The fabric fell away and he dropped forward, catching himself with one arm, and using his other hand to sweep up her skirts.

"Oh," she said again, realizing that *now* it would happen. Finally. Now. Her accelerated heart sped even faster, threatening to pound into one long, unbroken constriction.

She breathed in and out deeply, trying to remain calm. He plunged his hands beneath her skirts and deftly slid her drawers to the side. The strum of his fingers across her body introduced a brighter, more lovely burn, and she cried out again.

She wanted another strum, she wanted so much more of everything, but he was fumbling with his trousers again, taking himself in hand, and then he dropped down, burying his face in her neck, and pressing inside her with one deep thrust.

Sabine cried out, shocked by the jab of pain amid something that otherwise shimmered with pleasure. Stoker froze. His sawing breath stopped.

She tried to turn, to see his face, but he burrowed deep against her neck. She stared at the ceiling, waiting for more pain or less pain or some other sensation that no one had ever mentioned. He was petrified inside her and above her and silent. For an indeterminate number of minutes, they hovered there, fraught and breathless, and Sabine realized that she could engage her brain again. The pleasure had abated.

It was not so terrible, the pain. Tight and new and nothing like the swirl of sensation and mounting . . . something that made her press and arch and beg him to reach this point.

She was confused by the cause and effect of her body's want and the resulting dissolution of all pleasure, and she was frustrated with Stoker for burying his head, departing from her for all practical purposes, in this of all moments.

But perhaps this was what he was trying to warn her against all along. This stabbing moment of pain? That made no sense; it was unpleasant but it was hardly worth demanding some jewel or service in exchange. All the lovely moments leading up to it had been an equal trade in her view, and even now, it was not terrible, being so very close to him, locked in his muscled arms, with the glorious heavy weight of him pressing her down, safe and secure, into the bed, his face against her neck. It was so far and away, more intimate than their long talks or even the emotional theatrics they had navigated tonight. All of it was essential, she thought, including this, *especially this*, and she would tell him all about it, if ever he—

All of a sudden Sabine realized that the pain had subsided to a tiny sting of sensation, and the flicker of pleasure had returned, now rapidly overshadowing. She breathed deeply and moved her right leg, pressing Stoker's hip with her knee.

She'd meant to animate him, but instead she set off a spill of sensation inside her own body. She squeezed again. Now she pressed the other knee. More—better, so much better.

Sabine experimented with a small thrust, raising her hips as before.

Stoker swore into her neck when she did it, a long, breathy sound that ripped from somewhere deep inside him.

Sabine smiled and continued to move, delighted that the sensations had resumed and the pain was gone. After the third or fourth rock of her hips, Stoker's body answered back with a thrust of his own.

This, Sabine realized, was even better.

"Oh," she cried.

Against her neck, his breath had begun to saw in and out. His excitement stoked hers, and she felt herself get caught up in the thrilling mix of urgency and pleasure and the rising pressure of before. Stoker was up now, pressing above her slowly, inch by inch, centering over her while his hips thrusted.

He rose so slowly and evenly, she thought for a moment they had reinjured him, that his wound or ribs hurt, but then she caught sight of the expression on his face—an eye-closed twist of restraint against desire—and she realized he was invoking all of his strength to hold himself back.

"Stoker?" she panted.

His eyes remained shut.

"*Stoker?*" she repeated, her voice high and desperate.

"I'm sorry," he rasped.

"It's not a moment for sorrow," she managed. "Please."

He laughed without humor. "Do not say that."

"I will say it." She surged upward with her hips. "It's what I want. Stop restraining."

"You don't know what you want."

Now it was her turn to growl. "Do not *tell me* what I want." She grabbed him by the hips and moved his body in rhythm.

Something seemed to snap inside him. He didn't let go so much as hurtle forth. His thrusts increased in speed and strength; he fell against her bared breasts, slavering them with sucks and nips. If he kissed one, he touched the other. This attention shot a new jolt of desire through Sabine, and the drive of his body was suddenly, exactly, perfectly right. She heard herself cry out and call his name. She screamed *yes!* more times than strictly necessary, but she didn't care. Every care and inhibition and anxiety left her, pounded away by Stoker's body and the command he took of their combined pleasure.

His ferocity allowed her to lie back and receive and receive and receive, and her only thought was that she could take him forever—except they were building toward something that had a definite end; she could sense that now. She knew it as surely as she knew the next thrust would take her another rung higher.

She matched Stoker thrust for thrust, reaching for each rung, delirious with the anticipation. When finally, she reached the top, Sabine experienced an explosion inside her body—an actual explosion; why hadn't her friends been more clear about this?—and she surged up one final time, floating on a mist of sensation and release and languid, molten *yes* . . .

Stoker sensed her release and finally opened his eyes, watching her with something like disbelief, but the look of rapture on her face was clearly too much; he tore his gaze away and drove into her again, only a few more thrusts, and then he cried out, seeming to float on the same mist before he collapsed on top of her, panting.

By some miracle Sabine managed to muster the strength to toss her boneless arms across his back and hold him, opening and closing her hands on fistfuls of his loose shirt.

"Well done," she said after a moment. "I think. Would you say, Jon? Well done?"

"Oh my God," he breathed, and he rolled off her and lay beside her, staring at the ceiling. He fastened the buttons of his trousers quickly, efficiently, without sitting up. He jerked his waistcoat back in place.

"You may cover yourself," he said softly. He reached out with a weak hand to tug ineffectually at the side of her skirts.

Sabine dropped an open hand over her eyes and rolled her head back and forth on the pillow.

Now this? she thought as her levitating heart sank.

CHAPTER TWENTY-ONE

———————————————

Stoker had ravished her, plain and simple. He'd worn his boots—*his bloody boots were on still*—as he'd pummeled her virgin body. He'd ripped her silk gown like a lunatic.

They were in a strange bed, in an anonymous room, with only a low fire, no basin to wash, no wine to dull the pain, no lady's maid to attend her.

He'd ravished her. As he'd known he would, given half the chance. And now it was true.

It felt wrong; he'd known it was wrong. But self-control was but a faint notion in the corner of his mind, a discarded tool he'd forgotten how to use. And yet while he was in the moment, it had also been . . . glorious.

He sat up, cringing at the pain in his rib. He deserved the pain. He deserved to suffer a relapse and perish by morning. He deserved the bloody Duke of Wrest to seek him out and shoot him with his own gun.

"Will you lie back down with me for a moment?" she asked quietly, reaching for his hand.

"Let me call a maid to attend you," he said.

"I don't want a maid."

"Your dress is in ribbons."

"So it is," she said.

She sounded irritated. He glanced at her, trying to seek out her face. The fire had burned nearly to ash and the room hung in shadows. He was glad; he could not look at what he'd done to her dress. He didn't want to look at her body. He'd feasted on the sight of her body like a blind man who had just been given sight. He dropped an arm over his eyes, trying to erase the image of how he must have looked, staring down at her.

Sabine said, "It was worth it. To me."

"What was?" He struggled to follow the conversation, and he owed it to her to behave like an articulate person in this moment. He owed her whatever she wanted.

"The ruined dress. I'm not sure how I will get home, but perhaps if we hide here until—"

"Elisabeth can loan you a dress," he said and then he pressed his arm against his eye sockets until he saw stars, realizing what he'd said. He made an anguished sound.

"*What?*" Sabine demanded. Now she sounded angry.

"I can't face Elisabeth with this request. I've delivered so many girls to her who required new dresses because some . . . brute had ripped away their very clothes."

"Stoker, we will not entertain this line of thought," she said tightly.

"It's not a way of thinking, Sabine. It's the precise animal behavior I have fought my entire life. I am no better. I am the same. Elisabeth was a fool to think she could truss me up and send me to school and pretend that I have any place acquainting myself with well-bred ladies."

Sabine gave a shout and bolted from the bed so quickly, Stoker jumped too. They squared off across the twisted coverlet and decimated pillows.

"That," she said, gesturing to the bed, "was too . . . wonderful for me to allow you to proclaim it a . . . a gap in your character." She glared at him, yanking up her corset and clutching her bodice to her chest. "You did not inflict animal behavior on me, Stoker, we *made love*. You are my husband, I am your wife. We are realizing our . . . relationship in an unorthodox way, but we are married. We have spent the past six weeks together, and I have said that I love you and I mean it. There is a world of difference between making love to your wife and attacking a strange girl."

"Did we make love?" he asked. "Or did I go out of my head, risking your safety, paying no regard to injury, spoiling your dress. I . . . I unfastened my breeches like a randy soldier with only three minutes to spare and a guinea for your trouble."

"Is that *really* what happened?" she challenged, pulling pins from her hair. He'd never seen it long and loose, and he was momentarily distracted by the sight of it dropping around her shoulders in black rolling waves.

She smiled. "You see, I am happy. We've shared this

moment. I am taking down my hair because I am a real woman who is irritated by hairpins after four hours, and I feel as if we have passed the point of your not seeing me perfectly coiffed and kempt and pilloried by pins."

"I don't understand," he said, staring at her hair.

"At the threat of *assuming* what you think, Stoker, I believe that you have positioned me on this pedestal in your mind—perfect and tidy and proper, but that is a character, not a human woman. I am not perfect. I am not tidy and I have very little use for propriety. Obviously. We are learning our authentic selves."

"My authentic self is not for your knowledge."

"If you withhold yourself from me in that way," she said, "we are doomed."

"Then doom it is," he said, his heart ripping in two. "Just look at you. Look what I've done to you." He gestured to her dress.

"You must forget about the gown," she sighed. "Perhaps you will buy me a new one. I have been told that you are among the richest men in England."

"Is that what you want?" This, he understood.

Sabine screamed and reached to tug off her slipper. "No!" she cried, hurling the shoe at his head. She took a deep breath. "Stoker? Did you hear me cry for help in bed? Or for you to stop?"

He thought back, his face burning at the memory of his passion. It had been a wave of glorious relief and cresting guilt. A blur of her nakedness and his red-hot desire. He'd been out of his head.

She slid from the bed with a thump. "Did you hear me shout, 'Stop, Stoker, please, I beg of you?' Did I lie there like a carp on a plate, quietly enduring while you pounded away?"

He stared at her, distracted by the terrible memory of him "pounding away."

"No!" she shouted, rounding on the bed. "I did not. What did I do instead?"

He watched her limp to him, her gait uneven in one shoe. She stooped to remove the remaining slipper, and he braced, ready to dodge.

"No, truly," she continued. "I will not provide the answers to this. I want you to tell me. What were my reactions when we were in bed together?" She nodded to the scrambled bed. "Just now. Not ten minutes ago. I would like to hear it."

"You . . . kissed me," he said.

"Did I? That's happened on three occasions now, hasn't it, so it hardly qualifies. Something *new*."

"You called my name."

"In horror?"

"Well—"

"Did I also say some version of, 'Please,' 'Yes,' 'Oh!' 'More'?"

Her voice was flat and matter-of-fact. It was almost comical the way she rattled off such intimate exclamations. But she did not look amused. She looked angry. Stoker endeavored to take her seriously, to answer her outrage, to be contrite. It was his fault entirely. And yet, he could not deny that she'd said these very things.

He ventured, "It's no excuse, but when you say these

things, Sabine, in the heat of passion, it magnifies my struggle to hold back."

"I believe that is the idea of succumbing to passionate lovemaking, Stoker. I am no authority—"

"Yes!" he agreed, "you were a virgin, and you've no idea—"

"What I was going to say was that I am no authority on anyone's pleasure but my own! I should like to be an authority on yours, but it would appear we must devote considerable time to assuaging your guilt instead."

"I have been broken," he said, turning away. He heard the hyperbole as it left his lips, but he couldn't stop. He *believed* the bloody hyperbole. "I am too broken for you."

"Do not," she said. Her voice was so vehement, he turned back. She marched across the room to a wardrobe on a far wall. Grabbing the knobs, she hurled it open and rifled through drawers and shelves, looking for—what? He could not say.

She pulled out a garment—a boy's morning jacket—and shoved it back inside. She resumed her search, speaking to the open furniture. "You asked me earlier not to pity you, and now I must ask you to refrain from pitying yourself."

"It's not pity, Sabine. I cannot describe my struggle beyond saying that I want what isn't decent. I don't come to the bed with no despair in my life—"

She spun around. "I know it doesn't warrant as much, but I was beaten for nine months by a sadistic uncle who is now trying to blow up England." She turned back to the wardrobe, pulled out what appeared to be an ivory choirboy's robe, and shoved it back.

"You said he never touched you in that way," Stoker said, rising from the bed.

"I suppose a slap across the face, or a fork to the hand, or a boot to the ribs is not horrible enough." She pulled out a small dark suit and shoved it back. She turned on him. "This room must belong to a miniature vicar."

Stoker held up a finger. "When I first came to you, you shrank away from me. I could barely lift my head from the pillow, I was completely harmless, and yet you resisted any closeness. Because of Dryden, you could not be crowded or trapped."

She closed the wardrobe and looked around the room. His jacket was in the middle of the rug in a wad, and she snatched it up and shoved into it. "Yes, *when you first came to me*, but then we *learned each other*. I saw, among other things, that you posed no threat. I found I *wanted* to be close to you. Now I find I *want* to be crowded and trapped by you."

He swore and turned away. She said the most incendiary things.

"I'm sorry but it's true."

"And what if mental damage caused by Dryden surfaces at a later day? What if a situation that you cannot yet conceive—my God, there are so many situations about which an innocent like you cannot conceive—triggers some memory that you have long hidden, something that will rise up and haunt you?"

"There is always that danger, I suppose," she conceded, "but this has not been my experience. It's been years, Stoker, and now I rarely think of Dryden."

"Except every day when you investigate him. We are here tonight because of Sir Dryden."

"Yes, but the investigation is meant to get rid of him so that I can return home."

"How will he haunt you after that?"

"Not at all, I hope!"

"There is a toughness about you, Sabine, but you are not invincible."

"Perhaps, but I am also not a victim," she shot back. "When you delivered me to London after our wedding, I went over and over what had happened in my mind. I walked the city from one end to the other, and while I walked, I reckoned with my father's death and my mother's decline and how Dryden took advantage of it all. I looked at each episode from every angle. Was I culpable? *No.* Could I have handled his aggression differently? Perhaps, but I was doing the best I could at the time. Would he have killed me if you hadn't come? Possibly."

"A conviction of treason is too good for him," Stoker mumbled.

Sabine pressed on, "But you did come, and I made the incredibly reckless and risky decision to leave home with a stranger rather than remain with a known tyrant. Perhaps that decision saved you and me both, and what luck. But I have not buried or disregarded my memories of Dryden. You must trust me when I say that I have reckoned with it and moved on. It was the long walks, I think. When my meanderings turned from angry thoughts and tearful resentment to writing and drawing, the healing began."

"Of course it did," he sighed. "You're so . . . practical."

"Oh yes, I'm so very practical," she said, but the words came out almost like a purr.

She had settled on a window seat and was running her fingers through her hair, settling it over her shoulder in a shiny cascade of black. She glanced at him and raised a suggestive eyebrow. She said no more, but her message was clear. How practical had it been to make love—here, now? How practical had it been to find themselves shut up in a room while revelers danced downstairs? And yet she claimed it was exactly what she wanted. Stoker looked at the tussled bed, her torn dress. *Could she actually want this?*

"I just don't know why," Sabine sighed, "all of this must be so painfully tragic. I've told you in no uncertain terms that I am unharmed. Stop telling me how I'm meant to feel, when I could not be clearer about what I want, and when and how."

"What about what I want?" he gritted out.

"Stoker," she said, her voice weary.

"What?"

"Tell me what you want. I'm waiting. Tell me."

He sucked in a breath, wholly unprepared to name anything he wanted—not from her, not from anyone. He'd learned long ago that what he wanted did not matter so much as keeping ahead of what he did not want. And he did not want to hurt her, or frighten her, or lose her.

"Wait, let me guess," she said, sliding from the window. "You want to buy me a diamond ring in exchange for our lovemaking. You want to be my chaste bosom friend and never allude to or repeat what just happened. You want to leave Belgravia and buy a villa in Portugal and sail away."

He wanted none of those things—unless they were what she wanted. But she did not like him to assume what she wanted. He lit on the last suggestion and said, "The attempt on my life has cast a stain on the notion of living in Portugal," he said.

She frowned. "Well. You cannot live in Portugal because someone tried to kill you. And you cannot make love to your wife because—"

"Don't say it, Sabine," he said tiredly. "Whatever it was, don't say it. You cannot possibly know. I don't want you to know." He stooped to pick up her shoe.

She huffed out a breath and dropped her face in her hands. "I'm sorry," she breathed. "I fantasized about this moment since . . . well, since our first kiss, and no part of the fantasy was to convince you afterward that no *crime* had been committed. You are only trying to protect me. I know this. But I have told you on more than one occasion that you may not decide things *for me*. If I tell you I am displeased, you may believe it. If I tell you I want more, wilder, harder—"

His head snapped up.

She shrugged. "Then you may be certain that more, wilder, harder is what I want."

He walked to the bed and dropped the shoes. He sat, holding his head in his hands.

"The question of what you want," she said, crossing to him, "is valid and perhaps what remains unanswered. If you have no desire to toss me down and have your way with me, I cannot compel you to do it."

He laughed a miserable laugh, squeezing handfuls of hair in his hands. It was, of course, the *only* thing he wanted. But he could not bring himself to say the words. He'd spent a lifetime trying never to admit it. She was asking him to undo years of restraint. His notion of himself as a—well, if not a gentleman, then a decent man, was so very imbedded in the idea that restraint was the thing that separated him from his mother's lovers and the men from whom he'd stolen away countless abused girls.

And now to have the most beautiful woman, with the highest spirit and the cleverest mind, the woman he desired most of all, ask him to let it all go?

There was too much at stake.

They sat on the bed, not touching, side by side. The room was almost entirely dark. A chill set in, and she pulled his coat about her, snuggling. She reached for her shoes and slipped them on.

"How will we leave here?" she asked, ever practical. "Do you think the ball has ended?"

"Who can say? Obviously, we cannot go down. You are only half-dressed and I cannot run the risk of colliding with the duke."

"What will you do about him?"

"I don't know. My investigator should arrive within the week. Before I knew he was my *bloody father*, I'd hoped to make a charge to the police and walk away. But now—? It's something to sort out, isn't it?"

"Do you still believe you are in no danger?"

"No. But now that he knows I am in possession of a wife—"

"I believe the term he used was *doxie*."

"A name by which you will never be called. I'll kill him myself, if he insults you again. Now that he knows about you, I should like some security detail with you at all times, Sabine."

"Not when I'm working on the smuggling investigation, surely?"

"Sabine—" he sighed.

"No." She stood up. "Why should he send someone to kill me? Honestly? I'm not one of the richest men in England."

"We will . . . come to some accord. Together. We will compromise."

"*No security*," she stated.

"That is not how compromise works."

"Perhaps we can arrange some *barter*, then," she said suggestively, and he raised his head. She was padding across the room to the door, her long hair swaying down the back of his coat. He watched her move in the dark through narrowed eyes. A small pulse of fresh desire flickered in his belly, as he knew it would. He was afraid. *Hope* always made him afraid.

She unlocked the door and cracked it, peering out. "I hear music," she said. "Perhaps we can slip down the servants' stairs?"

"I don't want anyone to see you, including servants."

"Do *you* want to see me?" she asked.

Always, he thought. He said, "You think I'm a prude," and barked an ironic laugh.

"I think you aspire to prudishness."

"Bloody hell, Sabine. You shock me with the things you say. Sometimes you are very wise. But sometimes—? You have no idea."

"If you are not an aspirational prude, then take me out the window of this room," she said.

"What?"

She walked to the window and shoved the drapes aside. Moonlight flooded the room. She squinted in the silvery light and peered out. The sight of her there, draped in his coat, with her hair down and the remains of her dress hanging about her, took his breath away. A wave of lust surged inside him. She glanced away from the window and caught him in the hot look. She smiled and swept her hair over her shoulder. She raised her chin.

"It's only the alley below," she said levelly. "We can steal away under the cover of darkness and send a boy from the mews for your carriage."

"I'm not taking you out the window," he said.

"Because your ribs are hurting?" She made a weak imitation of concern.

"Because I'm not stealing my half-dressed wife down the side of a house at midnight and hustling her through a sodden alley."

"Because you are a prude."

"Sabine," he warned.

She reached out and jostled the latch on the window. It separated with a small creak. She pressed her fingertips against the glass, testing the give. It swung open.

"But perhaps you can no longer manage it," she said, kneeing onto the window seat. "Because you gave up rescuing girls when you married me."

"I cannot be manipulated in this way," he informed her.

"Elisabeth said you'd never come and gone from Denby House by way of the door until now."

He watched her plant her hands on the sill and lean out, examining the side of the house. "Oh, but there is a trellis. You needn't *steal me away*," she said. "I can climb."

He watched her sit squarely in the window seat, whipping the tails of his coat out of her way. He waited, determined to call her bluff. When she lifted her legs to swing out her feet, he swore and strode to her.

"Don't," he dared her.

"We cannot hide in this room all night." She began buttoning his jacket over her corset. "You've already said you will not subject Elisabeth to my depravity."

"You are not depraved," he said.

"Should I climb down *facing* the trellis or with my back to the trellis?" She scooted toward the sill.

Stoker made a growling noise and scooped her up. Every nerve ending in his body tingling at the feel of her in his arms again.

"Careful," he said, the only warning, and summarily pitched her, belly down, over his shoulder.

Sabine made an amused yelp and grabbed for his middle. She grazed his scar and he grunted.

"Sorry," she called. "Am I too heavy?"

"No," he said. She was too much of so many things, none of which prevented him from hauling her out this widow. He looped a hand around the backs of her knees.

"Hold still," he said, biting down against the pain in his ribs.

Sabine made an excited sound of laughter and anticipation and wiggled.

Chapter Twenty-Two

Perry and Bridget were waiting up for them when Sabine and Stoker reached Belgrave Square. Although Sabine had draped herself almost in Stoker's lap in the carriage, they'd ridden in sleepy silence. The dog's barking and Perry's horror over her loose hair and ruined dress were both jarring and unwelcome. Sabine scooped up the excited dog and thrust her at Perry, hoping the two would cancel each other out.

In the end she was given no choice but to allow Perry to attend her in her upstairs bedroom. She could not navigate the ripped dress or mangled corset alone, and she had ivy in her hair. For once the maid did not drill her with questions. She chatted pleasantly and helped her from the dress, agreeing it could not be mended. She brushed out Sabine's hair and plaited it in a single fat braid down her back. After she helped Sabine into a nightgown, Perry moved to turn down the bed.

"Don't bother," Sabine said. "I will sleep downstairs to-night."

"In the study, miss?" asked Perry.

"No," said Sabine simply. She handed the dog to her a second time with an imploring look.

"Very good, miss," said Perry and she bustled away. Sabine drew a deep breath, took up a candle, and descended the stairs to her old bedroom.

Stoker was in bed, reading correspondence. He looked up, his gaze capturing her eyes for a moment, then dropping to her thin white nightgown, her bare feet, and up again. His expression could not have been more alarmed if an elk had walked into the room.

Sabine had already made up her mind not to discuss her intrusion in favor of simply doing it. They'd already discussed too much, for too long, with too little progress. She'd been unforgivably rude, heartless, really, not to mention brazen and demanding. If he had deserved it, well, it did not mean he enjoyed it.

She approached the bed and blew out the candle. The room fell to half-light. She settled the candle on the floor and regarded the bed. He was situated dead in the center, frozen in place, gaping at her. He wore a dressing gown open at the throat, and spectacles.

"I did not know you wore spectacles," she said. She drew back the covers. If he did not move, she would have only a sliver of space.

Can you scoot? The words were on the tip of her tongue, but—less talking. She was determined. When it came right down to it, she was certain he would make room rather than bump up against her.

She turned to sit on the mattress, her intention clear.

"You mean to kill me?" he rasped. "After I survived the morgue and the stabbing?"

She swung her legs beneath the covers and fell back on the pillow. She squinted at the letters in his hand. It was the report from Portugal by his investigator. "You will not die," she said.

"I am already dead," he mumbled, dropping the letters and spectacles on the nightstand. He turned on his side, facing her.

She had prepared a brief speech. She turned her head on the pillow. "I've not asked you how long you will stay here."

"You ask me every day if I am preparing to go."

"Perhaps, but I've not asked you how long you will stay," she repeated. To her horror, a lump was forming in her throat. She coughed. "I've asked many other things of you, but pride and the value I put on my own independence prevents me from asking this. As long as you remain, this is what I want. To share your bed. Even if it's only for a time. You said that the nature of our marriage would change if we made love. That has happened, and I agree. And I should like this to be part of the change. Do you mind so terribly?"

Her heart pounded. She was certain that he did not mind; yet it was one thing to be overcome by passion and quite another to deliberately slide into bed with some measure of calm.

She'd vowed she would not launch into a lecture if he began down the road of wanting her too much or not trusting himself, etcetera, etcetera. She would not indulge him, but she was weary of all of the talking.

He stared at her, saying nothing, and the thought *I have no idea what I'm doing* flashed in her brain. Thank God she'd fallen in love with a man whose footing was as uncertain as her own.

"Sabine, I have wanted you in this bed every night that you occupied the chair instead."

"Well, then, we're in perfect accord."

"We are *not* in perfect accord."

"But we are in bed," she said.

"Where else am I to go?"

To the Courtlands'. To your own suite of rooms in Regent Street. To Cassin in Yorkshire. To Joseph in County Durham. To anywhere your ship will sail you.

There were so many places for him to go, but he remained and it felt significant, just as Mary Boyd had said.

"Did you discover anything new," she asked, "rereading your investigators' letters now that you know about the duke?" Her leg slid against his beneath the covers, and she was intrigued by the feel of hair and skin and tight muscle.

He cleared his throat.

"May I read them again?"

He handed them to her, the movement jostling them closer in the bed.

After a moment he said, "I cannot determine what Wrest

thought to gain from having me killed. I'd not acknowledged the claim of his solicitor that he was my father. I'd not even written the man back. I never corroborated his claim, even verbally, and certainly not in some document he could show at the reading of my will. I thought he was a charlatan—you saw my shock when I realized that he was likely my actual father. He had no proof. There is no record of my birth. I don't even know my birthday."

Sabine gasped and set down the letters. "You don't," she said.

He shrugged.

"We shall pick a day. What day would you like?"

"I have survived this long without a birthday. I see no direct need to fabricate one at this late date."

"Think on it," she said, taking the letters up again. She began to read. She could feel him watching her. She raised a few questions, asking about details that confused her, and they discussed the duke's motive until his bedside candle was nearly gutted. It was the same discussion they might have had if he'd been in the bed and she curled up in the chair; only now they enjoyed the intimacy of entangled legs and shared warmth.

He was tenser than normal. He paused before answering her questions, speaking haltingly as if they held the conversation underwater or on the moon—somewhere requiring careful balance and no guarantee of the next breath.

When she tossed the letters onto the floor and yawned, he said, "I'm careful not to drop my correspondence in piles around the room, if you don't mind."

She yawned again. "It will still be there in the morning, I assure you, and you may whisk it away to your fastidiously filed order." She turned to face him. "You may kiss me good-night."

"You are killing me," he said gravely, all trace of teasing gone. He sounded as if he truly believed she was doing him harm.

She ignored the agony in his voice, ignored the pang of guilt in her own chest, and leaned in to kiss a playful nip on his lips. He clamped a hand down on her waist, and Sabine felt a jolt of anticipation. But he merely tipped her forward to meet his lips and kissed her again, a more thorough, closed-eye kiss, and he rolled her back. He released her and blew out the struggling candle on the table beside the bed. The room went dark.

"Good-night," she whispered.

Stoker let out a belabored sigh as if she'd said, "Enjoy the dungeon."

Some hours later, the dawn sky just pinkening through the break in the curtain, Sabine awakened to Stoker's hand rubbing up and down her arm. She blinked at the ceiling and turned on the pillow.

"I've awakened you," he whispered. "I'm sorry."

"What's happened? Is your wound—?"

He laughed a wicked sort of laugh. She squinted at him. "Did you sleep?" she asked.

"No," he said.

"Why not?"

"Because I have you in my bed."

"It is still a bed, despite my presence."

"Sabine?" he breathed. A question.

"Oh," she said, her heart rate picking up.

She felt for his hand between them and took it up.

He said, "In view of what we discussed after we—"

He swore.

He started again. "What we discussed *after*, I should like to have another go. That is, I can only guess you would not have crawled into this bed if you were not amenable to—"

"I am amenable, Stoker." She slid her leg over the top of his, tracing his calf with the arch of her foot. It was an unbelievable luxury. She should have gotten into bed with him weeks ago.

"I have given it hours of thought," he said, "and I am going to endeavor to approach it from a less raw, more measured sort of way."

"Oh," she said, her foot going still. This did not sound like any fun at all.

"I think I shall feel less conflicted about it, if I try to be . . . refined."

Sabine tried to think of any "refined" element of Stoker's character that she found explicitly arousing. He was very well spoken and well-read, which she liked. He looked rather adorable in the spectacles. He had been handsome in the suit he'd worn to the ball, although she far preferred it when his jacket was on the floor and his trousers had been around his hips.

She cleared her throat. He was awaiting some response.

Already, this disappointed her. It was less exciting for him to wait.

"Whatever you wish," she whispered.

He moved in to kiss her then, one slow, soft kiss. He pulled back and looked down at her expectantly. *Survived it!* she wanted to say, but he descended again. Another slow soft kiss. This melded into more kisses, still slow but less soft, and she had the thought that this might be rather nice. It was nice in the way that plum-bolster pudding was nice after spicy soup. Or a rainy day when you were too tired to go out.

She reached for him, hoping to recapture some of the ardor of the ball, but he caught her hands and pressed them to his chest, holding them there as if she was taking his pulse.

And then he touched her. His free hand descended onto her face in the way a widow may grievingly touch a corpse in a casket one final time.

Sabine blinked and jerked her head, trying to keep his fingers out of her eye and ear. Finally, reverently, he moved his hand to her shoulder.

Now he will touch me, she thought, and he did touch her, but it was a slow, soft glancing sort of *drag* down her arm through the sleeve of her gown. He touched her the way a concerned mother might touch a child's bruise. Not so much a caress as a gentle assessment.

Sabine tried to wiggle her hands free, to reach for him, but he held them firm against his chest. This spiked her irritation, and she jerked away, opening and closing her hands, wiggling fingers. She settled her hands on his shoulders, determined to knead the way around his neck, but it felt strange and out of balance for her to frantically paw at his body when he continued the glacial, measured smear of his hands up and down one fully explored arm.

She let her hands go limp around his neck and tried to focus on kissing him, but now she had begun to itch. Her hair was itching, and she could not seem to find the correct spot. Now her wrist itched. Her leg.

Next her foot fell asleep. Now she was hot, kicking off covers, and then cold, scrambling beneath them. Stoker bore it all patiently—although, was he sweating?—and she finally forced herself to flop onto her back and simply allow him to rub and mush-mouth kiss and devote considerable energy to holding any body part below his chest *away* from her.

When at last he moved to lift the hem of her gown and settle over her, she welcomed the weight of him, because at least it was strong and heavy and she could trace the muscles of his back with her hands, which she had fantasized about repeating since their very first kiss.

He entered her with the slow press of a dull spade digging into dry earth. Sabine winced, but accepted him, wondering how this could be satisfying for him in any way. It wasn't unpleasant so much as a waste of their time in the bed. They could be tearing at each other's bodies as they'd done in Denby House, burning with pleasure—they could be sleeping, for that matter—instead, they were *refined*.

When finally, he finished, rolling off her to breathe

deeply at the ceiling, his hand sought out hers beneath the covers. It was, for Sabine, the high point. She had the idle thought that she would not mind asking for a piece of jewelry in trade for this experience. Or perhaps a new drafting kit. Or—

She drifted off to sleep before her wish list was complete and dreamt of their first time.

CHAPTER TWENTY-THREE

Stoker said the next day that he would simply apply to the Duke of Wrest's front door and ask for an audience. Sabine was resistant to a security detail or even Stoker himself hounding her every step. He would not feel easy about her safety until the strange, unexplained threat posed by the duke was solved.

And he simply wanted to know. He'd been casual about the attack when he thought the duke was a desperate old man, wasting money on a mercenary in the madcap murder of a stranger. But now there were deeply personal layers of complication that made the murder attempt not only dangerous, but haunting, as well.

Stoker had to know.

Sabine, not surprisingly, insisted upon accompanying him to the duke's home in Chelsea. They waited until afternoon, when they felt the hungover duke might be the clearest-headed, pounding on his peeling front door at two o'clock. They were admitted by an unhappy female servant, a woman-of-all-work by the looks of it, and led through a dingy vestibule to a dank parlor with water-stained walls and threadbare furnishings.

For half an hour they waited with no tea and no word. Sabine sat formally beside Stoker, beautiful in her yellow day dress, a gloved hand on his knee. With her other hand she held a handkerchief to her nose. The odor in the parlor was an eye-watering mix of chamber pot and unaired mildew. Twice Stoker asked Sabine if she would like to be taken home. She refused, and it was impossible to hide his relief.

Six weeks ago he could not have imagined relying on anyone to help him interrogate the man responsible for his half-dead arrival in a morgue—but to rely on Sabine Noble Stoker? The woman he held apart from anything dark or mean or haunted? It was unthinkable. But Sabine had made it very clear that he should not think on her behalf. If she wished to accompany him, he should not tell her that it was not really her wish. The problem with spending any time at all with a living, breathing person (rather than the idealized refuge built in your own mind) is that they thought for themselves.

Oh but her thoughts. She had asked a million questions about his boyhood association with the duke. She had hypothesized and speculated and helped Stoker anticipate any number of things the man might say. It had been useful. It had made Wrest seem less like a phantom and more like a nuisance, a problem to be solved.

Stoker had the urge to pluck her hand from his knee and kiss the small circle of exposed wrist below the pearl button of her glove. But who would welcome a kiss in a room the color of a scab that smelled like Newgate Prison? He was trying so very hard to be civilized.

"I was waiting for you to lose heart and go," said a voice at the door, and they looked up. Sabine removed the kerchief from her nose.

Stoker stood. He didn't know why. The old duke studied him.

"Little Johnny Stoker, all grown up," the duke mused. "Made good."

"Why were you waiting for us to lose heart and go?" Stoker asked. He felt odd standing while Sabine sat, and he reclaimed his seat. The duke swayed drunkenly in the doorway. His clothes were a better fit than the terrible formal suit from the ball, although he was again wrinkled and smudged. His watery eyes suggested drink, even in the middle of the day.

"I'm a very busy man," the duke said dryly, an obvious joke. He appeared, in every way, idle.

"Last night you wished to speak to me."

"Yes," he said, "and we spoke. I wanted you to know you were sired by a duke."

"That remains to be seen," said Stoker. He studied the man, looking for resemblances in his ruddy, hunched form. Sabine said she'd seen it now that she knew his claim might be true. The green eyes, the expanse of their shoulders. The duke was hunched and thick, but the shape was the same. His nose, his hairline.

"And you wish to . . . claim me as your bastard and challenge the law that forbids inheritance by an illegitimate son, is that it?"

"That depends," said the duke, stepping into the parlor. "How inclined are you to rescue me from my most current run of bad luck?"

Stoker and Sabine looked around the sagging room. *Bad luck?* Sabine brought the kerchief back to her nose.

"There will be no bailout," Stoker drawled. "Not from me."

The duke slapped his knee. "The devil you say! Well, we have nothing to discuss."

"On the contrary," said Stoker. "There are several more things I wish to know."

The duke ignored him and made a show of stepping to the side to gesture down the corridor. "The butler has the day off, but you may show yourselves out."

"Sit down, Sauly," Stoker commanded.

The duke's watery eyes expanded. "I'll not take orders from a whoreson. Not in my own home."

"If you do not sit down and answer my questions," Stoker said menacingly, "I will twist your arm behind your humped back, and we will learn how far the bone will bend until it snaps."

"You wish to speak?" asked the duke. "Fine. Speak. I cannot see what more there is to say." He backed into the wall and began inching to the side. "Perhaps that that mother of yours was a nutte—"

"You will not speak of my mother in unkind terms."

"Ha! Would that she had never *spoken to me* with unkindness! I was her best customer. I was pleasant to her brat—that's you, by the by. I set her up in a little room in Blackhall, remember? And yet she tossed me out, time and again. She'd move me along for the next bloke without a backward glance—"

Stoker shoved up. "I said I would not hear insults against my mother."

"And why not?" spat the duke. "You'll not stand there with a straight face and claim she was more than a common whore, would you? And you, her silent, soulful boy. I don't care how rich you've become. I've seen the pit from whence you came. I've seen you fight other whores for food.

"And now, here you are," he continued, "with your pretty wife, casting smug glances around my house as if you are *superior?* You forget yourself, Johnny." He made a sound of disgust.

To Sabine, he said, "Did you know that when Marie first showed him to me as an infant, he was so covered in flea bites, I thought he had the pox?"

Sabine rose to stand beside Stoker. He turned to her as if in a daze. They locked eyes. *Let's go*, he wanted to say.

Take my hand, he begged in his head. *Take any part of me. Deliver me.*

Subjecting her to this man went against every wish he'd ever held for her, but he couldn't have come without her. But perhaps that would have been a better plan. To simply release any thought or speculation or question from this part of his life and stay the bloody hell away.

He knew now why he'd been so ambivalent about the duke's original overtures. He hadn't wanted to remember any detail of his mother's myriad men, real or imagined. He'd hated those men. He hated this man.

"Your Grace," said Sabine levelly, "I think perhaps Jon wonders what has become of you. Clearly, you are . . . bitter and out of funds. What has happened, in thirty years?" She looked around.

"What's happened?" he asked. "*What's happened?* Bills and debts and money lenders have happened. The property and farmland that was meant to sustain me, sent me to debtor's prison! I was brought up to believe a great fortune awaited me, but that money goes to repairs and tenants and blights and taxes, taxes, taxes—so many bloody taxes. My father installed an idiot manager who bankrupted our seat in Devon. I hired a steward who was a liar and a thief. I had a run of bad luck at the card table. Women require money. Horses require money. The obligations of a dukedom require clothes and carriages and staff. From where is it all meant to come, I ask you?"

"I see," surmised Sabine. "It has all been someone else's fault."

Stoker looked at the duke. "What of your family?"

He waved the question away. "Wife—dead. No children, thank God. When I die, the title may go to a distant cousin in America."

"Have you asked him for a loan?"

Another dismissive wave, Stoker said, "You have."

But now Stoker wanted to be clear. "Did you really believe that *I* would deliver you? When you were such an unreliable figure in my mother's life? When you knew you had a son, and yet allowed us to carry on living in a brothel?"

"But this is where whores and their spawn *live*," said the duke. "In a brothel."

Stoker lunged. The duke's eyes bulged and he tried to slide right. Stoker grabbed him by the jacket and hauled him off the floor. Holding him eye to eye, he said, "My mother loved you. I'm glad I did not truly know you, because it would have taken no effort for me to love you, too. Whatever your financial woes, you had more than she ever did, and you gave her pennies and broke her heart. How dare you come after me for money now."

"I will do as I please, and you'll have no say in it," the duke gurgled. "Put me down or I will call the authorities. You may not assault a peer of the realm. Rank still means something in this count—"

"You'll report me?" scoffed Stoker. "You'll report me." He shoved him deeper into the wall. "I've a sworn statement, *Your Grace*, from a man called Roberto Giuseppina, who said you paid him £250 to stab me in the spleen and leave me for dead in Portugal."

The duke's cracked mouth fell open and his red face went purple. Stoker shoved once more and then released him, turning away as he slid down the wall.

"Now . . . now you're making up slanderous lies!" blustered the duke.

"A sworn statement," repeated Stoker, shouting now. "And a scar in my side and a month of doctor's care to corroborate it. Tell me, where did you get £250? And why, when you are clearly living in penury, would you spend it on a mercenary? I had not thought of *Sauly New* in thirty years, and good riddance. Did you believe I named you in my will?"

"No," spat the duke, "you could be named in mine!"

"Ha!" scoffed Stoker. "To inherit what? This squalor?" He threw out his arms.

"The title, you ungrateful, self-important gutter rat!"

"How can a bastard inherit a title?"

"And what if I say we were married for a time?"

"My mother never married," stated Stoker. The thought of his mother as a duchess was a cruel joke.

"Think of what an enterprising young man could do with an ancient title!" the duke boomed. "Think of your wife. She could be a duchess. Your children would inherit piles of money from you, and from me, they would inherit entrée into the highest rungs of society."

"You're hobnobber with nothing higher than the privy pipe, Sauly, so spare us the suggestion of societal triumph. There was no marriage, and there is no deal. And if you ever threaten me or my family again—in person or with a hired man—I will turn in my evidence of the murder plot and then come back and kill you myself."

"You'll never see the marriage document if I'm dead!" Wrest threatened.

"You and your phantom license may rot in hell for all I care. Stay away from me and stay away from my wife. Do not mistake my seriousness, *Your Grace*."

"Oh, why not simply kill me now?" the duke bellowed, rolling against the wall, turning his face to the plaster. "Run me through, see if I have a care. See if anyone in the world will care."

"I won't kill you," said Stoker, reaching into his pocket for a £20 note, "for two reasons. First, I'm not a murderer, and second, I owe you one significant debt. You taught me the alphabet and gave me old newspapers, once upon a time. Literacy has made all the difference." He flung the money at the old man.

"Eh?" asked the duke, craning around to swat the air for the fluttering money.

"That's it, Wrest. No more, so do not make trouble for me, on threat of prison or the noose. I'm preparing my statement today and sealing it. It will go by private courier to the authorities if ever I hear so much as a gurgle in my direction."

"Get out!" shouted the duke, and Sabine stepped forward, reaching for Stoker's hand. He clasped it, and they wound their way out of the parlor, down the corridor, and out the front door into the sunny October afternoon.

Stoker was gasping for air, walking without direction, staring without seeing. He pulled Sabine along, keeping pace as if the duke might overcome forty years of bad habits and give a decent chase.

"Stoker, wait," said Sabine, struggling to keep up on the uneven cobblestones.

He slowed down but did not stop. She wrapped her free hand around his wrist, trying to loosen his hold on her fingers, but he held her in a vise grip.

"Stoker, you are hurting me."

He came to an abrupt halt and turned to her, taking both of her hands between his own. "That is not the worst of it," he said, looking at every part of her face. *Eyes, green,* he thought, cataloging her features; *nose, perfect; lips, pink; hair, ebony; skin, creamy.*

"That is not the worst of it," he repeated. "That interview was wretched and mean and an embarrassment, but I want you to be aware . . . before you take another step by my side . . . that Sauly New and his hateful memories and extortion scheme and ridiculous rants barely scratch the surface of what terrible things are part of me."

"I do not see terrible as part of you, Jon. I see pain, survival, your love of your friends. I see you trying very hard to protect every part of me. There is no *terrible.*"

"It was all so bloody terrible," he told her slowly.

"Yes, I've gathered that. I did discover you in a morgue. But it is not so terrible anymore. Is it?"

"There is no map for getting back from it."

"Oh, but a map can be made for any journey," she said. "And I am an excellent cartographer."

"I don't need a cartographer. I need . . . I need . . ." He scanned the small, out-of-the-way road lined with modest houses and struggling shops. An alley opened behind the next block, and he strode to it, dragging her along. When they reached the alley, he whipped around the corner and pressed her up against the wall.

"I *need*," he breathed, pouncing on her mouth, kissing her with all the fervor that he'd locked away in bed last night. "I need a wife," he finally said, coming up for air.

"I am here, Jon," she gasped, kissing him back with the same ferocity. "I am here."

CHAPTER TWENTY-FOUR

In its five years since completion, London's showy Regent Street has distinguished itself as the city's shopping centre. Arching from Piccadilly to Oxford Circus, the John Nash–designed thoroughfare boasts modern shops and exclusive craftsmen. Also new is the esteemed Royal Polytechnic Institution for Machinery and Mining.

Perhaps the greatest harmony of Regent Street is the road itself, which represents the boundary of affluent Mayfair to the west and working-class Soho to the east. This arrangement draws luxury shoppers from one side of the street and employs shop clerks from the other.

Polytechnic scientists, by and large, hail from outside the city.

Public street with shops open daily except Sundays, several with extended evening hours till five o'clock.

Royal Polytechnic Institution features a public exhibition hall with working models of machines and scales, a lecture theatre, museum shop, and tea room. Open daily,

check postings for special presentations and frequent pho-
tography exhibits.

—From *A Noble Guide to London*
by Sabine Noble

The fervent need and passionate kisses of the alleyway did not, Sabine was disappointed to discover, carry over to the remainder of the day or the night. They had kissed against the wall until children ran past, laughing and jumping in a puddle that splattered Stoker's boots and Sabine's hem. Sabine had giggled and Stoker had muttered something in French, but the moment was broken. They had straightened their clothes and emerged from the alley a little disoriented but arm in arm.

Something about the meeting in Wrest's dark, filthy townhome made them crave daylight and fresh air, and they'd elected to walk the distance to Belgrave Square. Stoker had tucked Sabine tightly against him and she'd held fast to his arm, but they did not speak, not really. More than penury at the old duke's house, they'd encountered an alternate history of Stoker's entire life. The whole of which had been recounted in one afternoon. So much talking, so many revelations, so much to think through.

And so they had walked in silence, and when they reached Belgrave Square, Stoker had sat behind the bedroom desk and began writing letters. Sabine had offered tea or even brandy, but he'd declined. He'd wished, she sensed, to be alone, and she left him for her own work.

When the sun set, he'd asked if she would join him out

of the house for dinner—in a café or the dining room of an inn—and she had agreed. They settled on a public house not far from Belgrave Square, where the food was bland but fortifying and a little band of musicians entertained the room and removed the opportunity to talk.

When they returned home, Sabine hadn't asked his preference for sleeping alone; she'd simply changed into her night rail and climbed into his bed. He'd scooped her up at once, burying his face in her hair. Sabine's heart had soared. Her body strummed in anticipation of the passion and emotion that would, surely, invigorate their lovemaking.

But alas, no. After his first commanding gush of enthusiasm, Stoker seemed to take stock of himself and his passion, to steel himself, and then to gingerly undress Sabine and reverently, placidly, make love to her as if she was a fragile paper doll.

Sabine had been crestfallen and almost, *almost*, called him out on it, but she'd worried the revelations from his father had been enough burden for one day. It would have been overwhelming, she was afraid, to hear his wife heap on demands about the way he gave and received love in their bed.

She awakened in the morning, anxious to make progress with her own investigation. She would use the day to call on Regent Street and visit the young chemist, Dr. Birdall. There was more to learn there now that she understood the gunpowder plot. Considerable days had passed since she'd lurked about him in his laboratory or in the pub, eavesdropping about his work in explosives. He would not remember her; perhaps she could approach him. She was motivated to learn everything she could about the London network before finally making a journey to the Dorset coast to have a look at the Isle of Portland.

After she visited Dorset, she hoped her investigation could feel complete enough to be presented to the police, and she could wash her hands of it.

Stoker teased about how she would spend her time when she'd finally given the authorities the mural of damning evidence to which she'd devoted months of her life. She was a cartographer, she reminded him, not a detective. Besides, the thrill of vengeance against her uncle had waned considerably since she'd fallen in love with Stoker. His daily struggle to put all of his terrible past behind him had affected every part of her life.

Now her investigation meant only one thing to her: ousting Dryden from Park Lodge so she could return to her home, look after her mother, and restore her father's body of work. And if she could continue to publish her travel guides—who could say, perhaps a rural England edition?—even better.

But thinking about returning to Surrey meant speculating about a future with Stoker there. Would he consider life so far from the ocean? Would Park Lodge be equal to this Portuguese villa he'd been endeavoring to buy? If not, would he consider taking her with him when he sailed on to find the home of his dreams?

Sabine could not say. And she would not ask. She could tell him of her plans for her own life, she could suggest openness to compromise, but only *he* could declare his intentions.

Quietly, Sabine slid one leg from their warm bed, hoping

to disappear from the room without waking him. Stoker made a lazy sound and crept a hand beneath the covers and caught her wrist. She went still, heart pounding, and waited. If he yanked her back, if he rolled her beneath him, if he made love to her in the same way he had kissed her yesterday in the alley, she would be delighted to postpone her morning in Regent Street to toss about in bed with him.

However, if he embarked on another of his light touch, gentle kiss, half-asleep sessions, she was afraid she'd have to beg off on threat of the day's pressing schedule and the lateness of the hour. She might even claim she had a headache.

It pained her to avoid him; in fact, she wanted nothing more than to lie with him. But she could not tolerate the civilized . . . *hesitancy* that pervaded their lovemaking since they'd left the ball. The contrast between their first time and the following nights was so stark, they almost seemed like different activities. Last night he'd benignly *convened* with her (really, there was no other word) with more of the same. And now he wanted her again.

Better than nothing at all, she reminded herself, but she held her breath, waiting to see what level of "refinement" he would invoke in these early-morning hours. When he began to slide a faint, gentle hand up her arm, Sabine had her answer. She bit her lip, wondering if she could doze through another softly pressed ministration. When he slid a second hand beneath the covers to ineffectually massage her hip, like a groom polishing the side of a carriage, she tugged her wrist from his hand and stood up.

"Stoker," she said, "I can't."

He sat. The look on his face was pure horror.

"Wait," she said, "do not panic. It's not what you assume."

"Ah . . . how could it be any other?" A harsh laugh. "Please don't explain. You are weary. Or busy. Or *disinclined*."

"I am not weary or busy or disinclined," she said. "I don't like the way you touch me."

And now he was on his feet. He stared at her across the bed. "I knew it—"

"That is, I don't like the way you've touched me here, in this bed. I loved it at Denby House during the ball, and every time we've kissed, including yesterday in the alley."

"What? Wild and unchecked?"

"*Yes*," she said resoundingly. "Wild and unchecked. That is what I like. Have *you* enjoyed this . . . other?" She pecked a curled finger at the bed, pointing at it like it was infested. "This tickle-touch . . . chaste . . . slowness? Because I cannot believe that you do. Not when you are so masterful at the other."

"I love any opportunity to touch you," he said cautiously.

"Right. And I enjoy the closeness of you and the weight of your body . . . but that is quite all I enjoy. The other is not bad so much as . . . boring."

"*Boring?*" His voice cracked.

"And unsatisfying," she said, looking away. "If I'm being honest."

"Unsatisfying?"

She swung back. "Surely, you have noticed."

"I am working so very hard to not manhandle you."

"But I *want* to be manhandled, don't you see?"

"You cannot."

"I can and I do, and you are capable of thrilling me so thoroughly. When you do not, all I can think of is . . . that I wish you would."

"Sabine, I could damage you. I could—"

"You *won't*."

He made a scoffing noise, "You have no idea."

"Would you believe that this very statement—*you have no idea*—is exciting to me. Doesn't the promise of . . . whatever ideas I don't yet know *excite* you?"

He stared at her a long moment and then turned to the wall. He pulled his nightshirt over his head, revealing his muscled back and half of the serpent tattoo. Sabine almost sighed out loud. She wanted to launch herself at him. But this would only confuse matters; she'd only just rebuffed him. He was clearly in no mood. Besides, her passion was not in question; this must come from him.

"I am not prepared to discuss this with you," he said. His morning jacket was draped over a chair, and he shrugged into it.

"No one is wearier of talking about sex than I am, Stoker. But it seems unfair to both of us not to force out some . . . preference. It would be one thing if I felt you were incapable of satisfying me in a wilder, *less refined* way. But we both know that you are so very up to the task. In fact, I think we are of the same mind on the topic."

He walked to the window and moved the curtain, looking out on the autumn color tingeing Belgrave Square. It would rain today; she could smell it in the air. An otherwise perfect day to pass the morning in bed. Was she a mad-woman to criticize him? Too demanding? She sighed, wishing her friends were closer so she could ask them.

Sabine bit her lip and ventured, "I'm going to the Royal Polytechnic Institute in Regent Street today. Would you come with me?"

"No," he said shortly, biting the word. Sabine was not accustomed to terseness from him, and she felt her stomach drop.

"I've business with my brig," he said. "It should arrive today or tomorrow."

And it will take you away from me, she thought, fighting back tears. She could not accuse him of this. She could not *order him* to love her.

She was so very weary of giving orders. She just wanted to be swept up and carried away.

She backed from the room and trudged upstairs.

Dr. Jarius Birdall of Regent Street's new Royal Polytechnic Institution told Sabine that he could offer ten minutes, and ten minutes only, of his valuable time, as he was expected in an important meeting. (And, by the by, female tourists generally kept to the shop and tea rooms and were not known to approach faculty.)

She smiled sweetly and thanked him, lucky even for ten minutes. Her question for him—*How might her father blast the limestone outcropping from an otherwise fertile field in Dorset?*—had been rather weak. She'd invented it on the spot when she'd come upon him outside his office. He, in turn, showed weak interest. It wasn't every day that a pretty girl with a strange dog asked a stupid question of a man of little authority. Ten minutes was likely more than most people of any gender received.

"Limestone detonation is not an undertaking that one man, alone, with no training, can accomplish," he told her in his cramped, acrid-smelling office. "Your father should seek out any of several mining companies with offices right here in London and negotiate a price for the explosives and a crew to manage it."

"That sounds expensive," she mused. "Are there no men who could be hired to work alone? For example, could my father simply hire *you*?"

"That depends," Birdall hedged, considering this, and Sabine gingerly opened her notebook and dabbed her pen, waiting for him to think out loud or rattle off stray facts— anything new she could learn about how the charcoal of Hampstead would meet the sulphur and saltpeter from Mr. Legg's boat to become gunpowder.

At her feet Bridget stood at attention, sniffing the air. The dog would truly miss this investigation when it was over. There was virtually no subterfuge or stealth involved in cartography. Thank God.

Ten minutes later Sabine had a page of notes about the amount of each chemical compound required to make gunpowder and the way they were combined. She was just about to ask him if such an operation could take place in, for example, a barn or even out of doors, when the door to

Dr. Birdall's office opened and in walked the last man on earth she expected to see.

Her uncle, Sir Dryden.

He stood distractedly in the doorway, tapping rain from his hat and stomping mud from his boots.

"Entertaining females in the office, Birdall?" asked Sir Dryden with irritation. "I came all the way from Surrey for this meeting."

The sight of Dryden struck Sabine with a throat-closing gush of fear. Her heart lurched, stopped beating, and then leapt into a mad spring. Unwelcome tears burned her eyes and she fumbled with her pen and notebook.

Not now, she begged, *I am so close.*

And then she thought, *He will kill me. When he recognizes me and learns my purpose, he will not hesitate to kill me.*

She looked frantically around the room. There was no escape. The windows were sealed, and they were three floors up. The thick stone walls would conceal her screams. One glance at Birdall proved that he was as frightened of Dryden as she was.

Sabine pressed her notebook closed and blinked back the threatening tears, bracing herself, preparing for the firestorm that would follow when Dryden caught sight of her. She checked her dog. Bridget had never met Dryden and she was frantically sniffing the air, assessing potential threat.

I swear, she thought, *if he lays one hand on my dog . . .*

When Sir Dryden finally turned his attention to the small office, Sabine raised up in her seat, fear momentarily overshadowed by pride. On instinct, she flashed him a smile. She was careful to keep her expression serene and confident—Dryden's least favorite.

"*My God,*" he spat, "what are you doing here?"

"I moved here after my marriage, Uncle, or don't you remember? I've made London my home these past four years. What are *you* doing here?"

He made a dismissive noise and said, "I owe no explanation to you about my whereabouts. What are you doing in the professor's offices?"

To Dr. Birdall he said, "Why in God's name would you let my estranged *niece* in the Institution?"

Dryden looked back to Sabine, his gaze lighting on her notebook. "What are you taking down? Let me see that. Don't try to hide it." He slapped a bony hand on the notebook and Bridget let out a low, warning growl.

Sabine clasped the edge of the notebook, trying to slide it free. "Research. For my travel guides," she said. Bridget's growl changed to a bark, responding to the distress in Sabine's voice.

"The devil it is. *Let go,*" he demanded and yanked the notebook from the desk to flip it open.

"She's taking down notes on our compound, Birdall, you fool!" Dryden said, shouting over the sound of the barks. "What have you told her?"

Dr. Birdall was standing now, looking nervously between Sabine and Sir Dryden and the dog. "She said she needed advice about blasting limestone from her father's farm."

"Her father is *dead,*" said Dryden. "She has absolutely no need for this information, unless—"

He narrowed his eyes on Sabine, studying her face, her posture, the clutch of her hands. He squinted at the dog.

"Birdall?" he said quietly. "Get out. Take the dog."

"I beg your pardon?"

"I said, *get out*. Take the dog and lock the door behind you. I will attend to you in a moment. But first I must clear up some confusion between my niece and myself."

The younger man reached cautiously for the dog, and Bridget let out a vicious string of barks, baring her teeth. The professor drew back, edging away, and hurried out the door. Dryden slammed it shut and flipped the lock, spinning back to Sabine.

"What do you think you're doing, you meddling presumptuous bitch!" Dryden hissed. He slapped the heel of his hand between her eyes and drove two fingers into her nostrils. When he had a secure hold of her face, he jerked, giving her no choice but to stagger up. The pain and humiliation were immediate, and Sabine cried out, grasping his wrists with both hands. Bridget barked and barked.

"You think you can interfere with my business? A forgotten housewife, living alone in the cellar of glorified carpenters? You think I don't know? I look in on you each time I'm in London. I could snap your neck, and no one would even care."

He shoved hard, unhooking his fingers, sending her reeling. She collided with a bookshelf, knocking heavy tomes to the floor like apples from a tree. Sabine stooped to pick up a book.

She would throw it at him, she thought, trying to remain practical and defensive; she would use it to deflect him. He grabbed the book before she could get a proper grip, wrenching it free and drawing back to strike her in the head.

Sabine anticipated the blow and ducked just in time, sending him careening into the shelf, dislodging a second harvest of books.

Dryden swore and recovered himself, searching the small office for her. She had scrambled away, ducking behind a chair, searching the legs for a handhold so that she might heave it up. She would chuck it at him. She would—

"Let me tell you what will happen now," he said. "First, I will kill this dog."

"No," Sabine gasped, lunging for Bridget. When she stooped, Dryden grabbed her by a handful of hair and steered her downward, face against wood, to the desk.

Sir Dryden leaned very close to her ear. "You will return home with me to Park Lodge. Won't your mother be pleased by the visit? You will remain under lock and key until my business with the professor is finished. Then, we will discuss how you learned about it, *what* you know, and what you intended to do with the information. It is an understatement to say that I am *shocked* to see you here, but I am not disappointed."

Bridget's barking had reached deafening levels. The dog was maddened at the sight of her mistress under attack. She would not bite him unless Sabine gave the command, but she barked to bring down the Institute walls.

"Who," Dryden said over the sound of the dog, "have you told?" He resettled his hand and so his thumb pressed into a soft spot of her neck.

"Go to hell," Sabine choked.

"You would threaten me? Even now?"

"I will fight you until death," she said, fumbling her hands along the surface of the desk, feeling for some weapon. She felt a handkerchief . . . spectacles . . . the sharp point of a letter opener. *Yes!* Sabine rejoiced and walked her shaking fingers around the knife-like shape, searching for the handle. She moved slowly, trying not to draw attention; meanwhile her vision swam; she gasped for breath.

"Who knows about the gunpowder?" Dryden repeated.

"No one," said Sabine, homing her focus on the letter opener. The strange position disrupted her dexterity, and her trembling caused her to fumble it away. She swore and cast around, trying to recover it. Seconds ticked by. Dryden would not be satisfied with pinning her down forever. She let out an exaggerated sob, remembering how this thrilled him. He laughed and increased the pressure on her throat. Sabine saw stars but floundered on. Finally, after an eternity of glacially slow fumbling, she recovered the letter opener and squeezed the handle.

"*I said*," growled Dryden, "who knows?"

Taking a moment to gather her strength and consider the arc of her arm and the best target along his tweed-covered leg, Sabine sobbed again.

When he began to laugh, she sucked in a breath and cried out, "Bridget, bite!" The dog let out a ferocious half-growl, half-bark and sprang, fastening her jigsawed mongrel's teeth into Dryden's bony hip.

Sabine drove her arm down an instant later, thrusting the letter opener into his opposite thigh. The man shouted, jerked up, and then flailed backward. His hands dropped, and Sabine slid from the desk, sending papers and beakers flying. She bolted through the mess, scrambling for the door. The knob was locked, of course, and she began to shake it, too frantic to see how to unlock a door.

In the next moment she heard footsteps outside the door. Angry voices. Birdall must have gone for help. As she struggled to work the lock on the knob, someone rattled it from the other side. Pounding ensued, a frantic knocking that reverberated through the wood.

"Bridget, come!" Sabine cried, casting a glance over her shoulder. The dog had released Dryden's thigh and lunged for his jugular, a wiry ball of claws and bared fangs and sharp, feral eyes.

"Bridget, heel!" Sabine cried, trying to be heard over the pounding on the door. "Release, now! Come!"

Dryden pulled the letter opener from his thigh and used it like a dagger against the dog.

"*Bridget!*" Sabine shrieked, desperate for the dog's safety. Bridget skittered back and darted to her side, slipping on broken beakers and paper. Sabine turned her attention back to the knob and forced her hands and brain to work a simple lock on a standard door. When at last the bolt slid to the side, she wrenched the door open with a shout.

The sight beyond the open door took her breath away.

It registered slowly at first; Bridget's barking was the only phenomenon that seemed to evolve in real time.

Stoker was there, staggering back from the swinging door, his face torqued in fury and fear. Behind him crowded a small detachment of uniformed policemen. Scientists and students filled in behind the police. The corridor was mobbed with men in blue uniforms and white laboratory smocks.

Bridget barked at them all, squaring her small shoulders and lunging at the closest uniformed officer.

Sabine let her go and she reached for Stoker.

He took her by the shoulders and bent down, looking into her eyes. "Are you badly hurt? Where did he touch you? Your nose is bleeding. Can you breathe?"

"I'm fine," she said, clutching him to her for a quick, tight hug. His size and strength were like a sharpening stone to her own knife-like will to fight. She felt her dulling strength revive and she gave him a final squeeze and thrust him away.

"Dryden is there," she said quickly, breathlessly. "He has one of my notebooks. I can show the police some part—"

"I have the mural," Stoker said, pointing to a satchel on the floor. "I brought everything I could find and sent the local watchman running for a detective and a squadron of police." He reached for her again, taking her by the arms. "I'm so sorry you came here alone, Sabine. I'm sorry it took me so long to reach you. I'd never have found you in this building if not for the dog's barking."

"But how did you know to bring my mural or the police?" she gasped.

"Sir Dryden rode by Belgrave Square in an open cab. I

was staring out the window like a—well, you saw the wretched state I was in. When the cab circled the third time and I caught sight of his face, I realized. There was no guarantee that he would call to Regent Street next, but if there was the slightest chance, I could not but come to you. I gathered the mural and summoned the police as an afterthought. I'm too old to rescue girls on my own."

Sabine laughed, a gurgle of pride and gratefulness and relief, crying at the same time. "I managed," she said. "And you are not so old."

"You did manage," he said, hugging her fiercely again. "You certainly did, my courageous wife."

She gave him a squeeze and wiggled away. "Will you take the police in?" She nodded to the office. "I can't face him again." She wiped blood from her nose with the back of her hand and reached for the satchel. "Which one is the detective?"

CHAPTER TWENTY-FIVE

Stoker leaned against the corridor wall and stared down at Bridget. The dog ignored him; her unerring focus was on the closed laboratory door behind which Sabine stood. After the struggle they'd had, he did not blame the dog for wanting to be close.

Stoker had suggested that the detective might take her mural more seriously if she explained without the growling presence of a suspicious dog.

"It won't be long now," he told the dog, hoping this was true. A second and third detective had arrived shortly after the police cleared the scene. They introduced themselves as an explosives regulator and a detective who specialized in smuggling and joined the interrogation of Sabine. She now captivated a growing circle of men gathered around her mural. They were well into their second hour of questions and studying her evidence. The men had been shocked when Stoker declined to remain in the room for the discussion—in truth, they were shocked that he did not conduct the discussion—but this was her investigation.

Now he and the dog would wait. He wondered how Sir Dryden fared in his Whitehall holding cell. In the confusion of a dog barking, a bleeding woman, and a frantic professor who began a guilty recitation of ridiculous excuses, there had been ten stray minutes when Dryden had been left alone under very distracted guard. Stoker had used the time to slip into the destroyed office and have a few words with the sadistic git. A handy pen had somehow escaped the melee on the desktop. Stoker had snatched it up and dug it, nib first, into the shallow wound Sabine had inflicted on this thigh. While the older man tremored and begged for mercy, Stoker told him in no uncertain terms what would happen to him if ever he approached Sabine again. He assured him that the police would prevent him from ever residing at Park Lodge and the older man dared not contradict him.

Later, when the last detective had gone, Sabine asked Stoker if they might walk for a while before they made their way home. He wanted to ask her again to seek out a doctor, but she'd cleaned up her nose and swept up her hair, insisting that she was otherwise unharmed. He would not cluck over her, she didn't like it, and he was trying very hard to do what she liked.

A memory from the morning flashed in his mind.

"Remember this morning," he ventured, "when you referred to me as *unsatisfying* and *boring?*"

Sabine chuckled. "Of course this is how you would remember it. I did not assign these words to you, as a man. I was describing certain . . . er, interludes. Not all, just some."

"Forgive me if I saw only the forest of your message and not the trees."

"Actually, I was paying you a compliment."

"Oh yes, how complimentary to hear that I bore you and fail to satisfy."

"If you are waiting for me to say that I regret the conversation, I do not and I will not."

"Sabine Stoker," he sighed, "woman of no regrets."

She laughed. "I wouldn't say that. But I am decisive and I aim to be sensible, to consider cause and effect. I am not cavalier when I make decisions. What are you getting at?"

He stopped walking and turned to her. "At the risk of rehashing the topic of Sir Dryden, I merely want to point out that, if I bore you, I am endeavoring to be the opposite of your uncle. I endeavor to be the opposite of every terrible man I have seen bullying a girl—"

She tried to cut in, but he rushed to finish. "Certainly, I am big and strong and aggressive, and my desire for you is so great, it takes my breath away. But possessing these attributes does not mean it is safe or reasonable for me to inflict them on you."

Sabine nodded and looked away. Bridget paused on the sidewalk to drink from a puddle. A day of storms had washed Regent Street in cold rain. They stared down at the dog.

"Your caution is a gift. Truly it is," Sabine said. "Forgive me if I have not shown gratefulness in addition to my, er, demandingness. But what I endured under Sir Dryden has no bearing on what we enjoy when we are intimate. Sir Dryden's violence was about power. When you are passionate, your, ah, fervor does not come from a place of power, but of—well, I assume it is enthusiasm? Attraction? Passion for passion's sake?"

It's love, he thought, but he said, "Yes, it is all of those things."

"Power does not enter into our intimacy—not in my view. Well, perhaps that is not entirely true. If I'm being honest, *I* feel a small amount of power over *you*. That is, when you are doing it right—"

"Oh yes, on those rare occasions . . ."

She laughed and started walking again. "When we are both caught up in the moment, I feel as if I am irresistible to you. It is a powerful feeling, and an intoxicating one. I quite like being irresistible to you."

I have never known anyone or anything more impossible to resist, he thought. He said, "I'm sorry to raise the topic after the day you've had. But I felt compelled to mention it. In my defense."

Sabine paused and looked up at him. "I never meant for you to defend yourself, Jon. I only wanted you to love me the way you did the very first time. When we were hiding in that bedroom at the Courtlands', you touched me as if I was something that felt very . . . precious and almost fleeting. It was as if you wanted to swallow me whole, lest I slip way. And I had never felt more revered. Or looked after." She flashed an expression that said, *Don't you see?*

They stared for a moment and Sabine shrugged. She

continued down the sidewalk and Stoker watched her progress. "Noted," he finally said.

"But you raise an interesting point about power," she said when he caught up. "I've come to believe that how a man wields his power is a real measure of his character," she said. "Sir Dryden had a small amount of power over me, and he used it to terrorize and control. But look at someone like the Duke of Wrest. At one time he had considerable power and he chose to do practically nothing but serve his own folly. In the scheme of things, the amount of power a person has matters less than how he or she applies it." She shrugged. "But it's all relative, isn't it? A woman has very little power at all, not beyond her children or her staff. Women in particular are keenly aware of men who take advantage."

She looked up. "You never take advantage, Jon. Never. You have respected my interests and my intelligence. You have quarreled with me as if I am an equal."

"Only you would appreciate the manner in which I quarrel," he said.

"The way we quarrel," she listed, "the way we make love, the way you convalesce. Good lord, I am demanding."

"You are perfect," he sighed, and he scooped up her hand and tugged her against him. They walked arm in arm until they came to the corner of Regent Street and Great Castle. He stopped in front of the familiar millinery shop and collective of florist stalls that crowded the corner. The dog circled back and sniffed a lamppost. She looked at him expectantly and he realized he had run out of time to avoid saying the words that must be said. He wanted to say them. He would perish if he did not say them, but he was also terrified . . . as afraid as he had ever been.

If she rejected him because he amused her but she did not need him, not really . . .

If she sent him away because he was well and the investigation was over . . .

He felt himself begin to sweat. The bustle of the sidewalk and the noise of the road fell away. He cleared his throat.

"I wasn't sure where you wished to walk," he began.

His voice sounded odd and he cleared his throat.

He continued, "Regent Street is my neighborhood, actually, when I am in London. I think I mentioned the suite of rooms I keep for when I am in port."

"Oh right," she said, looking around. "I've never heard of anyone actually living in Regent Street. My research suggested that it is only shops and the science institution."

"Someone has to live upstairs," he said. His heart was pounding. "I knew I did not want to stay anywhere near the neighborhoods where I ran wild as a boy, and the stodgy squares of Mayfair did not suit me. No proper neighborhood seemed quite right, and I was so very rarely in the city. The traffic and commerce and life on this street appealed to me. I wasn't searching for a home when I let it, just an active, distracting place to stay."

He glanced at the shiny facade of his apartments above them. Someone had slapped on a fresh coat of paint and the windows looked clean. He wondered if she would like it.

"And now?" she asked, brushing away a stray lock of

hair. "What do you search for now?" She stooped to pick up her dog.

"I feel like I've spent my entire life searching for you," he whispered.

If he believed she would have some response for that, he was mistaken. She dipped her head into her dog's fur and looked up at him through lowered eyes. She waited. Stoker shifted on his feet. Two women rushed from the milliner's shop, and the bell on the door chimed. He swallowed hard.

"I climbed in and out of so many terrible places, searching for you, Sabine," he said.

She blinked, listening with fascinated eyes.

"Today," he continued, "when I thought my own vanity and . . . fear had kept me from protecting you—my fit of pique after you denied me this morning—when I thought Dryden would reach you before I could locate your mural and rally the police and be of some proper use to you, all vanity left me. And I knew the greatest fear of my life. I thought I'd lost you."

"We are both very difficult to lose," she said.

"When I found you, you had sorted it out yourself."

"There was no guarantee Sir Dryden would not have given chase."

"I should like to see him defeat you and your dog in a foot race, especially with a letter opener jutting from his leg."

She laughed.

Stoker exhaled deeply. "I honestly had no plan for where I would go or what I would do after I healed."

"I . . . I thought you were being very secretive about it or you had no idea. It was my very great hope that you had no idea."

He laughed. She was so honest and forthright and clever. She was everything he required. He said, "I wanted to come to some agreement with the duke. I needed to make certain my brig was not at the bottom of the ocean. After that my only plan has been to follow you, wherever you may go. If you will have me."

"Of course I will have you," she whispered, stepping closer to him. She stooped to release the dog. "I have been working very hard to hold you captive in my cellar for six weeks, or perhaps you haven't noticed. Pity you are so . . . virile. You healed and regained your strength despite my worst efforts. Now I must rely on you to willingly remain."

"You are a terrible nurse," he said, reaching for her, spanning her waist with his large hands. These admissions were halting and difficult to reveal, but touching her was the most natural thing. He lowered his head until their foreheads bumped. There was more. His chest felt as if it would burst with all he wanted to tell her. He closed his eyes. He opened them. "I love you, Sabine," he said on a rush of air. "I love you so much."

She sucked in a small breath and blinked. It occurred to him that he had surprised her. He was happy to reveal the unexpected but he marveled that she did not know. How could she not have known?

"I love you," she whispered back. The words flooded him with relief and hope and the courage to say the next harrowing thing.

"I will endeavor not to—" he cleared his throat "—bore you. Or leave you unsatisfied. If you will allow me. As an authentic husband. In every way. If you will be my authentic wife."

She pulled her head away to look at him. "Not bore me?" she teased. "I am very demanding, I'm afraid." But now she sobered. "I think some part of me always wanted to be your authentic wife. From the very first day."

"A large part of me wanted that," he said, and she giggled.

Stoker made a sound of exasperation and rolled his eyes. "How clever you are. Clever and naughty. What a lucky man I am to have such a clever, naughty wife."

"In all seriousness, Stoker," she said, "I will not hound you to, er, devour me. Of course, I will be happy to receive you however—"

"Do not insult me," he teased. "It was miserable—before. You were correct on every score. You are always correct."

"I am not *always* correct."

"Could I commission a mural with that headline?" he mumbled, looking around. "It's convenient that we should find ourselves on this corner. Do you know why?"

She studied the window of the milliner's shop. "Are we going to . . . buy hats?"

He laughed. "Perhaps later. My London apartments are here." He gestured above the shop. "Would you like to see?"

A slow drizzle began to fall, and Sabine shaded her eyes with her hand and gazed up. "May I bring my dog?"

"No," he said and took up her hand. She laughed, summoning Bridget, allowing him to pull her into a passageway beside the milliner's shop.

He unlocked the iron gate and they ducked beneath a stone arch. The gate led to a small brick courtyard blooming with roses. A stairwell led to a balcony and a wooden door. He scooped up the dog and deposited her beside a cat crouched disapprovingly in the corner. The dog ignored the other animal and sniffed around planters of roses and a stone bench. A sundial stood in the center of the courtyard, and Sabine stepped up to examine it. She brushed his shoulder, and he snaked out his hand to catch her wrist. Sabine looked up. He gave a demonstrative yank, snatching her to him.

She let out a satisfying little yelp and collided against his chest with a thud. He caught her up, digging his fingers into her hair and tipping her face up. Her eyes were bright with excitement and desire, and his own body surged, his heart thudding in his throat. They stood in the misty courtyard, frozen for a charged moment. He looked into the eyes that he hoped to see every day for the rest of his life and saw forever staring back. Autumn roses, the color of daybreak, bobbed around them, and the dog curled up in a dry spot beneath the bench and yawned.

Stoker gave a growl and swept a hand beneath Sabine's knees, scooping her up. She gasped and threw her arms around his neck. He brought his mouth down hard on her lips, kissing away any doubt about his ability to engage or satisfy, kissing her until she broke her face away to breathe.

She clung to him as he strode to the iron steps that led to his rooms above the courtyard. He turned the key in the lock and kicked the door open with his boot. Sabine laughed as he carried her inside. He tossed her on the first available velvet surface and followed her down.

Six months later

It was, perhaps, a great irony that Sabine Noble, the third and final Bride of Belgravia, the most reluctant and cynical, was the bride to insist upon a second wedding, a real wedding, with proper guests and a vicar, a breakfast feast, and music.

"Our original wedding was the most rushed of all," Sabine told Willow and Tessa as Perry dressed her hair. They sat in Sabine's old bedroom waiting for the summons to the tiny stone chapel on the grounds of Park Lodge. Maids rushed in and out, collecting parasols and shawls and chasing Bridget with a yellow satin bow for her neck. The gardener had come and gone three times with possible bouquets and a pail of flowers for Sabine's hair.

"I actually had a bloody lip and a black eye at my first wedding," recalled Sabine, frowning into the mirror.

The housekeeper came in to show off a tray of honey tarts, one of a hundred baked for the occasion. Willow approved the tarts and sent the servant away.

"Stoker," Sabine finished, "could not fill out the special license without sending a messenger to learn my full name."

"I think the second wedding is a brilliant idea," said Tessa, selecting fragrant purple crocus blossoms from the pail to tuck into her hair. "I might steal the idea and stage a second wedding of my own."

"Is it unseemly," wondered Sabine, "for the parents of three small children to indulge in a second marriage? Especially since their first wedding was one of the grandest in the country?"

Tessa tossed a limp flower at Sabine and then intercepted a maid who'd arrived with a note about the musicians.

When the servant had gone, Willow shut the bedroom door and clicked the lock. "I think it's wonderful that you're putting on a proper celebration, Sabine. And to include your mother, and the Courtlands, and my aunt Mary and uncle Arthur—all of us—it's sweet."

"Now you're gloating," teased Sabine, "because your master plan has come to such remarkable fruition. You are like Wellington, parading through the streets of London after victory."

"Stop. It is your wedding, and I am merely a guest," Willow said. "There is nothing about which to gloat. All I did was find a way for the three of us to leave Surrey. Falling in love was this magical thing we each managed on our own."

"We always had more to offer the world than Surrey could offer," sighed Tessa philosophically, gazing out the window.

Sabine and Willow exchanged a look. If Sabine's second wedding was her irony, Tessa's irony was that she'd gone along with Willow's scheme, despite never having given the world outside Surrey a second thought. The old Tessa St. Clair had wanted nothing more than to be someone's pretty wife and settle down on an estate in her serene hometown village of Pixham. Now she relished her job as Harbor Master in the bustling port town of Hartlepool on the coast of the North Sea.

"Will you take your children to Berrymede, Tessa?" asked Sabine casually, speaking of Tessa's childhood home.

Tessa shrugged. "I haven't decided. They've invited us to stay as their guests, but we are settled at the Pixham Inn. Joseph says that I may choose, but I shall consider it only after I've seen how they regard my children at the wedding— *all* of my children."

Tessa's oldest son, Christian, was the result of an attack she'd suffered before she was married. When her parents discovered her pregnancy, they had expelled her from the family. Willow's "Brides of Belgravia" scheme arranged for Tessa to marry Joseph Chance instead, and now he proudly raised Christian as his own son. Tessa's family had since become conciliatory and, in their own way, repentant for turning Tessa out, but forgiveness was a struggle.

"I hope you don't mind that I invited your parents, Tess," said Sabine gently. "They might as well see that all of us have succeeded."

"I look forward to showing off my children and my husband," said Tessa. "Of course you should have invited them."

"And your mother, Willow?" ventured Sabine, looking at her friend, now the Countess of Cassin.

"If ever I meant to promenade in victory, it would be before my mother," said Willow. "And why not? I've found happiness on my own terms, and become a countess along the way." She crossed the room to Sabine's vanity. "The only missing guest is wretched Sir Dryden."

"Indeed," Sabine said bitterly, "but they do not allow furlough from Newgate Prison to attend weddings."

"Will he hang, do you think?" Willow asked. "Your case for treason is strong."

"I don't know, and I don't care." Sabine waved the notion away. "When all trace of Dryden and his conspirators were removed from Park Lodge, I allowed myself to move forward and not dwell on him or smuggling or the rest of it."

Behind Sabine, Perry secured one final miniature daffodil to the crown of her head and then stepped back, clapping her hands together. "There you are, Miss Sabine, er, Mrs. Noble. Just look at you." She beamed in the mirror.

Sabine stared back, turning her head this way and that. "Lovely, Perry. Thank you. Having you travel from Yorkshire with Lady Willow was an unexpected gift."

"Oh, I couldn't have you marry Mr. Stoker a second time without being properly looked after." The maid turned to the other women in the room. "You should have seen Miss Sabine's hair the afternoon I arrived in London. It was like the hair of a wild woman, living in the forest, no hat, not a single pin. I've never seen so much wild, loose hair."

Sabine cleared her throat, hiding a smile, and Tessa said, "Well, there is a style for every occasion, isn't there? You will discover this after you are married to his lordship's valet,

Marcus. In the meantime, rest assured your current bridal creation is a stroke of genius. She looks beautiful."

"Simply beautiful," agreed Willow, coming to stand behind her friend.

There was a knock at the door and Mr. Fisk, Willow's manservant, could be heard calling, "They are ready for you, Miss Sabine."

"Thank you, Mr. Fisk," called Willow and she stooped to gather Sabine's long train. "Up you go," she said. "We mustn't keep them waiting."

"Flowers!" called Tessa, scooping up a bouquet of daffodils, purple crocus, and white snowdrops.

The trio of women bustled to the door, Perry rushing to keep up with her box of hairpins, combs, stray flowers, and handkerchiefs. Sabine allowed herself to be swept along but she paused when Willow reached for the knob.

"Willow—wait," said Sabine.

Willow turned back. "What is it?"

Sabine looked down at her dress and flowers and up to her friends. "Is this . . . silly?"

"Is what silly?" Tessa stepped around her.

"Making such a fuss over an event that, in the eyes of God and man, has already happened?"

Tessa said, "Sabine, you've always been too suspicious of things that might appear *silly*. Indulge yourself. Enjoy it. You've earned this moment."

"I am not suspicious," corrected Sabine, "I am practical." She gestured to the profusion of soft yellow silk that hung from her waist in frothy layers. "And this is not practical."

"Yellow can be worn all summer, Miss Sabine," recited Perry with authority.

Willow held out a hand to quiet the maid. "Forgive us, Sabine. We've dominated your dressing room with talk about ourselves and may have overlooked your . . . hesitation. But let us not be rushed. We will not lose this moment to flowers or cakes or the guests. Take a deep breath."

"I can't," laughed Sabine, wiggling her torso in the tight corset.

"Perry, fetch a glass of water—no, actually, is that champagne in the drinks cart? Yes, let us have a toast. There you are. Now, Sabine. *Mrs. Stoker.*" Willow winked and they laughed. "You have our full attention. What gave you the notion to host a second wedding?"

"Well," Sabine said, examining the vibrant flowers in her bouquet, "it would bring no end of joy to my mother. I was lost to her these past five years. And Stoker and I began our marriage under duress, as you know. He was quite literally my last resort. When I found him five years later, he'd been left for dead, so in a way, I became his." She shook her head at the flowers. "Surely, practicality can be put aside for one day to transcend these tragedies with something pleasanter?"

"Practicality can always be set aside," proclaimed Tessa, relieving Perry of the champagne glass and taking a sip. "Life will wallop us with tragedy whether we plan for it or not. It's our duty to fight back by making fun when we can, prioritizing celebrations, reveling in the happy times."

"The epitaph on your gravestone, Tessa, will read, 'Here lies Tessa Chance. She prioritized celebrations,'" said Willow.

"I love it," said Tessa, taking another drink. "Someone please make a note."

Outside the door, a servant knocked insistently. "The carriage is ready, ladies."

"*Another moment,*" called Willow, bracing her hand against the door. To Sabine she said, "But what has Stoker said about today?"

"He did not challenge the idea when I raised it," said Sabine, looking up. "The idea came a fortnight or so after we'd moved to Park Lodge from London. I was showing him yet another corner of the grounds when we came upon the chapel. I said something wistful about having a real wedding. I was thinking out loud, really; and he said, it should be done."

Someone knocked on the door again and Willow fell against it, her back to the wood. "*In a minute!*" she called with irritation. "But perhaps it is for him that you are doing it— for Stoker?"

Sabine turned and fell against the door beside her friend. She looked over, and her eyes were bright with tears. "So very few things were done properly in his life, don't you see? His childhood was horrifying. His father endeavored to claim him, but not before he tried to have him killed first. He was educated by a loving family, but their love feels like charity to him. I married him to save my own skin. I . . . I want him to have a fresh start that feels proper and legitimate and considered in every way. I want the vicar to say, 'You may kiss the bride,' and for him to feel as if I am his proper bride, in earnest, and that I long to be kissed. I want him to feel as if he is a part of this estate and this family and future that we build together."

"Careful, Sabine," said Tessa, patting her hair, "these reasons sound very practical to me."

Willow laughed. "There. You have your reasons, do you see? Now, let us enjoy this wedding and this day and each other. We've won this round, all three of us. It is Sabine's wedding, but we shall all celebrate today."

In the vestry of the chapel on the northwest corner of Park Lodge's estate, three of the wealthiest men in England, the so called "Guano Barons" of 1835, waited for their summons to the altar, a bridegroom and his two best men.

"Perhaps she's cried off," said Joseph Chance, taking a nip of brandy from a flask and passing it to the Earl of Cassin.

"Perhaps she prefers you unconscious and in bed," said Cassin.

She does not prefer me unconscious in bed, Stoker thought but he said nothing, accepting the flask from Cassin.

"I've something more to mark the occasion," said Joseph, reaching into his pocket. He produced a crumpled, faded piece of parchment, frayed at the edges, and unfurled it on a table. "I thought we would appreciate a look back at how this all began."

"*The advertisement,*" breathed Cassin, peering down. It was the notice their wives had posted on the London docks some five years ago, calling for investment opportunities for their dowries.

"There are two impossibilities here that I must point out," said Joseph, smoothing the parchment. "The first is that the money they invested in our expedition multiplied so exponentially. We knew the guano had potential but no one knew to what degree."

"Naturally, Joseph mentions the money first," joked Cassin.

"Stop," said Joseph. "I fell for Tessa within *minutes*. It took you, Cassin, months, and Stoker years. And a brush with death."

"If you would have told me we would marry these women and eventually find love," said Cassin, "I would have left the partnership. I would have considered you as mad as King George."

"And that is the second impossibility," said Joseph. "We *did* marry them and the marriages have revealed themselves to be love matches. Sometimes the impossible happens."

"I've a third impossibility," said Stoker, reaching into his own jacket.

"Beyond moving to Surrey to become a country squire?" teased Joseph. "Although, I'd consider that to be more of an inevitability. You were always bound to live with your mother-in-law in a musty pile in Surrey."

"No," said Stoker levelly. "This."

He dropped a second piece of parchment on the table. The paper curled, flakier and more faded than the first.

"What is it?" asked Cassin. "They are finally bringing you up on that larceny charge in Tobago?"

"*No*," whispered Joseph, carefully picking up the parchment. "It's a marriage license."

"The license from marrying Sabine? Don't tell me it wasn't binding. The union had to be sound for us to take her dowry."

"No," said Joseph, reading it again. "It's from the bloody *1790s*, more than thirty years old. It's a marriage license between Marie Stoker and Saul Newington, the Duke of Wrest." Joseph looked up from the paper. "Stoker, is this authentic? Your parents were *married?*"

Stoker shrugged. "I cannot say. When Wrest died last month, his solicitor posted the sealed document to me, along with a few other papers and a box of rubbish. There was no note."

"But is it possible the old duke and your mother were married for a time?"

"I refused to believe it before," said Stoker. "But perhaps I will look into it. For Sabine's sake. And . . . if we are blessed with children."

"But if this is legitimate, you're a bloody duke, Stoker. Does Sabine know?" Cassin reached for the document.

Stoker shook his head. "No one knows. I've only just received it here in Surrey. It had been sent to my London apartment. I will tell her tonight. We will . . . decide what to do about it together."

"I can't believe you bloody outrank me," said Cassin, scanning the document. "*Your Grace.*"

"I am the same as I've always been," said Stoker, folding the parchment back in his pocket. "No matter how authentic or forged. You are the same. Joseph is the same. We are not changed by who died and made us noble, but rather who we love and who loves us. In this, we are all kings. Remarkably, *impossibly*, as Joseph said.

"It's happened," he continued. "Remarkable, impossible thought it may be. Finally, after years of rescuing women and children, my own life has been saved."

**And don't miss the rest of the
Brides of Belgravia and their journey to love!**

ANY GROOM WILL DO

Lady Willow Hunnicut has always dreamed of living in London. With design talent and aspirations grander than London's finest houses, she knows an unmarried heiress will never be allowed to live in the capital alone. But a married woman may come and go as she pleases. With a little imagination, a lot of courage, and one carefully worded advertisement, Willow concocts a plan to get everything she wants . . . even if she must take a husband in exchange.

Lord Brent Caulder, the Earl of Cassin, is destitute, his Yorkshire castle is crumbling, and his tenants are without work. He has an ingenious scheme that's a surefire moneymaker—if only someone would invest. When he discovers an advertisement seeking adventurers to fund, he is determined to claim the money. But his world is turned upside down when the investor turns out to be a flame-haired heiress.

The deal is simple: In return for marrying Willow, Cassin will receive her substantial dowry—and nothing else. All she asks is that after the wedding, each go their separate ways. But for all her careful preparation, the one thing Willow couldn't have planned is the way she feels about Cassin . . . or the desire that threatens to enflame them both.

ALL DRESSED IN WHITE

Self-made shipping magnate Joseph Chance never planned on falling in love. He simply needed financing for a new business venture and a marriage of convenience provides it. Then he meets Tessa St. Croix, his future bride, and is instantly smitten. But when the angelic beauty reveals a life-changing secret on their wedding night, Joseph thinks maybe some dreams shouldn't come true. He leaves England, reconciling himself to a detached, convenient marriage after all.

Eleven months later, Tessa Chance has built a new life for herself in the heart of London. She's learned her new husband's business and is determined to support herself and her responsibilities. When Joseph returns to London unexpectedly, nothing is as he imagined. His estranged wife has become the one person who can help him secure his company's future, and her allure can tempt him still. Determined and hopeful, Tessa jumps at the chance to prove herself and justify the secret that tore them apart.

Although bruised pride and broken hearts lie between them, Joseph and Tessa realize the love they once felt has never truly left. If they can learn to forgive each other, they'll soon discover the truest love can heal all wounds.

Available now from Avon Impulse!

ABOUT THE AUTHOR

USA Today bestselling author **CHARIS MICHAELS** believes a romance novel is a long, entertaining answer to the question, "So, how did you two meet?" and she loves making up new ways for fictional characters to almost not meet but live happily ever instead. She was raised on a peach farm in Texas and gave tours at Disney World in college but now can be found raising her family and writing love stories from her screened-in porch in the mid-Atlantic.

Discover great authors, exclusive offers, and more at hc.com.